RISING Queen

BLOOD ⚔ EMPIRE

Rising Queen

BLOOD EMPIRE
BOOK ONE

By Alisha Williams

This is a work of fiction. Names, characters, places, and incidents are either the product of the author's imagination or are used fictitiously. Any resemblance to actual persons, living or dead, events, or locales is entirely coincidental.

For more information, please address:
alishawilliamsauthor@gmail.com

Cover design: Alisha Williams
Book editor: Lærke Gade Villemoes

AUTHORS NOTE

Please be advised. This is a reverse harem/why choose romance, meaning the heroine of this story does not have to pick between her love interests.

This book contains explicitly described sexual content and the excessive use of swear words. This is a dark themed book and contains a lot of things that may trigger some readers. It is not for the faint of heart, so please read the trigger warnings before you dive in.

TRIGGER WARNINGS

This book contains a multitude of possible triggers which include but are not limited to what's listed below.

**Knife Play*
**Blood Play*
**BDSM*
**Murder*
**Blood*
**Graphically described scenes*
**Sex trafficking*
**Kinks of many kinds*
**Sexual assault mentioned on a minor*
**Rape of past events*

Please go into this book with an open mind.
You have been warned.

RISING QUEEN PLAYLIST

Slave For You by Brittany Spears

Bang by AJR

Buttons by The Pussycat Dolls

Eye Of The Tiger by Survivor

WAP by Cardi B ft. Megan Thee Stallion

Bohemian Rhapsody by Queen

Shake That by Eminem ft. Nate Dogg

Cradles by Sub Urban

Check It Out by Nicki Minaj and will.i.am

I highly recommend listening to *Bang* by AJR and *Cradles* by Sub Urban before or during their scene to get the full experience.

DEDICATION

I'd like to dedicate this book to all my readers of the Emerald Lake Prep series. You all gave me the love and support to keep going in my writing career. You fell in love with Harlow aka Queenie in Into The Unknown and made me excited to share her story with you. Thank you all so much for being with me from the very start, and I hope I have you in my corner until my last book.

PROLOGUE

I HIT redial for the twentieth time, but this time it doesn't go to voicemail. Someone picks up on the other end but doesn't speak. After a moment, I decide to talk first. "Hello?" I ask, wondering why Dean would pick up, but say nothing. "Dean, are you there? I tried calling Cassius first, but he's not picking up," I try to look through the bars of the gate that surrounds the mansion in front of me. "I'm waiting out front. Why the hell didn't you guys pick up when I called the first time?"

"Just leave, Harlow, you don't belong here." Dean's emotionless voice makes its way through the phone. I'm taken aback by his cold tone. The man on the other end of the line does not sound like the Dean I know.

"What the fuck do you mean leave?! You guys told me I could come here after graduation. You said I could spend the summer with you while I work on getting my own place. Could you please put my damn boyfriend on the line? I want to talk to him."

"You don't belong in our world, Harlow. You don't have what it takes to survive this life. Leave now, before you end up dead, and we are forced to deal with the disposal of your body."

My stomach drops and I start to shake. Why is he talking like this?! Just the other day, we were talking about the college we were all gonna be attending, *together*.

I know exactly what kind of life the boys come from and what their fathers do. They didn't hide much from me, and they are all aware of my past, so they know I'd keep their secrets safe. This information is nothing new to me, so what brought on this drastic change?

"What's going on, Dean? Why the fuck should I leave?" I ask, trying to hold back my tears. "I have nowhere else to go since I'm out of the system. Just come out here and talk to me! All of you!" I don't cry, that's not my thing, but after everything I've been through with these boys becoming my entire world, falling in love with Cass, only for them to turn around and pretend it means nothing to them... It's a lot to take in all at once.

"So what, this is it? Cass is breaking up with me? The fucker should be out here saying it to my face like a grown man!" I yell into the phone.

"Cass doesn't want to talk to you. He's done with you, just like the rest of us are."

"I want to hear that from him!" I say, feeling a panic attack coming. I don't get them often, but if there was a perfect time to have one, this would be it.

"I don't give a fuck about what you want, Harlow. Just get the fuck out of my town!" Dean snaps before the line goes dead.

I won't do it. I won't break down. I won't give them that power over me. I knew I should have just kept to myself when I moved to this fucking place. But *noo*, I had to go fall in love with the tall and handsome, dirty blonde-haired, blue-eyed boy, giving him my heart, even though I knew better, while secretly crushing on his twin brother and cousins too. Trixie and Mouse were the only ones worth giving a part of myself to, but I went and made the dumb choice to trust someone else.

Bet you regret that now, huh?

Do I fucking ever. Now I'm left with no one and nothing.

There's no point in begging or pleading. Once those boys make up their minds, there's no changing it. Why would I want to beg someone to be in my life? Fuck that.

I pick up my backpack, sliding my arms through the straps, and walk down the long pavement drive, heading back to the main road.

This backpack holds everything I own, which is very little. Some clothes, a book, and a photo of me and the girls. It was taken at school when I was in 4th grade and Trixie was in first grade. It was Mouse's first day of Kindergarten. Her teacher took the photo and gave each of us a copy.

When I was 13, the group home we grew up in became overcrowded, so they started placing the older kids into foster homes. Unfortunately, I was one of those kids, but I was relieved to leave that nightmare of a place I grew up in. Safe Haven, what a joke. That place was the complete opposite of its name. If anything, it should have been called "*Hell*," because the Devil himself lived there.

So many monsters lived within the walls at Safe Haven. I know I was one of the lucky ones to get out and get placed in a home, but that meant leaving the two most important people in my life.

Every day that I've been gone, all I can think about is running back there to break them out and take them with me. But they're in Las Vegas, and I am in Long Beach, California. I have no means or money to get to them.

It kills me, knowing I am not there to protect them. I've failed them. But someday, I will make it up to them. I *will* find them.

After walking for a few hours, I reach the main bus station and use half of the cash I have to buy a ticket on the first bus out of here. I need to get away from this place, from those boys. Stupid assholes. They made me their best friend, their whole world, made me fall in love with them, and then they toss me out at the drop of a hat like I'm nothing but trash. *Well, fuck them. I don't need them. I've survived way worse than this before, and I will do the same this time.*

The bus is bound for Los Angeles. I grab my ticket from the lady and head out to the bus. I hand it over to the driver and take my seat.

City of Angels, here I come...

Los Angeles is overcrowded. The streets are bustling with thousands of men, women, and children. I've never been to a place with this many people. Fuck, I'm gonna get lost so easily, and my phone was just shut off because I couldn't pay the bill, so I can't even use my GPS.

We arrive at the bus station in what looks like a crappy part of the city. With my bag slung over my shoulder, I exit the bus and instantly the powerful stench of urine overwhelms my senses.

Putting my hand over my nose, my eyes sting while I try not to puke. I head into the bus station and ask the lady at the front counter where the nearest shelter is. There is no way I'm gonna sleep on the street. That's just asking to be kidnapped or raped.

She gives me directions to the nearest one. I make it there just before the doors close for the night and the place is packed. I'm lucky enough to get a bed for the night, though. Finding my bed, I get settled in for the night.

As I snuggle into my hoodie and the thin blanket they provided, I close my eyes, praying that nothing happens in my sleep. But no matter how long I lay there, sleep doesn't come. There are too many sounds around me. Wet coughs echo around the room. Babies cry in distress as their mothers try to soothe them. Hushed conversations between others linger.

Finding a clock on the wall, I watch the secondhand tick by slowly, as sleep finally takes me.

A few weeks have passed, and I've gotten into a little routine. I'm officially out of what little money I had left, so to survive I panhandle. I make sure to be back at curfew every night so that I'm guaranteed a bed. We have to leave during the day, and beds are first come, first serve, but thankfully they favor mothers with children and young women overgrown men.

Every morning I take my bag and head to the bathroom, doing my best to stay clean. I then head over to the soup kitchen down the street with my three-meal-a-day tickets. They don't give you much to eat, but it's enough to survive.

Thankfully, today is beautiful, and I decide to find a new place to panhandle for the day. I only need enough for some shampoo and a bar of soap, maybe even some cheap coffee. Getting money this way hasn't been too hard. Looking like I do definitely helps capture people's attention. My long black silky hair and ice-blue eyes have almost been more of a curse than a blessing, though.

I've had a few men tell me I'd make a fortune if only I was working the street corners rather than standing out here begging for money, but I have zero interest in being a prostitute. I'd rather die than sell my body to nasty ass disease-ridden fuckers.

After a long day working the streets, I take the fifty dollars that I've earned today and head to the nearest grocery store. When I come out of the store, I'm stopped by a man. A well-dressed man who looks like he should be on the cover of a magazine. His short dark chocolate hair is nicely styled, and he's wearing a light gray suit with polished black dress shoes.

I give him a once over. "Can I help you?" I ask, raising a brow and wondering what the man standing in my way wants.

He flashes me a smile that shows all his pearly white teeth. "Hi, I'm Triver." He introduces himself, holding his hand out for me to shake. I don't. I look at it, then up at him.

"And your point is?" I snark, growing annoyed. I just want to go back to the shelter before curfew, and this guy is standing in my way of a warm place to sleep tonight.

Still smiling, he drops his hand to his side, finally getting the hint that I won't be shaking it. "I've seen you around a few times on my way to work. The streets are no place for a beautiful young lady such as yourself. I have a job opportunity for you if you're interested," he says.

I narrow my eyes, not sure what to think of this good-looking man, who's randomly offering me a job. "What kind of job?" I ask.

"I own a little bar on the other side of the city, it's called Diamonds. We cater to a wealthier clientele. We are looking for some people to fill a few positions. Now I'm guessing you're not 21 yet?" he asks.

"No...18," I hesitate.

"No worries, you may not be able to bartend, but you would do well as a hostess or waitress. I can guarantee you will get good tips."

Standing there, I think over his offer. I could keep standing out here all day in hopes of getting enough money to buy a decent meal, or I could work for this man at his bar. It sounds way too good to be true to randomly fall into my lap.

"What's the catch? Why are you randomly offering me this job?" I ask, tilting my head to the side, trying to figure out this man's ulterior motive.

"I don't like seeing young women suffer. The streets are a dangerous place. I don't think I could live with myself if something bad happened to you. You could make enough money to get off the streets and into a place of your own in under a month."

I mean, my life can't get much worse than it is right now. If it means I can get my own place and a steady cash flow, it's worth a shot.

"Alright, I'll give it a test run, but I can't guarantee anything."

He gives me another beaming smile. "Perfect. Here's the address. Come by around ten tonight, and we can start you right away. I'll have a uniform waiting for you," he says, handing me a card that says "*Triver Berk*" on it with the address, number, and name of the club.

He says goodbye, and we go our separate ways.

It's almost ten, and I find myself standing in front of a dark building. For a club on a Friday night, it seems pretty dead to me. No lights, no sounds, not even people walking around.

I try to look in the windows of the building but can't see anything because they are all tinted. I decide to walk around the building to see if there is another entrance.

Luckily, when I round the corner, I see a few men standing outside a door leading into the same building. I make my way towards them with caution. Nothing good ever came from a pretty girl being alone in an alley with grown men.

"Excuse me," I interrupt the men, who are laughing and chatting away. They all look like wealthy men. Nicely tailored suits, elegantly styled hair, and watches on their wrists.

"Well, who do we have here?" The one with brown hair says, as he ogles my body like a pervert. I get the sudden urge to turn and run, but I need this job. I can't live on the streets for the rest of my life. At some point, I'm gonna get kidnapped or worse, wind up dead.

"I'm here for a job, I'm here to see Triver? Do you know him?" I ask.

"Oooh, Triver sent you here," he says with a creepy grin. There's something about the way he reacts that sets me on edge. I have to get out of here. I don't feel safe anymore.

"You know what, never mind. I'll come back another time," I say, turning around to leave. But, before I can make it two steps, the blond one grabs my arm so tight that it's gonna leave bruises.

"Not so fast, sweet thing. If Triver is expecting you, then I'm going to deliver," he insists, as he drags me inside.

My survival instincts kick in, and I thrash and scream for help, but it does nothing as they drag me deeper into the building. We come to an elevator, and I try to grab on to the side, hoping to keep them from locking me in there with them, but they're stronger than me. One holds my arms while another holds my legs to keep me from kicking him.

They say nothing and act as if this is no big deal, like it's something they do every day. A sick feeling in the pit of my stomach tells me it is.

When the elevator doors open, we enter the club. No wonder it looked abandoned from the street, it's all underground.

The place is packed with people, mostly men. I see some women dressed in skimpy, yet somewhat tasteful clothing.

I yell for help, but no one looks our way. I know they can hear me; my screams are loud. I start thrashing and kicking again, trying to get out of their hold.

"Stop moving!" an unfamiliar voice says, and I come face-to-face with a black-haired man. He then raises his arm to punch me in the face, but someone grabs it, stopping him.

"Do not touch her!" a voice hisses. Triver steps around the man and drops his arm, but I know he's not here to save me.

"This one is gonna make me a pretty penny, and if she can dance, she's gonna be a gold mine. If you damage her face or body, then I will lose money while waiting for her to heal," he snaps at the black-haired man.

"Sorry, Boss, but she won't stop fighting," the black-haired guy replies.

"Then give her this," Triver says, holding out a needle.

I panic even more, knowing that whatever is in that syringe isn't good. "No, please!" I beg, feeling small and helpless. I never begged before, but I need to survive. Unfortunately, I don't think Harlow will be making it out of this one.

"Hush now, My Little Hummingbird, so beautiful, so delicate. Such a rare sight to see. I'm gonna have fun with you, dear girl," he says in a sickeningly soft voice, as he jabs me with the needle and empties the contents into my arm.

I start to lose consciousness fast. "Fuck you!" I manage to slur out.

He chuckles darkly. "Oh, I intend to, sweet one, I intend to."

Then everything goes black.

My head feels like someone took a jackhammer to it while doing an Irish jig. *Where the fuck am I?*

I try to sit up and open my eyes, but the dizziness is too much, and I fall back onto the bed.

"Wow, take it easy," a sweet, feminine voice says. "You're gonna feel pretty out of it for a while, maybe even sick. What they gave you is some powerful shit," she says. Hearing that word coming from her mouth with that voice sounds so wrong.

I pry my eyes open and try to focus on the person who's speaking. Sitting on the end of the bed is a beautiful, dainty, delicate looking young girl. She looks to be about my age. Her long ginger hair hangs down over her shoulders.

Thousands of freckles paint her creamy pale skin. Her emerald-green eyes are filled with sadness and pity.

"Here, drink this, it will help," she says, holding out a bottle of water. She sees my hesitation and giggles. "Don't worry, it's sealed." I take the bottle from her and check for myself before opening it and taking a sip.

"Thanks," I say, swallowing the piss warm water gratefully. "Where am I?" I ask, looking around the room. It looks like I'm in a prison cell. No, wait, I am! There's even a toilet in the corner, and it appears that I'm lying on the bottom bed of a bunk bed.

"Well, you are in a cell with me," she smiles sadly. "Deep in the basement of the Diamond Night Club."

My stomach turns, and I feel like I'm gonna be sick, and not from what they drugged me with. I refuse to give up, but who am I kidding, I'm not going anywhere.

"What do they want with me?" I ask, swallowing the bile trapped in my throat.

She grimaces. "Do you want the good news or the bad news first?" she asks.

I give her a funny look. "Is there even good news in a situation like this?"

She nods her head. "Good point. You are now the property of Triver Berk. You will be sold at auction to some rich creep who will probably rape and beat you, and once he has no more use for you, he will kill and replace you."

My face pales and I have to swallow down another mouthful of vomit.

"Or, if you can dance, they will keep you here. They will make you dance for the richest and cruelest men in the country. Those men will pay to watch you and take you into a private room where they will fuck you. You won't have a choice, but at least you won't be beaten. Bruised women are ugly women, and they won't make any money off that," she says, shifting on the bed so that she's facing me better.

"So, the question is, can you dance? And by dance, I mean, can you move your body in a way that can seduce a man?" she asks, tilting her head to the side.

I think back to the times when I'd get drunk with the guys, and they would blast their music. I'd dance without a care in the world, feeling sexy and amazing. By the end of the songs, I was left with four hungry stares, so yeah, I guess I could dance.

"I think I can manage that," I say, my voice unsure.

"Good," she says, suddenly becoming perky. "I'm Evie by the way," she says, holding out her hand, and unlike with Triver, I take it. I don't get bad vibes from her.

I will survive this, just like I've survived every hellish thing that's happened in my life before. Sadly, this is nothing new. I left behind a life sentence in one hell, just to walk into another. God, how stupid could I have been? It's all their fucking fault! If Dean, Cassius, Axel, and Neo hadn't thrown me aside like trash, I would be working a summer job and getting a place of my own. *My heart still burns, decaying a little more every time I remember their betrayal.*

They told me to leave because their world was no place for me. Well, how the fuck is this any better?!

“I’m Harlow,” I say, releasing her hand.

“Nice to meet you, Harlow," she beams. "Stick with me, and I’ll be the angel in your hell,” she says with a wink.

I think this girl may end up being the only thing that will keep me going.

CHAPTER ONE

Harlow

FIVE YEARS LATER...

"Is everything good to go?" I ask Evie as she leans into me, trying to avoid the handsy men of the overcrowded club.

Today is the day. The day every girl in this place has dreamed about. The day that all of us girls in this club, who have been held against their will, either forced to dance or forced to be fucked by monsters, will be free.

Let me tell you, this was not easy. It will be one of the hardest things I've ever had to do, but I know that this is just a raindrop in all the oceans of things I'll be doing to survive from this day forward.

For the past five years, I've been here at the Diamonds Nightclub. I'm Triver Berk's personal girl. Because of my appearance, I was saved from being sent into the sex trafficking ring that they're running out of this place, but that only meant I was a showpiece for the club instead. Forced to dance almost every night, and when I wasn't dancing, I was auctioned off to the highest bidder for the evening. Over time, as these despicable men bought their turns to have their way with me, I've learned to numb myself. At first, I cried, but that only got me locked up in a tiny, dark room for days. With how lonely this world already was, I hated it. If I had to be locked up, I'd rather it be with Evie than be forced to relive every horrible thing that's happened in my life repeatedly in my mind, all the screams of my younger self echoing in my head.

Over the years, I've become more and more popular, and eventually I became the most requested girl. In a normal strip club, the other girls would be beating my ass for taking the spotlight away because they would be losing money, but here, it was the best thing for them. Normally, they dance and then go back to their cells, and if they were lucky, they would only get called on once or twice a week. Me? I was called on two or three times a day. Triver would talk me up like a prized pony, getting all the men to fall for my curvy hips, big breasts, and delicate features with my icy blue eyes and raven black hair. I was every man's fantasy.

After a while, I morphed into someone different. *Something* different. I'd been beaten and raped plenty of times as a child, and somehow that never truly changed who I was. But these past five years? I guess everyone has a breaking point. So, I put on an act. Did what he wanted me to do and took it like a good little girl because what else could I do?

That was, until last week. I overheard Triver talking to some important members of the corrupt society that he entertains, who were planning to hold their annual gathering at the club this year. Apparently, once a year, some of the richest men with the most sick and twisted minds would get together and have one of the largest sex slave auctions in the country. They make a whole show of it. Prance the prettiest girls around and show them off. Make the dancers put on an extra special show.

This year, it is expected that we do just that. But I have a plan, one that will hopefully get us out of here, all of us... the girls, I mean. The men? Yeah, they won't be so lucky if things go as planned.

"Yes, the girls all know what they're supposed to do," Evie says, giving Roxy, the bartender, someone's order. She knows it's time.

"I feel bad asking them to do this," I say, looking out over the crowd.

"They are okay with it. They know this is the last time they have to do anything like that, so if it means their freedom, they are more than willing to do this."

I turn back to Evie. "Dancing and flirting, that's all they need to do until it's time. I don't want any of them to go into the back rooms, or that will fuck up the entire plan. They need to be out in the main part of the club, ready to go."

Evie nods. "They know. They will do whatever they can to keep the men talking with their buddies to keep them distracted."

"Good. Where's Triver?" I ask, feeling a little giddy about this, but also scared as fuck because if this plan fails, we're all as good as dead.

"He's getting ready for the show and plans on being front and center. He's been bragging about showing off his prized possession to everyone," Evie says, rolling her eyes. She means me.

"Do you have the laptop?" I ask, ignoring that last part.

"It's tucked behind the trash can by the elevator. Tommy is standing guard, ready for his part in all this." Tommy is one of the club's guards. In all the years he's worked here, he thought this place was a normal strip club. He and his friends were the only ones who didn't know what this place was really about. I guess Triver needed some men to know as little as possible as a backup plan. They found out the truth by walking in on one of the dancers getting fucked against her will. Luckily, no one saw him, but he came to me, and I told him the truth, which he then told his friends. So, when I came up with this whole plan of escape, they were willing to jump on board. They will help keep up appearances, all the while making sure everything goes as planned.

"Don't leave that behind, Evie. Our chances of survival depend on that laptop and the magic you can work on it."

She lets out a little laugh. "Have I ever let you down, Low?" She smiles. No, she hasn't. She's become my everything and the only person I know I can count on for anything, even if it's just providing me with a bit of normalcy by laughing and talking about nothing in particular.

"Never." I smile back. She nods and we both down the shots that Roxy has placed down for us on top of the bar. I give Roxy a look as if to ask, "Ready?" She nods her head and puts her hand under the bar where her gun is hidden. Both

Tommy and Lucas were able to sneak in a gun each for tonight, and they were given to the girls who would not have access to the men here. Roxy, because she works at the bar, and Evie because she isn't dancing tonight. Triver also uses Evie to do some of his paperwork. Dumbass thinks he's scared her into never betraying him because she's been sucking up to him for a while now, when really it had been a ploy to get access to his computer.

See, Evie is a genius hacker. She could have gotten us out of here years ago, but Triver has backup plans in place, and if we tipped anyone from the outside world off, Triver would just have the ring shut down and the girls shipped off, never to be seen again.

So, when Evie finally got her hands on his computer, we had a talk with the other dancers. As much as they wanted to get out of here, they didn't want to risk putting a death sentence on the girls not lucky enough to just be kept in the basement at Diamonds. What she did was collect as much info on the men involved as she could find so that once we get out of here, the first thing we do is to take them all down, as well as do our best to locate and save any girls who haven't been sold. What Evie doesn't know yet, is that I also plan on finding each of the men who have ever bought a girl and killing them myself.

I haven't killed anyone, yet, but all the hours I've spent planning and visualizing slicing the throats of every man who ever laid their hands on me, will be more than enough incentive to carry through. To me, finally getting to bathe in the blood of my enemies will be like a little kid getting surprised with the trip to Disney World that they have dreamed of for so long.

"Showtime," I say, forcing a smile, even as I feel my stomach drop.

Evie hugs me tightly. "We've got this, Low, we're gonna make it."

Oh, Evie, Doll Face, I hope you're right.

I head into the back to get dressed for my dance routine. The girls from the last set are getting changed into their normal clothes. They won't be sent back to the basement until after the end of the event. They are required to wait here, in case one of the members wants to buy them for the night.

That works in our favor because Max is ready for his part in all this. His job is to get these girls out on his way back out from freeing the ones still locked in the basement. Thankfully, there are not that many being sold tonight, but unfortunately, some sales have already gone through. I plan to get them back as soon as possible. Lucas's job is to get the girls who are working in the main room of the club out safely, and Tommy's is to provide a clear path to the elevator, which is the only exit out of here, and help them all get to safety.

We whisper amongst ourselves as they let me know they are all dressed and waiting for Max. The emotions on their faces range from excited to terrified.

When I finish with them, I head backstage. Pulling the curtain back just a little, only enough to see into the club, I look around the room and see that all the girls are in position. *God, if you're listening, I know that what I'm about to do is gonna land me in like... hell or whatever, but please, PLEASE, let this work.*

I'm A Slave For You by Britney Spears starts to play, and I laugh thinking of the song title. Well, that's my cue to get this show on the road.

Entering the stage, I see Triver's gaze snap to my body with a sleazy and possessive expression on his face. I move my body to the beat, putting on the best show of my life. Seductively, I sway my body, dipping and turning, making sure to rub my hands all over myself. Halfway through the song, they're all eating out of the palm of my hand, panting over me like horny dogs.

Triver sits back in his chair, getting comfortable, while also adjusting his hard-on. I keep the sultry look on my face, giving him the illusion that I'm genuinely into this and loving every moment of this display of erotic dancing, but in reality, I'm holding myself back from just going over there and kicking the fucker in the face.

As the song is nearing the end, it's time to make my move. Crawling over the stage towards Triver in a sensuous way, I glance over to the girls, giving them the signal to be ready. Once I get to the edge of the stage, where Triver is sitting, I climb down and into his lap. His hands grip my hips, forcing me to grind into his cock, and I do it. I move my body against his and my hands glide down his legs. When I feel the handle of his gun, I wrap my hand around it, getting a good grip. Just as I'm about to pull it out, I hear gunshots go off.

My gaze snaps up, looking at the girls around me. They all stand there with raised guns in their hands, eyes wide as they stare at the men on the ground. Every single man here who had a girl on their lap is now dead. But this wasn't the plan, I mean it was, but they were seconds too soon.

The club immediately breaks out into screams, and more gunshots ring throughout the club.

"RUN!" I shout at the frozen women as Triver pushes me off his lap. They all snap their eyes over to me, then register what the fuck is going on, before taking off towards the exit.

"You little bitch, what have you done?!" Triver roars. He reaches into his gun holster to draw his gun, only his hand is met with nothing. Confused, he looks down, then back to me, understanding mixes with rage on his face. In my hand is his gun. I managed to get a good grip before he pushed me off.

His eyes go wide for a moment, and before he can say a word, I take off, immediately getting lost in the crowd.

Frantically, I look around to see if all the girls made it out. When I only see men, I'm confident that everyone made it, that is until I look down and see at least five out of the twenty girls lying on the ground, dead, while the men trample over their bodies, desperately trying to find a way out and not caring who they hurt on their way.

Bile rises up and gets caught in my throat. It's my fault they're dead.

"HARLOW!" I manage to hear my name being called through all the deafening noise that fills the air. Looking around, I expect to see Triver, but he's nowhere in sight. Turning around, I see Evie waving her hands at the back hall exit with Lucas standing right behind her.

There are two doors that lead to the one exit at the elevator. Both require a long walk down a never-ending hallway. One of them, the one everyone seems to be climbing over one another trying to get out of, we have made sure to block and lock. The other is in the direction where Evie and Lucas are.

As I start to make my way through the crowd, Roxy grabs my arm. "Come on, we gotta get out of here. I just lit a few Molotov Cocktails, so we have less than a minute before this whole place goes up in flames," she yells in my ear.

When we reach Evie, we rush to the only open door, bursting into the hallway. Kicking off our heels, we start sprinting towards the elevator.

"Where are the girls?" I demand as we run, already out of breath from the dance before, but also feeling the high of the adrenaline.

"They made it," Evie huffs, laughing like she can't believe her words. "They are above ground a few blocks over, waiting for us with Max and Tommy."

"And why aren't you two with them?" I ask, looking at Lucas, who has the decency to look at least a little guilty about not sticking with the plan.

"There's no way I would leave this place without you, Low. There's no point in being on the other side if you're not there with me. Ride or die, Babe, ride or fucking die."

We make it to the elevator, and Lucas presses the button frantically to open it. Evie's words finally register, and I'm tossed back to the image of the girls' dead bodies on the ground.

The elevator doors open, and we all pile in. Lucas repeats the same motion on the opposite button to get the doors to close.

Looking over at her with sorrowful eyes, I say, "Not everyone."

Her eyebrows pinch. "What do you mean?"

"I'm guessing with all the craziness of tonight, you haven't had a chance to do a headcount, but at least five of the girls were shot and killed. I couldn't see their faces, there was too much commotion going on."

Evie's eyes start to tear up. "No!' she whispers.

Just as I'm about to say something, I hear the dreaded nickname Triver has for me.

"HUMMINGBIRD!!!" he bellows.

My eyes snap to the elevator doors, and I see him running down the hallway towards us. There is only a small opening between the almost closed doors. I make a quick decision to use the last few seconds I have left and pull up the gun I slipped off him, and fire off multiple shots. A few make contact, sending him sprawling on the ground. The last thing I hear, before the doors close completely, is his agonized scream.

My face morphs into the most sinister smile. That soothes my soul just a smidgen, and the sound is music to my ears. Knowing that he will suffer until the blaze makes its way to him, burning him alive, is the biggest and sweetest cherry on top. Feeling relieved and triumphant, I lean back against the wall.

Everyone is all talking at once, but it's just a dull pulse in my ear. All I can do is stare at the closed doors and smile, knowing that most of the men who thought it was their right to lay their hands on me are now burning alive. Smoke cutting off their ability to breathe. Flesh melting off their bones. Completely aware that their time on earth has come to an end. It's one of the most excruciating deaths a human can experience. That thought is a sweet bliss that I would happily drown in.

When we get to the top, the elevator dings, and the doors slide open. Lucas pushes the emergency stop button. “Just in case.” He shrugs when he sees me looking at him with a cocked brow.

“Come on, the girls are scared out of their minds and refuse to go to a hotel without you. The guys tried, but they wouldn't budge,” Lucas says as he heads off in the direction of where everyone is waiting.

We follow behind, and I look around at my surroundings. This is the first time I've seen the outside world in years. Breathing in fresh air, my eyes stop at a hotel not too far from here. It towers over the other buildings and has a perfect view of the club.

“There,” I say, pointing to the building. “We’ll spend the night there. I wanna stay closer to the club than at the other hotel we’d intended. I wanna watch it all burn down...”

Lucas doesn't ask any questions, just nods.

“The guys and I can use our credit cards and get the girls a room,” Lucas offers.

“We will put as many as we can in each room. That will save you from having to spend too much. And once we are situated, we will pay you back,” I assure him.

“It’s really not that big of a deal Queenie, we don't mind. We’re just glad you all made it out of there safely,” Lucas says, using my stage name. He doesn't know my real name. No one except Evie and Triver do. The day after I was taken, Triver asked me to pick a name, a name I would go by from now on, one that everyone would call me. I chose Queenie. But now that I'm out, I think I'll keep it. Harlow McKaven died in that fire as far as I'm concerned. Queenie is the one who made it out, rising above it all, like a phoenix from the ashes.

“Not all of us,” Roxy mumbles numbly, still reeling on tonight's events.

“I’m sorry about your girls,” he says, looking at each of us.

“We will find and save the other girls who were sold. That's how we will pay our respects to the ones we lost. If it wasn't for them, we wouldn't have made it out. They died so that we can live, and I plan on making good on this new-found freedom.” The girls nod in agreement with me.

When we make it over to the rest of the girls, they rush to meet us. We all hug and cry. They start to cry even harder when they find out about the ones we lost. Every one of us is like family, connected through all the pain we've had to suffer, so it's like we've lost our sisters.

After we get all the girls settled into their hotel rooms, Evie and I go to our own room, and she immediately sets up the laptop and gets to work.

Making my way over to the window, my eyes lock on the sight before me. I have a perfect view of Diamonds. The whole building is on fire, orange, red, and yellow flames engulf the structure. The upper level of the building is actually a business. It's a fancy little restaurant called Berk's Bistro. It serves as Triver's legal facade to cover up the fact that he was selling girls, with twenty-three kidnapped and held against their will in the basement.

Fire trucks, ambulances, and police cars have arrived and surround the outer building, but no one is rushing in to put it out. What's the point when there is nothing left to be saved. The building is too far gone to risk any personnel going in. Good. They shouldn't have to risk their lives to save the monsters below. They're exactly where they should be, burning in hell.

"It's done," Evie says. Taking my eyes off the beautifully destructive flames before me, I turn my gaze to her.

"How long?" I ask.

"Not too long. I say we wait a bit, let things settle down. Might look a little weird, all of us popping up out of nowhere. I transferred some money to the guys so that we can have something to live off until then. We will get them to help set us up in some place to stay. But we can talk more about that tomorrow. Right now, let's just get some sleep." she says, giving me a sad, tired grin.

Nodding my head, I make my way over to one of the beds and fall back onto the plush material.

While I was busy watching the pretty light show below, Evie was hacking into each of the men's accounts and transferred all their personal funds to offshore accounts. If you ask me, we deserve to be compensated for our pain and suffering.

Once it's safe to start using the money, I plan on finding a place that can hold all of us. These girls are *my* responsibility now. I'm making them my responsibility. They're my family, after all. And, like hell, will I ever let them suffer again in their lives.

Evie bustles around the room, getting things put away and ready for bed. I don't move from my spot on the bed. I'm still in my dancing outfit. One of the guys gave me a hoodie to put on before coming to the hotel. I was the only one still dressed like that, thankfully.

I'm too tired to change, so I don't. I just close my eyes, mumble a good night to Evie, and go to sleep. Tomorrow, I can let reality hit me. Tomorrow, I can acknowledge the lives that were lost. But tonight, I'm gonna take this win and get a good night's sleep on the most comfortable bed I've slept on in over five years.

CHAPTER TWO

CASSIUS

THREE YEARS LATER...

"Damn it!!!" Dean roars, smashing his fists on the keyboard before swiping the desk clean, sending the laptop crashing against the wall and breaking into pieces. "FUCK!" he bellows as he rams his hands into his brown hair, grabbing handfuls.

"What the fuck is going on?!" Axel demands as he bursts into the office, taking in the destroyed room before locking eyes on Dean.

Me? I'm just sitting on the office couch, sipping my bourbon, and trying to process this clusterfuck of epic proportions.

"They fucking destroyed it all!" Dean whispers in shock and disbelief. "I can't believe they would do that."

Neo enters the room and whistles when he sees the state of it. "Oooh, Daddy Dean is mad," he taunts.

Axel slaps Neo on the chest, but Neo just chuckles.

Turning his attention back to Dean, Axel asks, "Who the fuck are you talking about? And what the hell did they destroy?"

Dean is too far gone in his own head to answer, so I do. "Our fathers," I say calmly, swirling the golden-brown liquid in my glass before taking another drink. This problem that Dean is losing his mind over? I'm the one who found it and brought it to Dean's attention.

Axel's blue eyes turn a stormy gray at the mention of the monsters who helped bring us into this world. "What did they do?" he asks in a low grumble.

Neo dances his way over to the couch and plops down next to me, putting his arm around the back of the couch where I'm sitting. "What did our dear old pops do now?" he asks, grabbing my drink and downing it, then handing me back the empty glass. "Thanks," he says with a smile, patting my cheek. I glare at him in annoyance. But this is who Neo is, a carefree, lively, in-your-face kind of person... or rather psychopath.

Turning my eyes away from Neo, I acknowledge Axel's question. "They took everything. They drained the company accounts when they took off, disappearing to God only knows where. Apparently, we have been living off credit since they left."

"But that's six years?! How the hell have we been able to do that for so long? And not know about it?!" Axel growls.

"From what I've gathered, they set up a bunch of credit cards with large limits. That and the money we make from the businesses did a good job of masking the truth. But we were spending more than we had and, since we went legit, we haven't been making as much money."

"So, what do we do?'' Neo asks, his playful facade fading a bit.

"We need to find a way to acquire the money to pay back our debt, or we lose everything."

Everyone's faces fall, and the fear we never show takes over.

"We could ask for a loan?" Neo says.

I shake my head. "No, that won't work. When they do a credit check, they will see how much we owe. Plus, getting a loan to pay back credit doesn't change anything; we would still owe the same amount."

"I know we want to keep being legit, but I think we need to consider asking some of our old business partners for help."

Shaking my head again, I say, "That won't work either. Our fathers ruined all their relationships before taking off. All the bridges are burnt; they would never help us."

"Not everyone," Neo says, his face turning into a wicked grin. "There's still one person who our fathers never worked with. We could see if they are willing to help out."

Dean narrows his eyes at Neo. "Who?"

"She's known as Queenie. Over the past three years, she's been building a pretty hefty empire. She now owns all the strip clubs in Kingston Heights and has started collecting some in L.A. She's not well-liked by the men of our world, but no one dares to mess with her because she's fucking crazy! The stories I've heard about this chick..." His eyes light up.

The man is a sadist, and based on what he's saying, she sounds like his perfect match.

"She turned all the strip clubs into burlesque clubs and is crazy strict when it comes to the girls who work there. If you disrespect them in any way, she gives you a warning... and by warning, I mean she beats the crap out of you. If you fuck up again, you're swimming with the fishies," he wiggles his hand back and forth, mimicking the movement of a fish.

"She's a borderline billionaire, and here's the kicker, other than the little murdering sprees she goes on, her businesses are all 100% legit. Rumor has it, she only kills "evil" people, mostly men. Rapists, murderers, anyone who touches children." He uses his hand to mimic someone slitting a throat.

"And how is *she* gonna help us? What do we have to offer *her* in order for her to loan us money?" I inquire.

"I haven't thought that far yet, but it won't hurt to ask," he shrugs, leaning back into the couch.

No one bothers to ask him how he knows all this information, and I don't think we even want to know.

"Where can we find her?" Axel asks, leaning himself back against the now empty desk.

"There's a club called Evolution. Supposedly that is where she conducts all of her business," Neo answers.

"Do you think you could get a hold of her?" Dean asks, pacing around the room.

"No," Neo says, looking at his nails then back up to our frustrated faces. "But I know someone who can."

"Get in touch with them, have them set up a meeting. Anything is worth a shot at this point, but I'll keep looking for other options in the meantime," Dean says, storming out of the room with Axel following after him like a good little lapdog, leaving me alone with Neo.

My brother is a brooding asshole that doesn't take orders from anyone but Dean, so being his second in command, he likes to follow rank and keep order.

"Soooo," Neo says, looking at me. "You think someone that batshit crazy is hot?" he says, wiggling his eyebrows. "*I* bet she's a fucking vision." His eyes glaze over in a dreamy state. The fucker's probably imagining himself going on a murdering spree with the woman.

We have to keep Neo on a tight leash; otherwise, he takes off like a rabid dog, looking for a fight with any poor soul who dares to mess with him.

On more than one occasion, we've had to clean up his mess and get rid of the bodies. He doesn't set out to kill, but when he's in a certain mindset, and we aren't there to put an end to it, he doesn't stop until there's nothing left.

If he's not beating someone, he's fucking women as if he's on a mission to break a world record or something.

Women are definitely charmed by his playful personality and good looks. Neo works out like a beast to work off his extra energy, so his body is ripped and bulky. We are almost certain that he has undiagnosed ADHD. He can't sit still for shit.

We are all attractive men and are pretty popular with women, though none of us are looking to settle down.

Neo with his short black hair and clean-shaven face. Dean with his brown hair and stubble beard. Then there's Axel and me. We are identical twins. The only way to tell us apart is our hair. Though we both have the same toffee-colored hair with natural blonde streaks. I wear my hair long, just past my shoulders, and Axel wears his just below his chin. Both still long enough to put in a man bun that women seem to go crazy over.

None of us want to make a commitment, not after losing the one woman we all loved.

She was *my* girlfriend. This feisty, take no shit, gorgeous girl. With her long black raven hair and piercing blue eyes, she stopped any boy in his tracks.

Harlow was new to Long Beach, just starting at our high school when we met her. Even though most of the students at the school were pretty wealthy and entitled assholes, she always held her ground, never letting any of the students make her feel less for being herself.

The guys and I took a liking to Harlow from the moment we set eyes on her, much like every other guy, but the difference was we were the only ones she *wanted* to get to know.

That very first day, we invited her to sit with us and, with caution, she accepted. It took a long time to tear down some of the walls she had built around herself. We worked hard at gaining her trust and breaking her out of her shell.

At first, Harlow became one of us, a part of our little group. Over time, we all slowly fell in love with her, but none of the others wanted to admit it. I, on the other hand, saw an opportunity to be with the girl I was head over heels for, so I took it. She became my girlfriend, the person I lost my virginity to, and the one I told all my darkest secrets to.

Even though my cousins and I grew up with money, our lives were anything but glamorous.

In the beginning, our family money was just something our mothers and fathers inherited from their own wealthy families, but over the years, it became blood money. After some bad business decisions, much like the situation we are in now, our fathers chose to go dark.

By the time they handed everything over to us, they had involved themselves in every wrong, dirty, and illegal kind of business dealings you could think of.

Our mothers were all sisters whose parents married them off to wealthy families. Our fathers formed a bond and combined everything they had, as well as our mothers' wealth, to create Pentagon Industries.

Once each sister gave them a son, they were no longer considered useful. The men had their money and an heir for their family.

We were raised by ruthless men. We spent every day not wanting to be anything like them, but we had no means of escape. We just dealt with what we had to to survive. Surviving was something we had in common, Harlow, the guys, and I.

That is, until she was forced to leave our lives eight years ago.

I had no choice but to end things between us without any explanation. I still hold a massive grudge against Dean for forcing my hand.

After a long, heated discussion that involved things getting smashed and a few broken noses, we all decided that because we were set to take over the family businesses as soon as we were out of high school, it would be safer for Harlow to be completely gone from our lives. Our world consisted of rape, murder, and violence. Not by us, but by our fathers and the world they were so deeply woven into.

We always planned to turn the company around and go legit, but it would have taken years of being in a very dangerous world before that could happen. We couldn't risk the one person who meant the world to us, even if that meant breaking our own hearts as well as hers to keep her safe. We would rather her have a broken heart than ending up dead because of us.

Harlow was meant to stay with us the summer after graduation. Our fathers had never been around much, always traveling around the world, but they had recently decided to start spending more time at home. It was no longer possible to keep her with us safely.

Not knowing if they were going to stick around or not, we were compelled to put our plan into motion sooner than we expected.

When Harlow came knocking at our mansion gate, Dean destroyed her. He told her we didn't want her anymore, that she wasn't meant for our world, to leave and never come back. Breaking up with her on my behalf, much to my protests.

When she left, I spiraled downhill fast. As time went on, I became detached from my job, from my family, and spent my days drinking until I passed out—anything to numb the pain.

We sent someone to track her down, with money to give to her so that she could start a new life. That was the last time any of us mentioned her name.

One night, I got hammered and did something I normally don't do. On the three-year anniversary of Harlow's leaving, I picked up this pretty blonde at the bar, went back to her place, and fucked her until I was numb and went home.

A few months later, she showed up at our office, claiming she was pregnant, and that the child was mine.

I instantly demanded to have a DNA test done once the child was born. Six months later, she gave birth, and the test came back stating that the baby girl was indeed mine.

My heart broke all over again because I always pictured myself starting a life with Harlow and her having our babies, but the moment I laid eyes on my daughter, it was put right back together.

Rose, or Rosie as I always call her, became my entire world. I knew in that moment that I would do anything for my little girl, and I'd kill any motherfucker who would dare to even think about causing her harm. She's my little princess, and I'd die for her.

Rosie's mother saw this more as a payday, demanding a large amount of child support on top of whatever I'd spend when she was with me. Of course, I didn't hesitate to hand it over, anything to avoid a custody battle.

I can't allow that woman to take my daughter away from me and have been keeping up my payments to avoid any trouble. So, we need to find a solution to our problem as soon as possible, and if getting down on my knees for this Queenie woman gets us that money, I'd gladly kiss her feet to do it.

"Well, that went well. This whole thing is a fucking disaster, but I'm gonna go make that phone call and see if I can find an answer to our *little* issue," Neo sarcastically says, getting up off the couch, while making obscene and unnecessary noises as he does.

When he gets to the door, he turns back to face me. "Do you think she's as crazy as Harley Quinn?" he asks with wishful eyes. "Oh, I really hope she is," he groans.

"You've always liked the crazy ones. The more mentally unstable, the more obsessed you are," I comment.

"Well, anyways, off I go. Bye, Cassy," he says in a girly voice, as he wiggles his fingers at me in a wave goodbye before exiting the room with a manic laugh.

Damn lunatic!

But I find myself chuckling anyways.

CHAPTER THREE

Harlow

"**PLEASE! STOP**, I'm sorry, I won't do it again!" The silly little fat man sobs as I backhand him across the face again with my brass knuckles. Normally, I do this with my daggers, but I'm tired, and this fucker thought it would be a good idea to put his hands on one of my girls, right as I was going to call it an early night for the first time in weeks. I've had a very busy week slaying monsters. But nooooo, this fat fuck had to go and screw up all of my plans.

"Oooh, come on now, don't start with that! You know very well that's a lie," I say in a cheery voice. With my sugary sweet smile in place, I punch him in the jaw, sending his head snapping to the side. He grunts in pain as blood splatters across my black corset top. *Good thing black hides blood well.*

"I promise," he slurs, head bobbing back in place, then whines, "I was stupid and drunk." His pleas are getting weaker the harder I hit.

"See, that's what you said last month when you got your first warning for cat-calling my girl Roxy and saying very ungentlemanly things to her," I tsk. "You signed an agreement saying that you know and understand the rules upon entering my club; otherwise, you wouldn't be allowed in here. You break them, I break you. It's only fair."

"Stupid whore," he hisses, spitting a glob of blood that lands on my shoe. *Seeeee, I knew he was lying; they always do.*

"Well, that's not a very nice thing to say to a lady now, is it?" I pout, bending over to wipe the blood from my heeled, knee-high boots with a rag. Sighing, I stand back up and cross my arms, shaking my head at the pathetic excuse of a "*man*" in front of me. "These are new boots and you, rudely, just got them dirty. I think I've been nice enough. Playtime's over; any last words? Not that I care, but I feel like I should ask, maybe earn some brownie points with Karma."

"Fuck. You!" he slurs again through his swollen lips. *Poor guy's face looks like it's been in a fight with a meat tenderizer*, I think to myself, then remember that's exactly what I did to his face earlier. I giggle as I remember the first swing meeting his face and his howl of agony when he cried out like a little bitch. *God, some men can't even take a little bit of pain!*

"Nah, dude, fuck you," I say, losing my patience with this man. *How dare he talk to me like that, where are his damn manners?!* I'm so over this whole thing.

I pull out my pretty red gun and aim it right between his eyes. When he realizes what's going on, he lets out a frantic cry as a last-minute attempt to call for help, hoping someone will save him. *Not gonna happen, Buddy, not with me.* Never *with me.*

The smell of urine fills the air. Looking down at his crotch, I see that he's pissed himself. *What a dignified way to go out*. Pitiful man, such a waste, but most are. Oh well, not my problem anymore.

"Oh, come on, that's just fucking nasty! Where's your self-respect?" I say, wrinkling my nose then, wasting no more time, I pull the trigger. Thanks to the silencer, all that can be heard is the dull sound of the bullet making its way through his skull and into the wall behind him. Because I'm so close to him, his blood splatters all over my chest and a little on my face. The feeling of the warm, sticky liquid on my skin fills me with a rush of adrenaline. I close my eyes, smiling wide, letting out a breath as I bask in the glory of my kill. *I will never get tired of this feeling.* I imagine it's like getting that touchdown or home run. This feeling of being proud of what you've accomplished is amazing.

When I know in advance that I'm gonna kill a man, I get his blood work done to make sure he doesn't have any diseases. If he's clean, I get to play; if not, I just do it quickly. A shot to the head, heart, or lungs usually does the trick. Depends on how much I want him to suffer. If I *really* want to make things quick, a clean slice with my katana works perfectly. *Off with their heads!*

"Well, that was fast." A feminine voice comes from behind me. Still smiling, I open my eyes and turn to see my favorite person in the whole world, Evie.

"Well, hello there, Doll Face," I greet her.

She smiles back. Her long red hair is piled up on top of her head in a messy bun, her reading glasses sitting on the edge of her nose. She must have just come from the office, up late doing paperwork for the club. She works too hard. I try to tell her she doesn't have to, but she loves keeping things as easy as she can for me, and I love her all the more for it. "Normally, you're a little longer with your... play dates," she laughs.

"Well, he caught me at a bad time, and I just want to go to bed. I like sleep, I need sleep, and if I don't get enough, I go a little crazy," I point out.

She quirks a brow, her smile changing to one filled with humor. "As opposed to your normal, everyday crazy bitch self?" she asks, holding in a giggle.

"Whatever do you mean?" I ask, feigning innocence. I take a clean rag, rubbing my bloody fingerprints off my gun, and ignore the blood starting to dry on my skin.

Shaking her head, she hands me a stack of papers. "I looked up everything on the guy. Name's Toby Richards, 38, from out of town. The guy was here visiting his aunt. Still lives with his mother. He's on a watch list back in New York. Three counts of assault on his ex-girlfriend and was even accused of touching her seven-year-old daughter."

As soon as Evie mentions the little girl, my stomach goes sour, and I feel sick. Blood, guts, and gore I can do, but when it comes to harming kids in any way, I get extremely ill. Pedophiles are my number one prey.

Curling my lip, I turn back to the dead body tied to the chair. I take a few steps closer and spit right on his mangled face, returning the favor from before.

“The guys are waiting outside to clean up. Come on, let's get you showered. Lola just came in, and she’s here with Penny, her cousin that she was talking about. Better to just tell Penny about the place and let Lola set her up at her house,” Evie says, wrapping her hand around my arm. Her delicate pale fingers make contact with my skin, causing it to tingle. Quickly pushing all other thoughts out of my mind, I turn to face her. Sighing dramatically, I realize that I won’t be going to bed anytime soon.

“Do I have toooo?” I whine with a pout. “I just wanna sleep!”

“Yeah yeah, let's go, you big baby. After this is done, you can go to bed.”

“Fine,” I pout playfully, sticking out my lower lip. Her eyes zero in on my lip, and she bites her own, then quickly looks back up at me.

She shakes her head as if clearing her thoughts a little. “Shower in your office bathroom; it will be faster. I'll have Penny and Lola meet you at the bar,” she says before turning around and taking off without another word.

Leaving through the same door as Evie, I turn to my crew, giving my men a nod, letting them know they are free to dispose of that body as they please.

Heading up the stairs, I can hear the bass of the music from the main part of the club. Closing time was about a half-hour ago, so they should be cleaning up the place, getting it ready to go for the next night. My clubs must always be cleaned and sanitized every night. If not, I can't sleep, and I end up in the club myself, cleaning until I feel its cleanliness is up to my standards. I won't let any of my clubs be sticky and gross like most others. At Evolution, you get class. Sure, most of the girls are half-naked, but that's their own choice, and there's nothing wrong with a woman showing off her own body if *she's* the one who chooses it.

I enter the main space that leads out to the dance floor, aware that I'm covered in blood, but none of my people react, not anymore. They're used to it by now. However, I hear a little gasp, causing me to look to the right in the direction of the bar. Lola is standing there, slapping a younger girl on the arm, yelling at her in hushed tones.

The younger girl, who I'm assuming is Lola's cousin Penny, looks from me then to her cousin with a look of fear. *Good, she should have at least a little*. They all should. I don't harm women, but they need to know that just because I haven't yet, doesn't mean I won't. Cross me and live to regret it, if you're lucky enough to live at all.

A wicked smile spreads across my face and I give Penny a wink, just to fuck with her. She quickly averts her gaze to the ground. Letting out a cackle, I head down the hall and into my office.

Stripping my clothes off, I toss them in the laundry basket. I have my own personal cleaner for my clothes, so I give her a quick call, letting her know to pick up my corset before the blood sets in and will become a bitch to get out. I take pride in what I wear, so none of my things are cheap, which means I take proper care of them. Like I do with my girls.

Turning on the water, I make it so that it's just a few degrees shy of burning human skin. I love hot showers. The pain reminds me that even after everything I do, I'm still human. If it weren't for Evie, I would lose myself and just become a different version of the very monsters I set out to kill.

Quickly, I shower and get dressed into something a little more comfy. I love my burlesque outfits. They've become like a second skin to me, but sometimes a girl needs some baggy sweats and a hoodie.

I throw them on and pad barefoot back out to the bar. I don't bother with shoes because by now, the floors should be clean enough to eat off.

"Toss me a bottle of water from the fridge, please?" I ask my bartender, Roxy, then turn to the two ladies next to me. "So, you must be Penny?" I ask the trembling young girl.

"Y-yes," she stutters, refusing to look at me.

"Enough of that now," I say playfully. "I'm not gonna hurt you." I laugh.

She looks up at me, still wary of whether I'm fucking with her or not. "I don't hurt women, and definitely not kids. And by the looks of it, you're pretty young. How old are you? 15, 16?" I ask.

She shakes her head. "17."

"Well, Lola told me about your situation. You are more than welcome to stay with her at her place. Each of my girls has a townhouse to themselves with three bedrooms, so there's space for you. You're too young to dance, not that I'd ask you to if you were old enough anyways. Dancing is completely voluntary. You can't serve alcohol, so that leaves two options. You can serve food, or you can help clean up the club at night. All jobs pay the same, and it's good money. Whatever you feel more comfortable doing. As for anyone who may be looking for you, if they come sniffing around, I'll deal with them."

Her whole body relaxes, as if I just took the weight of the world off her shoulders. "Thank you." She smiles softly.

Nodding my head, I continue. "What you saw before, the blood?" I ask, and she nods, letting me know she understands what I'm talking about. "Don't ask questions. Lola can fill you in on what you need to know, but shit like that is an everyday occurrence, so prepare yourself for it now." I open my water bottle and take a big gulp. When I'm done, I cap it off and look back at Penny.

"There are rules for working and living on my property. What goes on in this club, stays here, no matter what happens. *Oh, and no* drugs of any kind are allowed. You do not touch any of the men. You're underage, and I don't want to make unplanned kills if I don't have to." Her eyes widen at my words, but I ignore it. "You do not bring outside people into my community. These homes are for my employees only, my family. No one else is welcome."

"Okay," she nods.

"Every woman who works here comes from an abusive past. Almost all the girls here were held captive by sick, evil, disgusting men, and we almost died trying to make a better life for ourselves and to be free. You will fit in fine; no one will judge you on how you ended up working here. As for the men, every guy who works for me is gay. We don't trust men as it is, and straight men are a big no-no for employees." She looks at me with a million questions in her eyes.

"Another story for another time, or Lola can tell you if she wants to. But don't bug her about it. There is one man who is bi-sexual, but he is an exception to the rule, for one main reason you don't need to worry yourself with."

I spend another ten minutes explaining a few more things before sending her off with her cousin to get settled in. My skin is crawling with pent-up energy that I didn't get to burn off with my usual after kill fuck, but I'm too tired to find Garrett and get rid of it.

I hate feeling like this—tired, weak, and in need of sleep. Normally, I'm my bubbly, sassy self. Sure, I can snap at the drop of a dime, but that's nothing new.

Just as I'm almost out of the door that leads to my attached penthouse suite above the club, Connor stops me.

"What do you want, Connor?" I snap.

"Sorry, Queenie," he says, stepping back. "I just need a quick minute of your time, and I'll leave you alone."

"What?" I growl, just wanting him to spit it out so I can go.

"Well, you see, I have this friend," he says, growing nervous, scratching the back of his head, his shaggy black hair covering half his face.

"And?" I ask in a bored tone.

“Well, he and his cousins, they own this company. And they ended up getting majorly screwed over and are in a lot of debt. Their fathers made it impossible for them to get help with any past business partners, legal or not, and well, they are hoping to set up a meeting with you.”

I narrow my eyes at him. “Look, I'm just the messenger, Queenie. If it's a no, I'll call Neo up right now and tell him. I just thought I’d ask for a buddy. They are good men. One has a little girl, and I know how much you love kids. I thought maybe you might be interested in helping. I'm sorry if I overstepped,” he stammers out, growing more apprehensive and disappointed the longer he talks without me saying a word.

At the mention of that name, Neo, my spine snaps straight. I haven't heard that name in years, haven't even let myself think of it or any of their names. They don't deserve to be a thought in my mind.

“Who are his cousins?” I say in an eerily calm tone, a complete one-eighty from the irritated one I had only moments before.

“Umm, there's Dean, Axel, and I think his twin brother’s name is Cassius.”

I guess this day had to come one way or another. No doubt, they would have come across my path eventually. So, in trouble, are they? Well, I guess those brownie points with Karma worked out in my favor after all. They don't deserve to live in that big mansion of theirs, living the high life. But I’d be lying if I said I wasn’t curious about this whole thing. *Do they know I’m Queenie?* No, they can’t know that. No one knows my real name or who I am, except for Evie and the girls. Not even the guys who work for me know my name, except for Lucas, Tommy, and Max. Everyone who does knows not to speak it when there are prying ears listening. *And did he say there was a kid?* A pang of hurt hits me at the fact that they started a family without me. I shouldn't care. *Actually, I don't care.*

So, should I take this meeting? What the hell, why not. They should be useful for *something* and if not, I could always just get my revenge. My position in their world is proof enough that they were wrong about me, and the pain they caused me needs to be returned. Maybe then, they will finally understand that women are not playthings.

"Call your friend back, tell him I'll meet with them tomorrow night, 9 pm."

He looks at me, confused. "But tomorrow's D-Day. Don't you normally do your show around that time?" he asks.

"Yes, and nothing about that has changed. We just have some extra guests to entertain." My smile grows so big and sinister that Connor looks like he's about to shit his pants. He spins and takes off running.

As I head up to my place, I can't help but laugh the whole way there.

Locking the door behind me, I make my way to my room. Black brick walls surround one big rectangle. The kitchen is to the left of the main door, all new and fancy and shit. On the other side of the room, on the left side, is a flat-screen TV with a couch in front of it. Between the kitchen and the living room is a little hall that leads to my room, the guest room, and the bathroom.

Crawling into my big four-poster California king. I snuggle under the blankets, closing my eyes and trying to go to sleep. Only, I can't because my mind is racing a mile a minute as I come up with all the ways I can use this situation to my advantage.

Buckle up, boys; you're in for the ride of your life!

CHAPTER FOUR

DEAN

I CAN'T believe our lives have come to this. I did not expect much from my father as a parent, but I thought he would at least have been a smart businessman, no matter how dirty the dealings. You would think with everything they did to get to where they were, they would have been a little wiser.

Everything makes a little more sense now that I know why they were so eager to hand over their company to us and leave town. They knew that at some point everything would be going to shit, and apparently, they would rather we be the ones left to pick up the pieces, while they live god knows where, with at least a few million to survive on.

With them having ruined every partnership they ever had, legal and underground, we're now left with no other option than to seek out help from this Queenie woman. I'm surprised I haven't heard of her, but I'm not surprised at all that Neo has. The twins and I like to be professional. Neo, on the other hand, well, there's no hope with the professional aspect. Neo's a wild card who says everything and anything that comes to mind and tends to venture outside our little group, so he has all kinds of friends, from all over town that are more his speed.

When we took over the business, we noticed right away that this was not something Neo seemed interested in. Even though this was what we were raised to do, he's not the kind of guy to sit still in a boardroom and talk business. And the last time he tried that, he cost us a contract due to the way he was staring down the group of men we had the meeting with. Afterwards, we decided it would just be best to leave Neo to do his own thing.

Don't get me wrong, he's a smart guy, but with his ADHD, sometimes it's like herding a cat. He's anywhere other than the place you want him to be, specifically his mind.

I, on the other hand, like control. I *need* it. Since our fathers left us in charge, and we were finally free of those toxic men, I promised myself that no one would ever control me again.

Having to go to someone we don't know and never had dealings with before leaves me uneasy. Asking for help makes me feel weak, and I *hate* feeling weak. But we have no other choice; if Queenie can't help us, we are done for. Even if we sold everything we own, it still would not be anywhere near enough to pay off the amount of debt we are in.

We need this money; we need to save our company. Not for me, and not for the guys, but for the little girl who has me wrapped around her little finger. Rosie. From the moment Cass told us about her, our purpose has been to make sure that little girl has everything she could ever need. As we are right now, if Cass can't pay Rosie's mother, Brianna, she has threatened to try and take Rosie away from him, from all of us. I won't allow that to happen. Cass would be destroyed and to be honest, so would I.

Rosie is the only thing that's made him happy since I ran off the love of his life... of all our lives.

I don't want him to go down that rabbit hole again, so here we are, headed for Evolution, a burlesque club owned and run by Queenie. We have an appointment with her in an hour, but Neo wanted to come beforehand to check the place out.

The club is located at the edge of LA. From what I gathered from the research I did on the place, this area was meant to be built into a new housing community, but it was all bought out and taken over by an anonymous buyer. Guess we know who that was now.

We pull up in front of the big black building with big gold neon letters that read "*Evolution*" above the blood-red diamond-shaped padded doors. The only thing I can see around for miles is this club and what looks to be a heavily guarded community located behind it.

Everyone but Axel gets out of the car and stands in front of the building, checking the place out, while Axel drives off to find a parking space. The valet offered, but we don't trust just anyone, and I'm not risking my silver Mercedes-AMG S63 Coupe.

Neo lets out a low, appreciative whistle as he takes in our surroundings. “Damn, this is a nice place. A hell of a lot more ritzy ditsy than I expected for a burlesque club.”

“Burlesque is more modest than stripping, and even though they both take talent and skill, with burlesque, you're normally not fully naked. At least not at Evolution or any other clubs owned by Queenie,” a voice says from our right, coming around the side of the club. The guy from which the voice came is tall with short black hair and a solid build. Tattoos cover every inch of visible skin on display below his face. As he walks towards us, I feel Axel taking his place at my side.

“What can I do for you?” he asks. Two other men come around the same corner, taking a spot on each side of the red doors and crossing their arms.

“We have a nine o'clock meeting with Queenie,” I answer with my guard up as I take these men in. They don't look like the type who are looking for trouble, but they would surely be able to take care of it, if some found its way to them.

The black-haired guy looks back at the other men. They both gaze at us intently, then shift their eyes to their friend and nod. The black-haired man looks back at us with a slowly growing smile.

“You must be the Pentagon cousins,” he asks. *Pentagon cousins? That’s a first.*

“If you're referring to the fact that we are cousins, and we own Pentagon Industries, then I guess yes, that would be us,” I state, crossing my arms, lifting my chin as I narrow my eyes. I don't get what is so funny and why he is smiling like the cat that caught the canary.

"A little early, are we? Your... *meeting* isn't for another hour."

"We were hoping to come in and enjoy a few drinks, watch a few dances beforehand," Cass answers with a casual tone, but I know him well, and I can tell by the clenched hands that he hates not knowing what these guys are thinking or planning to do next.

The men study us for a moment. "Alright, I guess I can allow that. My name is Lucas, and I am the head of security here," the guy with the black hair says.

"Are you Queenie's personal security guard?" Cass asks, wanting to get as much information from him as he can to file away for later.

Lucas looks back at the other guys, and they all burst out laughing. My cousins and I stand there, confused about what is so damn funny. After Lucas calms down, he looks at Cass. "Ahh, no," he smiles, shaking his head slightly. "Queenie has no personal guards. We work to keep the women safe, keep the peace, so to speak."

"To run a billion-dollar empire and not have anyone watching your back doesn't seem to be very smart, or safe for that matter," Axel grumbles more to himself than anyone else, but the guards at the door hear him.

"Trust me, buddy, if anyone can handle their own, it's Queenie," one of the guys by the door says.

"Anyone sane wouldn't dare fuck with her anyways," the other one says.

The guys lead us into the club, down a long, doorless hallway. Upbeat music with a heavy bass meets my ears and gets louder the further we head in. At the end of the hall there's a black door. *I feel like this is starting to become a recurring color scheme here.*

Lucas stops with his hand flat on the door and turns to us. "Before you go in there, you need to know the rules," he says, all the playfulness from before gone. "They're pretty simple. Respect the girls. No touching or asking to touch. If they want you to put your hands on them, then they will have to ask you themselves; otherwise, keep them to yourself. No catcalling or shouting disgusting comments. However, after each dance, you are allowed to clap and cheer if you want to."

"Not saying I would, but what happens if you break these rules?" Neo asks with curiosity, one brow raised and a twitch of his lip. He'd better watch his mouth before he screws this all up before we can even get to our meeting.

The guy turns his attention to Neo. That slow, creepy smile finds its way back onto his face. "Then Queenie makes an example out of you. Could go one of two ways. Leave with some broken bones and your life, or her pretty face is the last thing you ever see. Depends on what rule and how severely you break it."

"Fuck, that's hot," Neo groans, clearly turned on. Scoffing, I turn to him, ready to tell him to smarten up, but Axel beats me to it.

"For fuck's sake, Neo, get yourself together," he growls.

Neo adjusts himself in his pants and smiles. "I'm not even fucking sorry. She sounds like a sinfully delicious monster."

Lucas ignores his comment and continues, "Make sure you stick to the rules, and you should be fine." Turning back around, he pushes the door open, leading into the main club.

The music is loud, and the club is pretty crowded for a Thursday night. The entire club is lined with black and red. Red chairs at every black table, red and black leather couches on the far-left wall. There seems to be three levels with a single row of tables and chairs on each one. On the far right is a bar with what looks like high-end liquor.

The guys come to stand next to me, looking around at the very classy club. It looks pretty clean from what I can see. A subtle hint of cinnamon flows around the room.

"I'll come back and get you when it's almost time, but for now, you can hang out at the bar." Lucas says, before heading off down another hall to our left.

After about forty minutes of sipping a drink or two and making small talk with the twins, while Neo lights up like a kid in a candy store as he takes in all the surrounding women, Lucas comes back with the two guys from before. He has that same smile on his face, the one that says he's enjoying some inside joke that we are not privy to. "Queenie is running a little late. Her previous... engagement is taking longer than expected, but we can take you out to the back, and you can watch and wait there."

"Watch what?" Cass asks.

"You'll see," Lucas says with a hint of mischief.

We follow them down the hall that Lucas exited through earlier and stop next to a door with a sign that says, "*Employees only, enter at your own risk*". What the hell is that about?

"Know this now, anything you see in there is to be kept private. If you tell anyone about what happens in that room, may God have mercy on your soul." I can only guess that he's insinuating that if we talk, Queenie will make sure it will be the last time we do.

We all agree, and he leads us into a small viewing gallery. And what we lock our eyes on sends chills running through every cell of my body.

CHAPTER FIVE

Neo

HOLY FUCKING shit! I think I just died and went to heaven...nah, hell. Definitely hell because what I'm looking at is a work of art created by a mesmerizing creature from the underworld. She must be.

The guys and I are in some kind of viewing area, overlooking a large room with a small stage. It looks like it's some kind of dance studio or something. This room looks a lot like the rest of the club. Black and red all over. Red curtains line the back wall, and in front of it are six men, bound and gagged to chairs. Each man is spaced equally away from each other in a row. A clear plastic tarp lies underneath their chairs with extra space all around the men as if to make sure no mess is made.

You can hear the faint sounds of their struggling and their muffled screams as they try to get free. The look of pure fear in their eyes makes my body tingle in delight. I know for a fact that what's about to happen is gonna be fucked up and bloody. I can practically feel it in my soul. And I can't fucking wait.

"What the fuck is this?!" Axel demands.

Looking back, I see Lucas, the giddy fucker, light up like a Christmas tree, causing me to smile my own wolfish grin. He looks to be just as excited for whatever show we are about to see.

"Well, you see, today is D-Day," he says cheerfully. The guys frown at his words, not having a clue what he's talking about, and me, even though I don't know shit about what that means either, I can't help but get excited along with the guy. I mean, whatever D-Day is, I love it already.

"Each man down there, tied to those chairs, are all very bad, evil men," Lucas says, stepping up to the window. "The first guy, he raped five teenage girls after almost beating them to death. He got away with it because, as you know, money can buy a lot of things and make problems disappear."

I start to grow enraged. I may be a sick fucker myself, but I'm not that kind of sick. I would never hurt a woman or child. Never lay my hand on any of them. As Lucas tells us what the rest of the men's crimes are and why they are strapped to those chairs, I'm shaking with fury. I'm impressed that I actually have any self-control left, stopping me from going down there and slitting each of their throats myself, so I can watch as it runs red and life drifts out of their eyes.

Guy number two touched his young sons, and when they tried to get help, the CPS worker did nothing. The CPS worker just so happens to be guy number three. Number four beat his wife, then forced her to have sex with him, every night. Number five murdered his whole family but got away with it, all because of some tampered evidence. And number six is the cop who helped number five get away with it. Lucas said they didn't find anything on him like with the rest of the men, but he was a very dirty cop that let way too much fucked up shit slide.

Music starts playing in the room below, and I immediately know what song it is. It's *Bang* by AJR.

All of the vile creatures snap their attention to the front, a moment later, a woman comes into view as she dances and sings along to the music.

The moment my eyes take her in, my cock grows hard. This is Queenie, I just know it is. I can't see her face, but I've got a perfect view of her long, black hair hanging down her back in curls. She's dressed in sexy, lacy, black panties that show off her plump and mouthwatering ass, paired with a red and black corset. Mid-thigh high boots hug her legs, and on each thigh there's a gun holster strapped, just above where the boots end, with a bright teal pistol in each one. The color clashes with the room but draws in everyone's attention.

As the song continues and hits the main chorus for the first time, she takes both hands, wrapping them around the handle of each gun, whipping them out, and aiming at the men's thighs, and as the song plays the next bit of lyrics, she shoots them every time the song says "*bang*".

Groaning, I rub my hand over the bulge in my pants. This is the most erotic and sexy thing I've ever witnessed. For the rest of the song, she keeps singing and moving her body to the beat, but it's almost like she's in the circus or something because the way her body twists and turns as she prances around is almost unnatural. As the bangs go on, she shoots them all in different parts of their bodies. Blood is splattering all over themselves and onto the plastic below, making a perfect work of art.

As the song comes to an end, she uses the last bangs to do a headshot in each person's head. Their bodies slump forward as their life is immediately snuffed out. I can't help but clap enthusiastically at the perfectly executed show that she just put on.

The sexy, little vixen, the star of the show, lets out a whoop of excitement. “Fuck yeah!” she shouts. “That was fucking amazing, the rush I got with every shot. Never gets old.”

She still hasn't faced us long enough for us to get a good look at her. She’s talking to the people that work for her, but her voice... I’ve heard it before, only it’s more mature than the one my brain remembers. Like a freight train, the memory of where I’ve heard that voice comes crashing into me.

My eyes go wide, and I want to refuse to believe it, but I know it’s true. Turning around, I ignore the guys trying to talk to me about what the fuck they just witnessed and look at the three men watching me with small smirks on their faces. Like they were all waiting for one of us to catch on.

“It’s her, isn't it?” I growl, needing them to confirm what I already know. I don't understand how in God's name this is real because all logical sense would have her far from here; she should be married with kids, happy and safe. Not be a well-known, murderous empire queen that makes men piss their pants at just the mention of her name. But deep down inside, I know it's her, there's no doubt in my mind.

The three guys just smirk at me, not confirming or denying my question.

"What the hell are you talking about?" Dean snaps, his control slipping slightly. He has no clue what's got me all worked up like this, and being in the dark is killing him.

Ignoring his demand, I turn back to the woman in question below us. She turns around to look right up at the gallery. Every visible piece of skin on her body has specks of blood painted on it. She's a vision with her black hair still perfectly styled, not a single hair out of place. Her piercing blue eyes are sharp and hardened, with a mix of playfulness and wonder buried deep beneath them. She has grown into a goddess of a woman. Large, lush breasts, the same ones I used to dream about licking and sucking. I've imagined gripping her tits as I fucked her like an animal from behind. Her waist is still slim, but her hips have filled out and are now curvy. The one girl we were all madly in love with but couldn't have.

The guys haven't noticed her yet; they are still looking at me, as I am caught in her powerful, beautiful gaze. "Neo!" Cass yells, shaking me, trying to get me to talk, to look at him. But I won't, I don't want to look away from her, in case she disappears again. "What is going on?"

Without breaking eye contact, I say, "It's her."

The guys immediately stop talking. "Who?" Dean asks, looking confused, his gaze quickly sweeping the room, not quite picking up what I'm putting down.

"Harlow," I say. As the words leave my mouth, the guys slowly turn their heads to look in the same direction as me. Harlow's hold on me breaks as she spots my cousins standing around me. Her eyes give nothing away, that is until they lock with Cass's. I see fury in them for half a second before she locks it away again beneath her amused stare, and I hear him suck in a little gasp.

She turns away from us again and heads through a side door on the left, leaving her men to clean up the mess of bodies she left behind.

CHAPTER SIX

AXEL

MY MIND is trying to play catch up with what the hell I've just witnessed. The moment she came into view, I was in a trance. As if I was under her spell without even having to look at her face. Her presence alone commanded the room. The way her body moved so effortlessly and the timing of each shot she took was breathtaking. She makes the word 'monster' into a compliment of the highest honor, seeing as she is the most beautiful monster I've ever seen.

When she was done with her performance and went off to the side to speak with someone, I assumed that was the end of the show. I turned my attention to Dean, who was commenting to himself about what we just saw. Neo's demands of Lucas earlier were confusing to me. Neo asked if it was "her" down there, and I had no idea what he was talking about. When our eyes followed his gaze, I never in a million years would have thought that the woman down there, the woman who had just tortured and killed six men, would turn out to be Harlow McKaven.

I thought my eyes were playing tricks on me. But when my gaze devours her gorgeous body and I reach her piercing blue eyes, there is no doubt in my mind that this is Harlow. The question is, what the fuck is she doing here, and how the hell is she Queenie?

"This can't be real. There is no way that this is really happening," Dean says, heavily in denial. "No, it's just a big coincidence. She just happens to resemble her, that's all," he rambles on. Being blindsided by something this big is making him lose control, and he's not handling it very well.

Lucas and his buddies are leading us away to start our meeting with Queenie officially... or should I say, Harlow. What the hell is going on?

"Sorry to break it to you, Daddy Dean, but that was absolutely the one and only Harlow McKaven. No mistaking those eyes," Neo says with a splitting grin. He is beyond excited about the revelation, not seeming to care that the girl we thought we sent away to have a better life is smack dab in the middle of the very life we tried to spare her from. Hell, she's pretty much running it!

"Don't be foolish, Neo! How are you not more surprised or shocked that it's Harlow, for fuck's sake, and she's turned into a fucking cold-blooded killer?" I seethe, grabbing him by the shoulder to stop him so that I can look at his face and into his eyes.

His smile turns from giddy schoolgirl to dangerously lustful. "I know. It's amazing," he sighs. "You have no idea how many wet dreams I've had of us fucking bareback in a pool of blood." His eyes hold a faraway, dreamy look before looking back at me. "And now it's so close to becoming reality, I can taste it."

Lucas lets out a huffed laugh under his breath and shakes his head.

"What?!" Neo asks, his smile slipping from heavenly to murderous psycho like a light switch being flipped. "What's so funny, pretty boy?" Neo asks, cocking his head to the side.

"You, pretty boy," he mocks back. "If any of you think you have a chance in hell at having your teenage dream fantasy playing out, you're dead wrong. Queenie hates men, especially straight men. You will never lay your hands on her without her eating you alive. I've seen what she does to her play toys; you wouldn't survive one night in her dungeon." Lucas smirks in an almost teasing way, like he's trying to get a rise out of us.

"Dungeon?" Neo asks, groaning like he just came into his damn pants. Fucking crazy bastard.

"Of course, that turns you on," one of the other guys utters.

They lead us through a door and down to what must have been the basement, the same level where Harlow just put on her show. Harlow. How strange it is to say her name again. Shaking my head from my thoughts, I follow along, grumbling to myself, wondering if she's going to off us like she did those men only moments before. After what we did, I wouldn't be surprised. From what I just saw, it seems like she would kill a man for far less.

We come to a stop in a little waiting area. A black leather couch sits against a wall, and on the opposite side of it is a door. “Have a seat; Queenie should be done soon.” Lucas nods his head in the direction of the couch. Neo plops down on it, stretching his legs out to rest on the edge of the coffee table and relaxing back into it, putting his arms on the back and arm of the couch. Cass takes a seat next to him, but Dean stays standing next to my brother while I stand next to Neo, content with staying right where we are.

As I think to myself and wonder what else she would need to be doing before this meeting, I get my answer with a loud bang. All our heads snap to the door where the noise emanated from. The banging continues, followed by, “Fuck yes! Pound my pussy harder, Garrett, make me cum like a river,” a voice shouts. The banging gets faster, and male grunting starts up.

Fury takes hold of me, filling my veins at the idea of someone touching Harlow, the woman I’ve been in love with since I was a teenager. I’ve always pushed her to the back of my mind, never wanting to be consumed by her like my brother was, but hearing this has brought everything back full force. Looking over at the guys, I can tell by the looks on their faces that they are thinking the same thing.

The sounds of pleasure grow louder, then the sexiest cry is released. As much as the idea of someone plowing into her makes me want to commit a murder of my own, that cry turns my cock rock hard. Dean stands there, completely rigid, with his hands fisted at his side and his jaw clenched as he takes deep breaths trying to keep himself under control. Not from anger, like myself, but because of all the surprises that were thrown at him tonight. He's just about ready to explode. Throw in the fact that the woman he's also been in love with for years is with another man at this very moment, and yeah, I don't think he's going to last much longer.

There's some rustling going on in the room, and a moment later, a man with short blonde hair, big muscles, and an earring exits the room. Neo and Cass stand up. Dean and I take a step closer to them. The guy buckles up his pants before nodding to Lucas and his buddies, not even bothering to look our way.

"Sorry about that," an out of breath giggle comes from the doorway. Our head snaps over to the door, away from that guy, to find Harlow leaning against the doorway.

Her hair is tousled and sweat lines her hairline, giving her a freshly fucked glow. Seeing her up close, I don't know how I could ever deny that this is indeed Harlow. Our Harlow. Same height, same build, only more mature. She wears a smile, but it seems to be masking a darker side of herself. Not just the killer within, but something much more gruesome.

She looks at all of us as if we were just any other group of men, she's having a meeting with. Does she even know it's us?

She turns around, heading back into the room, leaving the door open. "Come on in, boys," she calls in a cheery voice, then looks over her shoulder, her smile turning a little crazy. "I don't bite... much." Fuck. I can see why grown men piss themselves at the mere mention of her name. This girl is terrifying.

THE ROOM smells of sex and cinnamon. I'm still deliciously sore between my legs. Garrett fucked me hard and dirty, just the way I like it. Just the way I demand him to. But I still find myself wanting as I look at the four boys turned men who I hopelessly and oh so very stupidly fell madly in love with. *What? I'm not fucking blind; they are fine as hell.* Don't worry; I didn't forget what they did. I'm imagining fifty-two different ways I can slice and dice their bodies as we speak.

Taking a seat in my chair, I lean back and prop my feet up on my desk. I'm in a pair of sleep shorts and a loose top. No bra.

The guys walk into the office and over to the chairs in front of the desk with caution. To say I've shocked them would be an understatement. My face shows no emotion, but underneath, I'm going off like a slot machine, only instead of shooting quarters, I'm shooting feelings... *Eww.* When my eyes find theirs, my heart drops into my stomach. All the pain they've put me through comes rushing back—the phone call from Dean, the homeless shelter, Triver. I quickly shove them back down, *deep* down. But when I see Cass, that one hits the hardest—our first time making love flashes before my eyes. He told me that he wanted me to be his first and to show me what it was like to have sex with someone you cared for and had a choice in. Something I never had before in all the years I could remember. I don't like being reminded of how human I really am. Feelings blind your judgment. Impact your decisions. I can't afford that. I'm already pushing my boundaries with Evie, but she's different. She's a special case when it comes to my emotions.

They made me lower my guard; they made me feel things I told myself I'd never allow myself to feel. Then, they destroyed me. That won't be happening again. They will leave here *wishing* they never came in the first place. They're mine now, but not in a way that's gonna be pleasant for them.

They each take a seat and I pull a lollipop out of my drawer, ripping off the wrapper before popping it into my mouth.

"So... What brings you to my humble abode?" I ask, moving the sucker around with my tongue, making it clink against my teeth.

No one says anything. They're just staring at me. Well, Neo is staring at my pebbled nipples that are on full display through the thin top.

Cassius clears his throat, the look on his face is packed with guilt and longing. I plaster on a carefree smile as he starts to talk. "We have unfortunately run into a bit of a situation, and we have exhausted all our options. With nowhere else to go for help and the bank not being an option, we come to you, asking if there is any way you could help us?" Cassius says, shifting in his chair.

Neo barks out a laugh. "What Cassy Boy here is trying to say is, our daddies fucked us over good, like a Sunday whore, and we are millions of dollars in the hole. Our dads also fucked over every person they ever did business with, both legal and illegal dealings, and now you're our only hope from losing our company, home, and everything we own," Neo says with a shrug. He smiles at me like he's ready to pounce over my desk and take me in front of everyone. Oh, silly man, you can't handle me. I'd swallow you whole.

Smiling to myself, I turn away from the sinfully sexy, black-haired man in a leather jacket and over to the sexy man in a gray suit. He's always so formal.

"Is that right?" my tone playful. I let my feet drop from the desk. "Oh, how the tables have turned," I say before bursting out into laughter. Lucas, Max, and Tommy laugh with me. They all know what the guys did to me. I don't handle my liquor well, and I made the mistake of letting my guard down and letting loose one night when we started this new life. I blabbered on about my past, told them everything, but they never saw me as anything less than what I was to them sober. But they were, of course, on my side. They can't help but laugh with me at the irony of this whole situation.

The guys look at me like I'm crazy... they're not wrong. Neo, the fucker, is just sitting there all relaxed and smiling like he's the same breed of deranged as I am. He's always been a little fucked in the head. This I can have fun with.

"What the hell is so funny?!" Axel growls. The sound goes right to my clit, and I hold back a moan. Fuck them for still having this effect on me.

Sobering up from that feeling, I wipe the tears from my eyes. "You," I say, cocking a brow. "All of you."

"Care to enlighten us?" Dean says through clenched teeth.

"Happily!" I chirp joyfully. "It's simple. You sent me away. You told me that your world was no place for someone like me, that I'd never survive. The funny thing is, you tossed me right into the belly of the beast that was your world, by doing that," I say, leaning back into the chair.

"What do you mean?" Cassius asks, his long, light-brown hair falls into his face, and he tucks it away behind his ear. "How did you get here? How did you become this-" he says, his hand gesturing in my direction, "...killer? You *should* be married by now, with kids and a house of your own."

My eyes go wide, and my brows fly up, so high I'm surprised they didn't hit the roof, and stare at them for a brief moment before bursting out into another fit of laughter. I laugh so hard I fall out of my chair. I lay there, laughing like the fucking crazy person I am. I take the hand Lucas is holding out for me and let him help me up.

Standing next to Lucas, I slap him on the arm. "Me, married with kids," I laugh out. He shakes his head with a smile, knowing that idea is ludicrous. Turning back to the guys, even Neo is sitting up in his chair, his playfulness gone.

"Why would something like that be so funny to you?" Neo asks.

"Well, one thing I can tell you for sure is that there is no husband, no kids."

"Then what did you do with the money?" Dean snaps. "Twenty grand should have gotten you a good head start in life!"

The laughter stops, and my face goes blank. "What money? What are you talking about?

"You didn't get it," Cassius breathes in disbelief.

"Get what?!" I snap back, not liking that I don't know what they are talking about.

"We paid someone to track you down and give you money to start over somewhere else," Axel answers for his twin brother.

"I don't know what you're talking about, but no one tracked me down, no one gave me any money. I went to LA, lived in a homeless shelter for a few weeks before being kidnapped and held against my will," I say as if it's nothing. And at this point in my life, I've changed so much since then that I don't even care who knows *how* I became who I am, as long as they know what I can do now. I have nothing to hide, nothing to be ashamed of. None of the women in this place do. We are survivors, and I stand tall and proud of it. Also, I'm blunt and don't give a fuck.

Dean lets out a curse. "He must have taken the money and ran."

"Well, yeeeah," I taunt. "You gave the guy a crap ton of money; who wouldn't?"

"Wait, kidnapped?" Cassius asks, face pale.

"Yup," I say, popping the P. I sit back in my chair and start spinning myself around. I'm still restless from my kills, and if it weren't for this meeting, I would have taken Garrett for another few rounds. I have about another hour of sexual energy left in me, and these guys, as much as I hate them, are dripping sex appeal, and that isn't exactly helping.

"Har..." Cassius says in disbelief, using the nickname from when we were teens. I stop spinning, plant my feet on the ground, reach for one of my daggers in my desk, before gripping it and bringing it down on the desk hard, stabbing it a good centimeter into the wood.

"Don't. Call. Me. That!" I growl, eyes deadly, and with a sudden urge to take this dagger and ram it into his neck and watch the blood spurt out like a water fountain.

He tries to school his expression, but I still see a little fear in his eyes, and it makes me fucking soaked.

He clears his throat. I sit back down, leaving the dagger where it is. My eyes drift from one guy to another. They all look pissed, but not at me.

"Who?" Axel growls.

My eyes find his. The thought of saying Triver's name out loud isn't helping me feel less stabby. "Triver Berk."

His eyes widen slightly, indicating that the name is one he knows. "Our fathers used to buy women from him," he snarls, eyes furious. "He owned an underground sex trafficking ring."

"And a strip club where he forced the prettiest girls to dance for the sickest men," I point out.

“Is that where you were?” Dean asks, his face blank. Dean always likes to show he’s in control, but I can tell I’ve thrown him for a loop. Wondering how long until I can make him crack completely, I give it another ten minutes. *If you win, next kill, we hang him from the ceiling and beat him like a piñata,* I say to myself and grow excited and determined to win my own bet.

I mask my excitement and shrug. “Maybeeee,” I taunt with a smirk.

“Just answer the question,” he demands, and I laugh at how brave he is for thinking he can demand shit from me. *Oh, I'm sooo winning this bet!*

“Nope,” I smile, and he narrows his eyes at me, making my smile grow.

“If you were there, then that means...” Neo says, his face turns so dangerous that if I were a normal chick, I'd shit my pants. “I'm gonna fucking murder him!” Neo roars, jumping out of his chair, breathing heavily, ready to burn down the world.

“Oh, calm down, Hulk,” I giggle. “No need. He’s already dead.”

Neo looks at me, but I can see that Neo is in the back of his mind, and his monster is present. My own beast calls to him. *Down girl, he's the enemy, no matter how fucking hot it would be to rip each other apart and fuck like the world is ending.*

“How?” is all he asks.

“Well, me, duh,” I say, rolling my eyes.

“You killed him?” Axel asks.

"Yup! Burned the place to the ground with all the bad, bad men inside." I start spinning on my chair again, not giving any more information.

"Would you stop spinning and take this seriously?" Dean snaps. Stopping the chair facing away from him. A wicked grin splits across my face, and I tilt my head up to look at him upside down.

"Or what?" I ask, cocking a brow.

"You're so damn infuriating!" he says through a clenched jaw. "I don't remember you being this difficult."

Standing up, I step into his personal space. We're toe to toe now. "That's because the girl you knew was Harlow McKaven. And Honey, that poor girl died around the 100th time she was held down while rich, sick, entitled men stuck their tiny little cocks where they didn't belong," I say, licking my lips. His breath hitches for a moment. Just when I think he's about to show some kind of sympathy, he turns around and storms towards the door.

"Finish the fucking meeting without me; I'm done with this day," he shouts before disappearing out the door.

I won my bet; he snapped in eight minutes. But the win was not as sweet as I expected it to be. Oh well, I still can't wait to see whether if I hit the body hard enough, if it will explode like a real piñata. I have no fucking clue, but it will be so fun to try.

Turning back to the guys, I see they didn't like that little bit of information I just shared. They can't look at me like that; they are not allowed to. Not when *they're* the reason all that happened to me in the first place.

Ignoring Neo's vibrating fury, Cassius's nausea, and Axel looking like his head is about to explode, I get back to the point of why they are here in the first place.

"Look, I've had a long day, and normally, I'd be getting railed good right about now, then going to bed, so can we get this show on the road?" I sigh dramatically.

"Like we said earlier, we need your help," Axel snips.

"No shit, Sherlock." I shake my head. "But how, pray tell, do you want me to do that? Are you asking me for money, for a loan, to work for me?"

"Honestly, we will do just about anything as long as we get the money," Cassius sighs, looking defeated.

"And why is it so important?"

"Because, if I don't get the money to pay everything off and then some, I can't afford child support, and I lose my little girl. Please, Harlow, she is my life and my world. I'd die without her, please, I'm begging for the first time in my life, please help us, so I don't lose my little girl," he pleads with his heart in his eyes, and I feel my resistance give. FUCK! He had to go and use one of my very few weaknesses against me. I love kids, and over half my kills were men who've harmed children. *Dammit! Fine, I'll help them, but they are gonna have to fucking work for it.*

"Alright, I'll help," I say after looking into Cassius's broken eyes.

"You will?" he breathes, shoulders relaxing.

"Yes, but there are a few conditions," I tell them.

"Like?" Neo asks.

"Like, you are now *mine*," I smile, looking over at him.

His eyes cloud over with lust. He grins and licks his lips. “And what would you have us do, Master?” he jokes.

“It’s Mistress to you,” I smirk back, and he lets out a groan. Oh, Neo is gonna be fun to play with.

“What, exactly, do you mean?” Cassius asks, leaning back into his chair, tilting his head to the side.

Walking over to him, I crouch down in front of him, placing my hands on his thighs. The contact causes him to shift as his eyes bore into mine. Out of my peripheral vision, I can see a rather impressive tent starting to grow in his pants. Giving him a half-smirk, I rub my hands up his thighs, causing him to inhale sharply. Leaning forward, I bring my face close to his. He doesn't move an inch. My lips brush against his cheekbone until I get to his ear.

“It means,” I whisper in his ear, causing him to shiver, “I own you now. *You* are *mine*.” Giving his thighs a tight squeeze, I suck his earlobe into my mouth, giving it a little nibble. He tries to hold in a groan, but I hear it slip. Chuckling lightly, I move away to sit on my desk, facing the others. My nipples are hard and pebbled, and my thighs are slick. I meant to fuck with Cassius but just fucked myself over in the process. Garrett is gone to pack for his move across the country, so it looks like I'll be taking care of this myself tonight. If I really wanted to, I'm sure I could get one of these guys to take care of the problem. I know Neo would bow down and lick my feet at the chance to have me. And I have every intention to use these men for my pleasure, but not yet, not now. Why waste perfectly good-looking men with large cocks.

Neo's eyes are glued to my tits, not hiding the fact that he's rubbing his cock over his pants. Axel is staring at me like he's trying to figure out what I'm up to. *Good luck with that one, buddy, even I don't know half the shit going on in my brain.* And Cassius is shifting in his seat, trying to hide the fact he has a raging hard-on.

"You four work for me now. You will do what I say when I tell you to do it. You will *not* ask questions; you will not second guess my actions. You will obey. In return, I will give you the money to pay off the debt you owe over a two-year period. I won't just hand over the money; you need to show me you want it, and that you really are willing to do what it takes to get it. But I will give you the money to pay for child support and a monthly wage I pay to my other employees. You don't get paid more than them. You are not better than them, if anything, you are less, so be happy you're getting that."

"Deal," Neo says immediately.

"Wait a minute," Axel protests to Neo.

"Deal," Cassius echoes.

"Cass!" Axel chastises. "We should be talking this over with Dean!"

"He's the one who lost his cool and bailed on this meeting. I'm going to do whatever it takes to keep my child. And I have a strong feeling Harlow is not someone to negotiate with."

"Nope!" My perky response earns me a scowl from Axel. Oh, he's gonna be so much fun to piss off too! This is gonna be sooo much more entertaining than I thought.

Axel looks back at his twin. They stare at each other, seeing who's gonna break first. It's Axel. He huffs out an angry sigh. "Fine!" he bursts. "But I know this is gonna come back to bite us in the ass!" Then he looks up at me with a smug grin. "Good luck trying to get Dean and me to bend to your will. We bow to no one."

How dare he talk to me like that? In front of my own men. Nope, not gonna fly. With reflexes like a cobra, my hand reaches out and wraps around the handle of my dagger still embedded in my desk, yanking it out, and flashing over to Axel. He doesn't see me coming; I have no trouble shoving his large body up against the wall. Placing the blade against his throat with a little pressure, not enough to cut him but enough to feel a little pain, I look him in the eyes. He's breathing heavily, his eyes wide, but he says nothing and doesn't move.

"I will *not* repeat myself, so listen and listen well," I say, my voice calm but deadly. "You *will* do as I say. You *will* bow down and lick my fucking feet if I tell you to. This is not a request; this is not an option; it's a demand. And if you fail to do so, I will show you *no* mercy in your punishment. Don't think for even a moment that just because we were friends in a past life that I will let any disobedience go. Because, *Buddy*, you would be sorely mistaken. Don't forget. When it comes down to it all, you all are the reason I am what I am today."

He says nothing as he breathes hard. Eyes looking like he's ready to murder me himself. I press my body against his, causing the dagger to dig into his skin, leaving a bead of blood to drip over the blade. Axel hisses lightly. I can feel his hard length against my belly. He's getting off on this... These boys are making this so much easier for me.

"Do. You. Understand?" I demand.

"Yes," he grinds out reluctantly. Looking at him a moment longer, I lean back, taking the dagger with me.

"Good boy," I praise him like one would a dog for obeying a command as I pat his cheek. He doesn't like that little move.

"Now, if you don't mind. This meeting is over. Leave your information with Lucas, and I'll be in contact with you in a few days," I say, not bothering to give the others a second thought as I exit my office and head to my penthouse.

Lying in bed, I take my favorite teal vibrator and pass out after three powerful orgasms as I imagine taking all four men to my dungeon, tying them up, and having my sick and twisted way with them.

CHAPTER SEVEN

CASSIUS

"**GET UP**, Cassy Boy. Time to break the news to Daddy Dean. I bet that the vein in his forehead pops when he finds out what our new job is. He's gonna lose his shit," Neo laughs and lays down next to me in bed; he rolls on his side to face me. My eyes are still closed, but I know he's staring at me.

Groaning, I rub the sleep from my eyes. "What time is it anyway?" My voice comes out groggy.

"No fucking clue. Suns up, and so am I," Neo says. I turn my head over and find Neo smirking at me, hands tucked under his cheek.

Neo is one of the oddest, scariest people I've ever met. He's not only my cousin but my best friend too. The guys and I are the only ones who are never on the receiving end of his crazy—at least not the dangerous kind of crazy.

"Isn't it exciting?" he whispers, and I cock my brow.

"What is?"

"Harlow. How fucking funny is it that she's our boss now?" he says, pausing, then bursting out laughing. "You think I'll get to fuck the boss? I really hope so. What do you think my chances are at having the job that numbnuts had in her office?"

"Job? You mean the guy who was fucking her?" I ask, grunting as I sit up. My night was shit and I got no sleep. My mind wouldn't shut down until 4 am because all I could think about was our new jobs and my weekend with Rosie. I miss my little princess more than any words could explain.

"Well, it must be. Harlow doesn't look like someone who would just let anyone fuck her, and I know for a fact she doesn't do boyfriends. Whoever that guy was, he works for her, and now that we do as well, I want his job," he states.

If he is right, and it is a job, he, out of all of us, would be the one to get it. She would never let us be in control of any aspect in her life, and Axel and Dean would never let a woman dominate them. I would, but something tells me she's not gonna let me back in, at least not without a lot of work on my part. I plan on doing everything I can to get back into her good graces, though, if I ever was in them. I loved that woman back then, and I still do now. I don't care who she's become.

When she told me, what had happened after leaving our front gate, it took everything in me not to puke. The idea of her being kidnapped and then raped on a daily basis made me want to claw off all of my skin just to twist the organs that lie inside.

No wonder she hates men so much. She has every right to, but she is still the love of my life, and I'm not ashamed to admit it. Not like Axel and Dean would be.

On the other hand, I also have to think of Rosie. Is bringing her into this life a good idea? We've worked hard to keep everything legal and stay out of shady businesses. Having a serial killer playing a significant role in *her* life doesn't sound like the best parenting move. So, I have no choice. I need the money to keep Rosie in my life, and there is no way I'm letting that money sucking leech have my daughter full time. There's something about her husband that rubs me the wrong way.

"What the hell are you two doing in here?" Axel grumbles as he steps into my room. He looks over the two of us and shakes his head like none of this surprises him.

"Alright, let's get this done and over with. Fill me in on what I missed, and then we can set up a game plan and get things in motion," Dean says, making his way into the room and around Axel. He looks at Neo in the bed with me and raises a brow but says nothing.

"Oh, lighten up, Daddy Dean. Pull the dildo out of your ass. We have fallen down the hole into a wonderful land of possibilities. This is gonna be awesome," Neo says, jumping up onto the bed, bouncing a bit. "Like talk about a total bombshell of a boss. I'm never gonna get any work done. All I'm gonna be able to do is think about how perfect those pretty tits would look as I thrust my cock between them." Neo's grin splits his face.

"Neo, now is not the time for games or your fantasies. I'm being serious. Tell me what she said after I left," Dean says, his voice stern as he steps closer to the bed.

"Boooo! You're such a buzzkill. Chill the fuck out," Neo says, then bends over and grabs a pillow. "Pillow fight!" Neo crows before whacking Dean across the face with the pillow.

I choke on a laugh and Axel groans, knowing what's coming next. Neo just has to poke the bear, even if it is this early in the morning. Dean is already walking a fine line when it comes to his control.

Dean's face turns red in anger, and Neo bites his lips, holding back a smile. "Now, now, Daddy Dean, calm down before that pretty blue and green vein in your forehead pops. Although, then I'd win my bet, so never mind," Neo shrugs. He jumps up and lands with his butt on the bed.

"Fuck. Off," Dean seethes, his jaw clenched tight. "And stop calling me that stupid nickname."

Neo smiles. "Oh, Daddy Dean, I've been a bad boy. Spank me," Neo says, then bends over and sticks his ass in the air.

I need to put a stop to it before Dean murders Neo... it's not even noon yet. But Dean brings up his foot and kicks Neo in the ass, sending his body forward on the bed.

"Harder," Neo groans. Thankfully, he's joking because if this were Harlow, he would have already busted a nut.

Dean growls. Neo chuckles. "Alright, alright."

"What you missed was these two asshats accepting a deal with her before talking to you," Axel says, stepping forward, crossing his arms, and giving us a look as if he were a parent scolding a child. I roll my eyes.

"It's really not that big of a deal. We went there for this very reason anyways," I say, getting up and grabbing my robe off the back of the door.

"You agreed to her terms for all of us, and that's not how things work!" my twin snaps.

I sigh. "We went there to make a deal and get the money we need. She is gonna give us all of that. Money to pay off our debts, to pay for Rosie's care, and money to live on. I don't get what the big deal is."

"Are you stupid? You signed us all up to be her slaves for the next two years!" Axel shouts.

"You what?" Dean asks, trying to keep his cool.

"We agreed to be Harlow's lapdogs, and honestly dude, I think this is the best job I could have ever dreamed of, like really, who needs stuffy boardrooms with ugly, old dudes in expensive suits when you can look at a goddess with an ass that could cause another world war," Neo groans.

"And what exactly do we have to do for her? What does this job entail?" Dean asks, looking at me for answers because Neo is useless right now, so Axel answers.

"That's the thing; we don't know. It could be anything from cleaning the place to burying the bodies," Axel grumbles.

"Oh, don't be dense, she would never bury bodies. Too easy to trace back to her," Neo scoffs, grabbing a handful of candies I have on the side of my bed and eating them all at once. I swear that man is always eating. I don't get how he's not a thousand pounds.

"Look, I don't think it's gonna be too bad. She doesn't trust us, so it definitely won't be the body thing."

Just then, all our phones go off. I grab mine off my nightstand and open the text message. *"Morning, boys. Work starts tonight at 9 pm sharp. Be warned, it will be a packed night, and you'll be shadowing Lucas. I'll meet up with you after my performance."*

"Fuck yes," Neo groans. "I better get front-row seats to this, or I'll stab someone."

"I don't like this," Dean says, turning around and leaving the room. "I don't like this one bit!" he shouts as he takes off down the hall.

My brother turns to me. "If we get fucked over by this crazy bitch, *you're* the one I'm blaming."

"I'm not the only one who agreed to this," I say. His attitude is not welcomed. We may be twins, but we're not best friends. Neo is mine and Dean is his. I guess they are each a better personality fit for us. But he's still my brother, and this is my family.

"I'm not going to hold that one accountable for anything. This is something I'd expect from him. He bought a llama in an online auction. Of course, he's gonna agree to be a slave to sex on legs," Axel snaps.

"Hey! It was an alpaca, not a llama," Neo defends.

Axel narrows his eyes. "The point is that you spontaneously bought a wild fucking animal out of nowhere!"

"I don't regret it. Susie is adorable. And smart. She probably would have gotten sent to some zoo, just to be gawked at by a bunch of crotch goblins."

"And how is that better than her living in our backyard by herself?!"

"I take good care of her, thank you very much," Neo growls, getting into Axel's face. "She has her own pen and everything. She's my baby. I was also thinking of getting her a little friend. Do you think Harlow would spot me the cash to get a donkey?"

"We're not getting a damn donkey," I groan. It is way too early to be dealing with the typical Neo crap.

"You're right; they're too loud." Neo snaps his fingers. "Oh, oh, I got it. A goat. One of those baby ones, and we can dress it up in a onesie!"

"No goat!" Axel snaps.

"Well, you're just gonna have to tell Rosie that and break her little heart," Neo says, then picks up the phone and makes a call. "Hey, my little Posy Bear, guess what, we're getting a baby goat friend for Susie!" Neo says into the phone. For a moment, I think he's fucking with us, then excited girly squeals come from the other end of the line. Fuck, we're getting a baby goat...

"Fuck this shit. I'm done with you two today. I'll see you later for our first day in hell," Axel seethes, clearly done with the day already.

"Neo, give me the damn phone," I tell him as he chats up my daughter.

"What was that, Rosie? You want to name him Bob? I think Bob is a perfect name," Neo smirks, ignoring my request as he darts around me and rushes out the door. I'm honestly surprised Rosie's mother hasn't taken away the phone I bought for her. She uses it to FaceTime us whenever she can. And almost every time, her mother asks for more money on top of the agreed upon amount. Working for Harlow is what's gonna fund me, keep that selfish bitch at bay, and my daughter close. So, I'll do whatever she wants of me.

The place is more packed tonight than it was last night. There's extra security in every corner of the room.

"So, what are we doing tonight? Queenie is busy, so what exactly is our job?" Dean asks, looking around the room. People from all different walks of life have shown up for whatever kind of show is happening tonight. I'm pretty intrigued to see what goes on in this place. You know, when Harlow's not murdering people.

When she left the room last night, leaving Lucas behind to explain a few more things to us, he made one thing very clear. We are NEVER to use her real name in public. Everyone who works for her knows her real name, but that's it. Unless we are 100% sure no one outside her little family is around, we must always refer to her as Queenie.

"Tonight, all you're gonna do is observe. What you saw last night might be a big part of what goes on around here, but it's not the main thing. This club is everything to these girls. It's their whole lives. They work hard to do something they love, and Queenie makes sure they have a safe environment to work in. Not every night is going to be soaked in blood. Most nights, it's simply this," he says, gesturing to the crowd of people laughing.

When the girls aren't dancing, it is just like any regular club. People dancing to the music, letting alcohol consume their minds, letting loose and having fun. I do like the idea that none of these girls have to worry about letting their guard down and getting taken advantage of. I have no doubt that these people have some idea of who Queenie is and what she's capable of.

"So, take everything in. Pay close attention to the inner workings of this place. And enjoy the show. But remember the rules. Just because you are on the payroll, it doesn't mean you are exempt. We all live by these rules. It's literally life or death. If you have any questions, feel free to ask Tommy or Max. I'll be in the back, making sure the girls have everything they need for the night," Lucas finishes explaining.

So, that's their names. Now, who is who? I contemplate, looking at the two guys at our side.

"So, where is she?" Neo asks, ignoring everything Lucas just said. He's on his tip toes trying to get a better look at the crowd. He looks like an eager puppy who's desperate to lay eyes on its owner. It's only been a day and Harlow already has Neo eating out of the palm of her hand. I've never seen him obsess this hard over anything in his life.

"She's backstage getting ready with the girls. It's group dances this weekend. Sometimes Queenie joins. Max and I are normally watching the crowd. But I guess tonight we're on babysitting duty." So, that would mean *he* is Tommy, the guy with a buzz cut, and Max here is the guy with the brown hair.

"Well, if we get to watch, I want a front-row seat," Neo says, his tone leaving no room for discussion. Max stares him down, contemplating if it's worth the argument. Trust me, it's not.

"Well, normally VIPs pay triple the regular admission, but Queenie did say to show you guys how things work around here, and the shows are a major part," Max says, sounding more like he's trying to convince himself.

"I wholeheartedly agree," Neo says, his face splitting into a grin.

"Also, I'm not really sure what is going on with you guys and Queenie, but to avoid any unwanted bloodshed, on you or someone else, I'd keep away from all the women in here," Max says and smiles at the shocked look on both Axel and Dean's faces.

Me, I have no interest in being with anyone right now. The one-night stands have slowed since Rosie was born. Once in a while, when the need is too much, I'll let a girl take me home, but that's become few and far between.

Neo already has their wedding planned out in his head, and probably some fucked up joint mass murder as his present to her, so there's no worry about that with him.

The other two, however, that's not gonna go over well with them. Axel is with a new girl every other week, and Dean has a few girls he calls whenever he needs to let off steam. Unlike the rest of us, he was never really the type who would just go out and pick up some random girl. Instead, because of his need for control, he hires a high-end escort service with background checks and regular testing.

"You're kidding, right?" Dean asks.

"When it comes to Queenie, I never joke," Max says, and I believe him.

"So what? We're not allowed to have sex now? This was not what I signed up for," Axel growls.

"I mean, you can always ask Queenie to make sure," Max chuckles. "But is that really something you wanna risk?"

"Your best bet is to accept that she owns you in every way, and I'm pretty sure, if I'm not mistaken, that includes your balls," Tommy says.

"Among other things," Max adds, and they both have amused grins, loving every moment of this.

"Fucking bullshit," Axel grumbles. Dean's nostrils flare, and I can see his mind processing what he's gonna do now, and if there's any way around it.

"I'm not fucking her," Dean says through gritted teeth. "And she can't make me."

The two guys' brows lift. "And she would never try. She may be a cold-blooded murderer, but she would never force anyone to do anything sexual against their will," Tommy says.

"She doesn't just sleep with anyone anyways. She has someone special to give her what she needs. But the guy who had that job is now moving for personal reasons, so she will be looking for a new reliever," Max throws out. Neo instantly perks up.

"And is there some kind of paperwork I need to fill out to apply for that position? Because I very much would like that job." he says.

The guys smile and shake their heads.

"Well, seeing how everyone else who works here is gay, and I don't think the other three of you can handle her... unique brand of... pleasure," Tommy says, picking his words carefully, "Something tells me *you* would be perfect for the job."

"Damn right, I would be. I'd be the best damn reliever she's ever had. I'd relieve her real good," Neo grins, and I can tell he's thinking about all the fucked up sexual things Harlow would do to him.

A pang of jealousy hits me because these guys are right. Harlow isn't the type of woman to let a man be in control, and that's exactly what Dean and Axel thrive on, Dean more so, but in the bedroom, they are both very dominant partners.

There's no way she would allow me to get close to her, either. Not after how things ended with us, and our past together, so Neo would be the perfect fit. Plus, they seem to be a similar brand of crazy; perfect for each other.

Tommy looks at his phone. "Alright boys, showtime," he grins.

Max and Tommy get us a few seats upfront. It's a tight fit, but we make it work. Red velvet ropes block the VIP section, while matching padded chairs line the stage, just inches away. One of the rules is *No touching*, and being this close, I could see how it might be tempting to just reach out and touch. Maybe that's what Harlow wants. To see if someone is dumb enough to try it, so she can get her pound of flesh. She's crazy enough to do it. And I know in my heart that we haven't even scratched the surface of this girl's brand of insanity.

The lights dim a little, causing a chain effect as the room starts to descend into silence.

"Ladies and Gentlemen. Welcome to Evolution, where we bring you Burlesque with a sexy twist. Tonight, you're in for a treat. Our wonderful Queen will be joining the show. So, sit back, remember the rules, and enjoy the show," a blonde woman with a pink corset outfit and a feather boa to match announces.

The lights dim more, engulfing the room in almost complete darkness, before a red tinted light illuminates the stage, casting a shadow over someone showing the outline of their curvy body. The music starts, and the song is one I remember well. *Buttons* by The Pussycat Dolls. When we were teenagers, Harlow went through a phase where she would listen to every song on repeat until it drove us mad. But the voice singing this song isn't coming from the original performer, it's being sung by someone else, someone on stage.

Half the stage lights up and some of the girls start to dance. Their bodies are in sync with each other as they flow perfectly with their music, and they are really good.

After a few seconds, the rest of the stage lights up, and the silhouette of the body is revealed. Harlow struts closer to the audience and joins the girls in the dance. When her eyes lock on us, it's as if this song and dance number is meant for us alone.

Her body twists and dips seductively, but not so much that it takes away from the grace of her movements. She's perfect. Her body beckons to me, like a siren calling to sailors out at sea. Beckoning them over to trap and kill. And at this moment, I'd gladly let her take me and devour me whole.

I've never heard Harlow sing before. Sure, she messed around and sang when we listened to music, but she never gave it her all. But right now, she's giving it her all and her voice is just as alluring as her dancing.

As she sings and moves around the stage, I look over at the guys. Neo is watching her with wide, hungry eyes, following her every movement. Axel's face is impassive, but I can see the glint in his eyes. He clearly likes what he sees. Dean is watching every girl on stage, except Harlow, as if to prove a point to himself. Cracking a small smile, I bring my attention back to the beautiful black swan on the stage. Graceful and mysterious.

The lyrics talk about needing help taking clothes off, and now, all I can think about is stripping her bare and having my way with her like I used to when we were teenagers. She used to have so much trust in me, allowing me to play with her body and make us both happy. Something tells me that is the furthest thing from being the case now.

Harlow dances her way over to the edge of the stage and locks her eyes with mine. She runs her hands up her body, but it fits with the choreography of the dance. She looks directly at me while singing lyrics that pretty much insinuate that the love I said I had for her, was never shown to her.

As she keeps singing, she pays attention to the other guys as if she's singing to them as well. A part of me thinks she picked this song just to rub the whole fucked up situation in our faces, but I don't care as long as it means I get to see her this way. Carefree and happy. I can see the joy on her face as she dances up there. Going through hell for all those years hasn't stopped her obvious love for music and its art.

When she's not looking, I sneak glances at the other women dancing. Not in interest, but with curiosity about what *their* stories might be. I know all these women were held captive with Harlow. Women she saved. So, what makes them want to keep dancing? And why did some of the others choose not to?

It's none of my business, though, so I shut that line of thought down quickly and watch the last little bit of the song. When they are done, the room erupts into excited chaos.

"Thank you, thank you, my lovelies," Harlow says, giving the audience an extravagant bow and a big smile. "Please enjoy the rest of your night! There will be a few more dances throughout the evening from our lovely girls; however, I am done for the night."

The room makes disappointed sounds, and Harlow chuckles. "Now, now, no need to be glum. I have some exciting news! Now that I've hired a few more capable men on my team, I'll have more time to perform for you all." The room starts to cheer again.

"Thank you again for coming." Her smile drops and is replaced with a spine-chilling expression. "And don't forget the rules. You will not be reminded." Her voice is low and dangerous. The room is silent, allowing me to hear a few people behind me swallow hard.

"Anywho, have fun! Toodles!" she says, now all bubbly and perky while waving. Something tells me this girl is gonna be giving me whiplash with her mood swings. This will definitely be interesting.

CHAPTER EIGHT

Harlow

THE WAY they watched me when I was up on stage gave me power. The lust and want was unmistakable, even Axel and Dean. They aren't fooling anyone, but I could also see they didn't want to react to me that way. Unlike Neo, who was salivating after me like a hungry hound does a bone. Then there is Cassius; he looked like he was watching his long-lost lover, who he still harbors feelings for. That, I don't like. I said it once; I'll say it again. Feelings, eww.

After I leave the room, I can hear the crowd pick up again once I'm out of sight. Bunch of pussies. Not like I'm gonna kill them... for no reason.

When I get to my office, I ask Lucas to grab the guys and bring them back here. Time to tell them their new jobs. This is gonna be good. They are gonna freak. Well, maybe not Neo. I can see him totally enjoying what I have planned for them.

I head into the back and wash off the sweat I've worked up from dancing. I normally have a bit of extra energy coursing through my veins after a show, but it's nowhere near as powerful as it is after a kill, so the need to fuck isn't as strong. I easily take care of myself with what I like to call rub-a-dub tug, or more simply put, a shower vibrator. It's a big black cock that uses suction cups to stick it onto the edge of my tub. I love the looks of shock when people go back there to use the bathroom, in between meetings, and are met with a thick, eight-inch vibrating dildo.

Still looking for a real one. A thick, eight-inch cock, I mean. Although, it would be fucking epic if cocks could vibrate. I mean, some twitch when they come, but that's not the same.

I wonder if one of the guys has a big cock like that. From what I can remember, Cass had a pretty big cock for an 18-year-old. It must have grown as he did. *Right?*

Shut the fuck up, Harlow, stop thinking about their cocks. They are naughty men who need to be punished.

That thought has me smiling as I think of what I'm about to tell the guys.

When I'm changed, I pull my damp hair up into a messy bun and head out to the main part of the office. As soon as I enter the room, all four men stop whatever conversation they were in the middle of and snap their gaze to me.

Neo's eyes light up with a hungry glint. I smile and roll my eyes as I plop down into my chair, spinning once, before placing my elbows on the desk and setting my chin on top of my hands.

"Hi," I say, my voice perky and high. "So, we meet again."

"Because you fucking called and demanded us to be here tonight," Axel grumbles. I narrow my eyes at him.

"Watch your tongue, Pretty Boy, or you're gonna find yourself missing it real quick," I warn, all playfulness gone because this ass-face just had to go and ruin my good mood.

Dean clears his throat, interrupting Axel's and my glare off. "We came like you asked."

I snicker at his words, and Neo looks at me with amusement, like he knows my dirty mind is interpreting what Dean said differently. "I'm sure you did." I wiggle my brows. Dean frowns.

"I mean, you asked us to be in attendance tonight, and here we are," he rephrases—Party pooper.

"Well, yeah." I say, "You work for me now. So, when I say jump, you need to say how high." I smile.

Cass snickers while Neo looks eager to obey. On the other hand, Axel is giving me a dirty look, and Dean's jaw ticks.

"Calm down, D. If you clench your teeth any harder, they're gonna fall out." I giggle with a wink. He clenches and unclenches his fists in response.

"You name it, and I'll do it," Neo pipes up.

Axel scoffs. "You just want to get your dick wet. I bet if she told you to suck her toes, you would," Axel sneers at his cousin and his easy betrayal.

"And your point is?" Neo smirks. He sticks his thumb in his mouth, sucks it with a moan, then pulls it out with a pop and bursts into laughter at the sight of his cousin's face. Axel is looking at Neo like he wants to murder him, but I'm sure they are all used to his behavior by now. I may hate these guys, but I hate Neo the least and Dean the most, but Axel might end up tied with Dean here soon.

"Focus, boys, we have important business to attend to," I say, leaning back in my chair and propping my feet up on my desk. "Tomorrow, I want you boys in here at 9 am sharp. For now, until I can find better things to do with you, you will be doing grunt work. Cleaning the club, stocking the kitchen and bar, cleaning the bathrooms, and changing rooms. Stuff like that. The girls are normally in for their shifts by 6 pm for their 8 pm shows. You are never to be alone in a room with any one of my girls. It's preferred if you avoid them completely until we are open to the public if possible."

"We're not gonna hurt them." Dean blinks at me, slightly taken off guard by my rules.

I give him a fake, sweet smile. "Listen, buddy," I coo. "You are a stranger to me. I don't know you. These girls have lived just as fucked up lives as I have, so most of them don't feel safe being alone around men. This club gives them the security to do what they love, while being safe and protected. Only a mindless moron would dare try to fuck with me or them. But that still doesn't mean you are an exception to the rule." I keep my fake smile on and rapidly blink at him. I probably look stupid, but it's pissing him off.

"We're not strangers," Cass says.

Now it's my turn to scoff and roll my eyes. "I stand by what I said. I knew who you were eight years ago, and that's sure as hell not who you are now, so yes, you're strangers. Anyways, the only women you're allowed around are Evie and Roxy, who is the bartender. If the other girls choose to be in the same room as you, that is up to them. If one of my girls makes a pass at you, do not touch them. They are off limits."

"Why would they try anything with us? Don't they hate men, like you do?" Cass asks with a raised brow.

I smile slowly. "We may hate men, but men have something most of us enjoy. A well sized cock. And I may not like you four, but I'm not blind. You are all hot as fuck, and I'm sure most of these girls would love to take a ride on your joysticks." I laugh. "But they won't. I'll make it known that you are also off limits."

"But if they choose to, why can't they?" Axel grunts.

I look at him, and my smile widens. "Because, as of right now, you are all cut off from sex."

Dean and Axel's eyes go wide. They both start to protest loudly, talking over each other. I start to cackle like an evil mastermind. God, this is fun. I mean, it's a dick move, but fuck them and everything they caused to happen to me. They deserve it and so much more. I'm sure they can survive a little blue balls. If anything, as long as they take turns switching hands as they jack off, they could build some serious muscles. Or get a pussy pump.

"You can't do that!" Axel growls.

I stop laughing and raise a brow with a smile. "Oh, but I can. And I just did."

"And what if we don't agree," Dean asks. I can see his control slipping, and he's ready to burst. I bet myself throwing star practice with a live target if he walks out again from this meeting. I need to find a new play toy soon. It's been a few days, and I'm starting to get itchy. Would be fun to use *him* as a target, turning him into a human piñata.

"Then I'll cut off your dick and put it in a jar on my shelf." I giggle. "Would make a great addition to my collection." Dean's face pales.

"Oh oh, can I watch?" Neo bursts in, bouncing in his seat.

"Mayyyybe," I say. "If you're a good boy and do what Queenie says, my new little pet." Neo smiles wide at my comment, like he's honored to be mine in any way.

"There's only so much shit I can take in one night," Axel says, getting up and heading to the door with Dean following behind him. My smile slips, and I quickly grab my dagger from my holster on my thigh, throwing it in their direction. It whizzes past their faces, right in between their heads, and lands in the door with a heavy thud. Their bodies go rigid, but they don't turn around.

"Walk out on me again after tonight, and I'll aim that a little further over," I warn. My voice is deadly, void of all previous playfulness. "Clear?"

"Crystal," Axel snarks, then Dean rips open the door.

"Remember, 9 am sharp. Don't make me come find you!" I shout at their receding backs.

"Well, then, now that the drama queens are gone, let's continue, shall we?" I ask the two remaining men with a bright smile.

"Umm," Neo says, raising his hand like he's in school.

"Yes?" I ask with a raised brow, a smile still in place.

"That was fucking hot," Neo groans. His attraction to violence supersedes mine. Yeah, I'm gonna need him as my new reliever. Something tells me he would kiss the ground I walk on. It would be nice to have a man follow with utter blindness.

"I agree." I bite my lip. Fuck, am I flirting? I don't do that shit. But his beast is calling to mine, like fated mates or some shit.

"Harlow?" Cass asks. "I need to talk to you about a few things regarding my daughter Rosie."

That sobers me up, and business Queenie takes her place. "Alright," I nod.

"Well, you see, her mother, Brianna, has been messing around with the agreed upon custody arrangements. She hasn't been sticking to it, and she knows she can get away with it because I don't have the money to take her to court to fight it. So lately, she's been picking up and dropping Rosie off at random times. I might not be able to be here with the guys all the time." He looks worried like I'm about to lose my shit on him or something.

"As long as you always let me know, and it really is because of Rosie, I'll allow it," I say, and he relaxes. "Also, if you ever need someone to watch her, I trust my girls, and I trust Evie with my life. Let me know."

He gives me a warm smile that does fucked up things to me. *Nope, nope, not happening. Shut that shit down, Low, we are not catching feels for this guy. Dude destroyed you, remember?* But fuck, he looks like a tasty treat looking all buff and stuff. I just wanna grab a fistful of that hair and use it as reins as I ride his cock like a bronco rider. At least he could be good for one thing.

"Thank you. I appreciate the offer. I'll keep that in mind."

"I mean, I could always watch her too," I say casually with a shrug. He makes a choking sound, sending Neo into a fit of laughter. I look at him annoyed. "Hey! I would be a kick ass babysitter. I love kids," I pout.

"Harlow, you murdered a room full of men all while dancing and singing just the other night." Cass points out.

"Like a fucking badass, I might add," Neo throws in.

"Yes, but she still murders people," Cass counters. He looks panicked and protective of his daughter.

"Cassius, I need you to understand a few things. One: I love kids. Two: I would rather die than allow or cause harm to any child in general, let alone one that is in my care. Rosie would be safe with me. Hell, the safest place for her would probably be with me."

Cass looks like he's about to go all Papa Bear on me. The first real defiant thing he's done since we reconnected. "Down boy!" I chuckle. "I'm not saying you can't protect your baby girl; I'm just saying that there's little to no one who would dare fuck with me. You guys will see that for yourselves real soon."

He nods. "Thank you for understanding."

"Alright, well, that's all I got for tonight. You can go, Cass. I'll be seeing you tomorrow." Cass gets up, and leaves. Neo gets up to follow. "Neo, you stay," I command and get a groan in response. Not out of disappointment, but full-on heated anticipation. God, he really is perfect to be my new pet.

"I have another job offer for you, if you're up for the extra workload." I smile as he turns around with blown pupils and an excited expression all over his face.

"Anything," he says eagerly. "Anything at all. I'll be your fucking footstool if you want." He's almost panting at the thought.

"Perfect," I smirk. "But this job would be more enjoyable than that, on both our parts." He sits back down but on the edge of his seat, as if ready to jump up and start worshiping at my feet anytime, if I'd only ask. I smirk at his puppy love.

"After I play, I always have this lingering adrenaline in my body. Garrett, the man you saw leaving my office the other night, used to help me take care of that. But he moved away, and now I find myself in need of a replacement. I'd like to offer you the job." I lean back in my chair, cross my legs, and place my arms along the arm rest, looking a little more professional despite my baggy clothes and messy bun. Even now, I know I'm a fucking bombshell, so who fucking cares.

"And how exactly do I help rid you of this extra energy? Just to be clear on my job description." He gives me a sly smile. The fucker knows exactly what I mean. I'm sure as fuck they all heard me getting my brains fucked out.

"To put it bluntly, I'm gonna need you to destroy my pussy. I'm gonna need you to fuck me so hard and good that I see stars, or at the very least until I cum hard a minimum of three times. Then and only then can you cum. Where, it doesn't matter. On me, in me, around me. As long as I get to cum, nothing else matters." That's not exactly true; I want my partners satisfied. But he doesn't need to know that part yet.

Neo groans as if he just came in his pants. Wait... did he?! He adjusts his pants, and my eyes zero in on the wet spot on his pants. The crazy fucker nutted into his pants like a teenager... *I guess he likes the idea then.*

"That *never* happens," he says, but he doesn't seem embarrassed. "I can usually go for hours. But hearing you talk like that, on top of me being hard as a rock ever since you walked out on stage, plus that little dagger trick you did, and well... there's only so much my sick, twisted mind can take..." His voice is deep and husky and, fuck, does it do things to my newly aching clit. Neo is a gorgeous man. A sinfully sexy man. Black hair, short on the sides, longer on the top. A Cali kissed tan and piercing blue eyes. I always had it big for Neo when we were younger. I know my body remembers him, but my mind won't let me forget.

"So, you want the job or what?" I ask.

"More than anything in the world," he replies.

"Alright, then you need to know about the rest of the rules. You *never* touch me without my permission. Even when I'm ramped up and ready to go, mentally, I can only handle you touching me if I give consent. It's just something I need, or I get... stabby." He nods.

"I would never touch you without your go ahead first."

"I don't kiss. Kissing is personal, and this is just a business arrangement." He nods again. "I already banned you from touching anyone else, but even if I didn't, being with me means only being with me. If you have needs outside our arrangement, suck it up. You will just have to wait until I need you to get off. However, your hand is allowed."

"Seeing how you're the only woman left in the world, at least in my eyes, that won't be a problem." He smiles adoringly. Eww, stop, stop being all sweet and shit. It's weird, dude. You're just as crazy and fucked up as me. I'm pretty sure you've killed your fair share of people too. Stop acting like a puppy! .... Or... Let's see if he goes along with...

"I am your master now, and you are my pet. You will obey my every command, even outside of sex," I demand, my voice heavy with authority.

"Whatever you say, Mistress." There's a tent in his pants again, and his breathing starts to pick up.

"You're gonna need to get that under control. I mean, it's hot how easily I affect you, but cumming in your pants every five minutes is gonna get old. And inconvenient."

He lets out a deep chuckle. "Trust me when I say that you will *never* have a problem with me getting it up," he says, then waves a hand in front of his dick. I raise my brows and shrug.

"Sooo, do you need any help tonight?" he asks hopefully.

"Nope."

"Oh," he says, sounding disappointed.

"Guess you're just gonna have to follow me around like a little puppy from now on, My Pet. Never know when I'm gonna need a good, hard fucking," I smirk.

"Done and done," he chuckles.

"I'm tired as fuck and need to sleep. Weekends are crazy around here."

"More crazy than tonight?" he asks with amusement.

"You would be surprised," I laugh.

"Alright then, the Queen needs her sleep. Don't let me keep you waiting," he says, getting up and heading for the door. He pauses just before he leaves the room.

"Harlow?" he says, all playfulness gone, his mood sad and remorseful.

"What?" I ask, not sure if I'm gonna like what he has to say.

"I didn't know," he says.

My brows pinch. "Know what?"

"What Dean did. Sending you away. I didn't know he did that. I didn't find out until a few days after when you didn't show up to spend the summer with us. Dean decided everything on his own and told everyone but me and Cass. Just so you know, Cass beat the shit out of him, and then I took my turn. I don't care what his reasoning was for what he did, I wouldn't have let you go," he says. "I never wanted you to leave, even if it might have been for your safety. I was and always will be a selfish bastard," he says before turning back around and leaving.

What the fuck are these guys doing to me! Fuck, fuck, fuck! That part of me died years ago, and here they are resurrecting what should be dead like some fucking necromancers or some shit. Fuckers really need to fuck right off, or I'll need to start chopping shit off!

"**YOU HAVE** got to be fucking kidding me," I growl, my voice echoing around the changing room. Right in front of us, hanging on the rack, are four maids outfits. "There's *no way* in hell I'm wearing that. That woman is delusional!"

"She's doing it to fuck with us, and we do deserve it," Cass says, taking one off the rack. I just keep staring at them in disbelief.

"Like fuck we do. We sent her away to protect her. We didn't do it to be evil!" I say.

"And look what ended up happening to her," Cass counters.

"How the fuck were we to know that would happen?!" I'm getting worked up now.

"We have to wear them; Queenie said so," Neo taunts in a sing-song voice, waving around a piece of paper. I snatch the note from his hand, and he chuckles, grabbing an outfit of his own.

He's right. She's left a note demanding we wear them, calling them our new work uniforms. There's no way I will let this become a regular thing. Hell no.

"I think it's sexy," Neo says, wiggling his eyebrows, then starts stripping off his clothes and getting dressed in the maid outfit. Once it's on, he does a twirl. "Perfect fit." He starts shifting his hips side to side. "Lets my nuts breathe and everything," he says, and then he shifts the wrong way and flashes us a clear view of his junk.

"Neo, dude, get your boxers back on. No one wants to see that. And Harlow would kill you if you flash her girls your dick," Cass laughs and tosses Neo his discarded boxers.

Neo pouts for a moment before giving Cass a wicked grin. "I bet Harlow would looove it," he winks excitedly.

The fucker has been bragging from the moment he got into the car about how he's now Harlow's new source of sex. I may not know this new version of Harlow because clearly this isn't the girl I fell in love with, and I'm not sure if I even like this new version of her all that much right now, but I'm not blind. She is a stunning woman in every way. Men would start wars for a chance with her, even if it's just for one night, so I get why he's so excited by this opportunity.

Cass changes into his outfit next, and the sight of my brother in that has me wanting to wash my eyes out with bleach. He looks like the bearded lady in a maid outfit.

"Damn, Cass." Neo whistles as he checks out my brother. "If it wasn't for the beard, and the fact that you're my cousin and a dude, I'd hit that." Neo then takes a feather duster and tickles Cass in the crook of his neck with it. Cass tells him to fuck off, and they both start laughing and messing around. *Where the fuck did he get that?*

I look over and see a box of props on the floor under the clothes. No fucking way. I'm done with this shit.

Ripping the outfit off the rack, I head for the door and out to the club floor. Harlow, Evie, and some other women are at the bar talking. When I stop in the middle of the room, they all turn to look at me.

"I'm not fucking wearing this!" I growl.

"Oh, poor Axel. Are you too *manly* to wear it? Are you too much of a man to wear women's clothes? My guys have all worn them, and they rocked the hell out of that outfit," Harlow smirks.

"Why are you making us wear these?" I ask, honestly needing the answer.

She hops off her stool and skips over to me. "Because, Silly, I can," she says with a sweet grin. Then she pulls a dagger from the holster strapped to her leg and runs the tip of the blade against my t-shirt. She doesn't cut me, but she does cut the shirt, leaving a big gash over my chest. "Now, go change, Pretty Boy." She flutters her long lashes at me and bites her lip.

"I won't do it," Dean says from behind me.

Harlow looks around me to Dean. Her face goes from sweet to dangerous in a second. "I've had just about enough from the lot of you. *You* came to me, asking *me* for help, not the other way around. Then you disrespect me in my own home *and* disobey my orders after we made an agreement. I gave you enough chances; I will not be ignored again. Most people would be beaten to death for talking to me the way you have been. Don't be mistaken. You won't get another chance. Now, do it, or get the fuck out of here, rendering your deal null and void," Harlow growls.

The bartender pretends to be busy behind the bar, but I can see her checking out the situation like she's ready to see Harlow bleed us dry right here and now. The girl with red hair sitting at the bar has her eyes locked on Harlow with a look of pure admiration.

Dean's jaw ticks for a few beats, and he gives her one last glare before turning around and heading back to the changing room. She looks back at me.

"Now. What's it gonna be?" She raises her brows and weaves her dagger between her fingers. My mind goes to Rosie. We desperately *need* this money, not just for our company but to keep her in our lives. Fuck... I gotta put the stupid, frilly dress on.

"You're just making us wear these for your own entertainment, aren't you?" I ask.

"Yup." She pops the P and smiles brightly, obviously enjoying holding this power over all of us.

Sighing heavily, I turn around and follow Dean. Just as I'm about to leave Harlow's line of sight, Neo and Cass walk past.

"So, ladies, what do you think?" Neo asks and twirls for them. They start whistling and clapping. Cass stands there with a smirk, looking like an idiot.

Turning around to go back and change, I'm stopped at the door by Lucas, Max, and Tommy. They have their arms crossed and look pissed. "We know what you did. And because of that, Harlow was in absolute hell for five years. Then you come here asking for help, and she is nice enough to do it. If she asks you to cover yourself in honey and let a bear maul you, you do it. Because you deserve anything that woman throws at you and more. It's the least you can do." Lucas takes off in the direction of the bar. Max and Tommy glare at me until I close the dressing room door.

Unfortunately, they are right. I may not like this new Harlow, but we are the reason she is the way she is now. Our Harlow is long gone, we did that to her, and the least we can do in respect for the girl we loved is to do as Queenie asks, even if it's beyond stupid and makes us look like freaks.

CHAPTER NINE

DEAN

"THIS IS degrading!" Axel grumbles as he puts all his force into the toothbrush as he scrubs the floor. "She is making us do this in the hardest way possible just to fuck with us."

After Harlow's warning, I didn't say anything more. I went back and got changed, although it's taking everything in me not to snap. I'm so far out of my element that I feel like I'm spiraling out of control. I'm the one in charge; I'm used to being the leader of our company and the one who makes the hard decisions that affect all of us. It's me who finds the best option for us to pursue. So, when Harlow said she would do to us whatever she does to others who disobey her orders, I believed her and did what was best for our family and company and forced myself to suck it up.

She owes us nothing and is doing us this favor. I'm not a fan of how she's going about it, but it's not like we don't deserve it. My idea and me forcing the others to comply with it is what sent her down a never-ending hole of horror. In a way, I killed Harlow, at least the one we knew. Queenie is a hard and ruthless woman, showing only a glimpse of humanity for the family that she's formed. We are not a part of that group. We lost that chance the moment I sent her away, and the others by default.

I know the things she's planning to make us do will be ridiculous, but we have to do it with no more complaining, or we will be screwed. Honestly, this company isn't worth the embarrassment we are going to have to endure. Normally, I would be stubborn enough to lose everything, just to avoid getting down on my hands and knees to scrub the bathroom floor in a maid outfit. But Rosie is on the line too, and I would do anything, and I mean every single gross, degrading, embarrassing, pathetic thing if it meant being in that little girl's life. She's our Princess, and we live to make her happy. She has kept us from becoming the men we were trained to be. Growing up, Harlow was the one that kept us grounded, and with her gone, for a while we started to slip, but the moment Cass found out about his daughter, we all started to change for the better.

"Just be happy that Harlow has a compulsion with everything being so clean you could eat off every surface," Lucas says from the doorway. He's standing there, leaning against the wall with his arms folded and a look of amusement as he watches over us. I don't think he was told to babysit us; he's just doing it, so that we have an audience for our humiliation.

"Yeah, every room but this one!" Axel growls. "There's so much fucking glitter! Who needs this much fucking glitter?!"

"How does she expect us to get all this out only with water and a toothbrush? Glitter is one of the hardest things to clean. And this is really more of a fine dust. It's never gonna come off," I say, sighing as I keep scrubbing with my own toothbrush.

"Stop being baby back bitches! It could be worse; we could be cleaning up piss or shit. And I do enough of that at home with Susie," Neo laughs. Lucas looks at me with a raised brow.

"His llama," I explain.

"Alpaca!" Neo growls as he stands up and looks in the mirror. He's covered in glitter. He has it all over his face too. Basically, he looks like a pile of unicorn shit.

Lucas looks even more confused. "Trust me, it's better if you don't ask too many questions when it comes to Neo. He's just as random as he is crazy. Essentially, he makes no sense."

Lucas huffs out a chuckle. "Maybe he is the perfect reliever for Harlow."

"Damn right, I am. Her crazy speaks to mine." Neo puffs out his chest and looks back to the mirror. "Hey look! I'm a vampire."

"What the fuck are you talking about?" Axel asks, irked that Neo has stopped working.

"A vampire, you know, like Edward from Twilight," Neo says, as he shifts back and forth so the light makes the glitter sparkle and shine around the room.

"You watched Twilight?" Lucas laughs.

Ah, fuck. Neo is in Lucas' face in a flash. Neo takes him by surprise and slams him against the wall, hand tightly gripping him around the neck. "You got a problem with that?" Neo asks, his voice deadly. Neo is an oddball. He loves what he loves, and just because he can snap someone's neck in the blink of an eye without thinking twice about it, doesn't mean he doesn't enjoy girly movies and tea parties with Rosie. If anything, I think he likes them even more than her.

Lucas tries to shake his head but can't because of the tight grip Neo has.

"Neo, man, let go of him," Cass says, his voice calm as if trying to coax a wild animal. Which is pretty much what he is. "He's turning blue, and if you kill him, Harlow kills all of us. Think about Rosie." With that last part, Cass's voice sounds panicked by the risk Neo is taking on his daughter's fate.

At the mention of Rosie, Neo relaxes his grip on Lucas, and when he finally lets go, Lucas bends over in a coughing fit as he tries to take in air. "Do that again-" he coughs, "And you're dead." Lucas staggers out of the room.

Fuck.

"Way to go, you crazy fuck. You're gonna get us killed," Axel growls.

"He laughed at me," Neo says with venom.

"He was probably just surprised that you would know what Twilight is," Cass says, trying to defuse the ticking time bomb that is Neo. Cass is the best one out of us all to coax Neo's monster into doing what is needed.

"The man is gay! He should never judge someone just by looks. Because he sure as hell doesn't look gay, but you don't see me assuming he's straight," Neo grits.

"So not the same, man," Axel says. "But let's not touch on that subject because none of us are a part of the community, so it would be disrespectful."

Neo bares his teeth at Axel. Cass puts his hand on Neo's shoulder, guiding him back to work. "Just think, Harlow is due for another kill soon, I'm sure, and then you'll get your moment to shine," Cass says, trying to get Neo's mind onto something else. Neo's smile is a scary, wicked one.

"I can't wait. She says she needs at least three orgasms before I'm allowed to come. I'm gonna one up it and make it four," Neo loudly cackles when Axel gives him a death glare.

"Lucky bastard," Cass huffs under his breath as he takes the bucket of glitter water and dumps it down the toilet in the changing room bathroom.

I'm not gonna disagree with him on that one.

"ALRIGHT, BOYS. You can leave now," I say, propping myself up against the door as my eyes roam over the four grown men in maids costumes on their hands and knees. It's so much fun watching karma slowly take her revenge.

Petty?

Abso-fucking-lutely. Do I care?

Hell fucking no.

"But we didn't get all the glitter cleaned?" Neo says, standing up and dusting off his hands.

"I know," I grin.

"But you said not to stop until everything was spotless," Cass says, looking confused.

"I know," I state again, holding back a giggle.

Dean narrows his eyes at me. Not in a glare, but as if he's trying to read me. After a moment, his face drops, and he gives me a blank stare and then looks at his cousins.

"She knew we would never be able to get all this crap off the floors," Dean says blandly.

"Then why the fuck did we just spend five hours scrubbing?!" Axel protests.

"Because," I shrug, looking at my nails as if all this is boring.

“You did it just because you could,” Cass says, and I look at him. He has a small smile on his face.

“Maybeeee,” I finally grin. Neo bursts out laughing.

“You sick, little thing,” Neo says with a big smile.

“Ahh, thanks, Sugar Plum,” I wink.

Axel and Dean don't say anything more and angrily grumble to themselves as they get off the ground and grab their clothes.

“I'm gonna have glitter in places I didn't even know I had,” Dean groans. I can tell I’ve tested his control really well today. Good, fucker needs to be pushed here and there, or in front of a bus.

“Bye,” I say sweetly, wiggling my fingers as they pass me exiting the door. “Keep your phones on you. I'll let you know when I need you next.”

“I hope it's for real work this time,” Axel says as he and Dean leave.

“So, is this what we're doing from now on?” Cass asks.

“Nah.” I smile. “Cleaning, yes. But I’ll mostly use you for heavy lifting. My guys do a lot around here because I don't trust that easily, so I don't hire that many new people. They work security for the club, and with you guys here doing the grunt work, it will help them be more focused on the important things. The girls do some work too, but I'd like it if they could just dance and relax when they aren't working. They deserve a break. They won't take it willingly, so I'm not giving them a choice. They feel like they owe me, and don't want to disappoint. They don't, but they’re stubborn. I guess we all are.”

"My Queen, you can tell me to do anything, and I'll do it. No complaining from me like these fuckers," Neo laughs, giving me an unmistakably hungry look. Fuck, I'm horny. It's been a few days since I've had cock, and this month seems to be low on playdates. But I don't trust him enough to have sex just for the sake of it. Not yet, at least.

"Soon, My Pet, soon. I'll tell you all the dark and dirty things you can do for me," I purr.

Neo groans and adjusts his hard-on in his boxers. I get a glimpse of what he's packing beneath, and fuck me, it's gotta be at least 9 inches. Garrett was only 8.

Biting my lip, I turn around and get the fuck out of there before I do something stupid, like jump him.

The guys have been working for me for a few weeks now. I have them stocking shelves, taking out trash, and Cass has even been helping in the kitchen.

Each night, when the shows are over, they stay here until 2 am cleaning everything to my liking. Cass has had to leave at random times because his ex keeps dropping Rosie off whenever she feels like it, which is really annoying.

I don't like this bitch. From what Evie has been able to dig up on her, she's nothing but a gold digger. What kind of mother holds their child over the father's head as a continuous source of money? From what I can tell, she doesn't even want her child full time, so she's just making empty threats knowing Cass and the guys won't risk it.

I don't kill women, but I have a feeling that maybe sometime in the future, she's gonna be my first. I don't know what for yet, but I can feel it in my bones. I'll get Evie to do some more digging on her.

"Come on, Neo, let's go for a drive," I say, coming out of my office. He looks over at me from his place behind the bar. He's helping Roxy with today's shipment of liquor.

"Sure thing, Mistress," Neo says with a grin and hops over the bar top. "Where're we going?" he asks like an eager puppy. He looks super happy to have some time alone with me. And he should be.

"Well, it's been too long since I had a playdate, and we are gonna go on an adventure to find me a friend," I say, my face slipping into a sinister grin. Neo's eyes light up with excitement.

"Fuck yeah," he whoops.

I live in Kingston Heights, just North of LA. Have for the last three years. It's where we settled and made our home. Evie and I felt it was safe here to start small and grow as time went on. We started off buying up the unfinished housing developments. Hired people to finish them, and then we built the club. From there, we've been buying properties like apartment buildings and renting them out to people who can't afford the high LA prices. I don't think people should have to live in crappy conditions just because they don't make enough even while working three jobs.

We have also been taking over several strip clubs and cleaning them up. We target the places that tear their women down and treat them like shit, like disposable objects.

Some of the owners go missing. I know, what a shame, right? Thankfully, I have a wonderful friend named Miller, who works for the LAPD, who's been keeping my extra-curricular activities under the radar. He's an older man, early fifties or so. He's been working as a police officer for thirty years and has grown sick of all the corrupt cops he works with. So, when someone caught wind of my earlier work and the cases landed on his desk, he did his own investigating and when he noticed what type of men I was killing, instead of arresting me, he offered to team up. As iffy on that as I was, I also wasn't in a position to say no. We agreed, he would overlook and bury my cold cases, and in return, I would slowly clean up his police department. So, here we are, still going strong years later.

My black, knee-high, leather boots click as we walk down the sidewalk. Neo says nothing, but is vibrating with excitement as he looks around at our surroundings. We drove to a shitty part of the city where it's less likely anyone will notice someone missing, but where we are sure to find some low life sack of shit doing something they shouldn't be. Sick fuckers are easy pickings out here.

The sounds around me fill the air. Dogs barking, people yelling, car alarms going off. I hate big cities; it reminds me too much of my time at the shelter. You know, before I was stupid and walked right into a trap.

As we keep walking deeper into the dark streets, I hear a muffled scream. It sounds too high-pitched to be a man, so that means there might very well be a damsel in distress.

My face splits into a wide grin. I look up at Neo, and his face is a mirror image of mine, indicating he hears the same thing and knows what it means.

"Sounds like we might have found you a playmate," Neo whispers.

Fuck, I can't wait to get my hands around who-ever-the-fuck-it-is's neck.

Since this is an unscheduled kill, I won't be able to have my normal fun. I won't risk any diseases. So, that means we only get to do as much damage as we can without spilling blood. That makes me a little sad. I'll have to work on another D-Day soon or have Evie find me someone we've vetted already. I've been so busy not wanting to leave the guys alone that I haven't killed in weeks. Lucas, Tommy, and Max say that I've been extra snappy, have jitters, and sometimes have an eye twitch. I'm not even kidding; when I don't at least have someone to beat the shit out of, I feel like a junkie being denied their fix.

We slow as we come to the alley. Peeking my head around the corner, I see a tall guy pinning a small blonde girl against the wall. "Shhh, you know you want this. Why else would you have slipped your thong into my pocket?"

"I just thought it would be a funny joke. I didn't mean anything by it," she whimpers. "My friends dared me to."

"Well, I don't think it's very nice to make a man think you want them, then deny him by having it be a joke. By giving me these," he holds up a bright red thong, "You were literally waving a red flag." The creep starts kissing the girl's neck. She's too afraid to move, petrified in place. He goes to move his hand down to her crotch, and that's the moment I decide it's time to step in. I quickly take in the situation, looking around, memorizing every detail of this alley. Just in case.

"You keep watch," I tell Neo. He gives me a little pout, like he's sad *he* doesn't get to play. "Not yet," I tell him. "Maybe sometime soon you can play too." I wink, then quietly sneak closer to the girl and the creep. They are in the far back end of the alley, tucked away in a dark corner with a streetlight casting a shadow over them, making them just barely visible.

I play out everything I'm about to do in my head, and as long as everything goes smoothly, this should be quick and easy. Unfortunately.

Okay, I'm gonna be honest with you. This isn't really a playdate. They last a little longer and involve blood in some way, but right now, I just need something to kill to keep the cravings at bay. The real reason is, I'm horny as fuck. I need a cock in me, bad. It's been too long since I've come hard around a real dick, not my silicone ones. Although they do the job, I can't quite seem to get the hard pounding part down.

The creep keeps fondling the girl, whispering to her to just relax and that it will be over soon. That part, I believe. He comes off as a two-pump chump, if he even manages to get it inside in the first place.

When I reach them, he shifts her head more to the side, so he can get better access, and that's when her eyes find mine. I give her a sweet smile, but it probably looks creepy as fuck to her, me just popping up out of nowhere.

I raise one finger to my lips, telling her to keep quiet, and the other hand points to the fucker sucking on her neck like a leech.

She gives me a tiny nod, letting me know she understands. And as if the gods have a sense of humor, the guy slips that bright red thong into his back pocket to get a better grip on the girl. I look to the sky with a smirk and a brow raised as if giving the gods a *'really?'* look. Shrugging, I get to work.

I take my brass knuckles out of my own back pocket and slip them on, then snatch the thong out of his pocket. I tap on his shoulder. “I'm a little busy here with my girl, fuck off,” he says into the woman's neck. I clear my throat, trying again. This time he turns around and laughs.

“Hey there, little lady. Let me finish here with her, and I'd be more than happy to have you next.” His pervy eyes look me over, taking in my tight, white top that shows my bra underneath.

“I'd rather eat dog shit, thanks.” My voice is like sugar with a just-as-sweet smile. I cock my fist back and nail him right in the face. I can hear the sweet sound of his nose breaking against my brass knuckles. The guy lets out a roar that he thankfully muffles by clutching his nose. The girl lets out a little squeal but does nothing.

"Umm, Hunny, this would be the part where you get the fuck out of here," I deadpan. Like come on, lady, I know you're in shock, but your fight or flight instincts should work.

She takes one last look at the guy and then takes off.

Taking advantage of his position, I jump onto his back, wrap my legs around his waist, and bring the thong around his neck, pulling it hard.

He starts to thrash, his hands frantically trying to loosen my grip. I cling onto him like a spider monkey, refusing to let go until he's at least passed out. Just as he starts to slow his movements, the motherfucking thong snaps. Like, come on! I mean, I knew it was a long shot, but it was working! Plus, it was fun to try. Death by thong would have been funny as fuck. But fuck this shit.

Before he can gather his thoughts, I hop off his back and grip his hair tightly. With all my strength, I smash his head into the brick wall.

He falls to the ground like a sack of potatoes. Crouching down next to him, I flip him over onto his back and make sure he is, in fact, unconscious. Then I wrap my hands around his neck and give it my all.

"Need any help, Mistress?" Neo asks from the alleyway entrance. I don't know why he started calling me that, but I like it. Maybe he *will* be able to survive my dungeon.

"Not right now, Neo, I'm in the middle of choking a bitch out," I shout casually as if it's something I do all the time... Actually, it kind of is. Silly me.

"Right," he says. I bite my lip in concentration as I feel his pulse start to slow. "It's just, watching you like this is a major turn on, and my cock is gonna burst out of my pants." Neo groans as I flex my arms harder, taking the last bit of life from this fucker. I let go and check his pulse again. Good, he's dead.

"All done!" I nod at the body as I jump up with a little bow and a big smile on my face. I look over at Neo and find him inches away from me. "Oh, hi," I say, cocking my head to the side as he devours me with his eyes. I really want to ride his dick, but we gotta get rid of this body fast.

"Okay," I sigh. "This is not how I normally do this, and trust me, this shit only gets more intense after a bloodbath, but I am still vibrating. So is my pussy, so show me what you got, Big Boy. Show me that I made a good choice in choosing you as my reliever," I taunt with a smirk.

His chest is heaving, and his cock is straining in his pants; so much so that I wouldn't be surprised if the thing bursts out and recreates that scene from Alien.

"Is this you giving me permission to touch you?" he growls, and the sound sends a shiver down my spine, right to my clit. I put my hand on my chin in the universal gesture for contemplation.

"I guess," I smirk, loving that I'm getting to him.

"Mistress, with all due respect, I'm gonna need a real answer. I don't want to break your trust and end up touching you without your clear consent." His tone is confident, yet strained. His words catch me off guard. He's so determined to follow the rules, no matter how much he wants me. I'm not used to that. Garrett was attracted to me, and he never left unsatisfied, but he also never looked at me how Neo is right now. With admiration, respect, and raw desire.

"Yes, you can touch me now." My pussy clenches in anticipation. I can't go this long without a dick in me again. Vitamin D is good for your health after all. "Fuck me, Neo, see how fast you can make me come. But remember, never pin me in a corner, just the wall, understand?" I ask, my tone deadly. Being trapped in a corner makes it harder to duck out if I need to.

"I'll never do anything you don't want or don't feel comfortable with," he says with fire in his eyes. Fuck.

I nod. "Same. Safe word is *monkey*." That gets a grin out of him.

I turn around and stick out my ass, giving it a little wiggle. "Come and get it," I grin. He's on me in seconds, ripping my pants down my legs in one swift pull. Thank god I went with leggings, or that might have hurt. He rips my G-string off me like it's a simple sewing thread and wastes no time before he rams his throbbing cock into my dripping cunt. I moan a little louder than I should have, seeing how we want to keep the body beside us to ourselves until the cleanup crew arrives. But fuck me, it feels so damn good being stretched like this. His cock is huge and is gonna split me in two. Just the way I like it. He grips my hips, but not as hard as I know he wants to, and starts to pound into me. He's grunting in pleasure and maybe some pain, like this is the sweetest ecstasy he's ever experienced. I let my eyes close, and my head falls forward, and I bask in the sensations he's causing to flow throughout my body. My pussy is humming from his touch. “Fuck yes,” I groan. “God, your cock feels sooooo good.”

“Like it was fucking made for you, My Queen. This cock is now yours to do with as you please.” He picks up his pace, his hips slapping against my ass. I feel an orgasm building already. Normally, it takes me a little bit longer. I don’t know if it’s because his cock is like some magic wand, or I've been without sex for too long. Maybe a bit of both?

I hear footsteps and two beeps. Neo goes on guard. “Don’t stop. It’s just my cleanup crew,” I say breathlessly. The beeping is a signal to let me know it's them, and so I don't get defensive and kill them by mistaking them as a threat.

“But...” he tries to protest.

“Damn it, Pet, fuck me. NOW! I'm so close to cumming, and I will chop off your dick and finish the job myself if you make me lose this orgasm."

That gets him going again. He fucks me like a wild animal and as if my crew isn't right next to us dealing with the dead body. It’s nothing new for them, they’re gay, and the only part that might interest them is the monster cock destroying my insides.

“Right there, fuck fuck fuck,” I chant. He reaches between my legs and gives my clit the attention it deserves. “Fuuuuck. This is better than taking a bra off after a long day of suffocating your tits,” I breathe.

Neo gives me a choppy chuckle, and with one last thrust, my core grips his dick almost as hard as I choked that fucker out not too long ago. He lets out a strangled grunt as he holds back his own release. He knows he can't cum without giving me my three mandatory orgasms. But we don't have time for that this time.

He rides me through my climax, and I almost black out, twitching on his cock like someone who stuck their fucking finger in an electrical socket. It would be an embarrassing sight *if* I gave a single fuck.

"Cum, My Pet," I tell him at the tail end of my relief.

"But you only came once," he says through gritted teeth, sounding determined.

"I know, but we don't have time; we need to get back to the club and let them clean up. I left blood on the wall, and us fucking out in the open like this is gonna draw attention to them," I moan as his cock hits me in my g-spot.

"Where do you want me to cum?" he asks.

"In me. I already had you tested back when you started, and I'm on birth control. Fill me with your cum, Pet. I want to feel it coat my insides." I let out a cry as another orgasm hits me out of nowhere. This sets him off, and his grip on my hips tightens, but I love the bite of pain as his nails dig in. He roars out his release like a lion who was victorious in battle. I feel jets of hot cum fill me, and fuck if it isn't hot. I'm fucking weird, but cum is almost as much of a turn on as blood is for me. I mean, coming from the right guy, of course.

If this is what it's like after only a drive by fuck, then I can't wait to find out what it's like when we have time for the whole show.

CHAPTER TEN

Neo

IF THAT'S what it's like as a quick fuck, I can't wait until she uses me for more. The feeling of my cock in her dripping cunt was the best feeling I have ever experienced. I swear that woman has a magical, golden pussy or something because once I'm in, it's like I'm under a spell.

I might be deranged sometimes, but I'm not stupid. I know this little outing was her way of getting sex without having to outright ask me. I asked Tommy and the guys if Harlow only fucked after a kill or dance, and they said no, that Garrett would be there for her anytime and for anything. Dickheads were trying to rub it in that she hasn't used me at will like that. But she will. I know it. I'll wait and do whatever she wants, for as long as she wants.

Never in my life have I ever submitted to a woman. I had no idea I would ever want to be dominated, but as soon as I laid eyes on this newly risen Harlow, something about her just called to me. Her beast matches mine. And she even has him whipped. The guys think I'm in it for the mind-blowing sex, and sure as fuck, that's a bonus, but that's not all it is. She's someone I can be myself with, completely and without restraint; with her, I will never be judged. She's just as unhinged as I am. My mind, body, and soul, yeah, all that shit's hers. She can have it.

We leave the alley as her men do their work. They are like fucking ninjas or some shit because if I were just some random person on the street, I wouldn't have any idea they were there. I love that she can just take a life and keep going, without worrying about the mess she's left behind. I get it; she's not the biggest person, so having to dispose of the bodies would probably be a bitch.

Harlow skips along the sidewalk next to me, a wide grin on her face. My chest swells with pride, knowing I had something to do with that... or maybe it was the thrill of the kill? Nah, fuck that shit; it was me and my electric cock. I felt how she twitched around it as I blew her fucking world to fucking bits and pieces. Like someone getting struck by lightning. It was fucking hot. *Just you wait, My Queen, you ain't seen nothing yet.*

"Can I tell you something, and can you promise not to stab me?" I ask with a grin.

She looks over at me with her own grin. "Can't make that promise, Pet. Not ever," she giggles.

I chuckle. "I'll risk it because I'll probably be turned on by that shit anyways."

Her eyes light up. “Really?” She licks her lips as I see her mind playing over all the different ways, she could use her daggers on me. “Because I can arrange that.”

“Please do,” I groan just thinking about it.

“So, what do you dare risk telling me?” she cocks a brow.

I push my luck. I mean, really it would be a win-win anyways and lean in closer. “Knowing that your panties are soaked in my cum as we walk down this street has my cock rock hard.” She shivers slightly, and I don't know if it's the leftover lust or if I really do have that effect on her. Again, I'll let my ego think it's me.

“You're a dirty boy, Pet. I may just have to wash your mouth out.” She bites her lip and smiles playfully.

“If it's with your sweet juices, then let me gargle that sweet nectar like it’s mouthwash,” I purr.

She stops and turns to me with a blank stare. I start to panic that I took it too far, too soon, but she just brings out my inner freak as well as my monster.

But then her face slips into a grin, and she bursts into a laughing fit. I don’t know if I should be relieved, laugh along with her, or be insulted. But honestly, like the guys said, I’d suck her fucking toes if she asked me to, so if I can get a laugh out of her, fuck my pride.

“You really are a nasty man, aren’t you?” she giggles.

“I can be anything you want me to be,” I smirk.

“So, tell me, Neo. Do you act like this with me because you think it's how I want you to act, or...?” She tilts her head to the side, and her eyes drill into mine as if she's trying to read every little secret that hides in the darkness of my mind.

I look at her, confused. "I'm not acting like anything but myself?"

"You act like this around the guys?" she smirks.

I shrug. "Like you said, I've got a dirty mind. But with them, I'm just joking around."

"And with me?"

"I mean every single thing," I say, locking my eyes with hers.

She just nods and starts walking. "I think we're gonna have some fun together, My Pet. I have so many... different things planned for you. But I have yet to find a man able to withstand my form of pleasure in its entirety."

"Don't take me out of the running just yet, Mistress. There's a lot I can handle," I grin.

"No matter how fucked up it is?" she grins.

I narrow my eyes. "As long as there's no shit or piss," I growl, and she giggles.

"Dude, I'm fucked in the head, but I'm not that fucked. I mean water play, sure. Not for me, but for anyone who does it, that's their own choice. But shit?" A disgusted shiver takes over her body, and she scrunches up her face, making the cold-blooded killer in front of me look so adorable. *Mine!* my beast screams from within me.

"I've disemboweled men before, and that image I just had in my head is far more disturbing." She shakes her head, and I smile to myself. I can't help but shamelessly check out her plump, round ass in her skin-tight leggings. I wonder if

I'll ever get access to that entrance? I already pushed my luck today; I'm not gonna risk asking that just yet.

Catcalling ahead of us gets both Harlow's attention and my own. "Hey, you sexy mama, why don't you bring that fine ass over here and let us show you what it's like to be satisfied by some real men," a guy shouts as he and his buddy get off the steps of the apartment building, we're about to pass.

Both are tall and buff, bigger than me, but I can take them down in two seconds flat. Something tells me that Harlow doesn't need, or want anyone to save her, but there are two of them, and I want some fun too. One for each of us. *Right?*

I look at Harlow, and she gives me a megawatt smile as if reading my mind. Slipping my hand into my pocket, I palm my switchblade, which I always carry around with me for fun.

As we come face to face with these men, they look Harlow over like she's a snack, and me like I'll snap as easily as a twig. Fucking dicks fucked with the wrong cuckoo's nest tonight.

We both just stand there and do nothing for a moment. As soon as they look at each other confused, Harlow and I pull out our weapons at the same time; a dagger for her and my switchblade for me. Simultaneously, we jam the sharpened metal right into their carotid arteries. They grunt in pain, but it quickly turns to gargling as we rip the blades back out. They drop to their knees while holding their necks, trying to stop the blood, but there's no point. The blood spurts out, gushing like tiny waterfalls. Harlow is watching the blood as if she's some rich bitch eyeing up some shiny-ass jewelry at Tiffany's.

She shakes her head and looks at me. We burst out laughing as we take off running. Me in deep belly chuckles and her in giddy giggles.

Harlow pulls out a cell, saying, "Hey, E. I need you to do a sweep on 51st on the west side." How the hell can she run so fast in those damn heels?

She hangs up the phone just as we reach the car. She hops in the front, and I take the passenger.

"Fuck, that was awesome," she cheers as she revs the engine and hits the gas. We race through the empty streets in the direction of her club.

"Umm, should you call your crew or something?" I ask, looking in the rearview mirror behind us.

"Nah. Miller will know it's me. He'll write it off as gang activity. If I make too many bodies disappear too close together, even Miller has trouble covering it up," she pouts. "I've had to start finding playdates around the country and bringing them to me. Not easy, but fun." She laughs. "Speaking of, I'll have to talk to Evie and see if she has anyone lined up for this month's D-Day." She is practically bouncing in her seat at the idea. I smile at her, knowing that that happiness comes from murdering another room full of men. True love is right here, even if she doesn't see it. Maybe she will someday. I know in the future, I'm gonna marry this woman, and we can spend the rest of our lives murdering people on a daily basis. Sounds like heaven... or hell.

Cassius

THE DOORBELL rings, and I open it to greet the wicked witch of the west, otherwise known as Rosie's mother, Briana. I'm about to say something to her when I get interrupted by Neo.

"Is that Bob?" Neo shouts as he rushes to the door. When he sees Rosie's mom, he sneers. "You're not Bob. My order was for a goat, not a snake."

Briana sneers back. "Aren't you a grown man? You're too old for a backyard petting zoo."

"But I love Susie," Rosie says quietly, peeking out from behind her mother's leg. My face splits into a wide grin.

"Hello, My Little Princess," I say, crouching down, opening my arms for her. Her face lights up as bright as mine.

"Daddy!" she cheers as she rushes into my embrace. I wrap my arms around her, and hug her tight to me. She snuggles into me, with her face tucked into my neck. "I missed you, Daddy."

"I missed you too, Sweetie," I sigh, feeling all my worries wash away for just a moment by her presence alone.

"Don't be silly, you saw him a few days ago," Briana scoffs.

"Well, if you ask me, with you dropping her off every other day to go off and do God knows what with your rich boy toy, you may as well just leave her here," Neo snarks. I give him a warning look. I don't need him poking the bear and pissing her off. I don't mind that she's been dropping Rosie off more. Harlow has been pretty chill with it. I mean she makes me show her proof because it really has been every second day recently.

We've been working for Harlow for a little over two months now, and she has been bugging me to see Rosie. I want to introduce her, but with Rosie's inconsistent schedule because of Briana's disregard for anyone other than herself, meeting someone new might be a little too much right now. And knowing Harlow, having Rosie around will become an all-the-time thing.

Our jobs have been a lot tamer than what we thought working for a serial killer would be like. Her club and her workers are her top priority, and because summer is here, tourists have been coming in more and more. This makes her club her full-time gig and leaves us having to work as security most of the time.

I can see that she's itching for a kill. She has had one mini D-Day since we first reunited with her. We weren't able to watch because we were working, but we did hear Neo fucking her brains out later.

He loves to rub it in any chance he gets that he's getting all the sex, and we are not. Axel and Dean have been real assholes lately, always bitching about her when we get home. We even got into some fights.

I feel like they may try and test her soon, and that's not good for them. Just because Harlow has seemed pretty tame these days, it doesn't mean she won't snap at any moment. Even Lucas and the guys think she's been acting too... normal. They told us not to be surprised if she explodes soon. So, for the sake of staying alive when she does, I'll stick to her conditions.

"Rosie, why don't you go out back with Uncle Neo and feed Susie, while I say goodbye to mommy and start your supper, okay?" I give her a kiss on the cheek and set her down.

"Come give mommy a hug, Rose," Briana says. Rosie looks at her unsure, then over at Neo.

"Last one to Susie's pen has to clean her poo!" Neo taunts with a smile. With one last look at her now annoyed mother, she takes off in Neo's direction, ignoring her mother's words.

"I don't like that man around my daughter. I don't feel like she's safe, and he is a terrible influence on her," Briana says in a snooty tone.

"Briana, I can assure you that Rosie is safe while she's here. My brother and cousins would die for that little girl, as would I. We would never allow harm to come to her; what kind of parent would I be if I did?" I sigh. Can the bitch just leave already?

She gives me a defensive look, but it's gone just as fast. "Of course, that's what a parent would do." She forces a laugh. She's acting a little weird, well, weirder than normal for her because this woman is already an odd-ball. I can see why it took me being drunk off my ass to sleep with her.

"Anyways, I'll be back in a few days," she says, handing over a bag for Rosie. I take it, knowing I won't be using anything in there. She claims it's all things Rosie can't be without, but all it is is some overpriced clothes that she can't even play in and a porcelain doll that Rosie said if she broke, her mother would be mad, so she doesn't bother to touch it.

She has everything she needs here. A little girl's room perfect for her age, all the clothes she would need for any occasion and season. She never has to want while she's here.

"When exactly will you be back?" I ask, knowing I'll have to tell Harlow I won't be in again. I really don't understand why she hasn't fired me yet. The guys have been doing most of the work.

"I don't know. Why? Don't you want to spend time with your daughter?" she bitches.

"Yes, but I need to tell my boss when I can and can't be in for work," I blink.

"Where is this new job of yours anyways? Must be something good if you can afford to keep this place, pay for stuff while Rosie's in your care, and keep up with child support. That's a lot," she smirks.

No shit. The witch demands five grand from me per month. Before her new husband came along, I only paid two thousand a month. Still pretty steep, but I didn't care because it was for my child. But Brad said that because Rosie was not his child, he would not be paying anything towards her care when they moved in with him. What a fucking jackass. And yeah, he pretty much made Briana pay him for Rosie's portion of the rent, utilities, and food.

Which, in turn, means I paid for it, and I couldn't exactly argue with him because he knows people who could seriously fuck me over. People that my father burned bridges with, and he could use them against me to get whatever he wanted. So, I give them the money, even though every few months it increases by a few grand.

I know if I don't tell her, she will find out on her own and rip me a new one. "I work at Evolution in Kingston Heights."

She looks confused before her eyes go wide. "Do you mean that strip club run by that crazy lady?"

"It's not a strip club, it's a burlesque club, but that doesn't matter. We do odd jobs and work security sometimes."

"And that gives you enough money to be able to save your company and pay child support on top of living expenses?" she raises a brow in disbelief.

"Well, my boss is rich, what can I say?" I shrug.

Just as she's about to start bitching, the buzzer for the front gate rings. I see a small animal trainer carrying a crate. Lovely, Bob is here.

"If you don't mind, can we say our goodbyes now? That would be for Neo. I need to deal with that and make supper for Rosie because I'm guessing you didn't feed her before coming here, again?" I ask, getting angry at the last part. She does it every time. Rosie is always hungry when she gets here, and she says that her mother said she doesn't want to pay for something when I could.

She glares at me but says nothing, before huffing and taking off towards her car. I buzz in the man with the damn goat and let Briana leave.

Well, it looks like we have a new addition to the funny farm. What the hell has my life become?

Neo

FUCK YEAH, *Bob is here.* I bounce around in excitement in my spot next to Susie's pen. Well, I guess it's both of their pen now. I spent last weekend adding on to it and made a gate to block the individual spaces off, if needed.

Rosie and I were feeding Susie some bark when I heard the truck pull up and then the sound of a bleating goat. Rosie heard it too, so I picked her up, and we jumped in excitement. Now, she's standing next to me doing a happy dance as she holds herself back from launching out of the backyard in search of Bob.

"I think this belongs to you," Cass says, sounding annoyed as he brings a cute little baby goat into the backyard, but Rosie's high-pitched squeal melts that away as he smiles in devotion at his little princess. She does that to us all. Being around her is the only time I'm normal. Well, as normal as I can be. I have to calm down my crazy because I don't ever want Rosie to look at me with fear or be uncomfortable around me. But I make up for it by letting my other freak flag fly. I am who I am. Sure, you could make fun of me, but you're likely to get stabbed if you do.

"I still can't believe you bought the damn thing," Axel laughs as he walks into the backyard. He smiles at Rosie as Bob chases her around. "Don't you think a dog would have been a better pet?" He cocks a brow at me.

"Maybe, but would it have been as much fun?" I grin. "Plus, have you seen the YouTube videos of them in PJs, fucking adorable."

"Bad word!" Rosie shouts as she stops in the middle of the yard, crossing her arms, and stomping her foot. The little thing has the sass of her uncle Axel.

I cringe. "My bad, Rosie Posy," I say and reach into my back pocket for my wallet. I know what comes next.

She holds out her little hand, waiting. I take out a dollar bill and place it in her hand. She gives me a big smile. "Thank you very much," she nods, then runs over to show her dad.

"Look, Daddy, soon I'll have enough to get my nails done with Uncle Neo," Rosie says excitedly. Cass smiles and shakes his head.

"You know, Princess, we can just take you. You should save your money," Cass says, ruffling up her hair.

"Nope," she shakes her head. "I don't want you to give me money. I want to earn it. You already give mommy a lot." Her voice goes low and sullen.

Cass looks up at Axel and me, and we are both pissed. Cass doesn't ask Rosie anything more, but I can see it in his eyes. He's wondering what else that woman has talked about in front of their four-year-old.

Rosie is crazy smart. She might be four, but it's like talking to an eight-year-old. She loves educational shows and is always watching kids YouTube on how to make things or learning about a new animal. So, it doesn't surprise me that she picks up on this kind of thing. It's also why we watch what we say and do. Making sure not to bring work home with us. When Rosie is here, it's all about her.

"Well, speaking of nails. I know someone who always gets her nails done, and they always look really pretty," I say, smirking at Cass as he narrows his eyes at me. Harlow has been bugging him to see Rosie for a while, but Cass is iffy on the subject. Sure, she slits men's throats and laughs while she does it, but that means nothing. I see her eyes light up every time she forces Cass to show her new photos. I know Harlow would be amazing with Rosie. I've killed people, and I'm not exactly what someone would call... stable. But I'm helping to raise her too. And I think we are doing a fan-fucking-tastic job at it.

"You do?" she asks, her bright blue eyes wide.

"Yup, her name is... Queenie," I say, catching myself because I don't want her to know Harlow's real name and repeating it to the wrong person. "She is the most beautiful person I've ever seen. Next to you, of course." I wink at her, and she giggles.

"Is she a Queen?" Rosie asks with a head tilt.

"She's mine," I smile. "And you're our Princess."

“Does that make you Kings?” she asks, looking around at the rest of us. Dean walks out into the backyard and leans against the pen’s fencing.

“He wishes,” Dean says, then looks around the yard. He sees Bob, and his eye twitches. “Now I remember why I never come back here. This place smells and looks like a farm.”

“Well, there are two farm animals here, so it's bound to happen,” I laugh.

“Couldn't you have gotten a dog?” he asks.

“That's what I said,” Axel mutters.

“Oh, come on,” I shout and open my arms, gesturing to everything back here. “It's our very own petting zoo. And we have tons of room for add-ons. We could get more animals.”

“NO!” Axel, Dean, and Cass shout as Rosie yells, “Yay!” They all glare at me, knowing they hate to disappoint her. I burst into a deep belly laugh. I love fucking with these guys.

“Hey!” Rosie shouts. Our heads snap over to her. “Give me back my dollar!” she yells as she starts chasing after Bob. The guys start trying to catch Bob as I stand there, watching everything play out.

Dean is in a suit, so he's no help besides yelling out what they should be doing. Cass is trying to stop Rosie from getting hurt as she chases after Bob, and Axel trips over the hose we use to fill the water bucket and ends up landing face first in a pile of Susie's shit. *Oops, I must have missed a spot.*

Axel slowly stands up and wipes the shit from his face. I bite my lip, trying to hold in laughter. But I fail as soon as he looks at me, and the sight of him has me losing it. I'm laughing so hard that my sides are hurting.

"I'm gonna fucking kill you!" he roars as he charges towards me, cursing up a storm. Rosie yells out, "Bad words!" in between her own fit of giggles. Dean shakes his head and takes off, and Cass is holding Rosie as he laughs with her.

I, however, run. I know I can take Axel, but I prefer not to kick his ass in front of Rosie, and Axel is definitely out for blood.

I run across the lawn and into Susie's pen. He hates her and won't come in here after me. Susie isn't a fan of him either; she bites him anytime he gets too close.

"I'm gonna kill you," he growls before taking off into the house.

"That's about a hundred bucks you owe Rosie," I call out.

"Yay! Pretty nails," she cheers and hugs Cass's neck tightly. He looks at me with a smile and cocked brow.

I shrug. "I saw the poop, I said nothing. Now Rosie gets her nails, and I bet Queenie would love to come." I grin.

"Sometimes I wonder who the bigger child is. You or Rosie."

"Uncle Neo," Rosie says, giggling.

She's not wrong.

CHAPTER ELEVEN

Harlow

"**SHOULD BE** good to go," Evie says through the phone. A case of déjà vu takes over as I stand in front of the guys' big ass, fancy mansion. The place I spent a lot of time in many years ago. In the exact place, I got the phone call that changed my life forever.

"What about the security cameras?"

"Did you want them taken offline too?" she asks, and before I can answer, I hear the clicking of her keyboard. Not even ten seconds later, her sweet voice rings through the phone again. "Did it, anyways. The cameras are now off, and the guard gate has been disabled. All you gotta do is give it a good push, and it should open."

Years ago, this place would have been flooded with security guards, housekeepers, and a chef. Now, because these guys have nothing left, all that remains in this shell of a house is the memories of the monsters that once inhabited it and a working security system. Other than that, it's just the guys. And Rosie when she's here.

Cass hasn't been in for a few days. Something about Rosie's mom dropping her off for an unscheduled visit. Again.

I decided to take this as my chance to meet her. I've hinted at it to Cass a few times, and I love getting new photos of her. She's the cutest little thing ever. Long, dirty blonde hair, big blue eyes, and a smile that melts my heart. Who knew I had one?

This is the new normal, and these guys are in my life for whatever reason, so I need to know everything about them. Including the little princess who has the number one spot in all of their lives. It's pretty fucking adorable.

"Perfect. Thanks, Babe. I'll call if I need anything else. Love you." I give her a phone kiss, and her musical laugh filters through the line before she hangs up.

Pocketing my cell, I put my hands on the guard gate and give it a hard shove. With a protesting groan, it opens just enough for me to slip in.

I could very well have called and told them I was coming over. Not like they would or could stop me, for that matter. But where's the fun in that?

Half the house is pitch black. No lights are on, except the living room light, which is shining brightly through the window, so I know someone is home. Where else would they be? It's eight at night, and they have a four-year-old, for Pete's sake.

With a smile on my face, I prance my way up to the front door. I love kids, and the way these guys talk about that sweet little girl, it's time I met her.

At first, when I found out Cass started a family with another woman, it hurt. Not like I'd ever admit that to anyone, ever! But it did a little bit.

Then, when he told me about the type of person she was, I was ready and willing to go out and kill my first bitch. But they asked me not to. They want to avoid hurting Rosie. So, I let it go for now. Although, I'm really fucking hoping that bitch slips up so I can fuck her up.

Giving the door three hard, loud knocks, I stand and wait for someone to answer with a big smile on my face. When no one does, I get impatient. I'm not gonna stand here like a fucking idiot and wait, so I let myself in, and to my surprise, the door is unlocked. Fucking dumb-asses. I am clearly proof that a locked gate won't keep someone out if they really want to be let in.

Pushing the door open, I take my first few steps in, smile still on my face, but it slips as I get farther into the house. Crying meets my ears, and I immediately go on defense mode.

Stepping into the open living room, I find the guys all crowded around Cass, trying to comfort a crying little girl who has a death grip on Cass's shirt.

"Please, Daddy. I don't wanna go back. Please let me stay here with you. I promise I'll be a good girl." She cries harder.

Cass's face looks crushed as he looks his little girl in the eyes. "I know, my little Rose Petal, but mommy called, and she wants you home tonight. I promise you can come back as soon as I can get you, okay?"

"Please, Daddy, I don't wanna leave." She's crying so hard that she starts to gag. These aren't the cries of a little girl who wants to spend some extra time with her daddy; no, this is more serious.

"What's going on?" My face is a mask, but inside I feel the rage building.

"How the hell did you get in here?" Axel grumbles, breaking away from Cass to stand before me. I give him a lifted brow and a smirk. He shakes his head and mumbles. "Never mind. I already know that answer."

Neo looks away from Rosie and gives me a heated look, like he always does, as he imagines all the dirty things, he wants me to do to him. Freak. I love it. I'll have to bring him to my dungeon soon. But now is not the time.

Dean says nothing, just moves away as I stand next to Cass.

"Hello, Queenie. Now is not a good time." He sounds exhausted and sad. He hugs Rosie close to him as he rubs her back for comfort. Her little sobs do things to my heart.

"Hey there, little one," I say, moving my face so that it's level with hers. At the sound of my voice, she slows her crying. Her face turns, and she looks at me with big blue eyes. They are red rimmed and blurry with tears. She says nothing but cuddles into her dad more.

"My name is Queenie. I'm your daddy's friend." I smile, showing her I'm friendly.

"Hi," she hiccups in a small, soft voice.

"Remember the lady uncle Neo told you about?" Cassius asks. She nods.

My smile turns brighter. "How come you're so upset, Sweetie?"

"I don't wanna go home with mommy," she says, and her voice wobbles like she's about to cry again.

"That's okay, Sweetie; you don't have to go home," I assure her. Her face brightens up.

"Queenie, her mom is on the way to pick her up; she has to go," Cass protests, and I give him a death glare.

"She is not going anywhere; do you understand me?" My tone is deadly and comes with a warning not to fuck with me. He purses his lips but says nothing.

"How about you show me to your room, and we can play a little bit before bed?" My smile is genuine again.

"Okay," she says softly, her crying has all but stopped, and she looks much happier.

Ignoring the annoyed men behind me, I hold out my hand for Rosie. She wiggles in her father's hold until he lets her down.

Her tiny little hand takes a hold of mine, and she starts to lead me in the direction of her bedroom. She brings me to the door with a sign that says *Princess Rosie's Room.* I smile as she pushes the door open. I giggle as I take in her overly pink room. Every single item is pink or Trolls themed. This little one is spoiled for sure.

"I see you like Trolls?" I smile as I take a seat next to her on the floor where her dolls lay.

"Yup! Poppy is my favorite. She's so pretty and funny and sings really good," Rosie beams.

We sit for a little while and play with her dolls. Yes, this big, bad bitch is making an inanimate object talk as if it was real. But I'm already batshit crazy, so is this really all that surprising?

"Rosie?" I ask, getting her attention as she puts her dollies away for bed. She's really smart for a four-year-old. She holds a conversation well and is very polite.

When she looks at me, I continue. "How come you didn't want to go home with your mommy?" I ask, voice coaxing.

Her face turns from happy to sad again, there's even a little terror making its way into her expression. She says nothing as she stands there like she's waiting to get in trouble.

"It's okay, Sweetie. You can tell me anything. I promise you won't get in trouble," I assure her.

She looks at me for a few moments before answering. "I'm not allowed to tell," she whispers, looking at the ground.

"I won't say anything if you do. I promise. Pinky swear," I say, holding out my pinky for her to take. She looks at it, then brings her small one up.

"Promise?" she asks.

"With my whole heart," I smile.

"Mommy is mean," she says, taking a few steps closer until she's in front of me. I hold my arms out, and she takes a seat on my lap. I like that she feels comfortable enough with me to talk and to let me hold her when she clearly needs it.

"How come?" I ask softly, brushing her dirty blonde hair from her face.

"She yells a lot. She makes me cry. She tells me that if I'm not a good girl, I won't ever see my Daddy again." She sounds like she's about to cry, so I shh her, soothing her.

"You will always get to see your daddy, okay? I'll make sure of it, no matter what she says."

Rosie just smiles. "Sometimes mommy is nice after my other daddy comes into my room to play at night. She watches us play, and when we're done, mommy tells me I'm a good girl, and the next day we get ice cream."

Her words make my heart stop, and my beast is scratching at the surface to be let out and murder everyone in its sight. I'm not stupid. I used to have the guards at my group home come into my room at night, and we would "play," and by play, I mean, the evil pieces of shit would touch me where they were not fucking allowed! Among other things. Trying to keep my control, I ask, "When you and your other daddy..." I try not to vomit on my next words, "play, what kind of things do you do?"

"He gets me to lay down, and then he massages my body," she shrugs.

"Like your legs and back?" I ask, so ready to break.

"Sometimes."

"Where else?" I ask, not ready to hear this, but I have to; I need her to say the words, so I know when I break these two vile pieces of shit, when I leave here tonight, they will deserve it. Of course, they fucking will, but at least I can look at Cass and tell him undoubtedly why. He's gonna be so fucking destroyed.

"Mommy said I can't ever tell," she looks up at me with her bright blue eyes.

"Remember, no one will know. You won't get in trouble."

She sits in my lap and plays with my fingers for a little while. I sit and wait patiently until she's ready. "He massages my gina. I don't like it. It hurts. But when I tell them, they tell me to be a good girl, and I'll get toys, candy, and ice cream."

My heart breaks, and I want to cry. I don't fucking cry. Ever. Even when I was taken by force every day for years. But this little girl here already owns me. I'll kill and die for her. I don't care that I just met her today. She's precious and innocent.

She goes on to tell me what he makes her do to him, and it takes everything in me not to lose the contents of my stomach all over her pretty pink floor.

I change the subject after thanking her for trusting me, and we talk and read books. I tuck her in and sing her a song of her choice. She asked for *Somewhere Over the Rainbow*, and by the time I was done, she's passed out cold. Giving her little cheek a kiss, I quietly leave the room.

The moment the door clicks shut, Queenie comes out. I'm a woman on a mission, and no one will get in my way. When I enter the living room, everyone goes quiet.

Cass gets up. "She's asleep," I tell him in a cold voice.

"Her mother is coming to get her, Harlow, why did you let her go to sleep?"

I get right in his face. "That little girl will NOT be going back to that bitch, and that monster she calls her husband. You will get everything that little girl needs to be here full time. I will give you anything you need to make that possible. But hear me now," my voice is dangerous and low. "By the end of the night, that woman and the perverted piece of shit she married will be dead and gone. And it will happily be done by my hand."

Cass's eyes go wide. He knows I don't just kill anyone. "What did she tell you?" he growls, but I can see his mind is running a million miles a minute.

"Let me do my job, Cass. Trust me when I say this; they deserve it," I say, my heart chipping at how his face drops.

"No," he whispers. "Please no. Not my baby girl." His eyes fill with tears and then with anger. "I'm gonna kill him. I'm gonna rip him to shreds!" he says through gritted teeth.

"I'll take care of them. Let their blood be on my hands," I say, taking one of his hands and giving it a squeeze. I'm not good with affection. I'm not in a place with these guys yet, where I'm okay with hugging them and shit.

"He is mine," Cass growls.

I look into his broken eyes for a moment before nodding. "But she's mine," I tell him, and he nods.

I walk past him and the others, heading for the door. They all start losing their shit. As I open the door, ready to call Evie and track down my new playmates, I'm met with a good-looking blonde woman. She looks me up and down with a sneer as she takes in my tight jeans and long-sleeved crop top. "Who the fuck are you?"

My smile grows into things nightmares are made of. Karma, I owe you one. Thanks for bringing her right to me. Without saying a word, a manic smile slips into place, and I head-butt her. Hard. I used all my force, sending my head crashing into hers. She lets out a high-pitched wail. Her hand comes up to cup her now broken nose as it gushes blood. "You crazy bitch!"

"Oh, Hunny, you ain't seen nothing yet!" I crow and let out a whoop of excitement as I bring up my foot and kick her with such force, it sends her flying down the stairs and right onto the lawn. Smiling wide, I jog down the stairs over to her. When she tries to get up, I push her down with my foot again, digging my heel into her chest. She lets out a pained grunt.

Straddling her chest, I lean over, bringing my face close to hers. "I know what you did to that beautiful little girl," I whisper. Her eyes go wide.

"I didn't do anything. Whatever she told you was a lie. Little kids lie all the time," she stammers. Even though she doesn't know who I am yet, she's no match for me, and she clearly knows it.

"Sitting by and watching as your husband does unspeakable things to her is exactly the same as doing those things yourself," I whisper. "So, here's what I'm gonna do. I'm gonna give you and your husband thirty minutes to get in a car and drive. You're not gonna get away; that much is a given, but it will give you some time to think about how much of a shitty human you are before I hunt you down, and then, we'll play," I grin. She's shaking now. Bringing my mouth to her cheek, I lick the side of her face like the crazy fuck I am. "Mhmm. Watching the life drain from your eyes while you beg and plead for your life is gonna taste so sweet," I whisper against her cheek, and she whimpers. Skimming my lips from her cheek to her ear, I bring her earlobe into my mouth, giving it a little nibble before sinking my teeth into the soft flesh and ripping it off. She howls in pain; sobs start racking her chest. I climb off her, and her hands fly to her ear as she continues to scream.

Spitting the chunk of ear out, I smile my bloody-toothy smile at her. "Run along now, little piggy. The big bad wolf is coming to gobble you up. And I'm famished," I taunt, grinning even wider, then I start cackling, making her even more terrified.

She scrambles away quickly, screaming and crying as she races off to her car. I pull out my cell and dial Evie. "Intercept incoming 911 calls. Send through any that are not a crying little cunt who may claim someone attacked her and bit off her ear," I say, smiling as I watch the car take off down the road.

"Do I even want to know?" Evie laughs.

My mood sobers. "It's not good, E. It's the ultimate sin in my eyes. I'm gonna need you to come down here soon and watch Rosie. I don't trust anyone else with her. Bring a few of the guys for backup if you want."

"No," she whispers. "Not Rosie."

"Don't worry, that little girl will *never* feel pain again in her life if I have anything to do about it," I growl.

"I know, Low. Have fun."

"I always do," I grin.

Hanging up the phone, I turn around to face the guys who are standing at the top of the steps, gaping at me. You would think they would be used to this shit by now. They have been to a few of my shows, and those are not short on the guts and gore.

"So," I say, clapping my hands as if my mouth doesn't have blood dripping from it. "I'm gonna let that Barbie Bitch have about..." I look at my wrist, looking at my non-existent watch. "About 28 more minutes to freak the fuck out while her life flashes in front of her eyes before I go all Fast and Furious on her ass. I called Evie. She's gonna come and watch Rosie."

Cass growls. His breathing is ragged, and his eyes are wild and feral. I have never seen him like this before. He's always the level-headed, funny one. But mess with his daughter and he will rip your head off. It's actually fucking hot; well, it would be if it was for any other reason.

"Evie is the only person in this whole world I trust with my life. That means something big. She would never let anything happen to your daughter. Rosie will be fast asleep, and you will be back here, with her in your arms, before she wakes. I know you all want to come, so someone needs to be here with her."

"Fine!" he growls.

"Now, I'm gonna go get a few things. I've got to call my men to get the showroom set up. When Evie gets here, meet me at the club," I say before turning around and heading towards the car.

"Hey!" Cass calls from behind me. I freeze but don't turn. "Thank you." I don't say anything, just nod.

"Come on, come on," I say to myself, my leg bouncing in anticipation. My phone says two more minutes. The phone rings, and I use the car system to answer.

"Are you ready?" Evie asks. I can hear the excitement in her voice. Evie set up her laptop at the guys' house and is gonna help track the car.

"Ready like a pussy loves cock," I say.

"What does that even mean?" Evie giggles. "Anyways. I found her car. I started tracking her once she left. She went to her home for a few minutes then left, and made her way to an office building downtown. So, with all the delays, she's only got a 5-minute head start on you. She's heading east on the 55."

"Perfect," I say, revving the engine. 5. 4. 3. 2. 1, showtime! I shove the gear stick in to drive and floor it. The car takes off with force. I zoom down the almost empty streets, dodging cars when they pop up.

"Alright, you're close. She switched cars, she's in a little red bug now. I don't know why the hell she would have chosen that car. God, she's stupid. She is literally putting a target on her back," Evie scoffs, and I laugh.

"I'm kind of disappointed that there won't be more of a chase, but I'm also excited I get to play sooner," I say, all giddy like.

"We need to get you regular playdates because you are way too excited," she laughs.

"E, I'm always excited to play. It's the highlight of my fucking life. But I have extra sick and fucked up things planned for these two. Evie, you have no idea the things they did to that little girl. They're getting a new fun package." My face morphs into a sinister smile as I play out all the fun things, I'm gonna do.

"Daaamn. Well, it sucks to be them," she laughs. "Alright, they should be coming up on your left," Evie says.

I look around, and just my luck, a little red bug zips out from a side street. The bitch sees me, and her eyes go wide. She quickly turns onto the same street I am, only able to go straight. Her car starts to go as fast as the damn thing can. And just for the sake of it, I make my pretty blue sports car slow, giving her the illusion that she has a chance. It makes things more fun.

I turn on the radio, and *Eye Of The Tiger* makes its way through the speakers. "Fuck yeah!" I shout and turn it up full blast. I scream out the lyrics as I bounce around in my seat. My adrenaline is off the charts, and I'm just a big ball of energy waiting to explode on their asses.

Rolling down the window, I stick my head out, feeling the cold air rush against my face. "Whaaa whooooo!" I yell into the night sky.

We're almost out of the city limits, and little does this bitch know she's bringing us closer to home. Good, less work for me to do.

There's a bridge up ahead, and I feel like this would be a good place to end this little cat and mouse game.

Pressing my foot harder on the gas, I speed up until I'm bumper to bumper. Her eyes snap up to the rearview mirror, and I give her one of my signature Cheshire cat smiles while wiggling my fingers hello.

The bridge comes into view, and I put the rest of my plan into action. I slow just a little and then floor it again. My car knocks into hers, sending it skidding to the side, right where I want it to go. The little red bug goes right up onto the guard rail before flying over the side, down into the shallow river below. I can hear the scraping of metal and their screams coming from the car. I start laughing like an evil genius.

"Showtime," I shout, fist pumping the air.

"Do me proud, Low," Evie says. Fuck, I forgot she was there. As if she could read my mind, she laughs. "It's okay; I know how you get. Your mind is in the zone. Keep me updated."

"Will do, Boo," I say, and the call drops.

Putting the car in park, I hop out and whistle my way over to the trunk. "Now what do I need?" I think out loud to myself. "Well, the dude is gonna be heavier than the barbie bitch, so I'll need rope." Looking over the rest of my toys, I pick out what I will need.

The car has smoke coming out from the hood, but I can still hear their screams, so I know they are still alive. Good, it would totally put a damper on things if they died before I got to have any fun.

Sliding down the bank on my feet and using my hand to steady myself, I make it down pretty quickly. By now, I can only hear Barbie Bitch yelling for help.

When I get to the car, I make my way over to her side. I crouch down and creep over to her window, and ever so slowly, I start to rise with the biggest fucked up smile I can muster. When my eyes make contact with hers, I say, “Heeeeere’s Queenie!” Her head snaps in my direction, and she screams at the top of her lungs. *I don't get it? Is it the smile or the fact that I still have her blood around my mouth?* God, what a fucking pussy.

CHAPTER TWELVE

SHE WON'T stop screaming in my face, and it's getting fucking old, fast. Rude bitch! I take a deep breath and yell, “Aaaaaaaaaahhh!” right back at her. She looks at me, stunned.

“Not so much fun having it done to you now, is it?” I cock a brow. “I think you broke my eardrum,” I say, tipping my head to the side and playing around with my ear using my finger, trying to get the ringing to leave. “I swear, if I have any permanent damage, I will hold a fucking séance to summon your ghost ass and make you possess some overweight dude with body odor. Don't try me bitch; I'll do it,” I promise, and she just stares at me like I'm crazy. Ha, jokes on you because I am!

“Now, can we please get on with the show? I have a busy night planned, and this is taking longer than I anticipated,” I say, standing up and walking around to her husband's side. With a good tug, the door flies open.

"Alright, big guy, time to go for a little ride," I say to the unconscious stack of shit, bending down and wrapping the rope around his feet, making sure to secure it tightly. I test the knot, and when I'm satisfied with my work, I smile and nod. "Perfect!"

Barbie Bitch just stares at us; I think she's in shock or something. I mean, I guess that's understandable? Weak ass bitch can't even handle a little car crash.

Taking the other end of the rope, I climb up the bank to my car and tie it to my back bumper. I hop into the front seat, starting the car up, and give it some gas. I drive forward until I'm met with some resistance. I give the car a little more gas, and after a few revs, whatever was stuck is no longer. After I think I've gotten far enough, I put the car in park and go check. I walk to the end of the rope to the body lying there. I can now see what was caught. One of his arms is missing at the elbow. I must have ripped it off. My bad. "Oops. Sorry about that," I say, bending over to check his pulse. He's still breathing, but I don't know if he's gonna wake up at this point. Hopefully, he does so Cass can play too. I don't want him to miss out on all the fun.

"Well, we can't have you bleed out before we get back, so hold on a second," I tell the unconscious body, holding up a finger, and rush back to my car. "This should do." I grab a belt I have in my car and tie it around his mangled stub. "That should do the trick for now."

I haul him back towards the trunk of my car, huffing and puffing along the way. It takes me a good ten minutes to get him in there. A lot of unattractive sounds on my part, and the sweat coming off me is just nasty. *Eww. B.O. is a no no.* I'll worry about that later, though.

Slamming the trunk shut, I take off in search of the missing arm. I find it wedged in between the guardrail. "There you are, silly! Can't leave you behind now, can we?" I smile at the arm, then wiggle it back and forth until it pops free. Placing my hand in his, we walk back down to Barbie Bitch.

"Hiya, Barbie," I say, popping back up into the window, waving her husband's hand at her. She looks at me with a yelp; then, when she sees the hand, she starts to scream like a banshee again.

"Alright, enough of that," I sigh. She's really becoming a party pooper. I reel back and with my free hand, I clock her in the face to knock her the fuck out.

"Better." I open the door and place the arm on top of the car. Using my dagger in my pocket, I cut the seat belt off her and drag her unconscious body out. I stand there, looking her over, trying to figure out the best way to get her up there. Dragging her by the arms or legs would be a little harder, so I just bend over and get a good grip on her long, blonde locks. It's long enough to give me some traction.

I hum to myself as I drag her up the riverbank, the arm in my other hand. When we get to the top, her body drops to the ground, leaving a chunk of hair and skin in my hand.

"Well, that sucks," I pout, then look at the hand. "Here, you hold it," I say, shoving the glob of hair into the hand and closing the fingers around it. "Thanks," I beam, giving it a little pat. Of course, Barbie is gonna make things harder for me, and now I have to drag her the rest of the way by her freshly manicured hand.

Getting her into the car is a lot easier, though; it's a tight fit with both of them in there. I toss the arm in on top and slam the trunk shut. I hop onto the trunk and bounce a little to make sure it stays shut. Note to self; next time, bring a different car with a bigger trunk.

Headlights blind me momentarily, and I bring my hand up to cover my eyes. When the truck stops, a few men hop out.

"Heya, boys. Just in time," I grin. "I'm heading home to play, but you do your thing. Get rid of the car and anything else I may have left behind."

"You got it, Queenie," Marty gives me a curt nod.

"We would never let you down," Billy smirks. I roll my eyes and get into the car.

Time to play!

Pulling around to the back of the club, I see Tommy, Max, and Lucas waiting outside for me.

"Hey, boys. I got a couple of playmates in the trunk. Mind bringing them down to my showroom? I think Barbie Bitch has some life left in her for some fun, but the big guy, well, he lost an arm and a lot of blood, so he doesn't have much left in him. What little he has left in him, I'm saving cause Cass wants a go at him."

“Do I even want to know how he lost an arm?” Tommy chuckles as he makes his way around the car to the trunk.

“Couldn't wait until you got here before they started losing body parts?” Max adds with a grin.

“Oh, hush you,” I giggle. “I'm not all big and strong like you boys, so I needed a little help getting him up the bank, not my fault that he got his arm stuck.” I shrug.

Tommy throws Barbie Bitch over his shoulder, and Max and Lucas each take an end of the sack of shit. I go over to the trunk to shut it and see if they left anything behind.

“Oh, boys,” I say, getting their attention. “You forgot something,” I say, making the hand wave at them. Lucas bursts out laughing, and the other two chuckle.

“Thank you!” I say. “It’s nice to know someone gets my humor.” I toss the arm on the body as I pass and take the lead.

When we get down to the showroom, the guys are all standing there with matching furious expressions as they watch a deadly looking Cass pace back and forth, angrily muttering things to himself.

“Tommy, hang her up by her feet.” I nod towards the hook and chain attached to the roof. “And you guys can-” My sentence is broken off by a roar as Cass comes charging over, grabbing Mr. Nub from the guys and lifting him over his head as he power-throws him against the brick wall. Clearly, Cass isn't Cass right now. He’s a broken father, a man on a mission. The mission: make his daughter’s abusers pay. And I’m just about ready to go all cheerleader on him and yell encouragements like, “Be aggressive, be-e aggressive!”

Cass's chest heaves as he takes in ragged breaths and rushes the body that's lying motionless on the ground. I don't know if Cass wanted this dude to be aware of the pain, he's putting him through, but he's way past that point now.

Cass picks the guy up and then starts chucking him around the room. After each throw, he lets out a roar, and I hear the pain laced in with his anger. It breaks my heart, but from this moment on, that little girl will never hurt again. I will do everything in my power to give her the life every little kid deserves.

I don't think torture is Cass's thing, or any of these guys', for that matter. They probably killed someone before, but not the way I do it. Well, except maybe Neo.

"Alright, well, while he does that," I say, hitching a thumb over at the raging bull behind me. "I'm gonna start on this." My grin is sinister as I point towards the blonde piñata hanging in front of me.

Lucas and the guys have gone, leaving me alone with my guys. *My guys.* I haven't called them that in years. I guess because I own them, they *are* mine. But not mine, mine. Because... just, no. They are quietly lounging against the wall, watching the show with solemn expressions.

I walk over to her, looking her up and down while circling her. I ignore Cass, thinking of what I should start with.

"First, we need to wake her up; it's not fun for me if she's out for everything," I say, then go to my table of toys that was so kindly set up for me, all ready to go. I pick up the syringe of adrenaline and stab it into her thigh. A moment later, she wakes up, sucking in a gasp of air and frantically looking around, confused as to what's going on. I bend over to look her in the face.

“Hiya, Barbie, I’m Queenie. Nice of you to come and play with me today. Sorry that this will be our one and only playdate, but I'll make sure to make it extra special just for you.” I pat her cheek and she whimpers. A grunt and the sounds of fists hitting flesh draws our attention over to Cass. He now straddles a mangled, bloody body as he pounds his fist over and over again into what, I think, is his face. I can't tell because there's not much left to it.

“Hey!” I shout so that my voice can be heard over the noise. Cass’s head snaps to look at me, his eyes feral. I cock a brow. He needs to stop; if he keeps going like this, he’s gonna lose himself, and I can't allow that, it's not fair to Rosie.

“Axel. Get him out of here.” He looks at me then Cass, unsure, but in the end he nods and grabs his brother. Cass starts fighting Axel, and Dean steps in and drags Cass out of the room kicking and screaming. Neo looks in his cousin's direction, but stays with me.

Barbie Bitch is looking at her husband's mangled body, and she starts to cry.

My eyes go wide, and I start laughing in disbelief. “Are you fucking kidding me?” I deep belly laugh. “Like, no really. Please tell me my eyes are playing tricks and my ears aren’t hearing you correctly. Are you honestly crying over your husband? The one who touched your four-year-old daughter in a way no one should touch another person, let alone a child, without consent. Your husband is a sex offender, and you would have sat there and watched your daughter get raped, just like you sat there and watched him do revolting, fucked up, horrendous things to that innocent, beautiful, little girl!" I scream.

She starts blubbering like a fish. All the blood is rushing to her head, and I need to get started before she passes out again.

"Alright, Pet, you ready?" I beam over to Neo, who has a wicked gleam in his eye.

"Hell fucking yes." He smiles a creepy as fuck smile, but I love it.

"So, I made a few bets with myself," I tell him as I grab a can of spray paint. "And I won, of course." I giggle.

"Oh really? And what might they have been?" Neo asks, amusement written all over his face.

I stop in front of Barbie Bitch and grin over at Neo. "That I could get Dean to lose control in a certain amount of time and that your cousins would walk out on yet another meeting."

Neo chuckles as I turn to the dangling body. She's crying, begging, and pleading, but I drown that out for now. Ripping her shirt down to expose some skin, I take the can of red spray paint and draw a bullseye on her belly.

"This was what I got for winning the second bet. The first prize we can save for the ending, so we still have something intact to play with," I say, backing away from her body and looking over the artistic, circle-like targets I've made, and nod, pleased with my work.

Looking over at Neo, I see his head tilted to the side as he looks the body over. "So, what are we doing exactly?" he asks, looking at me now.

"We are having target practice," I say. I'm giddy now.

His brow narrows. "But then she would bleed out before we get any real fun in." My face drops, and I roll my eyes.

"Not with guns, silly, with these!" I grab the little satin bag and dump out ten throwing stars onto the table.

"Nice!" Neo cheers.

"Five for you and five for me," I say, placing his in his hand. He looks at me with surprise.

"You're letting me play too?" he asks in disbelief.

"Well, yeah, sometimes it's nice to have someone to join in on the fun, you know, someone who isn't the person screaming bloody murder in protest." I laugh.

"Well, this seems just like the kind of game I'd love to play," he grins.

"Perfect," I grin back.

"So, what does the winner get?" Neo asks, checking out the throwing stars.

"To be on top." I give him a sexy smile and a giggle.

"Well, Mistress, then I guess even if I lose, I win," Neo chuckles. I just smile and shrug.

"Ladies first," he says, holding out his arm and pointing to the screaming target.

"Oh, Pet. I am far from a lady," I wink, and he groans.

I eye up the target, trying to get a good angle, but the bitch won't stop struggling, and it's making it very hard to get my aim right.

Huffing out a sigh, I turn to Neo with a pout. "Could you hold her still? Please, with a screaming orgasm on top?"

"My Queen's wish is my command." He bows with a grin, and I roll my eyes.

Once the bitch is still, I aim and throw, hitting her right in the belly button. She lets out a scream in pain, and I clap my hands in cheer. "Bullseye!"

Neo looks down at the star embedded into Barbie Bitch's stomach. "Perfect!" He nods his approval. We spend the next little while practicing, both telling the other where to aim and seeing if we can hit it, not bothering with the target anymore. I throw three stars in a row down her chest before I realize that she's passed out. Or is she dead? I don't remember when she stopped screaming, I was too into the game.

"Guess she didn't want to play anymore," I shrug. "Oh well, time for my next prize." I grin and pick up the metal bat off the table.

Neo looks at me with a raised brow. "I wanna see if she explodes like a piñata." My voice is excited as I get ready for my experiment.

"Fuck, now I gotta know too." Neo's energy matches mine. It's nice to have someone who is as enthusiastic as I am about my extracurricular activities. Sure, Evie puts on a supportive front and a smile, but it's not the same. She doesn't care for what I do, but she does accept and support me.

Gripping the bat, I stand next to Barbie Bitch, bring it back, and then swing, hitting her hard against the stomach. The sound of the metal hitting her flesh is like music to my ears.

I swing again, hitting her over and over again, in the same spot, but I don't think I'm strong enough. Frustrated that this isn't working, I hold it out to Neo. "You try."

He takes the bat with a fucked-up smile, and with as much strength as he has, he takes a swing, and I can instantly see that he manages to do more damage than I did. I start bouncing with excitement when the more hits he bestows her with, the more it starts working. Eventually, her stomach breaks open, and everything inside starts spilling out.

Neo is sweating and out of breath, but he looks at me with a smile. "Is this a good enough result?" he asks, sounding like he wants my approval.

"I'd say that's as close as it's gonna get. Sure, it's not as exciting as a bunch of candy, but it's just as much fun." But to be honest, I'm done with her now that both of them are dead. I'm vibrating with energy, and it's time I ride this stallion until my brain short circuits from too many orgasms.

Okay, there can never be too many, but you know, enough until I'm unable to move for a week.

"Wait!" Neo says as I dismiss the dead bodies and prowl towards him with a horny look in my eye. He has the same one, but keeps going. "We're tied."

That stops me. "What?"

"With the throwing stars, we each got the same amount of points. We need a tiebreaker. It's only fair," he says, walking over to the mangled body who used to be a human, but now he just looks like hamburger meat.

Neo drags the body by its feet over to the center of the room, then walks over to my table. I stand there intrigued, watching his every move. He grabs two daggers from the table and goes back to the body. With one, he cuts the shit down the middle, then holds out a dagger for me. "Tic-Tac-Toe?" he grins.

"What?" I huff out a laugh.

"You win, you ride me like a mechanical bull, making me give you as many orgasms as you can handle. If I win, I get to pound you into the ground until your voice is hoarse from screaming in ecstasy." His grin is sexy and hungry, and I know he doesn't give a shit which one we do, but options are always nice. Kind of like ice cream. Maybe I'll mix the flavors, do a little of both.

"Deal!" I say, snatching the dagger from him. He digs his dagger into the flesh, drawing the lines for our game. I was expecting more blood than what I'm seeing with how deep Neo is digging, so I look over to where the body was laying for a while and find a massive pool of blood with a trail leading over to us. Oh well, it should still be fun.

We sit crisscrossed on each side of the body and play a quick game of Rock-Paper-Scissors to see who goes first. I win and eye up my choices. Even though I'd enjoy it no matter who wins, I still want to kick his ass for bragging rights. I make my first move, then Neo does the same thing as I did, careful about his move. Only the fucker is mocking me. He pretends to look over the body, but has a fucking smirk. I let out a low growl, and he chuckles, finally taking his turn.

With my last X, I win the game. Jumping up, I let out *a "Fuck yeah, who's your badass bitch?"* Then look over at Neo. His pupils are blown wide, and he looks like he's ready to gobble me up. Or maybe for me to devour him. I like that last option. I pounce on him, sending us rolling away from the body, and when we stop, I'm on top.

"You caught me, Mistress. Now, what will you do with me?" Neo's voice is husky, and fuck if my pussy doesn't sing in response.

"No need to let a perfectly good meal go to waste now, is there?" I say, grinding my pussy against his rock-hard cock. He throws his head back, eyes closed tight, and lets out a pained moan. "Fuck."

"That's what I plan on doing," I giggle. With the dagger still in my hand, I wipe the blood from the blade against my pants, then use it to slice a hole in my crotch. Neo rushes to get his cock out, not wanting to risk the dagger anywhere near his man sub. Because trust me, that thing is a foot long. Pulling my panties to the side, I lift myself up, and when I feel his hot tip against my wet and ready center, I slam down onto him, impaling myself on his glorious cock. We both let out a loud moan. I immediately start to ride him, the extra adrenaline making its way back to the surface.

"Hands to yourself this time, Pet. This is gonna be hard and dirty, and I want it all for myself." I groan as I rock my hips, grinding my clit against him.

"Take it," he moans. "Take it all. Do whatever the fuck you want to me."

Wanting to make sure he does as he's told, I pull my shirt up over my head, getting a groan out of him, and use it to tie his wrists together and around the pole behind him.

"Remember the safe word?" I ask him as I see him zero in on my tits flowing out of my black lace bra.

"Monkey." He gives me a sexy chuckle, but it turns into a hiss as I rake my long nails up his shirt, then grab the dagger next to me and slice it open. His body is fucking fire. Muscles for days, black and white tattoos that I just wanna trace with my tongue.

So, I do. I continue to roll my hips as I lean over and trail my tongue all over his toned chest. His breathing hitches when I get to his nipple. I give it a flick with the tip of my tongue before sucking it into my mouth. When I give it a good hard nip, Neo lets out a *"Fuck!"* and bucks his hips, slamming into me hard. I moan against him and pull back.

"You like it rough, don't you, my Pet," I giggle and moan as his massive cock hits a good spot.

"Mistress. When I say you can do anything to me, I mean it. Any. Damn. Thing." he growls.

My senses are on overload, my mind is a haze of lust, and all I can think about is the powerful orgasms making me teeter on the edge of madness. I needed this. Normally, and only because I allow it, I'd let Neo take control and pound into me because like I said before, I can't seem to get that right myself. But fuck, do I ever love owning a man's body. And this man under me just gave me his on a silver platter.

Look, I know, I hate men. And I do. Well, most. But it's kinda hard to truly hate someone who submits to you in every way, shape, and form. I think I'll keep him because I sure as fuck won't find someone who is as fucked up as me and lets me do so many fucked up things to them, all while also begging for it. He's the ultimate unicorn.

My hips rock faster, I need to cum before I explode, and not in a fun way. I rake my nails harder down his chest, leaving trails of thin blood running down his body. He fucking loves it, if I go by the noises he's making, and knowing that I'm the one causing that pleasure gives me a power boost.

I cum, hard. Tossing my head back, closing my eyes, and gripping his sides to dig my nails deep in his skin as I scream my release. I don't even wait until I'm done, I need more, so I force myself to keep riding him. I lean back, hitting a whole new angle and, God, it's just the right one. I ride that man's body like there's no tomorrow as I start to play with my swollen clit. "Yes," I chant. "Fucking hell!" I scream as I cum again.

Neo is growling at this point. I know he's barely holding on. "Cum with me, Mistress. Take me over the cliff with you. Let me drown in ecstasy alongside you. Please," he begs. And something about the lust and need in his eyes makes me want that too. I untie him. But he doesn't move.

He looks at me with little restraint, but he won't do anything until I tell him. "Help me, Neo, and together we can cum." He growls as he grips my hips hard enough to match the marks I left on him with my nails, and I fucking love the pain.

He's an animal. He makes me fuck him hard. My nails are everywhere, marking my territory, leaving red lines all over his body.

Being so sensitive from my last two climaxes, it doesn't take me long before I'm ready to go again. I feel my walls clamp down around Neo's massive cock. He looks at me with a slight fear before he asks me, "Choke me, Mistress, please." Well, that's a bit of a surprise. But also, not really.

Well, since he asked so nicely.

I wrap my hands around his neck and squeeze. He lets out a lusty moan, gripping my hips. "Harder," he croaks, and I do. He lifts me up and slams me back down on his cock over and over. I'm done for. With one last squeeze, I strangle his cock with my cunt and cum again. Not as powerfully as the last, but still just as amazing. Neo grunts, his eyes rolling into the back of his head, and my god, I don't think I've ever felt a cock twitch out its release with that much power in my life. I can feel jets of warm cum coat my insides, filling me up and starting to leak out of me. Yup, I'm keeping him. This is the closest thing to a real vibrating cock I'm gonna get without added help.

My eyes snap open, and I realize my hands are still around Neo's neck. Oops. But he didn't try to throw me off him. I let go.

"Sorry." I cringe as he gasps, taking in air, trying to fill his lungs. "I've never choked someone before, unless it was to kill." I bite my lip.

"Don't be," he grins, getting his breathing under control, his voice still gravelly. "That was the hottest thing I've ever let a woman do to me."

I giggle. "Well, I'm happy to help."

"I don't think I've ever cum so hard in my life." He groans. "I really can't wait until you take me to your dungeon."

"You know, you would be my first," I shrug, aware that we are having this conversation while his still hard cock is buried deep inside me.

"Really?" He looks at me unsure.

"It's a lot harder to find men who would let you do anything to them. Word on the street is I'm a crazy bitch," I wink, and he chuckles.

"Well, that makes us each other's first in some kind of way," he says.

I give him a side smile. "I don't get to enjoy a lot of those." His eyes darken, but I do not want to talk about my past.

"Really?" a gruff voice comes from behind me. "And next to the mangled bodies too?"

I climb off Neo, his cum dripping out of the hole in my crotch and down my pants. "Hey, boys," I wave, standing there looking like a hot mess. But at least I'm still hot. Axel's eyes snap to my tits. I look down and see that my nipple is showing. "Nip slip," I shrug, tucking it back into place.

"So, how's Cass doing?" I ask.

"How the fuck do you think he's doing?" Axel growls. "He just found out his daughter was molested."

Snatching the dagger off the ground and slowly walking over to Axel, I point it at him casually.

"You really ought to learn how to fucking talk to me," I tell him. Why does this asshole always have to ruin my good mood? "The only reason why you get to keep breathing is because it would break that little girl's heart, and I think she's been through enough. But don't think I won't beat your ass down a peg or two. Remember who's in charge and who has your life in their hands."

He says nothing, just glares at me. I see Dean in the doorway. His face is unreadable.

"Anyways. They are no longer a problem. Rosie is safe with all of you full time, and I'll make sure no one ever lays another hand on her. Starting with them," I say, pointing to the body hanging from the roof. Well, what's left of it anyways.

"My job is done, and so is his," I say, pointing to Neo. "So, I'm going to get some sleep. And you all need to go home to that beautiful little girl." Axel and Dean nod.

"Hey!" Neo shouts, and I turn around to him leaning up on his arms, his cock still on display. I smirk, raising a brow.

"Thanks for letting me play," he grins.

I look at the bodies and then back to him. "It was fun. Next time I'll remember to add some music, and maybe we can dance." His face lights up with lust and excitement.

I smile and strut my way out the door, passing Dean, and say, "Later, boys."

CHAPTER THIRTEEN

I WAKE up with the sunshine warming the skin of my cheek. With a smile, I stretch out my arms and legs, making overly dramatic sounds as I do, but fuck, does it ever feel good.

Life is good. I have yet to have a fucking D-Day, though. It's been two weeks since I had one of the best playdates in a long while. It was fun having someone join me, and the sex was fucking amazing, so that's a plus. I've wanted to go and see Rosie, but Cass has locked himself in the house with her. He needs to deal, and he's gone into papa bear mode. He doesn't want anyone around her right now, and I can understand that.

But he's gotta get it through his head that I'm Rosie's mother now. I don't care what he thinks. That little girl is mine too. I want her to have everything I didn't get to. A real, loving, caring mother figure who will die before letting the monsters in the closet get to her, not invite them in for fucking tea. There's something about that little girl that just makes you feel things, good things, happy, sunny, unicorn, and rainbow type of things. Normally, I would rather get hit by a bus than feel this shit, but with kids, I'll allow it. With her, I'll even welcome it with my arms open.

There's a knock at the door, and I drag my naked ass out of bed. When I open it, not giving a fuck who sees me, I find Evie eye level with my tits. Her eyes are locked in on my nipples like a missile.

"Ahem," I say, with a smile.

Her eyes flick up to mine, and a blush takes over her cheeks. "Umm, sorry," she says, clearing her throat. "I didn't mean to wake you, but it's important."

I open the door, letting her in, and head into my closet to slip on a robe.

"You didn't wake me. I was about to get up anyways, but the bed was so warm and comfy that I just didn't want to. Maybe if you come over for a sleepover sometime soon, I'd have something else to keep me warm." Her eyes go wide, and I chuckle.

"So, what's so important that you're rushing over here at 8 am on a Saturday," I say, getting out my already brewed, iced coffee, and making her and myself a drink. "Not like I don't enjoy the time I can get with my number one," I wink, and she smiles.

"Well, since those guys came along, you haven't had much time for me." She sounds a little hurt by that.

"Aww, are you jelly?" I ask.

"No," she mutters, but I can see it in her eyes.

"Awwww, is my E a Jelly Belly?" I taunt.

"Low," she warns, but it's too late; I'm already on her, tickling her until she's laughing so hard, I'm sure she's about to piss her pants. I ease up, and she gasps for air.

"Alright, alright. Really, what's up?" I ask, taking a sip of my coffee. Her smile slips.

"Tracy didn't come home last night," Evie says, not meeting my eyes.

My brows furrow. "What do you mean?"

"Well, now don't get mad, but she went on a date last night with some guy from a dating app," Evie cringes.

I let out an angry growl. "I'm gonna kill that girl! She knows how I feel about them going out without me now. Or at the very least she should have taken backup, and now she's not back. Did you call her, track her phone?"

"Low, they are adults. You know the agreement we all have. We give her 48 hours, and if she doesn't contact us, then we worry. I know you want to keep them all safe in your Queenie bubble, but that's not what they want. They love you and appreciate everything you have done. You gave them their freedom back; now they have lives they want to live. Men they want to marry. Kids they want to have. They can't do that with you breathing down their necks," Evie laughs as I glare.

"I can try," I mutter, taking a sip of my coffee.

She raises a brow and smirks at me. "Fine!" I huff. "48 hours and that's it. Not a second more!" I say, pointing a finger at her. She nips at it playfully and then heads for the door.

"Come on. We got shit to do, like a club to run," Evie says.

"Oh! And people to kill!" I cheer.

"Not today, you don't," Evie denies as I lock the door behind us.

"E. You're really slacking on the D-Day front. We already skipped one. We can't skip anymore, or I'm gonna go nuts," I protest as I trail behind her.

"Babe, you're already a nut. Hell, you're the whole damn tree, plus the family of squirrels that lives in it," she laughs.

"True that," I laugh with her.

When we get down to the club, some of my girls are getting the stage set up for tonight's show.

"You dancing tonight, Queenie?" Lola asks as she hops off the stage.

I take a moment to think.

"I think you should. Would take your mind off Tracy for now," Evie says, taking a seat at the counter next to Roxy, who's behind the bar, setting up.

"Tracy has a solo tonight, doesn't she?" I ask Evie.

"Yeah," Evie makes a face.

Evie's right. I need to do something to keep my mind off shit, or I'm gonna lose my mind. And I guess there's no killing tonight, which is pure and utter bullshit.

"Yeah, why not. It's been a while since I did a solo," I say, and the whole room starts to cheer. I can't help but smile.

"Alright, back to work," I sing.

The TV behind the bar starts playing the news, grabbing my attention.

"Two more women have gone missing this week. That makes a total of four young women in the last four weeks... LAPD is working hard to find out what is...."

I don't hear anymore; just look at Evie. She has a guilty look on her face.

"Did you know about this?" I ask.

"Not about these two new girls. I promise," she defends.

"E," I warn in a low tone.

"Low. I wanted to get more information. Bad shit happens on that side of town all the time. Could have just been a few runaways."

"Doesn't seem like that to me." I raise a brow.

"I'm on it," she sighs and heads back to her office.

I start pacing, my mind going a mile a minute. I want to go hunting. Not only is it possible that one of my girls is missing, but four other women have also vanished. It's not like me to sit back and do nothing.

I get out my cell and call Miller. "I'm already on it," is how he answers the phone.

"Miller, I swear, if it's what I think it is, you know I can't stay out of it," I growl.

He sighs. "I know, and when I find out more, I'll let you know first."

"I'm giving you one week. If you don't have anything for me, and Evie can't find shit, I'm taking this into my own hands. And I have enough shit to deal with as it is."

"Like leaving me presents in the form of two grown men?" he replies blandly.

"Whatever do you mean?" I say, with a smile in my voice.

He chuckles. "You can't take out everyone who looks at you funny."

"Try me, buddy. I can and I will. Just sit back and watch," I sing.

"You don't pay me enough for this shit," he sighs.

"I don't pay you at all," I laugh.

"Well, maybe you should," he counters.

"Find out where I can find those girls, and I'll pay you more than a rich man pays for a top dollar whore," I chirp before hanging up, turning back to face my girls.

"Alright." I raise my voice. "Now I just need a song for tonight, I wanna do something different."

The rest of the day goes by fast. I help the girls with a few of their dance moves, enjoying the true moments of laughter as we work. They don't come so easily these days.

The guys are due to come in soon for their shifts, but Cass is staying home. I don't blame him. He's not ready to leave Rosie with anyone right now.

"So, what did we miss?" Neo asks as he walks towards me with a big grin, Axel and Dean following closely behind.

"Queenie is gonna dance tonight," Roxy says with a smirk, not looking at anyone as she dries some drink glasses, preparing for tonight.

"Oh, really now?" Neo says, his smile still in place. "Glad Cass convinced us to come tonight."

"That makes one of us," Axel grumbles, looking like he sucked on a lemon.

"Oh, Mr. Grumpy Guns, don't be so pissy," I say, walking over to him, then pat him on the cheek. He doesn't move away, but his eyes narrow at me, making my smirk widen. "Just sit back and relax. Enjoy the show. Your job won't start until after we're all done anyways." I pinch his cheek this time, making him let out a low rumble that does unwanted things to my pussy.

Neo laughs at how pissed off his cousin is over nothing. God, I love getting this man going.

"Ready, Boss?" Lucas asks. "The line-up is long tonight."

"Isn't it always packed in here on a weekend?" Dean asks.

"Yes, but word got out Queenie was doing a solo, so tonight is extra special. People are coming out of the woodwork to come watch her," Tommy says, all smug, and I give him a high five.

"People can't resist watching me up there. It's like waving a big, juicy steak in front of hungry lions. Maybe it'll even give me a reason to break some bones tonight," I say, bouncing with giddy excitement. I'm due for a kill, even just a teeny, tiny one. Hell, I'll settle for just kicking someone's ass. Anything to give me an excuse to ride that magic stick Neo has tucked into his pants. That gives me an idea.

"Neo," I say, and he looks over at me from whatever conversation he was having with his cousins.

"Yes, my Queen?" he smirks.

"I'm gonna get you a cock molding kit. I want to make a dildo so that I can use it whenever you're not here." Axel chokes on the drink that Roxy just handed him, and Dean's eyes go wide, while Lucas and the other guys just snicker and walk away.

"He's not gonna make a mold of his cock to give to you," Axel growls.

"The fuck I'm not!" Neo laughs. "Bro, if she wants my cock, real or fake, any time she wants it, then she sure as hell is gonna get it."

"You are fucking pussy whipped," Axel glares at his cousin.

"And I wouldn't have it any other way." Neo makes a whipping sound, and I burst out laughing.

"You're just pissed that Neo is the only one getting any. How's that going, by the way?" My smile goes wide and taunting. Dean and Axel give me a dirty look.

"Not good," Neo teases. "I'm surprised they haven't woken up Rosie with all that slapping of the salami they've been doing. God, the noises that have been coming from their rooms, I don't know if it's them or all the porn they have been watching," Neo snickers. I bite my lip, watching Axel and Dean's faces grow red. "I'm surprised they even have any skin left on their shafts. Probably have bad friction burns." I burst out laughing, poor babies.

“Shut the fuck up, Neo,” Axel growls. “Sorry, we can't all get our dicks wet on the daily.”

“Oh, come on, it's not on the daily. More like every second day,” I giggle as the blue balls crew turn their evil glares on me. “Too bad you’re not willing to submit to a woman because then I might be able to take care of that little problem for you.” I raise a brow, smirking at them.

“Oh, trust me, Honey,” Axel says, giving me a grin of his own. “There's nothing little about me,” he says, cupping his cock with his hand and giving it a little shake.

“Well, if everything is identical between you and your twin, then trust me, Buddy, I’ve had that cock. And no, there was nothing little about it. I bet it even got bigger too.” I bite my lip with a grin, and his slips at me talking about his brother's cock.

With that, I turn around and head backstage.

“Hey, ladies,” I say, stepping into the changing room. Everyone lets out happy *Hi’s* and continues to get ready.

“So, what do you have planned for tonight?” Lola asks, “Something serious and sexy, or something fun and flirty?” She gives me a knowing smile.

“Something that's gonna make jaws drop and cocks pop,” I giggle, and she laughs.

“And to make them men of yours drool?”

“They are not my men.” I glare at her.

“Oh, come on. They are fine as fuck. None of the women are allowed to touch them, despite how much a lot of them want to." I let out a growl at the thought. "Chill, they won't. They know that what's Queenie's is not to be messed with," Lola chuckles.

"They are my property, my workers, if nothing more," I huff, getting changed into my red, glitter bra and black, short shorts. I put on some bright red lipstick and take out my ponytail, letting my long, black hair hang down in loose curls. Slipping on my red, studded heels, I take one last look in the mirror before turning to the other girls.

"Showtime," I sing with a bright smile. I'm going to be the opening number, leaving me the rest of the night to hang out at the bar and drink until I forget. I know that Evie said to wait, but I know what happens to girls who go out thinking they are doing one thing, then wind up being a sex slave in the basement of a restaurant for five years.

My heels click as I walk down the hall and head backstage. Once I'm announced, the whole place erupts into cheers and whistles. I can't help but grin as I take in all the excitement for me. I miss dancing. As shitty as it was being forced to do it for all those years, I never lost the love for it. Being up on that stage, no matter the circumstances, gave me a sense of power and freedom, letting me get lost in the music, if only for a few minutes. Like the calm before a storm.

When we first started this place, I used to dance every night, but as my empire grew, so did my responsibilities. The more we expanded, the more time I spent in business meetings. Sure, half ended in bloodshed, but it was still work.

I enjoy getting up there and having fun with the girls. I don't go up there anymore for the entertainment of others,

I go up there with whatever song I'm feeling. Could be slow and sexy, or fast and silly. Upbeat and seductive, or I might just stand there and sing. When I perform, I do it for me and no one else. That part, I took back for myself.

The song starts playing before I step onto the stage, and the crowd grows even more wild. I mean, it's *WAP* by Cardi B and Megan Thee Stallion, so there's more than a few reasons to get excited about this song. I love dancing around my house naked, belting this song out, not giving two fucks.

With my mic in hand, I start to walk slowly out on stage as soon as the lyrics start. I try to look around the room as I sing, but my eyes can't help but gravitate to Neo and his cousins.

The look on their faces as I sing these dirty as fuck lyrics is priceless, and I'm loving it, every second of it.

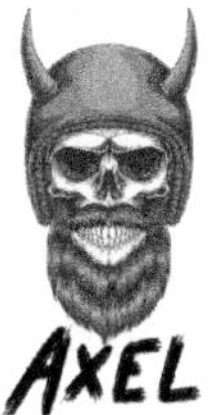

HOW AM I surprised, and at the same time not at all, by her choosing this song? She's up there singing about wet pussy and all the shit she wants a guy to do to her using his cock. The men around here are drooling like dogs looking at a bone while they listen to her sing the graphic lyrics as if they wish they could be the one to provide that for her.

Pigs.

But as I watch her, I can't help imagining it's my cock her mouth is wrapped around, or myself being strangled by her tight cunt. Look, I may not like this new Harlow. This isn't the one who we all fell in love with and were willing to break our own hearts to keep safe. Which, by the way, was the dumbest decision we ever made. Well, that Dean made; we didn't get much of a choice. My brother and Neo were the ones most broken by Dean sending her away. I didn't like it either, but I accepted my cousin's choice and understood the benefits of what he had done. At the time, he had a valid point. How were we to know that the guy with the money would screw us over and Harlow would end up in the complete opposite situation than what we had wanted her in?

This Harlow that I'm watching right now. She's not the young, damaged girl who stole my heart with her sassy, yet shy personality. There's no blushing when we check her out anymore; there's no hair tucking and stolen glances. All that's left is this hardened version of a woman who will slit your throat with a smile and not blink twice about it.

My dick sure remembers her, though. She's too fucking stunning to forget. There's just something about her that sets her apart from all other women.

I still don't like her, though. She's too controlling. There's no compromising with her, and everything has to be her way. I've never submitted to a woman before, and I don't plan on doing any more than I have to when it comes to her. I'll play her little games for the sake of our company and Rosie, but that's it.

Her little stunt of banning us from fucking anyone is downright inhuman. I mean, if she's not willing to let us fuck her because even if I don't like the woman, I'll sure as hell fuck her, then why not let us get it elsewhere? I get not touching *her* women, that's fine, no matter how hot some of them are, but all women? I could just fucking strangle her, but she would probably have my cock in one of her hands and a dagger in the other, ready to slice it off before I could blink. As much as I hunger for sex, it's not worth getting my dick cut off over, so I guess I'll have to keep using my hand for now.

Shaking my head clear of my wandering thoughts, I focus back on the woman of the house. The club is losing it for her, but she's not even really dancing. I heard her voice the other night, and the girl sure can sing, but this song doesn't show that talent. Although, she seems to be having fun. She has a big smile plastered on her face, and she just enjoys the beat. Shaking her ass and swaying her hips as her friend Roxy sings a part of the song.

Dean watches her with a blank face, but I'm sure his cock is just as hard as mine is right now. Neo wasn't wrong. I know for a fact that I have jacked off more in these past few months than I have in all of my teenage years combined. I crave a wet cunt to pound into and a fist full of hair that I can grab a hold of. Porn isn't doing it for me anymore, so moments like this where I can watch Harlow up there half naked, or when I catch the tail end of her and Neo's animalistic fucking, are things I can't help but store away for later. Yes, it's fucked up, but maybe so am I. I can hate a person and still imagine being balls deep inside them while they scream my name. After all, no one gets my blood boiling quite like her, and right now, that's all I have.

The night goes on, and Harlow sits at the bar laughing and talking with a few people. Neo is always at her side, like a loyal, little lap-dog. Ready to care for her every need. At first, I thought it was pathetic that Neo, Mr. Look-at-me-wrong-and-I'll-smash-your-teeth-in, was bowing down for some woman, but now I get it.

She may not be the same woman that we all used to love, but she is definitely the woman meant for Neo, at least. Her fucked up type of crazy matches his, if not more so. He's found someone that he can be himself with completely. I just feel bad for the poor sap that she won't give him *everything* he craves. She may enjoy fucking him and love having someone with an equally messed up brain as hers to plot her kills with, but she won't love him the way he wants her to.

The only people she really cares for are the people who work for her and Evie. I guess, Rosie now too. I can tell that it meant more than just killing perverts to her. More than just her everyday kills. She set out to destroy them and brought them down as if they'd hurt someone she loved. And I know that Rosie shot straight to the top of her list of people she's ready to die for.

She never asks me or Dean about Rosie, but I know she hounds Neo for updates and photos since Cass isn't here for her to do that to.

And Rosie is always asking about Queenie. *When is Queenie gonna come back over to play dolls with me? Or when can I show Queenie Bob and Susie?* Cass tells her, Soon, and I don't know if it's just to keep her happy or if he really means it, but I know Harlow will make sure it happens. One way or another.

We are all still trying to wrap our heads around what happened. When Harlow came out of Rosie's room with murder in her eyes and mentioned Rosie's mom and stepdad, I just knew. My heart was ripped right out of my chest, and I can only imagine what my brother must be going through. Harlow only kills sick and evil men, so when she said they were dead, I wanted to be right there alongside her to bring them down.

But that was Cass's place. He had all these things he'd planned on doing to that sick bastard, but from the moment he laid eyes on him, he just lost it. He saw red and didn't stop punching until Dean and I pulled him away. We didn't care what he did to the guy, hell, we all wanted to join in and help, but Cass was bordering the line of no return. A mindset that would be next to impossible to get out of once it traps you. So, we had to take him away to cool him down.

After we dragged him out of the room, he just went numb, almost robotic in nature. That was, until we got him in through the door to our house, and then he lost it again. He started smashing everything in sight. Nothing was stopping him. It took Rosie coming into the room and seeing her dad losing it and saying, “Daddy” for him to stop. The moment he saw her sleepy, little face and messy, blonde hair, he instantly stopped his rampage, just scooped her up in his arms and has yet to really let her go.

We all want to wrap her in a bubble, keeping her safe and with us at all times, but everyone but my brother agreed that smothering her isn't healthy. She doesn't know something is wrong. That something is different. We need to try to keep things as normal as they are usually when she comes over to our place. But it's hard when Cass won't leave Rosie's side except to shower and use the bathroom.

We’ve been doing his part of the work here at the club. We don't care, nor does Harlow, and I do have to thank her for that. She's been cool about the whole situation.

Harlow's about five porn stars, which is Roxy’s cocktail specialty, in, when she realizes Dean and I are sitting next to her at the bar.

“Oh look, it’s Captain Kill-Joy,” she cheers, and I frown at her. “You know, you would probably be more fun and have more friends if you took that dildo out of your ass. Or at least use it to give yourself a good fucking.” She starts laughing hysterically at her own joke. Evie takes the drink out of Harlow's hand.

“Q, you're done for the night,” Evie laughs when Harlow pouts at her.

“Fine. I gotta pee anyways. And I’m fucking tired,” she says, hopping down off the stool and wobbling a little. “You know, I'm not as bad as you make me out to be,” she says, putting her hands on her hips. She's a little tipsy, and it looks kind of cute on her.

"You sure about that?" I smirk.

"If you would just open your eyes, you'd see that the only people who face this monster you make me out to be in your head," she says, tapping my forehead with her pointer finger in between each word, "are those who deserve it. I would never hurt or kill an innocent person," she finishes with a flourish, throwing her hands out wide for emphasis.

I know that. But that doesn't change the fact that she's still a serial killer. I just lift my brow and sigh in response to her dramatic gesture, but she only looks at me with a blank expression on her face, as if she's lost her train of thought, while swaying gently on her feet, before changing the subject.

"Oh. Tell your brother I'm coming by this weekend. He's kept Rosie to himself long enough, and I miss her adorable face. Plus, I owe her another bedtime story. Cause let's face it," she sighs, leaning forward. "I'm gonna be the girl's mother from now on. I don't care what any of you think. She's mine, just as much as she is yours." With that, she straightens up, turns around, and leaves, and all I can do is watch in silence as the room parts for her like the Red Sea did for Moses.

I can't help but smile at her proclamation. I may not like this new Harlow, mostly because this one still has the body of the one we left behind but without the happiness that we tried to preserve inside her, but at least, I know my niece is in good hands. She has me, her dad, her uncles, *and* the most feared woman in the state, possibly even in all of the

USA, to protect her. Hell, even the world has her back, it seems.

So, I'll put up with her crazy ass. For Rosie.

CHAPTER FOURTEEN

Harlow

EVIE, TOMMY, Lucas, and Max have the club under control for the day. I'm heading over to the guys' house to see Rosie. I miss her, and I want to see how she's doing. Cass has kept her trapped inside that house long enough, and I need to work with the guys to have everything set up for Rosie. I found one of the best child psychiatrists that money can buy to help Rosie deal with any damage those sick fucks left behind.

Maybe if I had someone who really wanted to help me when I was growing up, I might not be as fucked up as I am now. Well, at least up until being locked away and used at that demon's disposal.

Tracy hasn't called, and let's just say that I didn't exactly take the news well, and as a result, we've had to order a new shipment of glasses for the bar. Evie has been working around the clock to try to get any leads she can, but she still only knows as much as Miller, which is next to nothing.

Evie's kicked me out of the club for the day, telling me to go see Rosie. With that in mind, my inner monster has agreed to go back into hiding, for now. But she also told me she was working on a D-Day for tomorrow night, which helped brighten my morning a bit more.

I feel helpless, and I fucking hate that feeling. It's not something I've felt or been in over three years, and I never wanted to, ever again. I made a promise to protect these girls with my life, to give them everything they deserve after all those years of living in hell.

Oh, and another girl went missing as well. So, that's five women in total, all between the ages of 16 and 25. This is exactly the kind of thing I would handle, but none of my contacts know shit. None of the regular players would dare try anything like this. So, whoever is taking these women can't be from around here. They are coming into my town to grab women from right under my nose and then taking them somewhere else, and they must be really fucking good at what they do for them to not leave any trails. But don't worry, so am I. Whatever the case may be, they will be dead as soon as I get my hands on them.

I will start storming the streets, beating any and every fucker I can, until I find not only Tracy but the other missing women too. But Evie is right, at this very moment, I can't do anything. And to avoid a few thousand dollars more in damages, I think I need some of those blinding smiles and giggles from that pretty little princess.

This time, when I show up at the house, I do it like a normal person. Odd for me, but hey, I'm always down for trying something at least once.

I ring the buzzer, waiting for someone to answer or open the damn gate. I look through the bars and tap my foot. I don't like to be kept waiting; it gives me too much time to think of fun and fucked up things to do.

I press the speaker button. "I know you're in there," I sing. "Open up, or I'll huff and puff and blow the mother fucking door down," I say in a sugary sweet tone. A moment later, the gate clicks open. I smile wide, happy with myself, and press the speaker button again. "Smart choice."

I hum to myself as I skip up the long pathway to the front door. Thank god, I chose sneakers opposed to a pair of heels. When I get to the door, I try the doorknob. And look at that, it's open. Good, saves me from having to pound the door down.

"Honey, I'm home," I call out. I hear a few voices in the next room, then the sounds of little feet hitting against the floor.

"Queenie!" Rosie shouts with the brightest smile that instantly melts my ice-cold heart. It's like that part in The Grinch where his heart kick-starts and grows three sizes; well, mine just grew one hundred.

"Hey, kiddo," I smile and crouch down as she runs across the room and into my open arms. I hug her tightly to my body, lifting her, and spin her around with both of us giggling.

"I missed you," Rosie says. "I've been asking Daddy for you to come over to play, but he said you were busy," she pouts. I look behind Rosie and find Cass leaning against the kitchen doorway, his arms crossed and with a guarded look on his face.

"Oh, he did, did he?" I narrow my eyes at Cass, and he does the same to me. "Well, not anymore! From this day forward, I'll never be too busy for you."

"Yay! Does that mean you're here to play?" she asks, her blue eyes shining brightly with hope.

"It sure does!" I say, giving her one last squeeze, and then put her down.

"I wanna show you Susie and Bob," she says, bouncing with excitement.

Chuckling, I take her hand and let her guide me to the backyard. I still can't believe they have zoo animals here. But I mean, they are Neo's, so I guess I'm not really all that surprised.

"Hey, can I talk to you?" Cass asks, placing a hand on my shoulder and stopping me from walking out the back door.

I see the importance of what he wants to say in his eyes. "Yeah," I nod.

Looking down at Rosie, I say, "Hey kiddo, why don't you head back there for a minute while I talk to your daddy, okay?"

She looks at the both of us. "Okay, but don't be too long," she admonishes.

"I won't." I chuckle.

Once she races off into the backyard, I take a seat on the stool at the kitchen island. "What's up?"

He sighs and takes a seat next to me, angling his body so that it's facing me. "First, I want to apologize for not being at work lately."

"Look, I get it. You don't have to apologize," I say, taking a grape from the fruit bowl and popping it into my mouth.

"No, I do. We have a contract, and I haven't been sticking to it."

I raise my hand in a stopping motion. "Don't. She comes first, above everything else."

"Why do you care so deeply for her? You only met her once," he asks with genuine curiosity.

"Because she reminds me of me, or at least the me, I never got to be," I say, looking out the window, watching Rosie running around and chasing the goat with Neo. His smile is bright as he runs around with her, and it does shit to my insides. Fuck. I told myself that these guys were in my past, but that crazy fucker in the backyard is making me feel things that I swore I'd never feel again. I mean, I guess I can hate him a little less, enough to be friends. He is loyal, fun to be around, and a fantastic fuck. And my god, his fucked-up mind is a fucking aphrodisiac to me.

"I don't know how I didn't see it," he says, his voice filled with pain as he watches Rosie through the window. "She never said anything. She never showed any signs. Well, maybe she did, but we all just missed it. I don't even know what they would have been." He sounds defeated, then turns to look at me. “How did you know? You took one look at her crying and knew something was wrong.”

I give him a sad smile. “Cass. You know my past,” I say, and fuck does it ever hurt to know that the first person, I spilled my hellish past to, would also be one of the people who crushed me the most.

“Right.” His face looks even more anguished as he looks at me as if he too is thinking about all those past moments between us.

“I knew because I was once her. But you see, no one was there to hear my cries, or if they did, no one cared.” Since the night I was taken by Triver and his men, I’ve stopped hiding my past and instead just owned it. I don't hide shit anymore. I'm an open book. I own my scars. I rose from the deepest pits of hell and climbed my way out, all the way to the top, where I am now untouchable.

“Low,” Cass says with pity.

“Oh, no, no, no,” I laugh. “Nope, not going there. I don't want your pity. But there is something you can do for me.”

“What's that?”

“Don’t fight me when it comes to Rosie,” I grin.

“She really can wrap anyone around her little finger with just a smile, can't she?" he says, sounding proud of his little girl.

“Dude, that girl owns my ass. She’s the one and only person who ever will.” I lean in close and, with a wink, whisper, “Just don't tell Evie that.”

Cass chuckles. “Yeah, something tells me shit’s about to get a lot more interesting around here.”

“Hell fucking yeah!” I cheer.

“Bad word!” Rosie shouts from the sliding glass door. I look at her then Cass with a raised brow and a smirk. He's smiling, trying to hold back a laugh.

“When we say a bad word, and Rosie hears, we give her a dollar,” he says with amusement.

“Aaah. Gotcha,” I grin, walking over to Rosie. I don't carry around a purse, but I always stash a few hundreds in my back pockets. Not like anyone’s gonna try and rob me. Pulling one out, I hand it over to her.

Her eyes go wide as she looks over the bill. “Daddy! This one has two zeros after the one!” she shouts and runs over to show her dad. Cass chokes on his drink that he just got out of the fridge.

“Wow. That’s... that’s a lot of money,” he says, looking at me with raised brows.

“Yay! Now I have enough to go get pretty nails with Uncle Neo and Queenie!” she cheers and runs out to show Neo.

“What was all that about?” I giggle.

“She has been earning her own money. She wants *pretty nails*. Neo’s tried to paint them for her, but she has small hands and yeah, no luck,” Cass laughs.

“Smart girl. I have a feeling she's gonna be richer than you guys. Especially with me and Neo in the same room,” I smirk.

Cass groans. “This is gonna be hell,” he complains.

"Nah, been there. Trust me, this is gonna be more like heaven."

I SIT in one of the loungers in the backyard, watching Harlow, Rosie, and Neo cleaning out the pens.

When Harlow saw the baby goat, she squealed like a sorority sister and started fawning all over it. And Susie, who usually hates everyone but Rosie and Neo, ended up loving Harlow just as much. Just what we need, someone else who supports these animals.

Watching Rosie giggle and laugh, acting so carefree with Harlow, warms my heart. Axel's told me what Harlow said. That she was gonna be in Rosie's life, whether we liked it or not. At first, I was pissed at her for inserting herself into that role, but as I started to calm down and think more about it, I realized that Harlow is exactly what Rosie needs. A loving, caring mother figure. Hell, Harlow is a stone-cold killer and still, she is a million times better at being a mother than Briana ever was.

Just thinking about her and that vile monster makes me wanna puke. Beating that fucker to a bloody pulp was the best feeling in the world, but it didn't take away the damage that's already been done. I can't help but thank god every day that the sick bastard didn't do more than what he did. I don't know the details of what happened exactly, and I don't think I want to know. All I needed to know was that it was enough for them to die by Queenie's hands. I had to know one thing though, but thankfully, when I asked Harlow if he had raped her, she told me enough for me to know that he hadn't gotten that far. Rosie hasn't once asked about where her mother is or when she's coming back for her, and I hope she never does. I could always tell how much she didn't like being with her mother, so I don't think she would be too upset if she never comes back. At least, I hope not.

Harlow may be one scary motherfucker, but it's in moments like these, when she is carefree and having fun with Rosie, that I can see glimpses of the old Harlow. The one I fell madly in love with. The one I had all my firsts with. My first real kiss, my first girlfriend, my first time having sex. She was my whole world.

I know my cousins craved to have the same with her, but I'm so damn lucky that I'm the one that she chose to be with. I don't know if what she felt for them was the same as what she felt for me, but I know she felt something. I saw the way they made her blush, the way she would steal glances when she thought no one was looking. The way she let the guys get just close enough without seeming too obvious or flirty. Someone might have seen it only as playful and friendly, but it was much more.

Funny thing was, I loved both her and my family so much that I would have shared her with the guys if that was what she wanted. I never told them, though. I wanted to keep her to myself for as long as I possibly could.

Seeing her now, the way she is with Neo, it hurts a little. I crave it; to be able to touch her again, to make love to her, to feel her lips on mine. But even with all that, I'm happy for him; I really am. He's getting something he's always wanted. Someone just as fucked up in the head as him.

But knowing that I was willing to share her back then and that I still am now, I'm holding on to the hope that someday, I might get a second chance to be with her too.

Now, I just need to find a way to break down her walls again, to earn her trust. She hates men, and knowing what she had to endure all those years, I can understand why. I can't even think about it without wanting to burn the world to the ground. I told her I would always protect her, and I failed in the worst possible way.

She doesn't need me to protect her now. She can do that better than anyone can, but I want a second chance to love her. I'll wear her down over time. She may not know it yet, but she's mine. Always has been, always will be.

"Daddy, Daddy!" Rosie yells, as she runs over to me.

"What's up, my little Rosie Petal?" I smile as she stops in front of me.

"Can we get a pony?" she asks me with her big blue eyes. Looking behind her, I see Harlow giggling and Neo with a shit eating grin plastered on his face. But fuck if I'm gonna let him get any more large animals. Someone needs to draw the line.

"Who needs a pony when you have a dad?" I say, then crouch down with my back to her. "Hop on," I say, patting my back. Rosie cheers and climbs on.

I pretend to gallop around the yard as Rosie holds on tight. Her giggling and cheering make looking like an idiot right now worth it.

"Alright! Now, this is something I can get in on," Harlow cheers, then hops on to Neo's back. "Giddy up, horsey," Harlow cheers, bending over slightly to smack Neo on the ass. Neo lets out a groan then a roar of laughter, but does as he's told. By the time we are done, we're all laughing, and it's nice not to be hurting for just a minute. I almost lost myself for a while, and if it wasn't for the guys, I wouldn't have understood how me keeping Rosie locked up inside the house to be safe would only cause her more harm than good in the long run.

Harlow found someone amazing for Rosie to go see, and it's taking a lot for me to admit, but I think I might find someone to talk to as well. I want to be in the best mindset for her, to be able to help her and to be there for her however she may need.

Neo

"**PASS THE** crumpets please, Princess Rosie," I say in a funny British accent. She giggles as she hands me a cookie.

"Would you like more tea, Princess Neo?" she asks.

"I would love some," I reply.

We're in Rosie's room, and Harlow decided to stay until Rosie goes to bed. Something about owing her a bedtime story or something, but I don't care; I would have her here all the time if I could. I can't help but look at that banging body and her constant smile. It's so genuine, it's enough to make a man go blind.

Rosie is dressed up in one of her play dresses, and Harlow and I have on tiaras. Look, you need to understand that I may enjoy smashing skulls and breaking bones, but if this little girl wants me to dress up and play tea party, you better damn fucking believe I'll do it, and I'll gut anyone who has a problem with it.

Watching Harlow with Rosie warms my damaged, black heart. I've seen how she acts around the little family she's made for herself. Most of it is for show. Always on her toes, always alert, but with Rosie, I can tell she's loving every moment of being here, with us. Maybe it's because she never got to be a child, or she's like me and just doesn't give a fuck.

Lately, I've been pretty tame. This new me with Harlow, fuck it's scary, but I love it. I would never ever in a million years be this way for any other woman, but there's just something about Harlow that sucks you in, and you just want to be consumed by her.

I'm in love, and I don't care if she ever loves me back. If what we have right now, me being used as a way for her to get off in her time of need, is all I get, then I'll take it. As long as I get some of her, that's all I care about. The rest is just a bonus.

But I feel him. My monster within. He's itching to come out, god does he ever want to come out and play! That time in the alley, and when Harlow let me play with her, killing those scumbags wasn't enough for him, he wants more. And I'm afraid that once he's unleashed, Harlow will put him down, ending one of the best things I've ever had. Maybe her monster will take on mine, and together we can be one fucked up mess. Hell, we're already halfway to a funny farm.

We play a few more games and watch a movie. When Rosie starts to get sleepy, Harlow gets her ready for bed.

"You love her, don't you?" Cass asks me quietly, referring to Harlow. He's standing next to me by the door as we both watch Harlow, who's snuggled up with Rosie, reading her a bedtime story.

"You do too," I point out, not looking away from the only two girls to ever own my heart.

"I'm not gonna give her up," Cass says. "I plan on getting her back."

"And I don't plan on letting her go."

"Then I guess we'll just have to make it work," Cass says.

"I guess we will," I say with a smile. I don't mind sharing Harlow. The idea of watching that goddess getting worshiped by my cousins gives me a fucking hard-on. Back when we were younger, I craved for Cass to share her. For her to want us, to want me, as much as she did Cass. But back then wasn't our time. Her beast wasn't yet formed, and mine was still growing by the day. I would have destroyed her without even meaning to if we'd started something back then. But now? Yeah, fuck that shit, she's mine. We've waited a long time for this.

"What about the others?" Cass asks.

I huff out a laugh. "I don't know who those fuckers think they are fooling. Axel may act like he hates Harlow, but he craves her. It might be just her banging body at this point, but it's something. And Dean? Being with Harlow means giving up control. That's his biggest issue, but I know over time she will wear them down. She's Harlow, how can you not want to bow down at her feet and offer her the world?"

"She told Axel she was Rosie's new mom," Cass chuckles.

"You have a problem with that?" I smirk.

"Not at all. Means I'm already getting one half of something I've wanted for a very long fucking time."

And now we wait. We give her time, wear her down. She puts on a big front, but I know we will break her, but this time we will be there to put her back together.

CHAPTER FIFTEEN

"**SO, WHAT** do you think?" I ask Rosie, holding out my hands, showing her my new set of nails. They are black with red glitter.

"So pretty!" she gasps. "I love them. Do you like?"

Her nails are galaxy colors, and I was kind of surprised that she didn't ask for pink, but she said the nail polish reminds her of the stars, and how she and Cass go in the backyard, laying down at night to look at them. It's fucking adorable.

"I love them! They look amazing on you," I smile, checking out her nails as she wiggles them in front of my face.

D-Day is tonight, and I'm so fucking pumped that I've been a bouncing ball of energy all day. The poor nail stylist had to redo my nails more than once because I couldn't keep still. I opted out of the full spa day, but Neo and Rosie didn't.

Rosie is on one side of me with her toes about to be painted. "Wait!" she shouts, and the nail stylist looks up at her, startled. “I don't want that color for my toes anymore. I want that color,” she says, pointing to my nails. I grin that she wants to be like me, then cringe. Let's hope she never wants to be exactly like me. Her dad would kill me, or at the very least he might try.

She beams up at me, then watches the woman with excitement as she starts prepping her toes. Rosie starts telling her about the *Trolls II* movie and all her favorite parts. I chuckle and look over to my other side where Neo is sitting.

He has cucumbers covering his eyes and headphones in his ears. He’s humming one of my favorite songs, *Bohemian Rhapsody* by Queen. I giggle at the sight of this sexy beast of a man getting pampered like a queen. It's kinda hot.

The door chimes, and I look over to see some snooty lady with fake blonde hair walk in like she owns the world. Two other women, carbon copies of the first, walk in behind her. My eyes follow them as they take a seat in the chairs across from us. Once they are settled in, they notice us. They all smile as they see Rosie getting her nails done, then look at me. The snooty lady gives me a pathetic attempt at a smile, but I don't smile back. When she notices Neo getting his nails done, she scrunches up her face in disgust and starts whispering to her friends. Nah, not on my watch. Like fuck if I'll just sit here and allow someone to be judged for something like this.

“Got a problem?” I ask sweetly as I lean right into her face, my hands on both sides of the armrest holding me up. She didn't see me there until the moment I spoke. Her head snaps over to look at me, and she lets out a yelp.

"What is your problem?" she asks. "Do you mind?"

"Not at all," I purr. "But I believe I asked you first."

"Excuse me?" she asks, her eyes wide when she sees I don't give a shit about being in her personal space.

"I said, do you have a problem with that man over there getting his nails done?" I repeat sweetly, my eyes never leaving hers.

She huffs. "Well, it's not very manly," she stammers. "Is he gay?" she lowers her voice for that part.

"No, he's not gay. I should know, I ride his dick like a carnival ride. Men don't have to be gay to get their nails done. It's a free fucking country. Sorry, but not all men are stuffy old rich perverts like I'm sure your husband is. I bet he's banging his secretary right now while you're out having a little girl time," I coo. The panic in her eyes tells me I'm fucking right. God, this is pricelessly predictable. "I bet your dusty old pussy is used up and useless to him now, so he tosses you to the side and pays you to look the other way to keep everyone thinking you have some amazing, loving marriage when really, your husband's tiny dick does nothing for your gaping hole, so you gotta go fuck the pool boy with a big cock in order to feel anything." I pat her cheek as I give her a fake pity smile.

"Who do you think you are, talking to me like that?!" she snaps, her face growing redder by the second in obvious rage and embarrassment.

"Does your husband work for any of the larger companies on Weston Avenue?" I ask, hoping it's a yes. From the looks of her fancy clothes, I wouldn't be surprised.

"Yes," she scoffs. "He runs the biggest one," she snoots, sticking her nose up in the air. Ah, she's Dick's wife then.

"You wanna know who I think I am to talk to you like this?" I ask. If my grin could get any bigger, I'd look like the fucking Joker. She just raises a perfectly manicured brow at me.

"Nice to meet you," I say, standing up and holding out my hand. She looks at it confused. "The name's Queenie."

Her eyes go wide with fear as she looks from my hand to my face, while she scrambles as far back in her chair as possible, desperately trying to get away from me. All the color has drained from her face, and she looks like she's gonna be sick.

When she doesn't take my hand, probably out of fear that I'd break it, I bring it up and grip her chin hard. "Next time you go around judging people, take a look in the fucking mirror. You're lucky I don't give women equal opportunity during my extracurricular activities like I do with men because if I did, I'd be taking you home and having my fun with you."

She whimpers, and I think she's pissed her pants. "Now, if you don't mind, I'm gonna go back to that sexy as fuck man over there with the blue nails and take him home, so he can rut into me like a wild animal and make me scream so long and loud that I lose the ability to talk. I'll black out from all the fucking mind-blowing orgasms he is guaranteed to give me."

I remove my hand from her face, and I'm pleased with the fingerprints I see left behind, marking up her face. “Not that you would know anything about mind-blowing orgasms, I’m sure,” I grin at her. With a perky smile, I wiggle my fingers in goodbye, my sweet smile back in place, as I take a seat in my chair.

Neo looks over at me with a smug grin. “Do you have any idea how fucking hard I am right now?” he says, lowering his voice, so Rosie doesn't hear.

I can't help but laugh. “What?”

“Watching you defend me like that, laying your claim on me. God, My Queen, I'm ready to bust a nut, right here, right now,” he groans, and the poor nail stylist looks like she's ready to bolt with how uncomfortable she is right now.

“Shh, you,” I giggle. “Rosie's gonna hear you! And don't think too much into it.” I huff.

“You like me,” he taunts.

“Do not,” I growl.

“Do toooooo,” he sings back at me. And I can't help but smile. What can I say, the crazy fucker is growing on me.

“All done,” the nail tech says. Rosie holds up her toes and wiggles them.

“They’re so pretty!” she breathes, looking up at me and beaming with happiness. “Just like yours.”

“Just like mine, Kiddo,” I smile back.

We gather our things and stop to pay at the front counter. “Your total is $115,” the lady says, looking at me. But Rosie steps in front of me and digs into her small Hello Kitty purse before handing over a bunch of bills to the lady. The lady looks at me with a small smile and a raised brow. When I nod, the lady takes Rosie's money and starts to count it out. Rosie watches her, waiting to see if she has enough.

While Rosie is distracted, I take two hundred-dollar bills from my pocket and discreetly slip it into Neo's palm.

"She's gonna notice that all her money, plus some, magically appears back in her purse," Neo whispers with a chuckle.

"Next time she helps you clean the pen, give some to her as a reward for all her hard work," I shrug.

"You're amazing, you know that?" Neo says, stepping up against my back, his lips grazing my neck. "She's lucky to have you in her life. No matter what the others might think, you're the best woman for the job."

A shiver takes over my body as it awakens under his touch. Neo and I have been fucking around for a while now, and it's gotten to the point where anytime I touch myself at night, his name is the one I'm calling out. I want him, and it's more than just for all the mind-blowing, amazing orgasms after a kill. I want him to be the one who gets me off for any reason, any time of the day. I really need that cock mold I told him to make. I don't trust him, and being with him in any other way would require that, but I will have to bring him to my dungeon. That will be the ultimate test. If he can survive that, then maybe I'll upgrade that dildo of his cock to the real thing. I mean, friends with benefits is a thing, and that's what we are now... right? Oh, fuck if I know.

When the lady gives Rosie a nod to say that she has enough, Rosie looks back at us with pride in her eyes. "I can't believe I got to pay like a big person!" she says, excitedly. Then she frowns. "But now I don't have any money left."

"Don't worry. Uncle Neo was just saying that because you help him with big people work for the animals, you should get paid like a big person does."

"Really?" She looks at Neo with wide, blue eyes.

"Yup!" Neo says, then picks Rosie up. She giggles as he maneuvers her onto his shoulders.

"Alright, Kiddo, we gotta go. Your daddy has been calling me like crazy, and I don't think he likes that I've been ignoring him," I laugh, and she giggles again as we walk out of the shop and head back towards the club where the other guys are working.

"He's gonna be mad at you," she snickers.

"I think I can take him," I say, flexing my arms. Rosie looks at my muscles and then looks back up at my face. I'm not crazy ripped or anything, but I do work out. And helping the girls with hours of practice helps a lot too.

"Yup, I think you could take him," she nods in approval.

"Trust me, Posy, Queenie could take on Daddy, Uncle Axel, Uncle Dean, and me all at once and not even break a sweat," Neo grins.

"Wow," she whispers in wonder. "I wanna be just like you when I grow up."

Neo bursts out laughing. "Oh, I bet your dad would *love* that," Neo cackles.

I pinch him on the arm, and he laughs even harder. I look up at Rosie. “How about we aim to make you a strong, independent, loving, caring woman; how about that?”

“I guess that works too. I hope I'm a good mama like you, though,” she says.

“But I'm not a mama, silly girl.” I smile, tilting my head to the side.

“Well, you can be my mama. Daddy says my mama is gone, and she's in a place that won’t let her leave. And that means I get to stay with Daddy forever!” She bounces up and down, and Neo has to get a better grip so that she doesn't fall off his shoulder. “I’m so happy my wish came true.”

“Your wish?” I ask, needing to know.

“Yeah. I wished to God every night before bed that when I go to Daddy’s, I’d never have to leave again.”

“You don't miss your mother?” I ask and then bite my lip because this is a sensitive subject.

“No,” she glares at me, and it's adorable. “She was a mean mommy. I hate her,” she spits.

“Well, you don't have to worry about that now,” I say, patting her leg, wanting to take this conversation in a new direction. “You’ve got your Daddy, Uncles, and me. And everyone at the club.”

“Uncle Neo says you have a dance club. Can I come dance there too?” I can't help but burst out laughing with Neo this time.

“Umm. We’ll see.” I shake my head at the shit eating grin on Neo’s face.

"Okay, but can you still be my new mama?" she asks hopefully. And fuck does that ever make my heart swell so fucking big.

"I'd love nothing more than to be your mama," I smile, holding back tears. Neo sees the emotion on my face and his eyes go wide with the realization.

I narrow my eyes at him and poke him in the chest. "Shut. Up." I demand in my scary voice, but I must be losing my touch because it only makes his grin grow wider.

Fucking dick head.

The club is full tonight, but that's nothing new. I'm so fucking ecstatic because my crew, not the ones who work at the club, but my outside contacts who collect my monstrous playthings and bring them to their execution block, brought in a new shipment from all over the country. I'm talking rapists, molesters, wife beaters, all that jazz. On the block tonight, we have six new playmates for me. All strapped in and ready to go. Tonight, I'm even letting Neo play again.

"You did amazing tonight," I praise Lola as she comes out of the dressing room and into my office, where I'm doing some paperwork for the club.

"Thanks," she smiles. "And thanks for helping me with that dip. I never thought I'd get the flow right."

"You fucking crushed it, girl," I say, giving her a fist bump, pretending to make it explode. "So, what's up?"

“I actually came back here to ask if you’ve seen Penny?”

My smile drops. “What do you mean? She isn't at the bar waiting for you?”

She shakes her head. “No. Roxy said she went to use the bathroom, and when she got back, Penny was gone.” With Tracy still missing, all the girls are on edge.

“Fuck,” I hiss, and Queenie is out. Grabbing a gun from under my desk, I strap it into its holster on my thigh. My daggers are strapped onto the other one. I'm already in my costume for tonight because I'm so damn excited, so they are all on full display as I stand up.

Storming out of my office, I'm on a rampage and god help anyone who gets in my way.

I beeline to Lucas. “Get the guys on all the exits. Check every room in this damn building. I want that girl found and safe,” I growl low and dangerous. They all take off at my order.

“What's going on?” Dean asks from behind me as he follows along.

“Penny is missing, and I'll be fucking damned if she’s the next one of my girls that disappears. She’s only a fucking kid.”

“I'll help,” he says.

I say nothing as I burst out the front door of the club. My eyes are everywhere, seeing if maybe she came outside for some fresh air. Shouting in the distance gets my attention, and I take off in that direction.

“Get in the fucking car, Penny!” a man roars, and as he comes into view, I see that he has a tight grip on her arm. She fights against him as he tries to shove her into a car.

“Please, just let me go,” she pleads.

“I’m bringing you home where you belong,” the man growls.

“Let me go,” Penny shouts, giving him a good kick to the shin. He curses with a grunt.

“You little bitch!” He goes to raise his hand to hit her, but I don't let that happen.

“Hello,” I say in my perkiest voice. “And what do we have here?”

The guy's head snaps towards me. I know who this is, it's Penny’s stepbrother. Penny ended up telling Lola everything a few weeks after getting to my club and once she settled in. After she realized that this was indeed a safe place, she opened up to her cousin about everything that had been going on at home and behind their parents’ backs. Her stepbrother was sneaking into her room at night, doing unspeakable things to her, and then would threaten to kill both her and her mother if she ever told a soul.

“It’s none of your business,” the man snaps, clearly having no fucking clue who he’s talking to. *But oooh, buddy, you're about to find out.*

“Scott,” Penny warns, but I raise a hand.

“You see, this lovely lady here, she is my concern. So, that makes this my business. So, you wanna tell me why you have your hands on her like that and where you think you're taking her?” I ask, my voice calm, but my monster is pounding at the trap door, wanting to be let out to try and sate the hunger that will never be satisfied. *Down girl, give me a few.*

"Penny, is this him?" I ask her, and she gives me a small nod.

"What the hell have you been telling people about me?!" he glares at her with fury in his eyes. "More lies? Just like the lies Lola told your mom and my dad? You know, they kicked me out. Disowned me!" he spits.

"I didn't lie," Penny says, trying to get out of his grasp once again.

"Alright, buddy, I think it's about time you let go of her," I say, stepping closer.

"Fuck. You." he hisses.

Dean lets out a dark chuckle from behind me as he watches me work.

Tilting my head to the side, I smile sweetly at him and pull my gun from its holster. I bring it up and level it with his head, switching off the safety.

"I said," my voice goes ice-cold as my smile slips. "Let. Her. Fucking. Go."

His eyes widen as he stares at the barrel of the gun. He lets her go and starts to back up.

"Not so fast, little mouse. We've only just begun to have some fun." A slow, sinister grin takes over my face. "Penny, dear, go back to the club with Dean, please. I'll take this from here," I tell her, leaving no room for discussion and never taking my eyes off this punk in front of me.

The sound of footsteps recedes behind me, and once they are gone, I continue.

"Look, just let me go, and I'll never come back. I'll leave Penny alone," he pleads, his *"I'm a man, hear me roar"* persona is gone.

"Did you enjoy sneaking into your stepsister's room at night?" I ask, tilting my head to the side, ignoring his words. "Having your grimy, nasty hands all over her as she begged you to stop?" I slowly walk towards him until he's backed up against the driver's door and the barrel is pressed against his forehead. "Sticking your tiny little weenie where it didn't belong?" He's shaking now as he swallows hard.

"You see, that's a big no-no for me. And because I know for a fact you did do those things to Penny, I'm afraid I can't let you leave here tonight," I sigh dramatically, loving every moment of this.

He whimpers, seeming to understand that no amount of groveling is gonna save him.

"Put your hands on the door frame," I smile, thinking of something fun I can do to get this party started.

"W-what?" he stammers.

"Come on," I motion with the gun and point to the door frame of the open car door. "Hands. Here." He gives me an odd look, rightfully so.

He stumbles to the door and places his hands where I told him to. "See those two hands right there," I say, nodding to his hands. "They did some very bad things. And I think they need to be punished, don't you?" I ask, raising my brows with a questioning smile.

"Ummm...?" he questions.

With my gun in my right hand, pointing to his head, I take my free hand and place it on the car door and with all my strength, I slam the car door onto his fingers, hopefully breaking a few. He lets out an ear-piercing howl as the door embeds itself into both his hands.

“God,” I groan. “Did you hear that? The crunch of your bones? That sounds so satisfying. It's like an ASMR wet dream.”

He crashes to his knees, screaming bloody murder, as he stares at his hands in horror.

“Enough of that,” I chirp. “You're gonna draw unwanted attention here soon, and I don't need anything derailing my plans for tonight. I've waited too damn long for this.”

I hear footsteps behind me as Axel, Dean, and Neo come into view.

“Perfect timing,” I beam over at Neo. “Pet, would you be a doll and bring him to the showroom with the others?”

“It would be a pleasure, My Queen,” he grins like a loon.

“I’m so excited,” I squeal as I do a happy dance. The guy's eyes go wide as I wave around my loaded gun. “Oops,” I giggle. “My bad. But I wouldn't have shot you... probably.” I shrug and put the gun away. Once Neo has grabbed the sobbing sissy off the ground and over his shoulder, I skip past him and all the way back into the club.

Looks like we have ourselves one more playmate for tonight; lucky number seven.

CHAPTER SIXTEEN

"**I WANT** to be there too," Penny says, trailing after me with Neo right behind her, as I head straight for my office. I'm vibrating with energy. I need the show to start very soon before I snap and hurt the next person who talks to me. "I have the right to watch as the person who hurt me finally gets what's coming to him," she says, folding her arms and giving me a look of determination.

I glare at her. "You're lucky I don't bend you over my knee and slap your ass for leaving the club with him! I don't care if he just wanted to talk, it was stupid to go! And don't give me an attitude. I might tame my beast for this club and the people who work here, but don't forget who you're talking to."

Her face falls and pales slightly. "Sorry," she apologizes. "I didn't mean to be rude, it's just..."

"I know, and it's not that I don't want you to be able to get the closure that you want or need; it's just that what happens in my showroom is something that will stick with you forever. Something you will never be able to unsee, forever ingrained in your brain. There's a reason why only a few people come to my private shows. I don't mind an audience, but most people can't handle what I do, and this is something I do for myself."

She sighs. "Can I at least see his dead body when you're done?" she asks, tucking her hair behind her ear.

Stepping in front of her, I place my hands on her shoulders, looking into her eyes. "That, I can do. I'll try to keep him... in one piece," I giggle, and her eyes go wide, clearly not getting my fucked-up sense of humor. No one really does. Except maybe Neo and sometimes Evie.

"Hey," Neo says, getting our attention. "If she doesn't want that spanking, can I take her place?" he grins wickedly at me, and my pussy pulses for this sexy male specimen standing in front of me.

"You, shut it!" I growl, only making his grin go wider.

He steps into me, as if Penny isn't right here next to us, and gets as close to me as he dares. "You know, My Queen, when you get all growly like that, you remind me of a little feisty Chihuahua. It's quite adorable."

"W-what!" I splutter. "Did you just call me... adorable and compare me to a tiny rat dog?!" I'm so not used to anyone testing my authority like this, knowing I slit throats for less. I should make an example out of him, but instead I do nothing as I get lost in his ocean blue eyes swimming with mirth.

Thankfully, I'm saved when Evie opens the door. She takes in the room and raises a brow at how close Neo and I are. I take a step back, needing space to clear my head. Fuck him and his psychotic, erotic charm. Why does he have to be so nutty, and why do I have to be a fucking desperate squirrel for it? My beast within approves, wanting to break out and lick him all over before devouring him whole. Traitorous bitch.

"Umm... everyone is gone now. We can start the show... if you're ready?" she says, sounding unsure.

"Perfect!" I cheer, quickly masking whatever the fuck this shit was. "Meet me down there and bring Dean and the others. I want everyone who's willing to be there for Neo's first performance."

Evie nods, giving me a smile. I give her a genuine one back. I miss her. Fuck, I'm a shitty best friend. Since the guys and Rosie came into my life, I've spent little time with my bestie. I can tell it's getting to her by the dirty looks she gives the guys and the longing stares she gives me. She misses me, and I miss her just as much. We're gonna need to have a slumber party ASAP.

She leaves, and I turn to Penny, my smile slipping when a dangerous look takes over my face. "If anyone asks, I kicked his ass for daring to talk to me like that. Understood?" Her eyes go wide, and she nods vigorously. "Alright, go find Lola, have her take you home." She says nothing, just scurries out of my office. I turn to Neo. The cocky fucker still has that grin on his face. Crazy bastard.

I push past him, and he follows me like the loyal pet he is. Ugh, awesome. Why does referring to him as a pet, outside the little dom-sub thing we have going, make me feel… iffy? Like I'm somehow degrading him? And better yet, why do I care? I should be hating this man. I should want to tear him apart for what his negligence caused me. But I don't… He's starting to grow on me. *Eeeeww, feelings*. Did I fall asleep and get abducted by aliens or some shit? That's gotta be it. It's the only explanation for it. Because there is no way that I'm actually starting to like this guy. *Is there?*

When we get to the door that leads down to the showroom, Neo steps in front of me, stopping me from entering.

"You know, you didn't really say no to that spanking," he grins as his heated eyes grow molten with need.

I can't help but smirk back. "Later," I wink, then push past him to head down the stairs. He lets out a whoop and practically skips down the stairs after me.

"Welcome, welcome everyone," I greet the room as I make my grand entrance. I'm all dressed and ready to go in my black, lace booty shorts and my black and red corset. Tonight, I did something a little different and slicked back all my long, black hair into a ponytail.

Muffled whimpers fill the room from the line-up of men on the other side of the room. All gagged and bound and ready for some fun. With the newest little pervert at the end. He has already pissed himself and is currently crying like a little bitch. He can dish it out but can't take it, I see.

"We're gonna do things a little differently. Tonight, I'm going to share my spotlight." Everyone starts to mutter in surprise. Lucas and the others are too busy to watch, but some of the girls who are done for the night, and the others who weren't working came to watch. “I know. This is the first time. But Neo here has been itching to play, and I’ve been dying for a D-Day. So, why not kill two birds with one stone.”

“Oh! Stones, can we use those?” Neo asks seriously. Hmmm, I’ve never used those before. Might be fun.

“Why not?” I turn to Tommy. “Be a doll and get me a bucket of rocks?”

He shakes his head with a smirk, but takes off, nonetheless.

“Let's all give a warm round of applause for Neo.” The room breaks out in cheers, everyone but Axel and Dean clapping after my announcement. With a grin, he gives an extravagant bow. I never force anyone to watch my shows; they are all here of their own free will. They love seeing sick and twisted fucks get their comeuppance.

I turn to Neo and clap my hands together. “You’re gonna go first,” I beam. He looks at the men strapped to the chairs and all the goodies laid out on the table, then to me.

“Umm,” he says, scratching the back of his head, looking unsure. “What do I do?” Aww, he’s nervous; how fucking adorable.

Neo

GOD, THIS is so fucking embarrassing. I feel like some virgin boy getting ready for his first fucking. I've killed before, even tortured a few here and there. But this is Queenie. She's a pro at this, and I feel like I'm learning from some kind of samurai master. I don't want to disappoint her or let her down. Or make a complete ass out of myself. God, I'd never fucking live that down, and the guys would make sure of it. Looking like a pussy in front of my girl. That's right, my girl. She just doesn't know it. Yet.

"Well, normally I pick a song to set the mood and let the music take over. Sometimes I just dance, sometimes I sing along too," she shrugs. "Do whatever you're comfortable with."

She's talking as if she's trying to pump me up for a school talent show instead of helping me get ready to torture and murder a bunch of men. God, I love this woman. I don't give a fuck who knows it. Well, maybe her; she's not quite ready for that yet.

"Okay," I say and walk over to the table of weapons. I don't dance. So, there's no way I'm gonna attempt that right now. Normally, I couldn't care less what people think, but this is a big moment right now with Queenie letting me in on something that is so important to her.

I can't sing worth shit, and I don't want to be disrespectful to any of the artists I know by trying to and butchering it.

Selecting the daggers in honor of this momentous occasion, I walk over to the men frozen in terror. Thinking of the first song that comes to my head, I begin, grinning at my choice.

“If you're crazy, and you know it, stab a pervert,” I sing. Then bring a dagger down into one guy's thigh while driving the other in the thigh of the man next to him. They both let out agonized, muffled screams. “If you're crazy, and you know it, stab a pervert.” I stab the next two and keep going down the line. “If you’re crazy, and you know it, and you are proud to fucking show it, if you’re crazy, and you know it, stab a pervert.”

Grinning like a freak, I step back and survey my work. Harlow lets out an excited cheer at my performance. “Fucking genius. I love it!” she giggles and runs over to the table and grabs two black handguns.

“If you’re deranged, and you know it, shoot a sick fuck in the foot,” she sings, then fires off two rounds into the first two guys' feet, then moves down the line. “If you’re deranged, and you know it, shoot a sick fuck in the foot.” Two more shots. “If you’re deranged, and you know it, and you couldn't give two fucks to show it, if you’re deranged, and you know it, shoot a sick fuck in the foot.” When she’s done, she fucking spins around to face me. Her eyes are wide with excitement, and I can practically see the energy dancing along her creamy smooth skin.

"This is so much fun!" she cheers and runs back to the table. "Come on!" she says, looking over her shoulders, beckoning me to join her. "I wanna try everything," she giggles. God, this woman owns my heart. My cock is so hard right now by watching this goddess at work.

By the time we're done, everyone is dead. Harlow goes around to the bodies lying on the ground and opens their mouths, then we take the bucket of rocks and make a game out of who can get the most rocks in their mouths. She's so fucking random and weird. She's perfect!

"Okay, now that was awesome. Totally not how I normally do my shows, but just as exciting and exhilarating." She beams up at me, her eyes heavy with lust, and I know now that the show is done, and the foreplay is over, it's time for my favorite part. She stands there staring at me intently, her breathing starts to quicken.

"Fuck me, Neo," she breathes, and I just about blow my load. What has this woman done to me? A door closes, and I turn to see that all of Harlow's people have left the room, knowing what comes next. Everyone but Axel and Dean. They lean against the far wall, arms crossed, watching us with unreadable expressions.

Well, if they wanna stay and watch, we may as well give them a show. I lean over and whisper into Harlow's ear, telling her my idea, and she grins and nods.

Her sexy ass struts over to the little seating area next to where the guys are standing. Their eyes follow every seductive move of her body.

She leans over the back of the couch that faces them and sticks her ass out. "Take me, Pet, make me scream your name while your cousins watch."

Groaning, I rub at my rock-solid cock through my jeans. Being a good pet, I do as I'm told.

She's given me permission to touch her, so I pull down her panties, not wasting any time. She wants it hard and fast, like always, and I'm more than happy to oblige, to satisfy her every need. Having my cousins watch as I fuck the girl they loved and still want in some kind of way is only icing on the cake. Maybe watching me have what they could have too, if only they'd get their heads out of their asses, they will see what they are missing out on, and maybe, just maybe, it might kick their stubborn need for control out of the way, so they can be happy too. They may not like being dominated by a woman, but Harlow isn't just any woman. Being under her control is fucking heaven. Best sex of my life, and trust me, I've had enough of it to know.

Taking out my cock, I give it a few strokes before lining it up with Harlow's beautifully glistening center. Once in place, I thrust all the way into her, her body presses into the couch from the force as she lets out a sexy moan of pleasure.

The guys shift in their spots, and I can see the tents rising in their pants. Between not getting any for months and watching the most stunning woman here on full display, it wouldn't be surprising if they end up cumming in their pants, just from watching.

They lock their gazes on Harlow, not wanting to miss any little thing. If it's a show they want, it's a show they'll get. Gripping her hips, I start to pound into her, pulling the most delicious moans from her. Her ass jiggles as my hips smack against her luscious, plump cheeks.

Despite the boner in Dean's pants, that looks very fucking painful, he does nothing. He stands there, still as a statue, with his hands clenched at his side. His jaw ticks as his eyes flick to me, grinning like a fucking loon as I plow into Harlow, who is now making all kinds of erotic noises. Reaching around, I start to play with her swollen nub.

"Fuuuck," she groans, pushing her ass further into me, making me take her deeper. "I'm gonna cum!" she screams before letting her head flop forward and biting the couch as she screams. Her pussy clamps down around my cock, choking it harder than she did that fucker in the alley. To stop myself from ending this way too early, I have to close my eyes and imagine naked, wrinkly, old people skipping in a field of flowers... Like I'd risk looking like a two-pump chump in front of the guys.

"On the couch," she commands, and I slip out of her, eager to obey. With my cock standing at attention, I walk around the couch, letting it bob with every step. I lock eyes with Axel and wink. If looks could kill, I'd be dying of a heart attack right now. Chuckling, I lay down and wait for my queen to ride my cock like a mechanical bull.

Harlow moves until she's standing in front of me, but she's facing the guys. Turning my head, I see their pupils are blown even larger, so that their eyes are almost fully black, making them look like creatures from the underworld as they watch Harlow give them a striptease. She slowly takes her panties the rest of the way off, letting them drop to the ground and kicking them to the side before unlacing her corset to reveal her large, gorgeous breasts.

Taking advantage of her being distracted with teasing the guys, I lean over to the juicy ass that's right in my face and take a bite out of it. Harlow lets out a yelp and turns to glower at me, but I just grin like a fool, biting my lip.

“Sorry, Mistress, but it was right there, just begging to be tasted.” A little smirk appears on her blood-red lips as she moves to straddle me. Grasping my cock with her soft, warm hands, she lifts herself up, placing the tip at her entrance. She turns back and looks at each of the guys with lust-filled eyes, biting her lip before slamming down and impaling herself on my cock, never looking away from my cousins. She lets out a moan as she starts to rock back and forth on me, her breasts bouncing with every motion of her hips.

Right now, this isn't about me, though. I'm being used for this little game she has going on with them, but I’m okay with that because I'm really enjoying this performance too.

Harlow runs her hands over her body in sensual movements, grabbing her tits, massaging them before playing with her already hard nipples.

Her eyes bore into Axel, daring him to leave, to be uncomfortable by what's going on and bolt, but he doesn't.

The stubborn, cocky fucker doesn't want Harlow to win at her own game, so he fights back. As he intensely stares at her, his hand moves to his jeans. He unzips his pants slowly and takes out his rigid cock, grasping it tightly in his hand.

Dean's eyes flick between the two, and with a growl, he furiously jumps up and storms out of the room like he always does. I bet Harlow loves that he lost just a little bit of his control because of her. She enjoys fucking with these two, but this is the first time Axel's really pushed back.

Harlow lets out a groan when her eyes lock on Axel's cock, as he pumps his length vigorously, taking all his anger at Harlow out on his cock. God, his poor dick, there won't be anything left by the time he's done. If he goes any faster, that fucker's gonna burst into flames.

I watch as Harlow parts her lips, panting as she gets close again, and watching Axel doing whatever the fuck you wanna call it seems to be getting her even hotter. I can't watch it. Not because he's my cousin, as we've shared girls before, no, it's because I pity that poor wiener of his. Slaying the Basilisk from the chamber of secrets isn't gonna help you get any pussy, bro.

She pinches her nipples hard, moaning as she bucks harder. One hand slips down between her thighs, and she plays with herself, causing Axel to bite his lip in concentration, probably in a desperate attempt to keep from cumming all over himself. I wouldn't be surprised if there's no fucking skin left on his dick. How the fuck does that feel good? It looks like he's trying to murder it. Dude should not go without sex anymore. I think he forgot how to use that thing. Now it's just getting embarrassing.

Harlow breaks apart with a scream as she gushes all over my cock. She keeps going though, not slowing even the slightest, taking no time to recover, and going after her third climax.

It doesn't take her long because she's already so sensitive after the first two, and like a domino effect, I burst like a fucking super soaker, spilling my cum deep inside her cunt. She milks the life out of my cock, and Axel lets out this fucked up, grunting noise as he cums on the floor right in front of him.

He's panting hard, his shoulders heaving as he tries to get a hold of himself. You can see when reality hits him because his face drops for a moment before he masks it with pure, unadulterated fury. Harlow and I burst out laughing at the rapid change, and Axel lets out a roar, before aggressively tucking his raw cock away, zipping up his pants as he yells, "I hate you. I fucking hate both of you!" Then he storms out of the room. Harlow beams with pride as she watches him leave, knowing that, yet again, she's won her own little internal game.

"What the fuck was that?" Harlow howls with laughter so hard that she falls off me and my still hard cock, landing on the floor, clutching her sides.

"Poor guy. It's gonna sting for a while when he pisses." Her laughter is contagious, making me laugh just as hard as she is.

When she's done, she sits back on the couch and turns to me with a smile. "Can we talk?"

"Always." I shift closer to her, giving her my undivided attention.

She bites the inside of her cheek. "Did you really not know what Dean was planning to do back then?" she asks, all amusement and playfulness gone from her when talking about our past situation.

I make sure she's looking me right in the eyes. "I had NO idea what he had planned or what he did until it was too late," I say, meaning everything with my whole, blackened heart. "I was starting to get worried when you didn't show up at the house, and when I was about to leave to go search every part of the city, Dean stopped me. He told me what happened. It explained the black eye he had and why Cass was practically missing in action. He went to look for you, you know." I give her a half grin.

She doesn't say anything, but her eyes widen slightly. "He loved you more than his own life; he would never have let Dean do what he did if he knew beforehand. Neither would I, for that matter."

She looks over at the bloody bodies on the ground as if she's looking off into the ocean or some shit.

"I don't want to hate you anymore," she whispers, her voice defeated.

"Then don't," I say, rubbing my thumb against her hand on the back of the couch, trying to ignore the fact that she's also still naked. Her tits are distracting, making me wanna lean over and take her nipple into my mouth and...

Shut the fuck up, Neo, this is serious. Don't blow it!

She looks down at her hand with mine still covering it, and then up at me. "I still don't trust you," she says, narrowing her eyes at me.

"I don't expect you to," I grin.

"If you ever do anything to hurt me again, I will kill you. I won't be taken for a fool again," she says, and I can see in her eyes that she really means it.

"I would rather chop off my own balls and eat them, then slice off my dick and fuck myself in the ass with it before even dreaming of hurting you again," I say with 100% seriousness. Her eyes go wide, and she bursts into another fit of laughter.

"Fuck, you're so weird," she giggles, shaking her head. "I fucking love it," she grins.

I give her a smile of my own, happy to know this woman really does accept every part of me.

She hasn't seen your beast unleashed; shit could still change.

"Alright, then," she nods. "Friends with benefits? This thing we have between us is no longer a job. If we are friends, I want you to do this because you want to, not because you think you have to."

"Oh, My Queen, you have me in every way, shape, and form. Whether it be business banging buddies or friends with benefits," I smile wickedly. "Or even passionate lovers who are head over heels for each other."

“Whoa now, buddy, don't get ahead of yourself there,” she raises a brow but still smiles. “That’s never gonna happen.”

“We’ll see,” I smirk.

She just shakes her head and holds out her hand. “Deal?”

I take it in mine, giving the back of it a kiss like the gentle-fucking-man I am. “Deal.”

CHAPTER SEVENTEEN

CASSIUS

WARM BREATH against my face wakes me from my sleep. Did Rosie climb into my bed again last night?

Slowly, I blink my eyes open and find myself staring right into a pair of bright blue eyes, but they're not Rosie's. My eyes widen, and I think my heart stops for a moment.

"Sweet mother of god," I breathe loudly. Harlow starts cracking up, only an inch away from my face. She's straddling me, and as she sits up to give me some space, she rocks against my morning wood, making me grunt.

She wiggles her hips back and forth, making me even harder. *Fuck.*

"Morning, Cassy. Looks like someone grew up big and strong. Did you eat all your veggies like a good boy?" she giggles and rocks her hips again. My hands fly out to hold her still, not wanting to blow my load. She instantly goes quiet, and I look from my hands to her face before quickly removing them.

"Sorry, I didn't mean to touch you, it's just... fuck," I breathe.

"From what I can tell." She rocks her hips again, making me groan. "You feel as big as Axel looked."

My heart stops for a moment. She's seen his cock? What the fuck?

"And how exactly do you know what his dick looks like?" I growl, feeling jealous at the thought that my brother's had her before me. But then I remember who Harlow is now, and there's no way she fucked him.

"You missed quite the show, Cassy boy," she grins, then falls onto the bed next to me. I roll over onto my side as she rolls onto hers, making us face to face. Her black hair fanning out onto the pillow.

"Oh really? And what show was that? D-Day, or your little show with Neo afterward?" I ask. The thought of Neo getting to fuck her doesn't bother me as much as it did before. The only thing I'm jealous over is that I don't get to touch her while he does. For now, she's ours, and I'll earn her trust back over time, and when I do, I'll let it be known that I'm madly in love with her. I don't want to own her, just love her, and be loved by her, like when we were kids.

Rosie adores her, not shutting up about her for even a second. The look on Rosie's face when she told me that Harlow agreed to be her mama made my heart explode. I know it sounds crazy; who lets a serial killer just take charge and demand that a child be theirs now? And I used to think the idea was absurd, but after seeing how amazing she is with my daughter and everything she has done to protect her, I know she's exactly what Rosie needs. Not once, since Harlow has come into her life, has she asked about her mother, other than when I told her she will be living with me full time from now on. It was nice, but sad, when I told her that her mother was gone and not coming back. She was happy and excited about living with me, but didn't ask anything more on the subject of why. That woman only did one good thing in her pathetic excuse of an existence, and that was giving birth to Rosie.

Harlow's smile grows wide with mischief and amusement. "Axel, the foolish man that he is, didn't enjoy my little challenge. Let's just say, by the end of it, I'm sure there was nothing left of his cock," she giggles.

My brows pinch. "Did you sleep with him?" I ask, holding my breath.

"No, silly!" she scoffs. "As if he would let me have any control over him." She rolls her eyes, then smiles again. "At least in the bedroom," she winks, and I chuckle.

"We had some fucked-up game of chicken during my post kill fuck with Neo. God, it was hilarious watching him whack his willy like it was gonna cum skittles." She breaks out into a fit of giggles at her own joke, and I can't help but smile at this really weird situation. We've found ourselves in some strange predicaments regarding Neo in the past, but with both of these oddballs in the same room together, I should get used to weird shit happening all the time now. Also explains why Axel looked like he was in a lot of pain last night, heard him cursing in the bathroom before I went to sleep. Stubborn fucker.

One thing I do love and appreciate from both Neo and Harlow is that their crazy personas get locked enough down to a safe and appropriate level when they are around Rosie. Another reason why I trust them with my daughter.

"So, what are you doing here so early... in my bed... with me?" I ask with a smirk.

She tucks a piece of my long locks behind my ear, like she used to when we were teenagers, as if out of muscle memory. When she realizes what she's doing, she retracts her hand.

"I'm having a girls' day with Evie today. With you guys joining our little rag-tag group of misfits and my spending so much time with Rosie, on top of all the club business and Tracy..." Her face flickers with pain and frustration at the mention of the girl who's gone missing. "I haven't had any time with my bestie. So, I came to tell you that I'm giving you guys the day off and closing the club for the night. It's a Monday, so it's really no biggie."

"I've had a lot of days off lately," I point out.

"About that. Penny can't do anything around the club with her not being legal age and all. So, I was thinking that if you're okay with it, she could watch Rosie while you work?"

She sees my immediate refusal coming and continues. "I know you don't trust many people with Rosie. But Penny is a good kid. She turns 18 next week, and she loves kids," she says. "You can bring Rosie to my place above the club. I have a top-of-the-line security system, we can get anything she might need while she's there, and she will be close by if anything happens. Keep in mind that you can't keep her locked up here forever, and I won't let this be an easy way out of the deal you made with me."

She does have a point. Rosie is already getting annoyed at my over-protectiveness, and she doesn't understand why. I don't want to overwhelm her any more than she will be once she starts going to therapy.

"Fine. But won't the music be a problem?" I ask.

"Ah, no," she laughs. "I have that place completely sound-proofed. Don't need anyone hearing my screaming orgasms now do I?" she giggles.

"Don't they hear that after your kills anyways?"

"Nope. Everyone has to leave for that part."

Wait, what? "We haven't been. And you've never asked us to."

"I know," she smirks. "I just thought you enjoyed watching. Also, it's a bonus having you watch Neo fuck me when you can't get any." Oh, she's evil.

I glare at her, but that just sets her off into another fit of giggles. I like seeing her like this; carefree and happy. Even if it's only for a moment, she's had enough heartache to last a lifetime, and I plan on making sure that I am never the cause of that pain again.

"Daddy?" Rosie calls from the doorway. Harlow and I both sit up to see a sleepy Rosie with a blonde bird's nest on her head.

"Hi, Baby Girl," I grin, but her attention is on Harlow.

"Queenieeeeeee," she cheers, running over to us. Harlow picks Rosie up when she gets to the edge of the bed and cuddles her close. Rosie squeezes Harlow with a big smile.

This moment could not be any more perfect, and I can't help the massive grin that splits my face, watching my girls like this.

"So, where did the family of birds that live in your hair go?" I joke.

"Daddy!" she giggles. "There's no birdies in there," she says, then her eyes go wide, and her hands fly to her hair. "Is there?" she looks panicked.

"No," Harlow laughs. "Daddy is just being silly."

"Come here, and I'll brush your hair for you," I say, reaching over and grabbing my brush from my nightstand.

"Can Mama Queenie do it?" she asks. Harlow's eyes widen, and she looks up at me, not really sure how to react to what Rosie just called her.

"If she wants," I say, holding out the brush to Harlow. Harlow takes the brush from me like it's a bomb, but relaxes when she sees Rosie's excited face.

Rosie gets into place and Harlow starts untangling her hair, being sure to be gentle with the knots. I just lay back and watch them interact, loving every moment of it. They talk and giggle, and by the time they are done, Rosie's hair is in fishtail braids.

"Look, Daddy. I look like Anna from Frozen," she gushes as she looks at herself in the mirror that's in the corner of the room.

"You look beautiful, Sweetie," I say, then look at Harlow. "Thank you."

She shrugs. “I do it for my girls all the time, plus I love hanging out with that cutie pie.” She gets up off the bed and holds out her hand for Rosie. “Come on, Kiddo, let’s get some food inside that belly. I'm gonna make you banana, chocolate chip pancakes.”

Rosie rushes to grab Harlow’s hand in excitement and practically drags her out of the room. Harlow laughs and follows the eager little monkey.

“Oh, great, *you’re* here,” I hear Axel grumble as he makes his way into the kitchen, where we’re sitting, and over to the coffee maker. He mutters to himself as he slams his cup on the counter, and as he bends over to get the spoon he just dropped, he hisses in pain. Harlow hides a grin as she takes a bite of her pancakes, and Neo chuckles as he enters the kitchen.

“How's the naked mole rat doing? Does it hurt to pee?” Neo grins as he prances over to Axel. Ignoring Axel's death glare, Neo snatches his coffee from him, which earns him a growl as he makes his way over to sit next to Harlow.

“Hi, bestie,” Neo grins like a lovesick fool.

“Hi,” Harlow smiles.

What the fuck is that?

“You know what, Neo,” Axel starts as he angrily starts making another cup of coffee. “It’s too early for your bullshit this morning.”

"Bad word!" Rosie mumbles around her mouthful of pancakes. Axel sighs and grabs his wallet, then hands her a dollar bill. "Thank you, Uncle Bear." Axel smiles at her nickname for him. She says it's because he's grumpy like a grizzly bear, but cuddly like a teddy bear.

Neo chucks a grape from the fruit bowl at the back of Axel's head, trying to rile him up more. Harlow giggles, and Axel spins around, getting in Neo's face. "Get out of my face and go feed your damn llama, Neo, I mean it. I don't want to deal with your brand of crazy this early in the morning," he snaps.

"Alpaca!" both Neo and Harlow shout back simultaneously. They look at each other with a grin and say, "Jinx" at the same time, too. Both burst out into laughter and high five each other. Axel lets out an irritated sigh and storms out of the room, almost colliding with Dean.

Dean watches him go with curiosity, before turning to see all of us sitting at the table, and raises a brow but says nothing as he makes himself a coffee.

"Where'd you disappear to last night? You missed the grand finale," Harlow asks with a smirk, and Neo roars with laughter. Rosie looks around, not sure what the heck we are talking about. I tell her to go out in the backyard to play with Bob while the big people talk. Our whole back wall is glass, so I can see the entire back end of our property from the kitchen table.

Dean shrugs, "Not my kind of show, made me feel a little sick." Harlow keeps her smile, gets up, and stalks towards Dean.

“Aww, don't be like that, *Daddy Dean*. You can just say it. You were a Jelly Belly that it was Neo I was riding like a pro and not you,” she purrs, tugging at his tie.

“Nah, I prefer my girls less... insane,” he says, and Harlow laughs.

“Hunny, all the best people are crazy,” she says, patting his cheek before her phone goes off. She checks it, scrolling for a moment before putting it back in her pocket. “Well, I gotta go. Evie’s up, and I’ve got a fun day planned.”

“Can I come?” Rosie asks hopefully as she steps back into the kitchen. Harlow's face drops, and she looks like she's ready to cave.

Quickly and very smoothly, Neo pipes in with a distraction, saying, “Not today, Rosie Posy. Me and you are gonna go to the movies!”

Rosie gets all excited, and Neo brings up the movie listing on his phone to pick one out.

“Thanks,” Harlow says. “Denying her anything is hard,” she chuckles.

“Trust me, I know,” I throw back at her, “And Har, thanks for this morning.”

“Anytime,” she says, then takes off. I don't know if I meant for our little morning powwow or for her helping out with Rosie, but either way, I'm grateful.

Harlow

"**OPEN UP!** It's the police," I shout in a really crappy impersonation of a man's voice as I bang on Evie's door to her townhouse.

A few moments later, Evie opens the door with a grin. "Well, hello there, officer, what can I do for you?" she says jokingly in a seductive tone.

"You know how to eat pussy, right?" I ask, pushing into her house like I own the place... well, I kind of do. "Because even though me and Neo are besties now," I say, opening her fridge and taking out the pre-made iced coffee, I know she always has in there, and pouring myself a glass. "We are not at that stage, and girl, I would love to be used as a meal, right about now."

I turn around to see her standing there with wide eyes and a deep blush staining her cheeks. "Who am I kidding, you're gay, of course you do," I say with a wink, then walk up to her, kissing her on the cheek before plopping myself down on the couch. "So, what do you wanna do today? I'm all yours." I lay back, widening my legs. Her eyes snap down to my crotch, then back up to my eyes. Poor girl looks like she's gonna have a stroke. What is up with her? I always joke with her like this, and she's never had this kind of reaction before. Or at least none that I've noticed.

"Evie, babe, breathe," I tell her, sitting up as she looks like she's about to have a panic attack or something.

She shakes her head. "Sorry, still early. My brain isn't functioning right, never does until I have my coffee." She looks at the glass in my hand and raises a brow. "The coffee you're so kindly drinking right now."

"I'll buy you one while we're out," I say, downing the rest of it, setting the glass down on the coffee table. I lean against the side of the couch, resting on my arms as I talk to her. "I wanna do something fun. We should go to a club tonight, but today let's take a drive to the Santa Monica Pier and play some games and do the rides and stuff," I suggest then pout, giving her puppy dog eyes. "Pleeeeaase?"

She sighs dramatically as if my idea is a big inconvenience for her, but I know she loves that pier. "Fine. But not only do you owe me coffee, I want cotton candy too!"

"Deal!" I grin, getting up and jumping at her, forcing her to catch me. She's taller than me, but not by much. She lets out a grunt but starts giggling as I kiss her face all over.

"Thank you, thank you, thank you. I love you!" I say, then detach myself from her then head over to the counter where she has her keys and toss them at her. "Let's go, you sexy bitch."

"Alright, just give me a minute. If we're going to the pier, we may as well go to the beach too."

"Fuck yes!" I shout, fist pumping the air, doing my best Jersey Shore impression, making her laugh even harder.

The pier is packed, and I can't even count on my hands and toes the amount of men I've wanted to stab already for looking at me like they wanted to fuck me, right then and there. I'm tempted to take them to the top of the Ferris wheel and watch them dangle over the side as they scream like little bitches. Why do men have to be such fucking perverts? I mean, I'm not even dressed suggestively, not that it would matter if I was, still doesn't give men the right to be pigs. I'm wearing jean shorts and a Mariana Trench band tee. Everyone at the club teases me about that one, but fuck them, that band is amazing! And I will continue to blast their songs as I get the club ready each day.

Evie, however, looks gorgeous. She's in an emerald-green crop top with her black bikini top underneath and a pair of jean shorts. Her long, red hair is pulled into a high, messy bun. My bestie is a bombshell.

"What do you wanna do first?" she asks me.

"How about a few rides, then something to eat?"

"Sounds good to me."

We head to the merry-go-round and get dirty looks from the kids as we cut in line. I slip the young man who is operating the ride a 20 and stick my tongue out at the snot nose punk who had the nerve to say, "Hey lady, you're too old for this ride." Fuck that shit. I'm *never* too old for anything. Evie gapes at me, then smiles as she shakes her head with a chuckle.

Pulling her along, we find a couple of horses as the ride begins. We never let go of each other's hands, holding each other with one and with the other, we cling to our horses the whole ride, laughing and being carefree for once. Sometimes I forget that at the end of the day, I'm a 26-year-old woman. I never had the chance to be a kid. My whole life was pain and misery. Evie has always been my saving grace amongst the demons in the pits of Hell that was my life. Without her keeping me tethered to reality, I would have gotten lost to my beast years ago.

After that, we make our way to the arcade, and I end up spending a half hour playing Whack-a-mole, competing with a ten-year-old boy while Evie just stands there watching in amusement. His mother is gonna need Botox for that resting bitch face she has going on. If she scowls any harder, her face is gonna be permanently stuck that way.

I won by default because she ended up forcibly dragging him away. Evie convinces me it's time for some food a little while after, but I think she just wanted to leave because I kept kicking her ass at Dance Dance Revolution. Not my fault, I dance more often than she does. The look I gave her when I accused her of this, along with her saying that she was letting me win, made her almost piss her pants laughing. She's lucky she's my ride or die because I was ready to punch her in the tit.

We eat at Bubba Gump's and fuck, I almost orgasm right there as I take a bite of my food, getting some disturbed looks and even a few heated ones. I don't give a fuck; their food is to die for.

"You know, I missed this," she says, sometime later, as we lay on the beach, soaking up the sunshine.

"Me too," I say with one arm over my eyes, blocking out the sun. My dumb ass forgot my sunglasses, yet I always remember my daggers. What can I say, perverts are worse for my health than a little sun in my eyes.

"So, you and Neo are friends?" she asks.

"Yeah, I guess we are. He's not what I expected him to be. He's everything that every man who ever touched me was not. Except Garrett, but he doesn't count. Neo won't touch me without verbal consent, or some kind of signal when I'm too far gone for words. He does everything I ask, with no resistance, and he's just fun to be around." I turn and grin at her. "Helps that his cock is like some magic wand doing some Hocus Pocus shit to my pussy."

She huffs out a laugh. "What about the rest of them?"

"Well, apparently he and Cass had no clue that Dean had planned to send me away. In the end, I guess they were kind of innocent. It was Dean who put everything in motion, and Axel by default because he knew and did nothing. Cass and Neo beat the shit out of Dean when they found out. And a lot of shit went down with them for a while after."

"Wow," she breathes, and everything goes quiet for a moment. "So, do you trust them?"

"Not a fucking chance," I laugh. "Girl, I'm so fucked up now that I don't even trust my bra to hold my tits in, let alone a man. But I'm tired of hating them all. Neo and Cass have followed my every command and at least earned me not wanting to kill them in their sleep."

"What about the other two?"

"Ah, fuck that shit. They can choke on a cock for all I care," I laugh. "I keep them around mostly for entertainment purposes." I tell her about the other night with Axel and Neo, and we spend a good ten minutes cracking up over it.

"Last one in has to tell Roxy that Dean broke her favorite beer mug," Evie grins as she takes off for the water. Fuck, she's gonna lose her shit. Roxy is almost as scary as me when pissed off. Almost.

I run after her, right into the water, only stopping when it gets to my waist. Evie squeals with delight as the waves splash her. She makes her way over to me, and we both relax in the water, floating as we look up into the purple and orange sky of the now setting sun.

"You know you're always going to be my number one, right?" I tell her as we collect our towels from our spot, looking like a couple of drowned rats. Note to self, don't wear makeup if you plan on swimming.

"No, I'm not," she says, giving me a half smirk. She stops me when I start to protest. "And it's okay. Rosie is way more important." My stomach drops a little.

"You two are the most important people in the world to me. You're not just my best friend. You're the Christina to my Meredith." Yup, I brought out the big guns. "With Rosie, I need her. And I need you too, just for different reasons." She looks at me, seeing how serious I am before nodding.

"I mean, she is adorable. I can see why she has all of you wrapped around her little fingers." She bumps shoulders with me as we walk back to my car.

"It's the big, blue eyes, man; they get you every time."

We end up back at my place, the idea of clubbing no longer on our minds. Drunk off our asses, we spend the rest of the night watching cheesy, scary movies and yelling at the dumb bitches who always think it's a fan-fucking-tastic idea to run towards the crazy killer. Nah, bro, you hear a noise when you're home alone, you get the fuck out of dodge.

That's not the case with me, though. I'll always find my target, no matter how long and far they run. Queenie always comes out on top. But I do love a good hunt before going for the inevitable kill. Nothing worthwhile in life comes easy. I enjoy working for my kills. *Why else do you think I love playing with my food?*

CHAPTER EIGHTEEN

CASSIUS

MY CELL phone rings, interrupting the board game Rosie and I are playing. "Daddy's just gonna get this, okay? Wait until I get back." I get up and go to exit the room and see her little hand sneak out to move a game piece. "No cheating," I call out, and she quickly retracts her hand with a giggle, turning her baby blues on me.

"I'm not," she says innocently, but the giggle is a dead giveaway. With a chuckle of my own, I shake my head and answer the call. It says private number, so I don't know who it is that's calling me.

"Hello?" I answer.

"Cassius, my sweet boy." A soft, musical, feminine voice makes its way through the line. I smile instantly at the familiar, soothing sound.

"Mother, how are you?" I ask. Normally, I would call her and give her updates on Rosie, but since Harlow's come back into our lives, the thought hasn't even crossed my mind. I feel like a shitty son, but I know she would understand.

“Unfortunately, not too good,” she sighs, her voice having a sorrowful tone to it. “I'm calling with some sad news.”

“Are you okay?” I ask in a rush.

“Yes, my dear, I'm fine. However, your grandfather passed away in his sleep last night.”

My heart is struck with a pang of grief. Our grandfather was a good man. Our grandmother passed away from cancer when we were in our early teenage years, and our mothers all went to live with our grandfather. His wife was his whole world, and losing her changed him in a big way. I'm sure he could have taken care of himself fine, but my mother and her sisters used this as an excuse to get away from the toxic relationships they were in with their husbands.

When they tried to take us with them, our fathers said they would kill them if they did. We told them to go without us, not wanting to see them unhappy any longer than they needed to. Seeing our loving, devoted mothers watch their husbands bring whores into the house every other day and pretend like they saw nothing while never being able to find happiness for themselves hurt us.

Our fathers couldn't have cared less about losing their wives, because it freed them to do whatever they wanted, but they would not allow their heirs to leave. At the time, we had a purpose. No one knew that it would all be for nothing because they fucked it all up with a few bad business dealings anyway. Draining the company, just to get the hell out of dodge, and leaving us to clean up their mess.

We were able to see our mothers during the summers, and those are some of the best memories I have. It was the only time we ever really got to be kids. Our trips slowly became few and far between as we took on more responsibilities in our everyday lives. Our visits stopped completely once we met Harlow because the idea of leaving her behind, stuck in her foster home didn't sit right with us.

"How are you guys handling it?" I ask with a softer voice.

"We knew it was coming. His health was slowly declining, but it still hurts," she sniffs.

"When's the funeral?" I ask, taking a seat on the couch in the office.

"In a few days. Your aunts and I are getting everything settled with all the arrangements and the lawyers. But I saw his will, Cass. He left everything to Rosie."

I suck in a breath. "But that's billions," I say in disbelief.

"He was going to donate it all to charity. But when Rosie was born, he left it all to her." We already knew that my brother and the others were left out of the will, as well as our mothers. It's not that he wanted to be cruel, but he knew that our fathers would find a way to control that money and use it for themselves, and we would never see a dime of it.

"She won't have access to it until she's 21, though."

"Wow. That's just... crazy." This is a lot to take in.

"We're selling the estate and moving to Ireland. We found a beautiful piece of land there."

"Well, I'm happy for you. But don't you think you might be happier finding someone you can actually love and grow old with?" I laugh, thinking about how she and her sisters are all joined at the hip.

She chuckles. "Maybe someday, my boy, but for now, your aunts and I have a chance to start over, a fresh new start, away from any reminder of them."

"You know, we still don't know where they took off to," I say, wondering if leaving puts them in danger.

"I don't know where they would have gone, but I know it would be somewhere no one would think to find them. I think we will be okay, but thank you for caring."

"You're my mother, and despite the lack of calling lately, I do love you with all my heart," I tease.

"About that. What on earth has kept you from me for so long?" she asks with amusement.

"I'll tell you everything when we get there. I'll let the guys know, and we will be on our way after getting Rosie settled." I'm going to have to ask Harlow if she would mind watching Rosie. I hate having to leave her for any amount of time, but this is not the best time to bring her with us.

"I wish your visit was under better circumstances, so you could bring that sweet, little girl with you."

"So do I. We will make plans before you guys move."

We say our goodbyes, and I head back to Rosie.

"I win!" she shouts.

"What do you mean, you win?" I chuckle.

"You took too long. So, I played for you." She giggles.

I shake my head with a smile. "Well, congratulations on your win. How about we celebrate with some tablet time while I talk to your uncles about a few things."

"Yay!" she shouts and takes off in the direction of her room.

I find Neo and Axel in the game room, where we have a bar and a few pool tables set up. "Take that, shithead!" Neo shouts as he takes the winning shot. "Bullseye, bitches."

Axel curses and tosses his pool cue on the table before chugging whatever is in his glass.

"Where's Dean?" I ask, getting both of their attention.

"Who knows, probably watching more porn. I think it's becoming a real problem, man. He spends all his free time in his room. Poor guy needs to get laid," Neo grins, knowing full well that's not happening.

"Fuck you," Axel spits. "You know damn well that we can't."

"I know," Neo laughs. "I just love reminding you. While you three have to live with this..." He makes a jacking off motion with his hand. "I'm doing this..." He holds out his hands as if he's gripping something and thrusts his hips back and forwards, fucking the air.

Axel growls and picks up his pool stick, readying to beat Neo with it. Neo ducks as Axel swings it at his head and dances off to the side with a laugh.

"Both of you, knock it the fuck off. This is important." I look to Axel. "Mom called." They both take me seriously now, letting me tell them what happened.

"Are you sure you can handle it?" I ask Harlow.

"You know, I find your lack of confidence in me insulting," she huffs.

"Have you ever actually watched a kid?" I smirk.

"Well... no. But Rosie is a good kid. Feed her, water her, play, and bed. It's like having a dog, right?" she smirks, and I hope to fuck she's joking.

"It's absolutely nothing like having a dog," I growl.

"Oh, chill out, Papa Bear; I won't let anything happen to our little cub. I'm a mama bear now, and no one fucks with mama bear, unless they want their heads ripped off," she says, matter-of-factly; a little over the top, but I love her enthusiasm and dedication to the situation.

She called Rosie hers, again, and I can't help the feeling of happiness that overtakes me. God, I wish this stubborn woman will let me in someday soon.

She goes back to reading the list of rules and Rosie's schedule that I put together, but we both know she's only reading it to say she did before tossing it aside and doing her own thing.

I'm nervous about leaving Rosie for any amount of time, but I know if she can't be with me, Harlow is the next best thing.

"Look. Go see your moms, say goodbye to your grandpa, enjoy some guy time. We will be fine," she says. Her face goes stone-cold, and I shiver at the death stare she's giving me. "But if I find out any of you go against me and fuck someone else, I will fuck YOU up! And not in a fun way."

"I don't know about that. Sounds like a good time to me," Neo grins as he enters the living room with his overnight bag hanging off his shoulder.

"I would give you the same warning, but I don't need to," she says, knowing there's no way in hell Neo would stray away from her to fuck some other woman. That would just be downgrading and risking his life. *Pointless.*

"Damn right, you don't," he says, handing her a cup of coffee. Harlow takes it eagerly from his hands and takes a sip. She lets out a moan, and it goes right to my dick. Neo sees me shift uncomfortably and gives me a slow, knowing grin. I flip him off and head to my bathroom to get this out of my way before we have to leave.

"I've missed my boys so much," my mother says as she hugs me, and then my brother.

"We missed you too, Mom. Sorry about Pop," Axel says. Our mother is the only person other than Rosie that he's never a grumpy fuck to.

She pats his cheek affectionately. "Thank you. I just wish you boys got to see him one last time before he passed."

We spend the day reliving old memories, enjoying the time we've missed together.

"So, how is my beautiful granddaughter doing?" my mother asks as she sets a plate of homemade spaghetti in front of me and takes a seat next to me at the dining room table.

"She's doing good," I say, not wanting to bring up anything upsetting at the supper table.

"Who is she staying with while you're here? Her mother?" my Aunt Linda, Neo's mom, says, giving me a stink face at the thought of the ratchet woman.

"Actually, she is no longer in our lives," Neo says, and I narrow my eyes at him. He just smirks and shrugs. "It's true."

"She just gave you full custody? After years of extorting money out of you?" my Aunt Rachel, Dean's mother, asks.

"Nope," Neo says. "She's dead." He just tosses out that little nugget of information like it's nothing.

"What!" my mother asks me, her eyes wide. "Since when?"

"A few months now," Neo answers for me.

"How?" Linda asks.

"Queenie," Neo says with a proud grin.

“Wait... Why does that name sound familiar?” Rachel asks.

“Because she rules Kingston Heights,” Dean mutters into his third glass of bourbon.

All three women's eyes go wide as everything clicks.

“I mean, I know Briana was a witch, but I thought Queenie only killed men. What did Briana do that would make her feel the need to kill her?” my mother asks, and my eyes darken.

“She doesn't just kill men for no reason, Madison,” Linda says to my mother. “She kills those vile wastes of space that have no right to even exist in the first place.” The venom in Linda's voice makes me wonder if this is where Neo got some of his crazy from.

“But again, why Briana?” my mom repeats.

I say nothing, avoiding her eyes, and the table goes quiet. “Cassius, what did that woman do? Did she hurt my grandbaby?” she gasps.

“Look, it's done and over with. She’s dead. Rosie is safe. Nothing bad will ever happen to Rosie again. Harlow will see to it.”

The look on my mother’s face makes me want to pull her into my arms and hug her. She doesn't say anything more, just wipes a tear from her eye and pats my hand that's resting on the table.

“Harlow?” Rachel asks. “Wait... Harlow? As in the girl you were all head over heels for as teenagers?”

“What do you mean? She was Cassius's girlfriend,” my mom says.

The three of them bicker about Harlow and who she was to each of us. Neo watches with a grin, waiting for one of them to catch on.

“What the hell does Harlow have to do with what Queenie did?” Linda asks.

“Because Harlow is Queenie,” Neo smirks.

“What?!” they all shriek at the same time.

I’m gonna fucking kill that fucker. Harlow is gonna decapitate us when she finds out we’re just giving her identity away.

“Yup.” He puffs out his chest.

“Wait. Is she the person helping you with the company?” Rachel asks.

“Yeah. We work for her, and she gives us the money that we will need over the next few years, as well as living expenses,” Dean says.

“It’s bullshit if you ask me. What's the point of saving the company when we're pretty much selling our soul to the devil,” Axel mutters, shaking his head.

“Why would you say that?” our mother asks.

“Because she makes us do stupid shit and banned us from having sex,” Axel growls, pissed off about everything like always.

“Well, that seems a little childish,” Rachel says. And Dean and Axel nod in agreement.

“Not really; we deserve it,” I say.

“Why do you say that?” my mom asks.

“It’s a long story, but pretty much Harlow didn't move away like we told you, we sent her away. Well, actually Dean did, and Axel let him." I narrow my eyes at my brother, and he flips me off.

"I was trying to protect her!" Dean says, raising his voice.

"You tossed her into the belly of the fucking beast! Because of you deciding for all of us, Harlow was raped multiple times a day and held against her fucking will for five years!" I bellow, leaning over the table, getting into Dean's face. At least he has the decency to look guilty.

All three women gasp with horrified looks on their faces.

My mother looks like she's about to ask more, but I shake my head. "It's not our story to tell, we've said too much already. We have no right to even try to discuss the horrendous things she had to endure," I say, leaving no room for an argument.

The funeral was a small, intimate gathering. A few of his friends stopped by, but other than that it was just us guys and our mothers. After we said our final goodbyes, our mothers took off back home, and we lagged behind, making plans to go out and eat. We invited them to join, but they declined, said they were too upset and just wanted to turn in early.

"Let's party," Neo shouts, jumping up onto one of the angel statues in the cemetery, then doing a backflip off of it with a whoop.

"We just buried a family member, you crazy bastard. Now you wanna go out like it's just some regular day?" Axel scoffs.

"Look, life's short. You never know when the grim reaper is gonna come and snatch your grumpy ass up. So, live a little. Plus, don't you want a night out with just us guys? It's been a while," Neo is bouncing around, jumping off anything he can.

"Dude, you need to chill. How do you have so much energy?" I ask as we reach the car.

"Well, with Harlow spending more time with Evie and Rosie, it's been a week since my cock has played hide-and-seek with her pussy. I have a lot of pent-up energy, and I need to get it out somehow. Seeing how I don't want to fuck it out of me, unless it's with her, that means one thing!" He gives me a manic grin in the rearview mirror as he slips into the back alongside Dean.

"The Devil's Pit," I grin back. The Devil's Pit is an underground club that holds very illegal fights. We started coming here when we were 15. In this type of life, money buys you everything, and that allows us access to a world unlike any other; it helps to throw our last names out there too.

Neo started fighting there any time we came for a visit. We made a deal. If he stopped kicking everyone's ass in school who looked at him funny, then he was allowed to fight at the Devil's Pit as much as he wanted when we came here.

I mean, he still got suspended a few times here and there for starting fights, but it lessened tremendously. It gave him something to look forward to and work towards. Neo needs to keep his beast tamed. Harlow unknowingly provides that for him now. He's been doing well. The violent tasks and sex with Harlow have been keeping his inner beast in check, while he gets to live and have some of the best sex of his life. Also helps with any pent-up energy he has. They use each other for the same reasons, only he needs her, not the other way around.

The warehouse is quiet; the only thing you can hear is the sound of the city traffic a few miles away. To anyone else, it's just an abandoned property, but there, deep in the belly of this building, is where all the people who don't feel like they have a place in the world come to get away from their shitty lives.

Neo leads us through a side door, down five flights of steps until we reach a door. Neo pounds on the door and we wait.

"Names?" a gruff voice answers through the little, sliding window.

Neo scrunches up his face. "Since when the fuck did this place start taking names?" Neo questions.

"Since the new ownership. Now tell me your names or piss off." Neo opens his mouth, probably to tell this guy where to go and how to get there, but Dean steps up.

“I’m Dean Beckett, this is Neo Hendrix, and the two in the back are Axel and Cassius Ledger,” Dean says, pointing to each of us.

The guy behind the door lets out a curse and quickly works to unlock the door. He swings it wide open. I'm guessing from his reaction, he knows who we are, or at least he has heard of our names.

He says nothing as we pass him, and I give him a curious look as he avoids my gaze. What an odd man. But what else do I expect in a place like this?

The deeper we get into The Devil's Pit, the louder the music gets. It’s practically deafening by the time we get to the second door.

Neo swings the door open wide, and a wave of nostalgia nearly knocks me over. It’s been years since I’ve been here. Neo has made a few trips back here when he needed to lie low. Normally, it was after he nearly beat someone to death. At least in this place, it's what they want, well, mostly.

The place is packed. The bar is against the far-left side, leaving room for the dance floor to the right, and the ring in the dead center of the room.

Shouts and cheers mixed with a few boos fill the room as the current fighters do their thing.

“I'm going to need a drink if I'm gonna make it through this night without killing anyone,” Axel grumbles loud enough to be heard over the music and heads over to the bar.

Dean takes a look around, locking his eyes on the girls dancing in cages over the dance floor. “Fuck,” he sighs, shoving a hand through his hair, then follows after Axel.

“Let's go see whose ass I get to kick tonight,” Neo grins, rubbing his hands together excitedly before grabbing my arm and pulling me over to the DJ, who it turns out is also the fight coordinator.

The guy gives me and Neo a once over and nods in greeting. “What can I help you two with?” he asks.

“I want in on a fight tonight, anyone. I really don’t fucking care,” Neo insists.

“Can’t. Sorry. All booked up,” he says and goes back to looking at his phone. Neo snatches the guy's phone, tossing it on the ground, making it shatter, then grips the guy's shirt, picking him up off his chair and leveling their faces.

“Let me repeat myself. Get me on the fucking list for tonight, or I’ll gut you like a fish. Got it?” Neo’s smile is equal parts crazy and unsettling. The guy is pale and shaking now. He swallows hard and frantically nods his head.

“Just let me move a few things around,” the guy stammers. Neo lets the guy down, dropping him on his feet, and then helps the guy fix his shirt before patting him on the head like a dog.

“Good boy,” Neo praises him. “Now run along,” Neo says, giving him a shooing motion with his hands. The guy takes off, practically tripping over his feet to get away from him.

“I need a drink,” I chuckle.

"Not me," Neo says, bouncing on the balls of his feet, checking the place out. "I need a clear head before I beat whatever poor sucker is placed in front of me." He looks back at me with a grin, and we head off to find the others at the bar.

"You might wanna slow down there. We've only been here ten minutes, and you're already three glasses in," I hear Dean say dryly, sipping a drink of his own.

"Because this place is full of women who would probably suck my cock if I ask nicely, but I can't do shit!" Axel snaps, downing a shot.

"Look, I'm not gonna judge, but if you're looking for something different than your old lady, here would be a good place to find it. No one's gonna rat you out," the bartender tells him with a grin.

Neo barks out a laugh. "Trust me, buddy, she would know. She has a way of knowing everything."

"I don't have an old lady," Axel mutters. "Just a crazy bitch who has me by the balls."

"She's not a bitch, but you got the crazy part right," Neo says, then asks for a bottle of water.

"Hey there, handsome, you wanna dance?" a blonde-haired woman purrs, rubbing her fake tits against Neo. Neo backs up, raising his hands in the air as if something gross touched him.

"Back the fuck up," he growls. "I have a woman, thank you very much. And there's no way in hell I'd ever stray, so fuck off," Neo growls. Damn, that was harsh, but it shows how dedicated he is to Harlow. If this was a few months ago, he would probably have her bent over the bar, fucking her without a care in the world.

"I'll dance with you, baby," Axel says, holding his hand out to the woman. Her eyes light up when she takes Axel in and gladly takes his hand. He pulls her into his lap, and she giggles as she starts to pat his chest.

"Well, hello, big boy," she purrs.

"Axel, I don't think that's a good idea," I warn.

"Good thing I'm not looking for your advice, brother," he says, cocking a brow. "Plus, she said we can't fuck anyone; she said nothing about dancing."

"Damn, whoever the woman you're talking about is, she sounds like she's a real peach," the bartender jokes.

"Yeah, that's not the word I would use to describe Queenie," Axel snarks.

The woman on Axel's lap goes rigid; her eyes go wide, her face pales, and she looks like she's about to be sick.

The bartender freezes, dropping the glass he was cleaning. "I'm sorry, I'm not sure if I heard you right over the music. Did you say Queenie?"

"Umm. Yeah?" Axel questions with a pinched brow, then looks at the woman. "Why?"

"Like Queenie, who runs Evolution?" the bartender asks.

"Yes."

"I gotta go. Bye," the girl squeaks, taking off in a rush, crying something about being too young to die.

"You have gotta be fucking kidding me!" Axel shouts. "Does everyone know who Queenie is?"

"Yes," the bartender laughs. "But this is also her club," he shrugs.

"For fuck's sake," Axel growls, downing another drink. "My fucking dick is gonna fall off from lack of sex at this point." The alcohol makes him more dramatic than normal.

"Nah, dude, that would be from all the jacking off you do," Neo laughs.

Axel gets up in Neo's face with a sneer, but Neo just laughs.

"Umm," a voice comes from behind Neo. It's the guy in charge of the fights. Neo turns to look at the guy, making him take a step back when Neo smiles creepily at him.

"Oh look. It's you. Find me someone I can fuck up?"

"Yes," the guy clears his throat, "but we're gonna need to find you someone else to fight to make it even."

"I'll do it," Axel says. "Pair *him* with someone else, and I'll take whoever that person was up against because I'm not fighting my cousin, no matter how fucking annoying he is." Axel won't be fucking anyone up. He's had too many drinks to be able to win a fight with a clear head, no matter how good he is, because this club doesn't just let anyone fight. You gotta be good enough to draw in a crowd. I say nothing to stop him. Maybe a good ass kicking will do him some good, or not. Either way, I'm gonna enjoy watching the asshole get his ass kicked for once.

"Oh... um, okay, yeah, sure I can do that," he says, taking a look at the sheet. "I can put you up against Jimmy Vic," he says, looking at Axel. "And you against Rob Nelson."

"No idea who the fuck you're talking about, but you got yourselves a couple of fights."

"You're on in five," the guy instructs Neo. "And you're right after him," he tells Axel.

Our day started with burying a body in the ground, and from the looks of it, it might be ending by adding two more.

Neo

I HAVE so much adrenaline coursing through my veins right now that I'm going to explode if my fist doesn't meet this cocky fucker's face here in a minute. Dumbass looks so stupid, growling like a rabid dog. Bitch, you're 5'8", and you look like you live in your mama's basement.

This fool starts beating on his chest like a gorilla, and I can't help but burst out laughing. He doesn't appreciate it because the moment the bell rings, he swings out in rage, and that's a dumb move on his part. I duck his right hook, punching him in the gut. He lets out a pained noise before stumbling back. I whoop, bouncing back and forth on my feet, taunting him.

Okay, this is fucking pathetic. One hit and he already looks out of breath.

"I'm a little offended that this is what you gave me," I crow. The guy lets out a roar before running at me, but I trip him easily and send him flying to the ground.

"This has gotta be some kind of joke," I yell at the crowd. "Where's the cameras; I must be on some kind of prank show."

The crowd wants a good show. Some are cheering, others aren't, but at this point I know who they are rooting for.

Fuck it. My beast wants out, and this place has no rules, other than when your opponent taps out, you win. Does everyone care or listen? No. Will I? Probably not. I mean, I won't kill the fucker... probably. But he came here, and this is the risk you take when you get in this ring.

He gets up, fury in his eyes, and charges at me again. I punch him in the face, then grab his head and knee him in the stomach.

Over the next few minutes, I pound into him, throwing him around from one side of the ring to the other, really letting loose. I feel free, alive, unleashed. Like I'm invincible and no one can touch me.

Arms come around my waist as Dean and Cass pull me off the guy. I fight against them at first until I see the whole club is silent.

Everyone stares at me with terror in their eyes. I look down at the guy, whose face looks really fucked up. "So... did I kill him?" I ask, raising a brow and looking around. Dean bends over and checks his pulse.

"No, but pretty damn close. You need to let your other side out more, or you're gonna keep losing control like this." Dean doesn't look too happy about the situation, but I am.

"Ah, give him a little ice and let him sleep it off." I wave my hand at him in a dismissive movement.

"You're kidding, right?" a guy asks seriously as he and another guy help the poor sap on the ground.

"No?" I answer.

They help their buddy off the stage, and we follow.

"I'm up next," Axel says, hopping into the ring and bouncing around, punching the air. Fucker is drunk off his ass, and I can't wait to see how this plays out.

A guy steps into the ring and Axel starts trash-talking him.

The bell rings, and the guy is on Axel, immediately pounding into him good. Let's just say, this fight is over before it even really started. With one last punch in the face, Axel goes down like a sack of rocks.

The guy gets called as the winner, and the crowd boos about wanting something longer.

I loved it. Watching the cocky bastard getting his ass handed to him. I love him, he's family, but the guy has been nothing but a dick since Harlow came back into our lives.

Laughing, I hop back in the ring and help him up. I'm sweaty, covered in blood, and just want a shower. I'm over tonight. As much as I've enjoyed this, and being back here, what I really want is to go back home to Harlow. I miss her crazy ass. Also, what if I'm missing the opportunity of a good dicking? It's a downright shame if I am.

"Come on, you lightweight." I smack Axel's face to wake him up. His eyes blink open slowly. And he looks at me, squinting.

"Did I win?" he slurs.

"If by winning, you mean had your ass handed to you in two point five seconds, then yeah, bud, you got the gold on that one," I grin as I wrap my arm around his shoulder, helping him down.

"So, I got the gold?" he asks, completely dazed.

I burst out laughing. "Take him, man; I just can't." I shake my head, handing him over to his brother. Axel starts mumbling something to Cass about winning a gold medal and how now he can go on a world tour.

Want some advice? Don't get smashed before going into a fight. Just... don't.

CHAPTER NINETEEN

"**WHAT DO** you wanna do today?" I ask Rosie as I comb her hair. When Cass asked me to watch Rosie for the weekend, I jumped at the chance. Evie is in charge of the club while I get to have a sleepover with my favorite, little lady.

The guys left after supper last night, and Rosie and I spent the rest of the night playing barbies and watching movies until we both passed out in Cass's bed. Rosie was a little sad to be away from her dad after being with him consistently for so long, so I asked if sleeping in his bed would make her feel better, being surrounded by his things. She loved the idea and settled down after that.

We woke up, ate some breakfast, and now we are getting ready for the day.

"I don't know," she shrugs. "Can we leave the house?" she asks.

"Yeah, I think a bit of fresh air would do us some good," I nod and check my phone to see if anything is going on in the area. Just my luck, there is a little community fair. The little flyer on the website states there are mini rides, games, and a petting zoo; perfect for a four-year-old little girl.

"How about we go to a fair?" I ask.

She spins around, her eyes going wide with excitement. "Really?! Yay!" she shouts and jumps up from the bed and races out of the room.

Chuckling, I follow her, finding her in her bedroom. "I want to wear these!" she says, holding up a pair of sparkly, ruby red cowgirl boots.

"I like your style, little lady; let's see what else we can find to go with those stunning boots." She nods as if this is a very serious issue that needs to be fixed. I giggle and head to her closet, throwing it wide open.

My eyes skim the line of dresses, she has hanging, and stop on a dress that is a white tank top connected to a frilly, red skirt.

"How about this?" I ask, holding it up to show her.

"It's perfect!" she cheers.

I help her change out of her PJs and into the dress and boots. She looks at herself in her little, pink mirror on the back of her door.

"It's missing something," she says, tilting her head to the side, then looks around the room until she finds what she is looking for. "That's it!" She races over to a big teddy bear in the other corner of her room and plucks a brown cowgirl hat with glittery red gems off its head and places it on hers, then rushes over to her make-up table, grabbing her black kitty cat sunglasses.

I grin as I watch this little ball of energy race around the room, trying to put together a perfect outfit. My arms are crossed, and I bite the side of my thumb, holding back a giggle as she grabs the last thing to make her ensemble complete.

"Now I'm ready," she says, stopping in front of me.

"Well, now I need to change," I huff jokingly.

"How come? I think you look very pretty," she says. I'm dressed in a pair of jean shorts and a black crop top that crosses between my breasts before wrapping around to the back, my hair in a high ponytail.

"You think?" I ask, tilting my head to the side.

She gives me one firm nod. "Like a Queen."

"Alright then, I guess we're good to go," I say, holding my hand out.

"How ya doing back there, kiddo?" I ask, as I pull her down the sidewalk in a wagon with a canopy top. Very fancy if you ask me.

"Good! Are we there yet?" she asks, just as we round the corner to the field, a few streets over from where the guys live.

"Yup, we're here," I say.

Rosie's eyes fill with wonder as she takes in the sight before her. Food vendors of all kinds, carnival games, rides, and the petting zoo fill up the big space.

"What do you want to do first?" I ask, helping her out of the wagon.

"Everything," she breathes, her eyes wide with excitement.

Laughing, I take her hand in one of mine and pull the wagon along with the other. "How about we ride a few rides first, games, food, then zoo before we head back home?"

"Okay," she agrees.

We pick the teacups first. At first, Rosie seems excited, but as the ride goes on, she starts to look panicked at the speed, so I pull her into my lap and hold her tight to let her know she's safe. By the end of it, I feel sick. Rides are not my thing, but I'll suck it the fuck up if it means this little girl has the best day ever.

Next, we go on the little trains. Rosie squeals in delight as I pray to god that my curvy ass doesn't get stuck in the seat.

By the time we are done with all the rides, Rosie is hungry, so we get food instead of games. "Hot dog, please," Rosie tells the lady at the food truck.

"Make that two," I say, handing over a twenty. "And two slushies, please."

"Do I get one?" she asks with hopeful eyes.

"Of course, silly, I wouldn't get one for myself and not you," I laugh.

"Daddy doesn't let me have sweets a lot. He says I'm like a puppy with a case of the zoomies when I eat it," she giggles.

"Well, today is just you and me. So, I think we can have a little sugar," I say.

Oh, boy was I wrong. A dog with zoomies? Hell no, more like a possessed chihuahua. She drags me from one place to another, not letting us stay long enough to actually do anything. I just laugh as I follow her while she talks a mile a minute about anything and everything.

We settle on a basketball game, and Rosie just chucks the balls in the air in hopes that they make it into the hoops, but I don't think she cares about winning, and as long as she's having fun, neither do I.

"Isn't she precious?" some soccer mom says as she gives Rosie judgmental eyes. I bet her name is Karen. She looks like a fucking Karen, hair and all.

"She is, isn't she?" I beam, not liking how she's looking at my kid.

"Hyper little thing," she mocks with a grin.

I look at Rosie. Her mind is no longer on the game, but on a butterfly, she's trying to catch.

Turning back to Karen, I get up into her face. "How about before you judge other people's kids, you take a look at your own," I say, cringing as I see the little boy, who I'm assuming is her son, picking a booger and then wiping it on her dress before using her skirt as a napkin to get all the chocolate off his face. At least, I hope to god that's what it is. God, kids can be nasty little fuckers.

She has the nerve to look offended. *Bitch, please.* She glares at me as if I'm being the nosy bitch.

"Oh, and next time, you might wanna be careful about who you feel needs to be called out, cause they may be bigger and badder than yourself. You never know who they are in the dark," I wink, pulling out my switchblade. Can't wear my daggers in these shorts, and I like to have at least a little something with me at all times. She lets out a gasp, and before she can blink, I bring it up to her face and flick it shut again, making sure the tip of the blade just nicks the tip of her nose.

Her hand flies to her nose as she looks at me in fear. "You're insane. I really think you need help," she says, before grabbing her son's grimy little paw and dragging him away.

"Ha! Jokes on you, lady. I don't want any help! I'm fucking perfect, just the way I am," I shout while laughing, earning me some horrified glares.

"What?" I say, puffing out my chest in a 'come at me, bro' gesture, making them flinch, and making me laugh harder. Okay, so I probably look like a nut case right about now. That may be the norm for me, but these strangers are probably not used to hanging around unhinged serial killers.

"It flew away," Rosie pouts as she watches the Monarch butterfly take off.

"That's okay. It's getting late. Let's go to the petting zoo; then we can go home, have a bath, and watch a movie before bed. How does that sound?"

"Yay!" she cheers, forgetting all about her little, flying friend, and grabs my hand, dragging me to all the animals.

"Maybe Uncle Neo can get one," Rosie says, as she pets a baby cow. The cow lets out a little moo before sticking out its tongue and licking Rosie's cheek. "Ewwwww," she giggles, wiping off the spit. "No, thanks," she shakes her head and moves over to the bunny pen. "Bunnies!" She sits down, and I put one on her lap. The cute, little fluff ball is surprisingly calm. Not sure if that's just its temperament or if it's in shock from having kids maul it all day, poor thing. As much as I love animals, and Rosie is having fun, petting zoos gives me uneasy feelings. I can't help but feel for them, having to be out on display all the time for everyone to touch them against their will. What can I say, PTSD triggers you when you least expect it.

Rosie picks the pony rides as the last thing she wants to do before we leave, and just as I help her off the pony, shouting gets my attention. It's coming from behind the trailer that is used to bring in the animals. "You evil little shit!" a voice growls. "When we get back, I'm putting your old, useless ass down."

Hold up, is this guy threatening to kill an animal? Hell, no. Grabbing a hold of Rosie's hand, we check out the situation.

An older guy with dirty jeans and a flannel shirt kicks a very angry duck. It's quacking at him as it flaps its wings, but it keeps trying to take a chunk out of his ankles.

"No!" Rosie shouts. "Stop. Don't hurt it!" Rosie lets go of my hand and runs towards the duck. Fuck, all I need is for her to get bit and for Cass to bitch me out.

But as Rosie gets close to the duck, she stops and crouches down like she's trying to call over a dog. "Here, ducky, ducky," she calls. The duck stops fighting the man at the sound of her voice and turns to look at her. It ruffles its feathers before waddling over to Rosie. Rosie reaches out to pet it, and it lets her, cuddling right into her. Rosie giggles as the duck quacks playfully and waddles back and forth, enjoying the attention.

"What the fuck?" the man says. "She is never that nice."

"Were you really gonna kill that duck?" I growl, making the man look at me.

"Yes. She's old and mean and no use to me anymore; can't have a duck at a petting zoo that bites people. Especially grown men."

Huh, looks like the duck and I have something in common. I enjoy taking chunks out of walking dickheads, too.

"Yeah, that's not gonna happen, but I'll tell you what. We will be taking her with us. And if you ever think about killing an animal because it no longer wants to be picked at by grabby, little crotch goblins, I'll find you and kill you instead. Got it?" I smile sweetly. The guy just laughs at me. I didn't want to do this in front of Rosie, like ever, but fuck if I'm gonna let this dick weasel go unpunished. Looks like my blade is getting a good workout today.

My smile drops and I stalk forward. When I get face to face with this smirking fucker, I take out my switchblade. Only I don't lightly cut him; I fucking stab him in the thigh. He lets out a pained yelp that I quickly smother with my hand. "Shhhhh. Don't want the little one to hear. So let me repeat myself, even though I really don't like to. We are taking the duck. Got it? And if you kill any of your animals, I kill you, got it?" I ask, my smile slipping back into place.

He nods rapidly. "Yes, yes, you can have her." His voice comes out all squeaky.

"That's better," I grin, then grab the rag from his back pocket and shove it in his mouth before yanking the knife out of his thigh. He lets out a muffled cry before clutching his leg.

"Drama queen much? Like the blade isn't even that big," I roll my eyes. Bending over, I wipe the blood on the blade off on his shirt and put it away. I turn to leave, but remember something. I bend over and take the rag out of his mouth. "So, what's the duck's name anyways?"

"Daisy," he grits out in pain.

"As in Daisy Duck?" I laugh, my brows flying up. "Fuck, that's amazing. Totally taking her now." I shove the rag back into his mouth and go over to Rosie, leaving the big baby whimpering on the ground.

Rosie already has her loaded into our wagon, feeding her leftover popcorn we were saving for later, giggling as she watches the silly way Daisy eats.

"Looks like we're adding to the funny farm, huh?" I laugh, grabbing the handle of the wagon, and we take off towards home.

"Uncle Neo is gonna be so happy," she says, giggling again at the duck.

"And your dad and other uncles are gonna lose their shit," I giggle to myself. Man, I really hope I get to see their faces when they see Daisy. We have a pet duck now. They are just gonna have to learn to deal with it because Rosie has already bonded with her. I mean, it's kind of like having a dog anyways, but cooler.

Just as I put the wagon away in the garage, my phone rings. It's Evie. "What's up?"

"Low, you gotta come down here. A few of the girls got into a fight. Something about one of them ruining the other's favorite pair of heels. I don't really know, but I do know that Alex has a black eye and Nikki has a broken nose, and the whole thing is going to shit," she says, freaking out. Fuck.

I look at Rosie and the duck. *Well, looks like we're going on another adventure.* "I'll be there in an hour." The guys live in Long Beach, about an hour away from Kingston Heights.

"Alright, Kiddo, you still wanna see what my club looks like?" I ask.

"Yes!" she grins, and I pile them both into my car. Once I decided that I was gonna be Rosie's new mom, I went out and bought a cherry red Toyota Highlander Hybrid. Not the fanciest, but gotta get something good for kids.

When we get to the club, Rosie trails behind me, talking to Daisy. Grinning, we head inside the club.

The stage is half set up, and Lucas and the guys are standing there, talking to a bruised-up Alex.

"Where's Nikki?" I ask Evie, who's stressing over her laptop in her office. She looks up at me and sighs in relief.

"Cindy took her to the ER," Evie says, then her face drops as she looks back at her laptop.

"Another girl went missing. From the same club the first girl went missing," she says, then slams her laptop shut in frustration. "I'm lost, Low. And I don't know what to do. I have no idea if Tracy is with these other women or just running off into the sunset with whoever she went to meet."

I pull Evie into my arms, rubbing her back to calm her down. "We'll find them. All of them. I won't stop until we do," I promise.

"Neither will I. I just need one lead, that's it, and I know we can find them," she says.

"If anyone can find it, it's you. I'll go to the club the girls were last seen at and see if I can find anything. If this is another ring being set up, I'll have better luck finding information than the police."

"I don't want to lose you," she whispers into my chest.

"Babe, this is me we are talking about. God help anyone who tries to cage me again. Remember, I'm a phoenix. I rose from the ashes before, and I will not be put down again. And if anyone tries, I'll come out on top, standing over the bodies of our enemies."

I left Rosie out there with a few of the girls, and when Evie and I come out to see what's going on, Rosie is sitting on the stage next to Tommy playing Rock-Paper-Scissors.

I grin, raising a brow at him. He shrugs. "What, I know nothing about kids. I don't know what to do with them."

"Mama, can I dance too?" she asks, looking over at a few of the girls setting up the stage for tonight's show.

Looking over at the bin of props, I get an idea that I know she will love. "Dance party!" I shout, and everyone cheers. I love random dance parties. I'm always in here during set up or when we clean, blasting the music and just enjoying the moment.

Picking out a few things, I put them on the table next to the stage.

"Here," I tell Rosie and help her into a pink tutu. Before we left the house, I changed her out of the dress and into shorts and a tee shirt because the duck pooped on her right as we were about to leave.

I slip a pink, feathered boa over her shoulders and top it off with a metal tiara. I match her outfit, but in red, then head over to the laptop hooked up to the DJ system and put on *Better When I'm Dancin'* by Meghan Trainor.

Rosie starts shaking her little butt, inviting Tommy to dance too. I think she's taken a liking to him. He may not know anything about kids, but this one seems to think he's doing an okay job.

We all dance around the room, laughing, singing, and enjoying the music. Evie sits at the bar, watching with a smile. *Nope, she's not sitting out of this.* I race over to her, pulling her off the stool and onto the dance floor.

She groans dramatically in protest, but lets me, nonetheless. I start to dance silly around her, trying to get a grin out of my overly stressed, overworked bestie. Sadly, she doesn't get her stress out by killing or fucking, much to my disappointment. I wish she was into the killing part, because how awesome would that be for friend bonding time!

The idea of her fucking anyone sets me on edge. No one's good enough for Evie, and I'll let that be known. In all the years I've known her, she's never had a girlfriend. Never dated, never had hookups. As a joke, I got her a big box of sex toys. She looked genuinely grateful for it.

I continue dancing like an idiot, not caring. I do some disco moves like the swim, twist the light bulb, and even the floss. The last one has her giving me a deep belly laugh, and I know I broke through. From time to time, she gets into these manic fits of stress and anxiety, and I always do whatever I can to distract her, bringing her back down to earth. Evie would do anything for me, and I would do the same for her. I would give her the world and slay anyone who tried to get in the way.

"I STILL think you're a fucking idiot for letting her watch Rosie alone for two days," Axel grumbles as we get out of the car and head into the club.

"I still can't believe she brought her here," Dean comments.

"Enough, you two. Rosie is safe with Harlow, and she's not that hard of a kid to take care of in the first place. Rosie loves Harlow. Also, who the hell else would I have gotten to watch her? We sure as hell weren't going to bring her with us." Yeah, no way. Last night was crazy. But both Neo and Axel needed it. Axel is still a grumpy fucker and looks like he's ready to kill anyone who looks at him wrong. Guess getting his ass kicked did nothing but give him a couple of black eyes and a fat lip. Neo, on the other hand, was able to let his beast come out to play for a bit, which buys him time. I told him that if he's at risk of the beast making an appearance when he's not welcome, he should talk to Harlow. I mean, if they really are friends now, she should understand. If anyone knows about controlling the beast within, it's her.

When we open the front doors, *Just Sing* from the Trolls World Tour is blasting somewhere in this building. How do I know that song? Rosie has it on repeat most days.

The guys and I all look at each other with raised brows, and Neo grins wide, racing off towards the music.

There, in the middle of the dance floor, are Harlow and Rosie, lost in the music. Both have massive smiles on their beautiful faces as they laugh. Harlow picks Rosie up, spinning her around as they dance, making Rosie break out into a fit of giggles. A smile takes over my own face as I see how happy my baby girl is, and it's all because of Harlow. Most people may see her as some unhinged monster, but me? No, she's a blessing in disguise. Even Dean and Axel can't help but smile. Not sure if it's because of Rosie or from seeing that the two ladies in front of them are having the time of their lives. Maybe both.

“Now, this is what I call a party!” Neo cheers and races over to a table with props on it. He slips on the bright orange tutu, orange feathered boa, and tiara so that he's matching the girls, Rosie in pink and Harlow in red.

Neo dances over to the girls and takes Rosie from Harlow, spinning and dancing with her around the room. Soon, he puts her down and starts dancing with Harlow, making her laugh as he dips and spins her around the dance floor.

Then I hear quacking and look down to see a white duck waddling around Rosie's feet, quacking to the music as if it's singing. Rosie bends over, picks it up, and tucks it under her arm.

“What the heck is that?” I ask, looking over to Evie, who is sporting a very amused grin.

"Rosie and Harlow picked up a new friend at the fair today. Congratulations, you're now a grandpa to a 5-year-old duck," she laughs. "Oh, and by the way, it hates men, so good luck with that," Evie cackles and walks away, heading into her office.

"That's it; I'm moving. I didn't sign up to live on a fucking funny farm," Axel says dramatically.

I should be more surprised. But honestly, I'm just happy that Harlow didn't kill anyone while we were gone. I call this a win.

CHAPTER TWENTY

CASSIUS

"NO. NOT happening." Axel shakes his head, pacing back and forth. We're back at the house after the little dance party, and Harlow gave us the rundown on how they came about getting the duck, Daisy Duck. Why am I not surprised?

"Oh, but it is," Neo grins. "Rosie is already in love with that duck, and there's no way you would break that little girl's heart, would you?" Neo makes his eyes go wide as he pouts, sticking his hands under his chin, mocking Axel.

"We already have two fucking farm animals; we don't need any more. Hell, we don't even need the two stupid ones we have!" Axel shouts, pointing in the direction of the backyard.

"Hey!" Neo steps into Axel. "Don't you talk about Susie and Bob like that," he growls.

Axel shakes his head, knowing better than to argue with Neo about his pets. He loves those two almost as much as he loves Rosie.

“The thing doesn’t even like men,” Dean points out. “How do we care for a pet that will only let Rosie and Harlow near it? One of us has to interact with it when Harlow isn't here.”

“Not it!” Axel says. “I get bit enough by the two freaks out there. I'm not gonna willingly get attacked by the duck.”

“I’ll do it; I'm sure after some time around me, it will love me, just like the others do,” Neo says, puffing out his chest, sounding sure of himself.

“Bath time!” Rosie shouts from down the hall. We all turn to look out of the office door to see Rosie in her panties running past, her feet slapping against the floor, followed by Daisy waddling after her, quacking like she's just as excited.

“I’m gonna give them a bath and put Rosie to bed before heading out,” Harlow says, grinning wide as she looks back at the two making a run for the bathtub.

“Thanks for everything,” I tell her. She shrugs.

“We had fun. I’m here to help with her any time you need me. It’s surprisingly nice to get away from reality,” she says, looking down at the ground like she's thinking about something. She shakes her head and smiles.

She goes to leave but turns back. “Oh, and the one rule I’ll make sure to stick to next time is no sweets.” She bites her lip.

My eyes widen, and I burst out laughing, and the other guys follow.

“He tried to warn you. Rosie is very... interesting when she gets some sugar in her,” Dean grins.

“You mean like a bat out of hell?” she giggles.

"Yeah, pretty much," Neo grins.

As much as getting another animal, that we really should not have, annoyed me at first, seeing Rosie with Daisy is kind of adorable. While Harlow was giving Rosie a bath, I checked on them and stayed a while just to watch. Seeing Rosie giggle as Daisy ducked her head in the water and ruffled her feathers, splashing Rosie in the process, warmed my heart. I mean, it's not a dog, but it's pretty close. Something tells me she won't be staying in the backyard with the other two.

Now they are both snuggled up with Harlow, reading a book. When they are done, I go in, give her a kiss, and almost get my face bitten off by the damn duck.

Harlow giggles while Rosie gives Daisy a firm talking to, saying that bites are for butts, not for faces; four-year-old logic.

I let Harlow say goodnight and tell her that I'll be in the game room. Axel is already there, having a rematch with Neo. Dean is probably being forced to be their referee.

Taking a seat next to Dean on the couch, I sigh and close my eyes, reliving the past few days of crazy. Tonight, I need to just relax and unwind because knowing our lives, there's not much time for it.

"Hey, so tomorrow, we're gonna do things a little different," Harlow says, walking into the room. We all turn to look at her. "There's a club I've had my eye on for a while. I'm putting my feelers out to see if it's a fit for my cause." Her cause refers to her turning strip clubs that treat their dancers like objects, not people, into one of her clubs. Harlow told me she's all for strip clubs. Women are welcome to do what they want with their bodies, as long as it's completely their decision.

"Anyways. You four will come with me. Evie will watch Rosie. Something tells me it's not gonna be an easy job, and I'll need back up... maybe... either way, you get a night out."

Axel laughs mockingly. "Yeah, a night out where we can't enjoy ourselves the way we want. We can't dance, touch, or fuck women. So, we just have to follow you around like a pack of lost mutts while you get to fuck Neo like a damn slut."

The room goes quiet. It's too late to tell Axel to shut the fuck up. He's drunk, pissed, and already crossed that line.

"We are forced to do what you want, when you want us to, while you prance around in your slutty clothes, call it burlesque when really it's just your excuse to be a glorified whore," Axel spits. His chest is heaving as he gets in Harlow's face.

The rest of us hold our breath as we wait for Harlow to kill Axel. Because I know for a fact, she's not leaving this house without causing him some damage. He's disrespected her too many times at this point, and she's not the kind of person to be walked over, not anymore anyways. He should be lucky he's still breathing.

She does nothing but blink at him, her face unreadable, before turning to the pool table, her back now to Axel. He can't see what she's doing, but I can. She wraps her hand around the pool cue, and then shit hits the fan. She spins around and cracks Axel across the head with the stick, snapping it in half, sending one end flying, making Neo duck, eyes wide in surprise.

Axel lets out a cry of pain. Harlow tosses the broken stick to the side and uses Axel's position to her advantage. He's holding his head as he curses up a storm. She grabs a hold of his long hair, getting a good handful, and pulls his head down until he's bent over, then reaching for something in her pocket. Fuck, it's one of her daggers.

She stabs Axel in the side, but from the angle I can see, I don't think she hit anything vital, not sure if she meant to or not.

Axel gives a pained grunt. I can see him gritting his teeth, trying to show Harlow that it's not affecting him, but he's not fooling anyone. He doesn't fight back, though. At least he did one smart thing.

Harlow yanks his head back so that she can look him in the face. Her face is fucking scary right now; pupils blown wide. Her playful and happy demeanor, whenever there is violence, is nowhere in sight.

"How fucking DARE you call me that," she says, her voice low and chilling. "You don't know me," she spits. "You want to know *why* I'm so carefree with my body? Why I don't care who sees it or how I use it? It's not because I want attention or that I want people to want me. It's not because I want to show it off. No, it's because for five fucking years, I was FORCED to strip bare for rooms full of men who looked at me with all the sick and twisted ideas they wanted to do with me. I was FORCED to give my body to monsters who had no fucking right to it. Now that my life is my own, I CHOOSE to do what I do. The difference between then and now is I have free will. I get to *choose* how I use my body. Who gets to see it and who doesn't. I fuck Neo in front of people because I can. Because it's *my* mother fucking body, and it's *my* choice! For the first time in my fucking life, *I* get to choose what to do, no one else!" She's yelling in his face now.

My heart is racing as she spills her heart out to us, and the sad thing is, I don't think she realizes she's doing it. She's just caught up in the moment.

"And fuck you! My clubs are meant to give women, who have endured the hell I have, a safe place to do the same fucking thing I do. We don't dance for anyone else but ourselves. We know when we get up on that stage and do something we love, we get to feel sexy and free, showing just enough without feeling like we're giving away our souls. Dancing makes us free to be whoever the fuck it is that we never got the chance to be. And I swear, Axel, insult me or my girls one more time, and I *will* end YOU!" With that, she rips his head to the side, sending him tumbling to the ground.

She storms past us, leaving Neo, Dean, and myself gaping at her back. "Meet me at the Rack Shack tomorrow night. Don't make me come find you," she shouts as she takes off up the stairs.

Axel groans, and as if being broken from a spell, we all snap into action.

"You're a fucking dumbass," I hiss as I help him over to the couch. He moves his hand, and blood pours from the wound. Dean comes back with some towels, and I take one, pressing it to his side. "You're gonna need stitches."

"I'll take him," Dean says, then looks at Axel. "You need to get your shit under control. I know being under her rule has been a mindfuck to our lives. But the thing is, no matter what, she will be in charge of us, as well as everything else around here. If I, someone who loses their shit when something isn't how it should be, have been slowly learning to deal with this situation, then so can you. I don't know why you hate her so much."

"You hate her too," Axel grunts, gasping in pain as he shifts his weight.

"Actually, I don't. I hate how I lose control around her. I hate how she isn't the woman we all cared for at one point in time. But her, as she is now? No, I don't hate her. How can you hate someone for who they are when you're the reason why they are the way they are," Dean says, then heads upstairs to start the car.

Dean is a quiet one, always observing things. He's not much of a talker and tries not to get involved when he doesn't need to. The fewer things he sticks his nose into, the less he has to try and control.

He is a good man. He's kind and caring. A lot like me, but more reserved. You just don't get to see that side or see who he really is unless you get to know him.

I find it funny how our whole little group works. Dean and I are alike, but so are Neo and Axel. Both of them are outspoken, always saying what's on their mind, going with the flow of life, not caring what shit storm they get themselves into.

Me, I'm pretty easygoing, but I'd like to think of myself as a kind and considerate person.

"Come on. Let's get this closed up before you lose any more blood," I say. Neo and I work together to get Axel up the stairs and into the car.

Neo has been oddly quiet. I thought he would be rubbing it in Axel's face that he got his ass kicked again, and this time by a woman, but I think that what Harlow said got to him as much as it did me.

We both love her. The Harlow she is now, because what the other two don't seem to see is that the old Harlow is still there, just formed and sculpted to have a hard protective shell around her. We see it every time she smiles and laughs with Rosie. Every time Rosie calls her mama, and Harlow beams like she's being offered the world.

But even if there wasn't anything left of the girl we once loved, we would still fall just as hard for this one. What she does for a living doesn't bother me. The people she eliminates are just a waste of space, who the world would be better off without. At first, I thought she was a heartless person who had nothing left in her soul, but seeing her with Rosie, I was completely wrong.

What I need to do is buckle the fuck up and try to get to know this Harlow better. I want to be friends with her, like Neo. Well, not exactly like Neo. Although, I wouldn't say no if she asked. I want to be someone she can talk to, and I want to be able to tell her things like I used to. She's still, to this day, the only person who knows my deepest, darkest, innermost thoughts.

I need to stop hiding behind my daughter, and *man the fuck up*.

FUCK HIM, fuck all of them! That rat bastard is fucking lucky I didn't end his life right then and there. I've killed men for less, but I stopped myself because I could never hurt Rosie like that. Those four men are her whole world. I would just be destroying pieces of her.

But *damn* him and his stupid, sexy face for judging me. He has *no* right. He doesn't know me and never tried to. I'm not saying that I want to be his friend, but from the moment he laid eyes on me, I saw nothing but lust and hatred, and it's fucking with my head. I don't like it. I don't know where I stand with this man, and I should not give a fuck, but a small part of me does.

I'm not stupid. I know Neo and Cass have stronger feelings, more than just friends type of feelings for me, but nope, I can't deal with that shit. Love leads to heartache, at least that kind does. Keep your heart to yourself, and no one gets hurt. With them, I know where I stand. Dean and Axel are a mystery that I just can't seem to figure out.

As much as I love the fucked up, back-and-forth thing, Axel and I have going on, today he went too far.

And I'm pissed at myself. Pissed for letting him blind me with things I didn't want to feel, memories I never wanted to re-live, and personal thoughts I never wanted to tell.

I poured out part of my soul to the very guys who sent me on the same path that fucked everything up for me. God, that was so stupid. I hate myself for slipping.

But then Neo tells me that he and Cass had no idea, and they would never have agreed.

The more time I spend with Rosie, the less I hate Cass. It's hard to truly hate someone for something they never actually did. When Neo told me the truth, I could see it in his eyes that he really meant it. So, here I am, besties with a psychopath and playing house with my ex-boyfriend.

The other two, however, fuck them. I won't forgive them. Not unless they bow down to me and kiss my feet. Even then, I'll never trust them again.

Do I trust Neo and Cass? No, but I don't hate them anymore, so that's a start.

Axel. Fucking Axel can go fuck himself because that's the only action he's gonna be seeing for the rest of his stupid life. Alpha asshole fuck face. Ugh, I hate that man!

Hearing that crack of the cue stick against his head was nice, though. And stabbing him felt amazing. I should do that more. Next time he talks to me like that, it will be his foot.

I'm a ticking time bomb by the time I get home. I stride past everyone working and head right to my apartment.

I'm too wound up. I need release, but there's no way my pride will allow me to call Neo up and demand him to fuck me. No, I'm gonna have to dig in my dick chest, a box full of sexy toys, and do the damn job myself. Won't be as satisfying, but it will have to do.

HARLOW STORMS into the club with a look of pure murder. I hate seeing her upset for any reason. She's normally a bubbly person with a side of crazy. She never used to show it when things got to her, masking it, and becoming Queenie in that moment. But ever since they got here, she's been changing, and I don't know if it's for the better, or if it's gonna blow everything up.

I hate sharing her. It's just been her and me for years now. From the moment she opened her stunning blue eyes on her first night in the cell, I was hooked. Her beauty, strength, and her dedication to never be fully consumed by the life we were forced to live had me wanting to bow down and follow her blindly.

She knows I’m gay, but she’s never seen me with a woman. Why? Because since she's come into my life, I’ve never wanted anyone else.

I’m in love with her, and she doesn't even know. Or maybe she's so damaged that she doesn't see it. Or it could be that she doesn't feel that way and wants to spare my feelings. Whatever it is, at the end of the day, I'm alone dreaming about what it would be like to be with the only person to own my soul.

She’s tried to hook me up with some of the girls who work here, but I don't want them. I want her.

Now the men who sent her away like she was nothing are back. Neo is a lovesick puppy, and I know he's holding out for one day to be loved by her the same way he loves her. I hate that he gets to be the one to bring her pleasure. To touch her in ways I can't.

Then there's Cass. How do I compete with her first love? I don't know much about her past with these men, because talking about them always had her shutting down, but I know that Cass was her first. Not the having sex part, but having sex with her permission.

Now he's back with a daughter who Harlow has taken on as her own. I'm not upset about that. I love Rosie too. She's an amazing little girl and deserves a person like Harlow in her life.

I’ve never seen Harlow love someone so much, other than me, but if anyone deserves what love Harlow can spare, it's that little girl.

I close my laptop and sigh with frustration. Girls keep going missing, and we have no clues at all. It's like they just vanished into thin air. No trace of evidence, no camera feeds. Just, one moment they're there, and the next they're gone.

Harlow hates not being able to do something to fix it. We have a suspicion that a new ring had been set up, we just don't know by who, or where, but I don't plan on stopping until I find them.

"Hey, are you going to check on Harlow?" Roxy asks from behind the bar.

"Yeah. She's been in a pretty good mood lately, but she looked like she was ready to burn the place to the ground just a moment ago. I'm sure it was one of those dumb boys saying something stupid, like always."

"My money is on Axel. Fucker is lucky to still have his limbs attached. If it weren't for Rosie, I know he would be a goner. Past history or not."

Letting out a sigh, I give her a side smile. "Wish me luck," I huff out a laugh.

"To anyone else, I'd say watch your back and be safe, but if anyone can get through to her, it's you," Roxy smiles.

I take off in the direction of Harlow's penthouse. When I get there, I knock on the door; nothing. I try again, but this time a little harder. When I don't get a response, I put my ear to the door, but it's pointless; this place is soundproofed.

Now I'm starting to worry. I take the spare key she gave me out of my pocket and let myself in. I look around the room, but she's not in the kitchen or the living room.

Then I hear it, a cry that I'm surprisingly used to but always try to avoid. I know Neo is not in there with her, so she must be taking care of herself.

I hear a lusty moan that echoes down her short hallway, and I can't help but clench my thighs. My mind immediately imagines that it's me between her legs, making her feel this good.

I know I shouldn't do it, but I can't help it. I have to see her in this rare state. I know she doesn't mind me seeing her while she's fucking, but I don't like it. It's not that I don't like seeing her body, because she has a magnificent and stunning body, but it's because it hurts to see her like that and know others can make her feel the way I wish I could.

No, I don't have a cock, but I would do anything to make her cum, make her cry out in ecstasy.

My heart starts racing, and my skin prickles with nerves. My pussy is clenching the more noise she makes, and fuck, I can't deny that I'm soaked.

When I get to her room, the door is slightly cracked, and the sight before me has me biting my lips to keep the groan from escaping.

Harlow is laid out on her bed naked, her legs parted as she fucks herself with a rather large dildo in one hand and a small bullet vibrator in the other. Her head is tossed back in pleasure, eyes shut, as she moans and pants.

Sweat covers her body, making her skin glow. I can see a wet patch under her, telling me she's already cum a few times.

The ache between my legs becomes unbearable, and even though I squeeze my legs and rub them together, it does nothing for me.

I should leave. I should go back to my house, go to my room, and do the same thing she's doing. Only my body won't listen to me; instead, I find my hand creeping down the front of my pants into my soaked panties.

Just a few strokes of my clit to make the aching stop. That's it.

It's only when Harlow starts thrusting the dildo in harder that my fingers move faster around my clit. I add pressure and almost buckle at the intense sensation.

"Fuck. Fuck, fuck, fuck!" Harlow chants, her head thrashing back and forth. She can't keep still; the pleasure is too much for her.

My fingers slip between my folds, feeling the wetness leaking out of me before coming back over my clit for lubrication.

I don't think I've ever been this close to cumming so quickly before. Normally, it takes me a good ten minutes and some porn to get me to cum.

My climax is creeping up on me. I'm breathing hard, and I have to lean against the door frame because my legs feel like they are about to give out on me.

My eyes rapidly look over her sexy body, taking her all in. Her plump breasts that I just want to suck, and her curvy waist that I would give anything to feel quivering underneath my fingertips. Her legs are shaking now, and I know she's about to fall over the edge again. Her lips are parted, her pupils are blown wide. Her black hair fanning out on her pillow, partly drenched in sweat.

My breathing comes in faster, and I can't help but bite my lip harder, knowing I'm ready to cum. And when she turns her head and locks eyes with me, I can't hold back anymore. She cries out her orgasm at the same moment mine overtakes me. My pussy pulses around nothing as my climax almost takes me to my knees.

Harlow cries out, never looking away from me as she twitches around the fake cock, she has deep inside her.

When we are both done, we sound like we've run a marathon, panting heavily.

"Well, hello there." She gives me a lazy grin, and fuck, I wish the ground would open up and swallow me whole right now. My face is flaming with the embarrassment of being caught fingering myself to the sight of her masturbating. How fucking creepy.

"Enjoy the show?" she giggles, making me blush deeper.

"I'm sorry. I'm just gonna go," I say in a rush and turn around to bolt.

"Wait!" she calls out. "I don't care that you watched. Actually, I think it's fucking hot that I could get you off just by watching," she grins.

"You're not mad?" I ask, turning back around to face her.

"At you? Never," she says, then pulls the fucking dildo out and tosses it onto the bed. She climbs off the bed, giving me a full view of her body, and fuck, I'm ready to go all over again. It takes everything in me not to get on my knees and beg her to let me have a taste.

Shaking my head from my wayward thoughts, I look back up at her. She's grinning like a madwoman as I get caught looking at her again.

"We need to get you a girlfriend. My girl needs some proper loving. But hey, if you ever want to watch, I'm happy to be your live porn," she says, giving me a wink before slipping past me and into the bathroom. "I'm just gonna hop in the shower real quick. Wanna watch a movie or something?" she calls out.

"Umm. Y-yeah. Sounds good," I say. My heart is breaking at her words. Her suggesting that I find someone else, someone who isn't her, to help satisfy my needs makes me even more certain that I'll never have her in the way my heart craves.

For the rest of the night, I keep stealing glances at her, watching her laugh at the movie, or boo at the TV when they do something she doesn't like. When she snuggles into me, I hold her and let myself pretend that this is what it would be like if she was my girlfriend.

"I love you, Evie. I know I don't say it a lot; it's not really my thing, but please don't ever forget it. You're my ride or die, Babe. You and me forever," she says sleepily before falling asleep next to me.

I know she loves me, but not in the way I want her to. And as much as I'd like to think that it's me and her forever, something tells me the guys will have something else to say about that.

For now, I'll just enjoy these little moments and hope it's enough.

CHAPTER TWENTY-ONE

CASSIUS

"**EVERYTHING FUCKING** hurts," Axel grunts as he climbs out of the car. Harlow told us to meet her at some place called the Rack Shack. What a dumb name for a club, but it is a strip club. Sounds like it was named by some pervy old man with greasy hair who makes his dancers suck his cock for a raise.

Neo laughs. "Probably has something to do with your dumb ass getting handed to you in the ring. I still can't believe you fought drunk off your ass," Neo cackles, slapping Axel on the back, making him groan in pain.

"Well, you just fucking stood there and watched! You could have stopped me," Axel growls.

"I could have," Neo smirks. "But it was more fun watching you go down faster than a virgin boy cumming."

"You're a fucking dick, you know that?" Axel shoots back at Neo.

"Maybe, but I'm also the only one out of us who's using it for something other than jacking off," Neo rubs in.

"Yeah, not sure if you should sound so proud of that. You sold yourself to the she-devil. All for what? Getting your cock wet?"

"Okay, fuck off with the insults. Yes, she's crazy and yes, she's scary, but she's not the fucking devil. And all for what, you ask? For the best mind-blowing sex a man could ever imagine, and even then, it doesn't compare to the reality. When I'm with her, I feel everything. My veins are filled with liquid fire, my mind in a euphoric comatose state. I would literally chop off my own fucking arms to be able to keep what we have. Hell, I'd chop off my dick and gift wrap it for her if she asked."

"You're fucking insane, you know that? Like there is something really fucking wrong with your brain." Axel shakes his head.

"Aww, thank you. That's so sweet!" Neo gushes, putting his hand on his heart. Neo's hands shoot out, grabbing Axel's face, holding him still, so he can place a big, sloppy kiss on his cheek before quickly licking half his damn face.

"Get the fuck off me," Axel shouts, pushing Neo away. Neo laughs as he dances away from getting backhanded. "I hate you, you know that?"

"Nah, you loooove me. You know it. Everyone does." He winks before ripping the door to the club open.

"Men pay $20, women get in free," the bouncer says in a monotone voice.

"Rip off," Dean mutters, and for a club like this, yeah, it is. We've only just walked through the door, and already I can see that there's nothing classy about this place. It smells like body odor, and the floor is sticky.

The guy cocks a brow and holds out his hand. Dean mutters to himself as he places $80 in his waiting hand.

When we get into the main area, I see that it has potential. It kind of looks like how Harlow does up her clubs. The dance floor is immediately to our left, the bar to our right, and the stage with the poles are on the far side of the room.

The interior is black and silver. It could be considered nice, you know, if it was actually maintained.

"So, when is she gonna meet us?" Dean asks.

"I think she's already here," Neo grins, pointing on stage.

There, in her signature Queenie outfit, is Harlow. Dancing on the pole like a fucking pro. We all just stand there and gawk. There are no poles at Evolution, so we haven't seen her dance like this, but I'm guessing with what she said about her past, she had to be good at both dancing on the floor and on the pole to avoid being auctioned up.

River by Bishop Briggs is blasting through the speakers as she does a very seductive dance number. Her fluid motions as she practically makes love to the pole, in a surprisingly non-sexual way, has my cock becoming rock hard. She hangs upside down, her breasts staying in place from her tight corset as she slides down to the floor, almost hitting the ground before righting herself, and gracefully starts dancing on the stage like she does at her own club.

People are throwing dollar bills at her, cheering, and cat-calling her. That's not allowed at her club. Well, that's not entirely true. Harlow allows it for group shows with her involved or her solo shows. She said she doesn't care, but some of the girls feel uncomfortable and uneasy.

But here and now, Harlow eyes up the crowd like she's hoping one of these poor fools would overstep and try something, so she can get a pound of flesh.

She can't be in a good mood, not after everything that happened last night. She unwillingly opened up big time, and I know she won't let any of us get away with my brother's stupid mistake. I don't think she's gonna do any more damage to Axel; at least I hope not until he's healed a little, then she can have another go at him.

His two black eyes are starting to yellow, and his fat lip is almost back to normal, but now he has a big lump on his head where Harlow hit him, and his side is sore where the stitches are. He came tonight anyways. Partly because he's trying to pull off some macho bullshit that none of this bothers him, and partly because he doesn't want to risk getting something important chopped off, even if he doesn't get to use it for fun things anymore.

When the song is over, she makes her way through the crowd, right to us.

"You made it," she grins, but it's not the happy kind. "Alright, I'm giving you a heads-up because I have shit to do, and I don't need anyone adding to my plate. I'm pissed. I'm feeling extra stabby today, and by the end of tonight, at least one person will be dead, beaten, and fucked."

"Like fucked as in fucked, or fucked as in *fucked*?" Neo grins.

Harlow turns to Neo, and her gaze softens slightly. A small part of me gets a little jealous of that. “Don't worry, My Pet. We will have our fun,” she winks.

“Are we really here to see if you want to take over this club?” Dean asks.

Harlow grins slyly. “Maybe, kind of. I mean, I’ve been here for ten minutes, and I know this place is trash. I’ve seen how the customers are allowed to feel up the dancers and even how the bouncers look ready to fuck them. Some of the girls look like they enjoy it; some are clearly putting on an act. Either way, I don't like it. This place will be mine. The foundation is set; all it needs is a good deep clean and some renos. The bouncers will need to be vetted, and the dancers will need testing for drugs and STDs. It’s all standard. Dean, if you don't mind, I’d like you to handle the bouncers. Evie has a lot going on, and you're the only other person who is good with looking into background shit.”

“Yeah, I can do that,” he nods.

“Good,” she says, turning to me. “Cass, you're in charge of finding me new men. They don't have to be like my guys. The reason why I have gay men is because the women who work at Evolution are the women who helped me through years of hell while enduring it themselves. They are special cases and will always get top priority. Also, this place needs a new fucking name,” she shudders.

“Oh, oh, can I name it?” Neo grins. “What about The Booty Bouncer?”

Harlow raises her brows and grins.

“No,” she laughs.

"Oh, come on! It's perfect. They're up there bouncing their asses anyways!" he pouts.

"How about Redemption?" Dean offers. "If you don't plan on keeping it a strip club."

Harlow looks at him, thinking over his suggestion. "I like it," she nods. "Look at you, Mr. Mime, you do talk," she quips.

Dean actually cracks a smile. Did I get sucked into some alternate dimension? "I do talk. Just normally, I don't have much to say." He shrugs.

"Challenge accepted," Harlow grins. Dean's smirk grows, and he shakes his head.

Yup, I've somehow ended up in another world and switched places with another dimension's Cass.

"Okay. Cassy Boy, you will come with Neo and me," Harlow says.

"Wait. What about us?" Axel asks.

"You're not useful to me, silly," she giggles, then pokes him in the side where he got his stitches, making him grunt in pain. "How you feeling, big boy?" Harlow grins.

"Like a million bucks," Axel grits out, nostrils flaring. Harlow steps up close to him and runs her finger over his chest.

"You know, if you weren't such a twat waffle, maybe people would want to stop kicking your ass," she purrs and pats Axel on the cheek, then turns to us, leaving a pissed off Axel behind.

"They will stay here. Let's go," she says, then takes off past us and through the crowd.

Neo takes off after her, but I linger a moment, watching Axel take off for the bar. He can't drink because of his concussion, so he's probably going to just sit there and sulk like a child and mutter to himself about how much he hates Harlow.

Dean watches Harlow leave. His eyes shine with longing, confusion, and hurt. He looks away from her, locking his gaze with mine. He gives me a nod before following Axel. Dean, however, yeah, something tells me he's gonna have a few drinks. I can see his control slipping, but not in the way it normally does. I think Harlow may just very well be slipping past his defenses.

"Hello boys," Harlow greets the room as she barges into the back office. A greasy fucker with a beer belly and slicked back, black hair jerks his head up. *Called it.* He's sitting at his desk, his eyes wide, clearly taken by surprise.

Looking around the room, I see two men in the corner. They have their hands resting on their guns in the waistbands of their pants.

"Ah, ah, ah. I wouldn't do that if I were you," Harlow sings, pulling out her own gun, pointing it at the guy at the desk, then pulls out another one and points it at the guys in the corner.

"Buh-bye," Harlow tells them, indicating they are no longer welcome. They look at their boss with an apologetic grimace. Guess they are not as dumb as they look. It's telling from how easily they run away that they know this is Queenie. I mean, it's kind of hard not to with the knee-high boots, guns strapped to each leg, lace booty shorts, and a black and red corset. Fuck, she looks so sexy right now. I can't keep my eyes off her. Her black hair falls down her back in waves, and her icy blue eyes sparkle with some kind of fucked up glee as she grins with a sick satisfaction at the men's fear. She looks really badass right now, and I'm loving this new Harlow. I don't get what my brother and cousin see wrong. She's fucking perfect.

"Umm. So, do I finish sucking you off?" a female voice asks from beneath his desk. He jerks his head down, then back up at us.

"No, Dina, you can go," he says, clearing his throat. Neo starts cracking up, and Harlow just blinks with a humorous smile.

A woman with long blonde hair, fake tits, and makeup that's caked onto her face pops out from under his desk. She pauses when her eyes land on Harlow and her gun.

"I gotta ask," Harlow says. "Why?' she sighs, shaking her head in disappointment at this woman's actions.

"She offered," the guy defends.

"Don't look at me like that," the woman sneers at Harlow. "He gives you an extra hundred on your check if you suck him off." She shrugs. "Always good to have extra cash."

Harlow just smiles and shakes her head. The woman rolls her eyes and struts past us, but Harlow sticks her free hand out, stopping her. Harlow leans in close to the woman.

"I'll be seeing you later," Harlow says, then backs away, giving Dina an air kiss.

Dina sneers at Harlow. "You don't scare me, Queenie. I know you don't kill women."

Oh, this girl has a death wish. That may have been true in the past, but after seeing what she did to Rosie's mom, I know that if you piss her off enough, she will gladly fuck a bitch up.

Harlow just blinks at Dina before bursting out laughing, making Neo join in, and I can't help but smirk. "Oh Hunny, you're so cute," she giggles. "Run along now. But don't leave, okay?" Harlow talks to her like you would a child.

"Whatever," Dina scoffs and leaves.

Harlow turns back to the creep at the desk. "Ballsy little bitch, isn't she?" Harlow says, sounding kind of impressed. "Too bad, it's gonna cost her her job."

"What do you mean? She's my best girl. Please," the creep begs, zipping up his pants.

"Well, not anymore. I'm thinking broken legs, a nice haircut, and I think that face could use a little work, don't you, Neo?" Harlow asks.

"Yeah, think she could use some facial reconstruction," he chuckles.

"Well, it just so happens I'm certified to do that." She gives a cocky smirk.

Neo walks around the room, checking the place out. He notices the private liquor cabinet and tries to open it, but it's locked. And rather than ask the guy for the key, Neo smashes his elbow into the glass and pulls out a bottle of bourbon.

"Not that one!" The guy starts to get up, but Harlow cocks her gun and the guy freezes in place.

"W.L. Weller," Neo reads, then looks at the guy. "Dude, this shit is like, super expensive. How can you afford a $7,000 bottle of bourbon?" Not waiting for an answer, Neo opens it and takes a swig.

"Fuck that's good," Neo groans. The guy sighs and sits back down. Neo goes over to the guy's desk and picks up a box that's sitting there and opens it. "Nice! Some Cubans too. Nice of you to take such good care of your guests." Neo takes the cigar, cuts the end off, then lights it up with a lighter from his pocket.

"You know, I'd like to know that too. How can you afford all this nice shit?" Harlow asks. His office is fancy compared to the rest of the place, all new furniture and everything.

"The club does good," he says, but this fucker's poker face needs work.

"Neo dear, do you mind bringing our friend over here?" she asks, grabbing a chair from against the wall and placing it in the center of the room. Neo goes over to the guy, pulls out his chair, and pushes it over to Harlow, with the guy still in it.

When the guy is face to face with Harlow, she hands Neo one of her guns and puts the other away.

"You see, I think it has something to do with whoever is taking all these young ladies who have coincidentally gone missing after spending a night at this club. You wouldn't happen to know anything about that, would you?"

"N-no," he stutters, shaking his head frantically. "I have no idea about any of that."

Harlow narrows her eyes and smiles. "Nah, you're lying," she laughs. "How can a bunch of girls go missing from this very club over the past few months, while you have no idea what's going on? Kind of fishy if you ask me."

Neo, the crazy fuck, leans into the guy and takes a big sniff. "Like a fucking fish market," Neo grins, and Harlow giggles.

"Pet?"

"Yes, My Queen?" Neo purrs.

"Hold him," Harlow grins. Neo chuckles darkly as he grips the guy's shoulders, holding him in place.

"Wanna know something about me?" Harlow asks, reaching for one of her daggers in its holster. She takes it out and holds it in front of her face, fixing up her lipstick in the clear reflection of the blade, before looking back at the guy. His eyes are wide as his gaze is fixated on the dagger. Swallowing hard, he looks back at Harlow.

"Well...?" she drawls.

"Sure?" he questions.

"Well, your lack of enthusiasm is kind of insulting," she pouts. "But I'll tell you anyway," she shrugs. "I love games. Do you love games?"

"Like board games?" the guy asks, confused.

"Well... no, not exactly." She looks up at Neo. "Remind me to try that sometime, though. Strapping them to a board could be fun."

"How about a board attached to a wheel? Like those knife throwers in the circus," Neo grins.

Harlow's eyes go wide with excitement. "Oh my god!!" she squeals. "Yes, yes, yes. We have to do that. That would be so much fun!'' She wiggles in her seat, doing a happy dance. "And we can use it for everything! Throwing stars, daggers, shooting practice..." she lists off a few more things, and I grin at her fucked up excitement for torture methods.

"Queenie," I chuckle.

She looks at me, blinking a few times. "Huh?" she asks.

"You're getting off track a little," I smile.

"Oh right, my bad," she giggles. "New ideas excite me."

I smile and shake my head.

"Anyways, back to my point. I love games, and I would very much like to play one with you." Her grin turns sinister. "Do you wanna play a game?" she says in a half decent Jigsaw impression. I smother my chuckle, as does Neo.

"No," he whimpers.

"Well, too bad for you," she starts laughing, and Neo joins in. The guy starts to fucking cry, and all I can think is *thank god, I'm on her side* because fuck, she's terrifying right now. Add Neo in, and it's like I'm looking at a real-life Harley Quinn and the Joker.

"So, here's the game. I'm gonna ask you stuff; you're gonna answer. For every lie or question you can't answer, I stab you in the leg, simple as that. Got it?" she quips.

"No, please no. I don't know anything, I swear!" the sad, little, fat man cries.

"Ready?" she sings.

And for the next 30 minutes, Harlow grills him, leaving him with multiple stab wounds in each of his legs that are gushing blood. Neo ends up stuffing that stripper's underwear, which she left behind, into the guy's mouth to muffle his screams. I pointed out that he can't answer her questions if he can't speak, but she just waves me off and keeps doing her thing. Who am I to question her?

During our little torture session, Harlow forced him to sign everything over to her. Well, more like to Ruby Snow, her alias, that Miller helped her get set up. It's what the professional business world knows Harlow as.

After a while, he passes out from the blood loss, and even slapping him in the face does nothing to wake him up.

"Well," Harlow sighs and looks up at me. "He really didn't know anything." She shrugs, then takes out her gun, raises it to his head and shoots him between the eyes.

"But, he was raping his dancers, so at least this little playdate wasn't a complete waste of time. I could have saved him for the next D-Day, but why waste a good opportunity."

She bends over and grabs a set of keys from the guy's pocket.

"Come on, boys, I'm pumped up and ready to go. I feel like dancing." She gives Neo a wicked smile, which he returns.

"Fuck, My Queen, you dirty girl," Neo groans.

"Sometimes, being clean all the time can get a little boring," she winks with a giggle. We leave the office and

Harlow locks it behind her. She takes out her cell and makes a call.

“Clean-up crew is on the way, I’m sending Axel out to wait for them by the back door,” she says when she gets off the phone, then sends my brother a quick text.

“Come on, you two, let's dance,” Harlow says.

“Both of us?” Neo asks with a surprised look.

“Yes, both. Is that a problem?” she bites her lip seductively, and I feel like I'm missing the meaning of the little telepathic conversation that they have going on right now.

“Nope. Not at all,” he grins.

“Good,” she purrs and heads towards the main part of the club.

I have no fucking clue what’s going on right now, but I sure as hell want to find out.

I follow them out to the center of the dance floor. The place is packed as the individual dance numbers are done for the night. Now the strippers dance to whatever is playing on the sound system.

I was expecting them to take off together, so Harlow can have her post kill fuck, but I guess we're dancing?

Shake That by Eminem featuring Nate Dogg is playing. Harlow wastes no time swaying her hips to the beat. When she stops, Neo takes the spot in front of her, but doesn’t touch her. His eyes drink her in as she gets lost in the song, singing along with the lyrics. "Dance with me, Pet," she shouts to be heard over the music. She waves her fingers, beckoning Neo closer.

He grabs her hips, crushing her to his front as she wraps her arms around his neck, and they start to move along to the music together, bodies grinding on each other. I stand there, okay with just watching, but then she looks over her shoulder at me and grins. "My back is getting cold, Cassy Boy; come warm me up," she shouts with a sexy grin.

My eyes widen, and I stand there looking like a fucking dumbass as I blink at her. Is she really asking me to dance with her, to touch her? Someone pinch me because I must be dreaming.

Her grin grows at my state of shock. "Well?" she asks with humor lacing her tone.

Not wanting to give up this rare opportunity to touch her, I step up close to her, enclosing her between me and Neo. Then it hits me, and I can't help the satisfied grin that takes over my face. She can't see it, but Neo can. His brows pinch in question, but I just grin harder.

Harlow, and she most likely has no idea she's doing this, is trusting Neo and I enough to be caught between us.

Our little serial killer's stone-cold heart seems to be melting a little. Maybe there is hope for something more after all.

I move my body with theirs, my hands tingle with the contact of her skin. I'm touching her for the first time in eight years, and the teenage boy who was madly in love with her is doing backflips right now. The man in love with her now has a fucking hard on that I'm shamelessly grinding into her ass.

After the song is over and another starts up, Harlow moves close to Neo's ear, and because I'm up close and personal with both of them at the moment, I'm able to hear.

"Fuck me, Neo," she tells him, licking his neck. "Right here in front of everyone."

Neo groans and looks at me. Feeling a little disappointed that I only got to hold her for one song, I start to loosen my grip on her hips and back away. "Stay," she says, gripping my hands, putting them back into place on her skin. An excited rush flushes over my body. I have no clue why she wants me to stay, but I do.

When I take my place at her back again, she leans into me and looks up. "While Neo fucks me, I want you to be the one holding me up." Her eyes dare me to say no, but if she really means it, then bring it on.

She takes my lack of response as my consent with her plan and wraps her arms back around Neo's neck to hop up into his arms, while also wrapping her legs around his waist.

Pressing myself closer to her, she moves her arms from Neo's neck and brings them back to wrap around mine, so that she can use me to hold herself up.

My heart is racing, and she's so close that I can't help but inhale her scent. She smells like fucking cinnamon, just like she did when we were younger. She always had a thing for that scent, getting anything that smelled like that.

Every Valentine's Day she would load up on the cinnamon hearts and pop the damn things like pills, all day, every day.

She would always get pissed whenever her stock ran out and didn't have anywhere to buy them, so the guys and I started ordering them for her online, so she always would have them available.

I can remember the spicy sweet taste of her lips when we kissed, the taste of her tongue dancing with mine.

Neo's eyes are half-lidded with lust as his eyes eat us up. Looks like this might be turning him on, but the dude has always been a horny fucker, so I'm not surprised.

Neo shifts Harlow a few times, and I'm wondering what the heck he's doing when Harlow suddenly grips the back of my neck harder, her nails digging into my skin. I hiss in pleasure from the slight pain as she lets out a moan.

Oh... well, I guess he didn't waste any time. Neo starts to fuck Harlow to the beat of the song, his hips thrusting into her, making her ass grind against my aching hard cock. It's the next best thing to being the one to fuck her. Also, I haven't gotten laid in months, and unlike my brother and cousin, I don't jack off like it's going out of style.

This whole situation floods my senses. My breathing is ragged, and every moan she lets out, it worsens. Neo is gritting his teeth as he fucks her like his life depends on it, and she's just along for the ride, holding on to me like I'm her life raft.

If this is a dream, I don't ever want to wake up.

Harlow tosses her head back, placing it between my neck and shoulder. Her eyes are closed as she enjoys everything we are doing to her body.

Her fingers slide up to grip the back of my hair, pulling at the long strands that are hanging loose behind my back. "Fuck," she groans, and I dig my fingers into her hips, holding her in place, so she doesn't fall as she starts to shake, then cries out as she cums hard on Neo's cock.

God, this is one of the sexiest things I've ever been a part of. If you'd asked me five months ago if I'd be willing to hold the love of my life up while my cousin plows into her in the middle of a nightclub, I would have called you mentally unstable. But if this is what crazy is, then sign me the fuck up and strap me in a straitjacket.

Neo keeps going, not letting Harlow down with her three orgasms rule. I used to think it was stupid because who has time to have that many climaxes in all the odd places, they do it, but I guess being sensitive from the first and never having time to recover lowers the time it takes.

Neo keeps fucking her, making her move against my cock, and I know I'm gonna cum if I don't move. But I can't move, not now. Harlow finds her release again, letting out a softer moan, and by the third song, I'm sweating, panting, and desperate to cum, and the look on Neo's face says he is too with the way he's biting his lip.

"God yes," Harlow screams as she falls apart in my arms during her final climax, triggering Neo. He lets out a hard grunt as he stills, cumming inside her. His hips start to move a little again as he gets the last of his release out.

Harlow untangles herself from Neo, then fixes her shorts that are probably already filling with their combined release. Not sure if that bothers her, though.

My hands are still on her hips, and she places hers over mine, then grinds her ass against my hard length, making me groan. I didn't cum, and fuck if it doesn't hurt to be in this state right now.

"Poor Cassy Boy didn't get to cum," she coos, her lips grazing my neck, making me shudder. "That just won't do. It's only fair."

She starts to dance, making sure that her ass is pressed against my cock good and hard. I breathe heavily into her neck, not daring to kiss it like I so desperately want to.

It doesn't take me long until I'm gripping her hips once again, and probably harder than I should, while I cum so fucking hard that I almost black out, leaving a big wet patch in my jeans. Like that won't be noticeable. At least the club is dark.

"There, that's better," she giggles when she turns around to look at my crotch.

"Fuck," I breathe, running my hand through my hair. "That was..."

"I know; no need to thank me," she winks, and I grin, shaking my head. "Come on, boys, let's go find dumb and dumber."

Neo barks out a laugh as we follow our Queen through the crowd, and everyone parts for her, knowing who she is and that she is not to be fucked with. If it were anyone else, they probably would have been caught and kicked out of the club for what we did. But Queenie owns Kingston Heights and everything in it. You don't challenge the Queen unless you're ready for it to be off with your head.

CHAPTER TWENTY-TWO

WOW... THAT was... yeah, I have no idea what came over me. I was so hyped up over killing the creepy perv that the idea of being between both their hard, muscular bodies, being held by one and fucked by the other, was just too tempting to turn down.

I'd be lying if I said I didn't enjoy being in Cass's arms again. His scent of mint and musk is like a fucking drug.

And I mean, it would have been rude of me to leave him with that impressively sized boner, so I did the nice thing and helped him out. Also, knowing I made him cum in his pants like a teenage boy was fun too.

A very cocky, satisfied Neo and a flushed looking Cass follow me through the crowd to see what Dean is up to.

The sea of bodies part ways for me and the guys. They know who I am, just taking one look at me, and it's a dead giveaway. Also, flashing my crazy ass smirk helps.

When we break from the crowd, my eyes scan the bar, and the blonde bitch from the office catches my attention. She has her fake tits pressed into a man, petting his arm like a bitch in heat. And that man is Dean!

Nope. Not fucking happening. *Not today, spawn of Satan, not today.*

Masking my fury, I beeline it right for them. He doesn't see me, too busy looking into the drink he's holding and ignoring the chick. I stop behind her, rolling my eyes as she babbles about how she can take him into the back and give him a private show. About how good she can make him feel and how she would be worth every little penny.

Only thing she's able to offer him is herpes.

Now, don't get me wrong. I'm all for my fellow women and supporting them in whatever makes them happy, but I don't agree when they turn on each other, using nasty language or phrases to purposefully put each other down. I refuse to be that kind of woman. That is, unless you piss me off. You wanna disrespect me; you don't get any of my *"I am woman, hear me roar!"* support. Nah, you get *"I'm a crazy bitch, watch me slit your throat!"* instead. Okay, so I don't plan on actually killing her, but I do plan on letting her know that if you fuck with Queenie, you will pay the price.

Plastering on my sweetest smile, I tap her on the shoulder. She stops mid-sentence and turns to me. "Yes?" she asks before seeing who she's addressing. "Oh, it's you," she sneers. "What do you want? In case you can't see, I'm kind of busy," she sasses. *Girl, watch that attitude, or I'll forget your fucking gender and shove a broken bottle down your throat.*

She turns back to Dean, flipping her hair back, Mean Girls style, hitting me in the face. She keeps going on with her conversation, although he's still not paying attention, but his eyes aren't on his drink anymore, they are on me, wide in fear of what I'm going to do to him. He has nothing to worry about, though. I could see he had no interest in this bitch; she's just too full of herself or desperate to see it.

Dean starts to open his mouth, probably to defend himself, but I raise a finger telling him to shush, and give him a wink. He looks at the woman, then back to me and grimaces at her.

She stops talking. "What's wrong? Why are you looking at me like that?" she huffs.

"Look, just remember I warned you. You didn't listen. You only have yourself to blame," he says, sounding a little sorry for her.

"What?" was all she got out before I reached out to grab a good chunk of her hair and yank her head down so that she is eye level with me. She lets out a shriek but shuts up immediately when she feels the blade of my dagger against her neck.

"You really should learn to listen more. Or is it that you just enjoy hearing yourself talk so much?" I coo.

She whimpers but gives me a dirty look. "Let go of me, you stupid bitch," she spits, desperately trying to get out of my hold. Fucking dumbass. I cackle like a lunatic as she struggles a little too much, causing my blade to graze her skin, cutting her slightly, and making a bead of blood trickle down her neck.

I tsk, "Now, see what you made me do?" I shake my head.

"What do you want?" she cries, wrenching away from the pain, but she has no chance; my grip is too tight. I'm not letting her off the hook that easily, no matter how much she struggles or pleads with me. This girl needs to be taught a lesson in respect.

"I want *you* to remember who runs this town. You seem to forget that just because I'm known for preferably *not* harming women, that doesn't mean that I'm any less of a ruthless killer. I dispose of toxic wastes of space. You need to remember that women can be just as evil as men. I recently dealt with one who was just as bad as the monsters I normally slay. So, I did with her what I do with all of them, I slayed. And I may not kill you tonight, but you *will* be learning a lesson."

With that, I rip her head back, then smash it down onto the bar top. She howls in agony, sobbing like a little bitch. Her nose gushes blood, and I think I see some teeth on the bar as well.

"Oops," I giggle. "I may have gone a little too hard there. Sorry about that," I say with a shrug.

Her hands fly to her face as she screams and yells and starts to draw a crowd. Good, let them look, and hopefully, they will remember who the fuck I am because I won't tolerate *anyone* doubting my authority. They are alive because *I* allow it. They own their little businesses because I say they can. And if anyone else wants to question that like this whiny, little, fake ass bitch, then I say *bring it on!*

"So, what did we learn today?" I ask, turning my head to the side, leaning my ear in so that I can hear her answer. She doesn't. She just cries harder.

"Noooeh, that's not the answer. You're supposed to say, *'Not to mess with the mother fucking Queen,'* and I wouldn't be opposed to an *'I'm so sorry that I'm a big, fat hoe bag who has no regard for anyone but myself. I've been a bad girl, so I need a good spanking',"* I say in a fake girly voice, mocking her annoyingly nasal one.

"But sorry, *no* spanks for you. I reserve them for My Pet only," I say, faking disappointment.

"Fuck yeah you do," Neo grins. I turn to him smiling, and blow him an air kiss while also giving him a wink.

"So, let's try this just one more time because I really hate repeating myself, and I'm not in the mood. What did we learn here today?" I repeat, mimicking a schoolteacher stare.

"Not to mess with you," she cries. "Not to look at you, talk to you, or fuck with you."

"Oh my god! You *do* understand basic English. I'm impressed," I nod. "Good. I'm glad we could clear up this little misunderstanding on your part. Don't let it happen again, okay?"

"I'm sorry. I won't ever disrespect you again," she promises. Something tells me she's full of shit, but I'll deal with that later.

"Good. Oh, and sorry, sweetie, he wouldn't have gone in the back with you even if he wasn't mine. Your breath smells like rank dick, and he has more class than that. Maybe you should try and get some too. Does wonders for personal growth." I give her a sympathetic smile. I'm just about to let her go, but then I remember something. "Oh, by the way," I say, grabbing the handful of hair I have even tighter and cutting it off with the dagger. Her eyes go wide, and she lets out another shrill scream. "It's rude to flick your hair at people, you snooty bitch," I say sweetly, tossing the locks of hair back at her, and hitting her in the face. A few stick to the blood covering her face, and I can't help but laugh at how ridiculous she looks.

The whole club start to break out into hushed conversations. Everyone still has their attention on us, though, so I take this opportunity to address the crowd. Pushing the bitch out of the way, and sending her flying to the ground, I climb on top of the bar.

"Listen up, fuckers!" I holler, cupping my hands. The room instantly falls silent. "Let this be known. Neo Hendrix, Dean Beckett, as well as Axel and Cassius Ledger are MINE. If any one of you dare fuck with them in any way, shape, or form, I will END YOU! Do NOT touch what is mine. Understand?" I say, locking eyes with as many people as I can.

The room breaks out in agreement, and I nod with satisfaction, "Good." I hop down off the bar and grin at my guys. "Well, that was fun."

"You know, My Queen. Seeing you be all sexy and badass while knowing my cum is soaking into your shorts is a fucking turn on," Neo groans, cupping his cock. I bite my lip and grin, looking down at the bulge in his pants.

"You really are a dirty fucker, aren't you, Pet?" I giggle.

"Only for you, Mistress," he growls, and the sound goes right to my clit.

"Alright, maybe we should go before you two start fucking on the bar," Cass laughs.

I look at the bar top and bite my lower lip, thinking about it. At that, Cass just laughs harder. I look back at him and grin. Tonight makes me like him a little bit more, but I still don't trust him.

"I'm sorry," Dean says, taking my attention away from Cass. "She just came up to me. When I told her I was yours, that just made her work harder. I didn't want to cause a scene without knowing what you would want done in the situation," he apologizes, and I can see he means it.

"You did good. And I told you, by the end of the night, someone was going to be dead, beaten, and fucked. So, check, check, and check," I say, making check marks in the air with my fingers. He cracks a small smile, and fuck, it makes my heart skip a beat. I'm not used to Dean smiling. He used to, all the time, back when we were kids, but since I've been back, he mostly wears a face of stone. Unless it's me testing his control, then it's an irritated scowl. His smile makes him even more handsome, and I have to remind myself that he was the mastermind behind sending me away. I hate him. He is just my property and nothing more.

But then why is he still able to have any effect on me? Damn it! Fuck them, fuck all of them, and not in the fun way!

"Come on, let's go. I'm full of blood, sweat, and cum, and the high of this whole night is starting to wear off. I need some fucking sleep," I sigh and take off towards the exit, and the three follow behind.

"Hey," Axel's gruff voice comes from around the corner. "What did I miss?" he asks, looking at all of us.

"Oh, you know. Just the same old, same old," Neo chuckles.

"Did you kill anyone else?" Axel asks with a sigh. "Because the cleanup crew just left."

"Nope," I chirp with a big innocent smile. "Nothing a little remodeling won't fix."

"Do I even wanna know?" Axel asks, raising a brow.

"Just showing everyone what you get for disrespecting me. You know, like I showed you last night," I smile sweetly, batting my eyelashes up at him, and he cringes.

"So, you stabbed another person?"

"Nah, just bashed her nose and teeth in," I grin proudly.

The guys and I part ways after exiting the Rack Shack. *God, that name is really cheesy.* Dean's idea for a new name was actually a perfect suggestion.

I was distracted the whole car ride, just reliving everything that happened tonight.

Being so high off the kill, the bass of the music clouded my judgment. Maybe it was my subconscious letting me know that maybe it's okay to be friends with Cass like I am with

Neo. Well, maybe not the friends with benefits part because there's way too much history for that, and it would make everything far too complicated, but spending all this time with him and Rosie has made me stop hating him.

And knowing I still have an effect on him was a big ego boost. Making him cum just by grinding my ass on his cock was the icing on the cake.

But where does that leave us now? I don't trust them. Yeah, yeah, I know I keep saying that, but it's true. I don't trust anyone but Evie. Even though everyone thinks I'm some cold-blooded monster, I'm really not. I used to think that feelings were just a straight path to heartache and destruction, but being a mama to Rosie has opened my heart up in so many ways that I didn't think I was capable of anymore.

I've never felt so free with a fuck buddy before. With Garrett, it was a friend helping a friend out. He never wanted anything more from me.

But Neo? That man worships the ground I walk on, and I'm not used to it. It scares the living fuck out of me, and I murder people for a living, so it takes a lot to scare me.

Then finding out my first love wasn't actually the one to fuck me over has been a blow to the walls around my heart.

I unknowingly opened myself up tonight, and I don't know how I feel about it, but what I do know is that I'm feeling things I don't want to feel. Things I never thought I would feel ever again.

Letting them in, in any way, even just as friends, gives them the power to fuck me over again, but I mean, I could always just kill them if they do. *Right?*

God, Harlow, get a hold of yourself. You're turning in to a hot fucking mess.

Whatever happens, I know one thing for sure, I won't let anyone control me or have any power over me, and I won't just roll over and take them back. I'm going to keep living in the moment because that's all we are guaranteed. We have today, but tomorrow isn't promised. I could keep hating them, although they aren't going anywhere. Not now that Rosie is the main part of my life too. Friends or enemies, I'll have to deal with them for the rest of my life. May as well make it the least stressful that I can.

Well, only in regard to Cass and Neo. Dean... he's not as shitty of a person as I've led myself to believe. There's a lot about that man I misunderstood, but in the end, he was the reason why I ended up where I did. So, can I ever really forgive him? Or any of them for that matter. He says it was to protect me, but it did the opposite. FUCK! I just don't know anymore! And I hate it! They are gaining this power over me, just like they had back then, and I... Fucking... Hate it!

Oh, and Axel, fuck Axel with a rusty pole. That fucker needs to get his head out of his ass. Until then, I'm going to enjoy fucking with him every chance I get. Bring it on, big boy, you ain't seen nothing yet.

Ugh! These thoughts are getting me nowhere, and with no idea, where to go from here or how to fix my problems, I need to think about something else. Anything else.

With that, my mind focuses on how much fun it was killing the greasy fucker in the office. It's my first messy kill outside my own establishment, and I feel a little bad for all the work my crew is going to have to do, but it's my responsibility because I'm the owner now. During our little torture session, I forced him to sign everything over to me. Well, more like Ruby Snow, my alias, that Miller helped me get set up. It's what the professional business world knows me as.

I changed my name because if they track Harlow McKaven back to me, they can use the only two people from my past that ever meant something to me, against me. And I would never put Trixie and Mouse in danger like that. So, everyone except the people who have endured hell with me know me as Queenie. To the outside world, Harlow McKaven is dead.

I've been slowly taking out all the men who were lucky enough not to attend Diamonds that night, and one by one, they have all fallen. I couldn't just lure them to me and kill them all at once because of how big of a splash their deaths would make. So, it's been an agonizingly slow process and sadly not as much fun, not like my normal playdates.

Their deaths are made to look natural or like some random accident, but sometimes I do switch it up a bit and make it look like they took their own lives.

Every year, we hold a celebration of life on that day in honor of the women we lost and to relish in the success of ridding the world of all those vile, evil men.

The ones we haven't gotten to yet still live large but try to keep their illegal dealings tightly sealed because they know I'm watching. I like to think they live in fear of when I'm going to strike. I do enjoy the look they get right before I take their lives.

When I finally get home, I take a quick, hot shower, washing the evidence of tonight off my body, reliving how it felt to have two sexy as sin, strong men holding me up as I was brought to ecstasy. I've never done that before, but I'd be lying if I said I didn't want to do it again. But can Cass kneel to me like Neo? And can I give my body to him, in any way, again if he doesn't?

Who fucking knows, I need sleep and to shut my damn brain off before it explodes.

Still wet, I climb into my silk sheets and close my eyes, reliving every scream, every sound of the blade piercing that man's flesh, and the cries that bitch made as I handed her her ass, falling asleep with a smile on my face.

CHAPTER TWENTY-THREE

CASSIUS

THINGS WITH Harlow have been kind of weird after that night at the club. When she's over, spending time with Rosie, she doesn't talk to us. We go into work, do our job, and then come home. Neo even said she's not as fun and playful as she normally is, but even so he loves to rub it in that the sex is still as mind-blowing as ever.

I think what happened with the three of us has scared her off a little. Or at least made her rethink things. I hope this isn't a step back. I'm willing to give her all the time she needs; that's why I haven't told her that I want to be something more than just friends in fear of freaking her out. She's not ready for any of that just yet. We've been back in her life for a few months now, but that doesn't erase the years of her thinking that Neo and I are as much to blame for getting rid of her as Dean and Axel are.

But I won't draw attention to it. I'll keep going on as normal and hope that everything works out in the end.

God, how pathetic do I sound? I'm stupid to have any hope at all, but that's what love does to you. It blinds you, consumes you, chews you up, and spits you out in the best way possible.

"Daddy, when is mama coming back?" Rosie asks. For a moment, my heart stops, thinking she's talking about Briana. "She told me she would be over yesterday. I miss her," she pouts.

"Well, mama has been really busy with work, but we are about to go to her place now. Penny is gonna watch you since Daddy and your uncles have to do a few things around the club."

"Yay! I like Penny. She does my makeup," Rosie says excitedly, jumping up from her spot on the couch and running down the hall in the direction of her room. Awesome, my four-year-old is wearing makeup. I'll have to mention something to Penny. Rosie is way too young for that.

I help Rosie get ready and load her into the car. "Wait!" Rosie shouts just as I'm about to buckle her into her car seat. She wiggles her way out and climbs past me, running back into the house. A minute later, she comes back with a big grin on her face and that damn duck in her arms.

Good thing I love my daughter more than my own life because I now know why that man wanted to off that devilish bird.

She hates men, alright. I have permanent bruises on my ass and ankles matching the number of times she's bitten me.

Rosie finds it hilarious when Daisy chases us around the house, flapping her wings and quacking at us.

She seems to love Harlow and Rosie and any other woman. Rosie will no longer go anywhere without her pet duck. And even though that bird is Satan reincarnated, I love how much Rosie has opened up since her new, little friend came into her life. Although it's not the most conventional pet, her therapist thinks it seems to be helping her to heal, bringing her out of her shell. The one she created to protect herself from her monster incubator and that disgusting bastard of a so-called step-dad, as well as all the vile things they did to her.

I can't even allow myself to think about it. I went to one session with my own therapist, thinking it would help, but it only made me so enraged that I ended up trashing the whole basement. We had to get all new pool tables and re-stock the liquor cabinet.

The guys said nothing, just cleaned it up as I slipped my mask back in place. I need to be strong for Rosie right now. I can't afford to break down and lose myself.

I'm not ready to go back for more therapy. Not yet. It's still too fresh, too soon, for me to talk about any of it without erupting again. But Rosie's therapist said that she already seems to be forgetting what happened. She's still so young that unless asked, it's not on her mind, which I'm beyond grateful for. I'm not sure what her therapist plans on doing, but I won't be bringing it up.

"We almost left Daisy behind!" she says, snapping me back into the present and away from my disastrous thoughts.

"Sorry, Daisy," she says, kissing the duck on the head. It lets out a quack and nuzzles its head against her neck, making Rosie giggle, and damn if my heart doesn't do a damn flip. I would do anything she asks, no question. And I know Harlow would do the same.

Chuckling, I shake my head, and Rosie climbs back in. She puts Daisy on the seat next to her, so I can buckle her in. Daisy nips at my hand, and I snatch it away, shaking out the sting. "Little bastard!" I hiss.

Rosie's eyes go wide, and she lets out a gasp. "Bad word!" she shouts, giving me a scowl. I think I shocked the girl because I rarely use bad language around Rosie. Axel and Neo typically slip up, not me.

"Sorry, sweet girl, but she hurt Daddy's hand," I apologize while handing her a dollar bill from my wallet. Rosie takes it, then looks from my hand, then to Daisy.

"That's not nice!" she scowls at her duck. "You hurt Daddy. Now say sorry."

I bite my lips, holding back a grin as my feisty little girl tells off her duck. Daisy lets out a bunch of squawks and then ruffles her feathers.

"That's better," Rosie nods and looks at me. "She said sorry," Rosie grins, taking my hand and kissing it where the duck bit me. "All better."

Fuck, I'm dead. My heart exploded in my chest, and now I'm a puddle of goo. I wonder if Harlow is up for giving Rosie a brother or sister someday.

When we get to the club, Rosie grabs her little friend and races for the front door. Once we're inside, she puts Daisy down. "Mama!" Rosie yells excitedly. Harlow is at the bar talking to a few girls, and when she hears Rosie, her head snaps over to look at her. A megawatt smile takes over her beautiful, delicate face, as she opens her arms. Rosie races across the room and launches herself into Harlow's waiting arms.

Harlow hugs Rosie right to her. "I missed you, my sweet girl," she says, kissing the top of Rosie's head.

"You didn't come over in forever!" Rosie wails, pulling back from the hug to look at Harlow's face.

"I know, Sweetie. Mama's sorry. I've been super busy, but I promise to tuck you into bed tonight, okay?" she smiles, rubbing her nose against Rosie's, making her giggle.

"You should just live with us," Rosie says.

Harlow looks over at me then back to Rosie. "How about we start with sleepovers first?" Harlow asks.

Rosie thinks about it, then nods. "Okay."

Harlow chuckles and lets Rosie down. Penny comes out into the room and Rosie rushes over to her, giving her a big hug too. We say our goodbyes, and Penny takes Rosie's hand, leading her up to Harlow's penthouse with Daisy waddling after them.

"Hey, Cassy Boy," Harlow purrs. "I can't get that night in the club out of my head. I think about it whenever I touch myself at night and when Neo pounds into me from behind."

My brain short circuits, and I let out a low groan as my cock instantly hardens while my mind flashes back to that night. Her screams as she came, her nails digging into my neck as she held on to me during her release.

Harlow grins as she looks down and sees the evidence of my arousal. She looks back up at me as she reaches for my cock. When I don't stop her, she gives it a squeeze and my knees almost buckle. I bite my lip and try not to come just from her touch alone.

She takes a step back, laughing at the state she's put me in. Little vixen, she is. She loves to tease and poke, but if it means more of little moments like this, I'll take what I can get.

She takes off, heading over to the girls who are getting up on stage, and leaves me standing there with a very uncomfortable boner.

Adjusting myself in my pants, I head over to the bar. "Hey," I greet Evie. She looks up at me, pushing glasses I've never seen her wear before, up her nose.

She closes her laptop and lets out a sigh. "Hey."

"You okay?" I ask. She eyes me warily. We've never really talked other than words in passing, but she's Harlow's best friend, and if I ever have a chance at being anything more with Harlow again, being friends with Evie can't hurt.

"Not good," she says, taking off her glasses, rubbing her eyes. She looks tired. Poor girl has been working nonstop. "Another girl went missing last night, and I don't want to tell Harlow just yet. She's been distracted with everything else, and although she hasn't forgotten about Tracy, keeping busy has lessened her fits of rage. She can get a little scary when she has them," she huffs out a laugh.

"You guys will find them. She won't stop until you do," I say, sitting down next to her at the bar.

"That's what I'm worried about. She's not used to *not* getting what she wants. And she really wants this, to find these women. We know bad things are happening to them, and with our past, it's fucking with her brain. She wants to save the world, but she forgets that she's only human despite what people might think."

Evie looks over at Harlow, who's now dancing provocatively with another dancer. I see a flash of hurt and jealousy in Evie's eyes with a mix of longing. That's not the way one would look at their sister or how a best friend would; it's the same look I find myself giving Harlow when she's not paying attention.

"So, how long have you been in love with her?" I ask, taking a sip from the can of pop Roxy hands me. Roxy chokes on a laugh and bites her lips shut.

Evie's head whips around, and she looks at me with panic but quickly covers it up with one of false innocence.

"What are you talking about?" she asks, opening up her laptop again, tucking her red hair behind her ear, pretending to do work.

"How long have you been in love with Harlow?" I ask again, trying to hide my grin.

"I'm not," she huffs out a nervous laugh, not meeting my eyes. "We're best friends, like sisters. She means the world to me... but not like that."

Roxy barks out a laugh. "Girl, please, you're not fooling anyone. Everyone knows you're head over heels for that woman. It would take a blind person not to see it, or Harlow herself."

Evie looks up at Roxy with wide eyes, then over to Harlow to see if she heard. "Shhh, I am not."

"It's okay, you know. No one's gonna judge you for liking a girl," I say.

"I know no one's gonna judge me, you dummy. I'm gay and everyone here already knows it." She rolls her eyes and Roxy chuckles.

"Well, I didn't. I've never seen you show interest in anyone."

"Because I don't have any interest in anyone," she says.

"Only Harlow," Roxy grins.

She looks between us for a moment, then sighs in defeat. She looks back at Roxy. "Everyone knows?"

Roxy gives her a sympathetic look. "Yeah, Babe, they do."

"God, I must look like a pathetic, little schoolgirl with a crush on the hot, popular girl," she groans, putting her head down on the table. "And what makes it worse, is that she doesn't even know it. And if she does, then she's damn good at hiding it," she sighs.

"Does Harlow like both men and women?" I ask, looking over at Harlow grinding her ass against one of the dancers, laughing and having fun.

"She doesn't really put labels on things. But I haven't seen her show any interest in a woman. She jokes around and has fun with the girls like she is now, but nothing physical.

She says she likes big, fat cocks too much to try anything else," Evie deadpans, and Roxy bursts out laughing.

My mind goes right to every man she would have been with before Neo, and I get jealous.

"Oh, chill out, jolly green giant," Roxy laughs. "The only cock she's riding is your cousin's."

"Yeah, that makes me feel so much better," I grumble.

"So, you want her too, then?" Evie asks, nervous of what my answer will be. Harlow isn't just any woman. With everything she's been through, she deserves everything and anything her little, blood thirsty heart desires. I love her, and I want her. But so do my cousins. Axel can deny it all he wants, but he's not fooling anyone. He gets off on the little bickering fits that he has with Harlow. And I'm not deaf; I heard him moan her name as he used and abused that poor cock of his.

I know for a fact that the only reason why Dean is holding back is because she challenges his need for control. She is very Alpha female and demands submission.

But if she feels the same for Evie as Evie does for her, that doesn't change anything about me wanting to be with her. I'm already hoping to share her with Neo. She can be with ten people, and I'd gladly accept it, just as long as I got to be one of those people. It's not my life to control, after all.

"I'm gonna be honest with you," I answer her. "Yeah, I do. And so do the others. I can't speak for them, but *I'm* not going anywhere. She's been my whole world from the moment she walked into our junior high school cafeteria.

With her long, black hair and that face with those ice blue eyes full of determination that just trap you," I grin.

"Alright, Romeo," Roxy laughs rolling her eyes, but Evie just scowls.

"Anyways," I draw out with a smile. "I want her. I don't care who else she wants to be with, if she even wants any of us, but I won't give up. I'm not going anywhere, not until she says to my face that she wants nothing to do with me in that way. If that's the case, then I'll just co-parent Rosie with her, but I'm not going down without a fight."

"Well, I'm not either," she says with sass, puffing out her chest. *Feisty, little redhead, isn't she?* But then her face drops, and she loses her sudden confidence. "That's if she even feels the same way about me," her voice filled with sadness as her shoulders slump.

"You won't know if you don't ask her," I say, not seeming to care that I'm helping out my potential competition.

"And what if she doesn't feel the same way? What if I spill my heart out, and she rejects me? Only sees me as a friend or sister. Then I ruin everything we've built," she rushes out, and I can almost feel her heart breaking, just at the thought.

"I might not know this new Harlow that well yet, but I do know, for a fact, that even though all these people work for her, they also mean a lot to her, and she would do just about anything for all of you; you are her everything. So, even if she doesn't feel the same way, you will never lose the piece of that woman you already have," I reassure her.

She looks away from me, biting back emotions. "I hope you're right," she whispers.

Not wanting her to feel awkward, I change the subject. "So... Rosie started calling you Auntie E whenever she mentions you," I smirk.

Her eyes light up. "Really?"

"Yup. She loves you almost as much as Harlow. I'm very grateful that she has two amazingly strong women in her life, even if this lifestyle is...."

"A really fucked up, warped version of *Alice in Wonderland*?" Roxy grins.

"Yeah, kind of. I mean she doesn't chop off people's heads like the Queen of Hearts though," I say. And they both look at me with amused grins.

My eyes widen. "Does she?"

"Not normally..." Evie giggles.

"But she has in the past," Roxy says, laughing when my face pales and I swallow hard. "She sometimes uses the heads as soccer balls too," she says, then takes an empty can and kicks it in the air mimicking a ball.

Sweet fuck, who is this woman?!

"Just don't fuck her over or be a vile waste of space, and you'll be fine," Evie titters, patting me on the shoulder and picking up her laptop, heading towards the back to her cave of an office.

Oh, trust me, I don't ever plan on hurting that woman again for as long as I live.

IT TOOK me a few days to wrap my head around the new changes between Neo, Cass, and I. I also think I'm done distancing myself from them because poor Neo looks like a puppy who got kicked.

I can tell he misses our normal playfulness, and I've gotten so used to it that I've actually missed it too. I've decided to just have fun and enjoy being friends with these guys. Just because I don't trust them with my heart, it doesn't have to mean that I can't trust them as a friend. *Or in bed.* They've shown how much they want to be in my life, as more than being just my employees, so I'm willing to give them a chance. They all know what's at risk if they fuck up.

I can see how stressed Cass has been while trying to deal with everything that's happened to Rosie. He's desperately trying to hold it all in, and that's not good. One day, he's gonna break down, and I don't know if he will be able to put himself back together. But I'd like to be there to help in any way I can when he does. I know what it's like to have to go through everything that Rosie went through. I've gotten so used to all the abuse that hearing her story only triggered me more to act in the moment. After ridding the world of those two fuckers, I knew *I* would be the best person to help Rosie cope with everything after that.

I'm not a professional, and I've never gotten any help to deal with my own trauma. I just learned to cope and deal, all on my own. Not really the healthiest way to survive, but the point is that's exactly what I'm doing. Surviving. And that's exactly what I want to help Rosie do too, only without carrying the trauma with her as she grows up. I want her to have a happy, safe, carefree life, basically everything I never got to have. But she deserves it, more than anyone I've ever known. And I desperately need her beautiful, innocent spirit to remain pure, and I'll be by her side every day to make sure that it does.

I had Trixie and Mouse to help me stay grounded in the group home, and the guys helped me through all those times when my PTSD was triggered; even though, I don't think they ever knew that they were such an anchor to me. I know that they all had a basic idea about my past, but the one guy who knows every dirty, little secret, or at least the ones I was strong enough to tell at the time, is Cass.

When I told him everything, he never once looked at me as broken. If anything, I think he loved me more, maybe because I trusted him enough to bear the burden of my trauma with me.

I think that's why *he* was the one who ultimately broke me when I left. He didn't tell me to leave specifically, but he wasn't there to stop me either.

Only, now I find out that he had no clue... So, here we are. Well, wish me luck with all this bullshit, and pray I don't kill the wrong person by the end of it.

After I'm done helping the girls practice for tonight's show, I take a quick shower at my place, giving Rosie a big hug and a kiss goodbye before I leave her and Penny on my bed to watch movies while I head back down to the club.

To make it up to my pet, I'm gonna bring him down to my dungeon and show him just how much I appreciate him. It takes a unique kind of human to be able to withstand my level of crazy, let alone crave and need it as he seems to do.

I went down there earlier this morning to set everything up. I've never used it. I bought everything in case I ever found someone who I felt comfortable enough to play with, but no one has so far. So, I'm really fucking excited to have Neo be my first, and I'll be okay with him being my last too.

"Hey, Pet," I purr, running my hand down his spine. He's facing away from me, wiping down the bar stools. His body quivers at my touch, and he lets out a little moan.

"Mistress." His growl is filled with lust and need.

"I have a surprise for you," I whisper into his ear before licking the shell of it and biting hard on his earlobe. He lets out a grunt that sounds more like a moan.

"For me?" he breathes.

"Only for you," I grin as he turns around to face me. His pupils blown wide with desire and excitement.

I cup his proudly erect cock, giving it a squeeze. "You have been a very good boy, My Pet. From the moment you signed yourself over to me, you have never once disappointed me. Never once disobeyed me, and you have been a very eager pet to please your master," I say seductively as I feather my lips against his stubbled jaw. I won't kiss him, but the pulse in his cock shows me that this is just as good for him.

"How, Mistress?" he breathes in a shaky breath.

"How would you feel about a session in my dungeon? I've been dying to use it. But it's just been sitting there waiting for me to find the perfect Pet to play with." I look him in the eyes, wanting to see his reaction.

"Please, Mistress, take me to your dungeon. I'm yours to do with as you please," he practically begs, and fuck if my pussy doesn't flutter at his raw desperation for me, and at the thought of all the potential dirty, fun, and kinky things I'm gonna do to him.

Without another word, I take his hand and lead him past the others who are working in different sections to clean up the club. They all look at us, taking in Neo's smug and excited face. I give them a wink and a wolfish grin before disappearing down the hall with the feel of their hungry gazes burning into my back.

We go through the door that leads down to the showroom. He looks around confused, like he's wondering why we are here.

I lead him to the other side of the room, to the door in the very back corner. Opening the door, I flick on the dimmed light switch, and the room lights up in a low, red hue. Neo steps into the room and takes a look around, running his hand over all the equipment, taking in everything.

In the far-left corner, there is a king-size bed made up in red, silk sheets with arm and foot restraints installed.

A sex swing hangs from the roof not too far from the bed.

I also have a wall of props, with a variety of things like a collar and leash, cuffs, whips, paddles, ball gag, and flogger; and on the table, I even have something more unconventional laid out to play with. I bought some new daggers just for Neo and our time here. He mentioned a while back that knife and blood play turns him on. Although we never really did it, I'm betting he would do anything to be able to do it with me.

On the other side of the room, there is a sex bench and a St. Andrews cross.

"Sorry there's not much here. I never had anyone to play with until now, and I didn't want to go out and spend a bunch of money on things I may never get to use, so... I only got what I thought I'd have the most fun using with my Sub," I tell him, running my hand across the bed.

"It's perfect," he grins, eager to get started, looking around like a little kid in a candy store, not sure what treats he wants to try first.

"There are a few things you need to know before we take this next step," I tell him, taking a seat on the bed, while he takes a seat on the padded bench.

"Of course," he nods.

"I need you to know that this won't be a regular Dom and Sub relationship. That requires a lot of trust on both ends, and that's just not something I can give you right now."

"Understood."

"I respect the Dom/Sub dynamic, but the complete practice… it's just not me. I'm not a "by the books" kind of person, you know," I grin.

"Oh, trust me, I know, and I wouldn't change you for the world," he chuckles.

"Okay. So, I don't know what you know about all of that, but you won't find that here. Yes, I have the equipment and the toys. But that whole "traditional" dynamic is not what you're gonna get here."

"But I'll still be your Pet and you my Mistress, right?" he questions.

"Yes," I laugh. "I will still be in charge, as always. And I fully expect you to submit to me in every way. We will still have a safe word, and please, if anything I do becomes too much, use it. I'm very big on consent and this won't work unless you agree. I'm all for taking you to your limits and exploring this with you, but don't endure anything you can't handle just to please me. I want this to be a pleasurable experience for both of us. I won't be able to enjoy this if you're not."

"I promise I'll use the safe word if it ever becomes too much," he says seriously.

"When it comes to sex, I'm dark and dirty, Neo. I love pain, and I love causing it. It's a big fucking turn on for me to have that power over someone else. But I will never abuse it in this way," I promise him.

"I'm okay with whatever you're okay with. You may not trust me. And I fully understand that, My Queen. We have a lot to do to earn that back, if we ever can, but I want you to know, I trust you. I trust you with my body, completely. I know how big consent is for you, and I will always ask for yours and give you mine. I know there's a difference between the playing you do in the showrooms and what we will be doing here. Out there it's torture to torture, to cause agony and to kill. In here, you torture to cause pleasurable pain. To push us both to our limits and into the oblivion of ecstasy," he says, his gaze intense and locked on my face.

My heart flutters at his words, and my brain swims with all the warm, fuzzy feelings. He understands my needs. What I want. What I can and can't accept, and he's okay with it. All of it. Fuck. Why does he have to be so fucking perfect for me? Pushing those feelings down, I stand up and start to stalk towards him with a smile that to anyone else would be deemed mental.

"Then let's begin, shall we?"

CHAPTER TWENTY-FOUR

Neo

SLAP MY dick and call me Santa, this is really fucking happening right now. Fuck! I've lain in bed so many nights thinking about when she would finally bring me down here.

I feel giddy, like a little kid on a rollercoaster for the first time, about the fact that she trusts me enough to take part in something so personal with her.

I get why this can't be a normal Dom/Sub relationship, but I'll take whatever I can get. I love when she calls me Pet, and her eyes light up when I call her Mistress. From what I've gathered over time, this is something she always wanted but never found, and I'm so fucking proud and beyond stoked to be the one to give her this experience.

I will submit in every way she asks me to. I really have no limits when it comes to her. She could cut every inch of my body and leave me bleeding on the ground, and I'd beg her for more. Yes, I'm a sick fucker, but really, have you seen this woman? My cousins are morons for not wanting to bow down and be owned by this goddess.

I sit on the bench, waiting like a good little pet for her to tell me what to do. She disappears behind a door on the right side of the room, emerging a few minutes later dressed in red leather pants and bra, wearing a black bunny mask and black, knee-high boots.

My heart stops. Someone call a code blue because the sight before me has stopped my heart. Sweet mother of god, she's every man's wet dream, and I'm about to have a throw down with my cock if it doesn't chill the fuck out, because if he cums right now, I'll disown the fucker.

I hold my breath, surprised I haven't passed out, as I watch her walk over to the table of goodies she set up. My cock perked up immediately when we first walked in, and I saw the daggers lying there. They looked new and shiny and ready to be stained with my blood.

"So many to choose from. Which one should we use first?" she asks herself as she looks over the assortment of toys in front of her.

"All of them," I answer her. "Give me everything you got." My smile is wide and wicked as she turns around to smirk at me.

"Oh, my silly little Pet. You can't handle everything I've got." Her smile turns into the thing of nightmares, and my heart starts to pick up, beating against my rib cage. Fuck me. Fuck me good. Fuck me with a dildo for all I care; just give me something.

“Tonight won't be a full session. This is new to both of us, and it will take some time to explore what we do and don’t like, but there is something that’s been on my mind since I got to wrap my hands around that thick neck of yours, choking you until we came so hard, we both saw fucking stars,” she purrs.

I grip my cock tightly as I think about that night. God, that was some of the best world-shattering sex of my life. If she didn't let go, and I died, I would have shown up at the gates of hell and high-fived the devil himself. Un-fucking-believable.

“Anything,” I breathe without hesitation. She looks down at my hand, that’s resting on my cock, and quickly takes a crop whip from the table to strike my hand, making me let go of it with a hiss.

“Don't touch! Mine,” she growls, but if that was meant to be a punishment, I didn't learn my lesson at all. If anything, my cock grew harder, if that’s even possible.

“Sorry, Mistress,” I say, holding back a groan.

“Strip and take your place in front of the cross,” she orders, and I quickly turn around, eager to obey my mistress, and it takes everything in me not to rush over there like an excited idiot.

My clothes are flying everywhere as I leave a trail of them behind me, as I hurry to do her bidding. She giggles at my eagerness. God, that sound does things to my heart and soul. There's a difference between her giggles when she's in one of her crazy moods and when she is genuinely laughing. It’s not something just anyone could point out. But spending enough time with her, like I do, gives me the ability to tell the two apart easily.

"Strap your feet in," she orders from where she's still standing by the table. I widen my stance, putting each foot in place, stepping into the leather cuffs.

Her heels click against the floor as she prowls her way over to me.

"Arms up, Pet," she orders once I'm done with my ankles, and I raise my hands above my head so that I now make a naked X with my body. She straps my wrists in and takes a step back.

She's biting her lip as her eyes devour my body. I stand here, bare and waiting for her, my cock standing proudly and pointing right at her.

"Now, normally I'd make this about my pleasure just as much as it's about yours. But tonight, because My Pet has been such a good boy, it's all about you." She walks back over to the table and picks up one of the daggers and the crop whip from before that she had to put down to strap me in.

Fuck, she's magnificent. Bring it on, My Queen, give me all you got.

"Question," I address her.

"Yes, My Pet," she asks, stopping before me with her head cocked to the side.

"Am I to be quiet while you have your way with me?"

She thinks for a moment before answering. "Sounds of pleasure and pain are okay, but no asking questions, no distracting me once we begin. It's already gonna take everything in me not to jump on that massive cock of yours and ride you like a cowgirl," she says, biting her bottom lip, taking another glance up and down my body.

I give her a nod, not saying a word, letting her know that I'm ready to begin when she is.

"First, I'm gonna have a taste of this glorious cock of yours," she says, getting on her knees before me, never taking her eyes off me as she flicks her tongue out, licking the pre-cum that's weeping from my cock.

Fuck, fuck, fuck. Don't cum, you fucking pussy. Yes, I know that the sight of this powerful woman on her knees before you is enough to lose your load, but not now! Blood first, cum later!

She groans at my taste, licking her lips before wrapping her plump, red ones around my cock. She takes me all the way in, and my hips try to buck forward, but I get nowhere. She chuckles with my cock still deep in her throat, and the vibrations make me moan.

"Fuck," I hiss.

"Not right now, Pet," she grins wickedly after pulling back. She abandons my cock and I almost cry at the loss of her lips when she goes to grab one of her daggers.

"I can see you're very worked up, Pet, and I have a feeling this session may be over sooner than we both planned. But that's okay, because I have a feeling we will be back here often, and we can try something new each time. Right now, let's give this a try," she says, taking the dagger and nicking one of my nipples. I grunt at the sting, watching her pupils widen while she watches the bead of blood pool and drip from my nipple.

"Do you want to know one of my favorite things?" she asks me, not looking away from the blood as another bead drips down again.

"Yes," I breathe.

"I love blood, the color, the smell, the taste. Some might call that odd, others say it's downright fucked up, but that's me. There's nothing normal about me, Pet," she says before leaning over and sucking the bloody nipple into her mouth. She moans against it as her tongue swirls around it, soothing the sting of the cut left behind, making my cock jerk against her belly.

"Does that freak you out?" she asks, releasing my nipple, leaving a little smudge of red on her lip. I wish my hands were free, so I could grip her face and lick her lips clean.

"No," I shake my head. "It's sexy as fuck. My own little vampire."

She smiles at me, a real genuine smile, and all I want to do is shout "I love you" like a freak, but I keep my mouth shut, not wanting to ruin this moment.

My cock is throbbing painfully with the need to cum. I want to let go and fall into the high of a release, but I also want to see what else my Mistress has planned for me.

While I'm not paying attention, she does the same thing to my other nipple, and my head falls back as I stand here at her mercy.

"You taste divine, Pet. Like the most lavish, red wine money can buy," she breathes. She looks down at my angry cock.

"He seems to be impatient. Perhaps he needs to be punished," she takes the crop whip and with more force this time, she hits my cock, and the pain makes me moan. Seeing that I like it, she whips my cock again, watching it as it bobs back up.

"You like that, don't you, my dirty, little Pet?" she grins.

"Fuck yes," I moan.

She does it a few more times, stopping when it starts to go red, and only then does she go back to nicking my skin, leaving little cuts on my abs as she laps up anything that falls. She trails the blade down the length of my cock, causing me to gasp in a breath. Partly in fear, but mostly in pleasure.

Her tongue and mouth lick and suck at my body, and I'm panting with need, breathing heavily, and gritting my teeth, trying desperately not to cum. I don't know how much longer I'll be able to last, though. My mind is on overload and my skin is on fire.

Before Harlow, my stamina was idolized. But now, this woman has such a strong effect on me that I have no control over my cock anymore, she owns me.

She licks down my jawline as she trails the tip of the dagger up my inner thigh.

She takes a step back, her eyes black with lust, and I have a feeling that tonight isn't about just me anymore.

"You've been such a good pet. Letting me play with your body. I think you deserve to cum. So, cum for me, Pet. Show me just how much you loved what I did to you," she flashes me a hungry grin.

With that, I can't hold back. She doesn't even have to touch me because I'm already to the point of bursting. With a loud desperate cry, I roar out my release as my cock jerks on its own, shooting ropes of cum like a fountain up into the air and splashing onto the floor next to Harlow's feet.

I'm gasping for air by the time my cock is done releasing itself. Harlow moans before stepping over the puddle of cum at her feet and letting me loose from the cross.

"More. I'm gonna need more of that another time," she breathes, her eyes wide with want, with need, and I think I even see a bit of fear in there. Fear of what's changing between us, the intensity of what's growing. God, I wanna kiss the crap out of her right now.

"On the bed," she demands. "I know this was supposed to be about you, but I'm so fucking turned on that I'll stab the next person I see after leaving this room if I don't get to cum. I'm wound so fucking tight that these leather pants are sticking to my legs as my juices drip from my cunt."

Oh, fuck. Yup, just like that my cock is standing proudly for her again, ready to be ridden by my Queen.

She starts to strip as I climb onto the bed. I lay back, my eyes taking in my Mistress as she stalks towards me, her breasts swaying with every step.

She climbs onto the bed, then straddles my hips. Wasting no time, she impales herself on my cock and starts to ride me with no restraints. Her moans mix with mine, and the dirty words that fall from her luscious lips spurs me on.

I lie there as she uses my body for her pleasure, and I enjoy every fucking moment of it.

She tosses her head back and lets out a cry, "Yes, fuck yes!"

Her pussy clamps around my cock, and I curse at myself as I cum again, only giving her one orgasm.

"Fuck. I'm sorry, Mistress," I apologize, hating myself for ending this so soon.

"That's okay. I'm exhausted anyways," she breathes, plopping down next to me. "Just remind me to spank you as punishment next time," she mumbles, and excitement fills me as I imagine her turning my ass red.

When she doesn't say anything, I look over at her, finding her passed out. I just blink at her in shock. This has never happened. When we fuck, we go about our day after. Or we part ways and go home. Never once has she ever stayed with me like this.

Smiling, I mentally do a happy dance as I enjoy this clear sign of trust. She might deny this ever happened if someone asks her, but that's okay. I'm just happy I got this.

I get out of bed and look around for something to clean her with. When I see nothing, I head over to the door she went through earlier to change. It's a little bathroom. Perfect. I see clean towels and facecloths on the sink.

Wetting one with warm water, I go back over to my sleeping beauty and carefully clean her up. She mumbles but doesn't wake up. I do the best I can to clean my cum from between her thighs before pulling the sheet up over her to cover her gorgeously naked body. Then I sit there, like a fucking creep. Butt-ass naked, I just sit there with my legs crossed and my elbows on my knees. My face in my hands as

I smile contently, searing her face into my mind. The way her lips part as she breathes softly. The way her black hair covers some of her face. The way her long lashes rest against the skin right above her cheek.

A fucking vision. After an inappropriate amount of time of just watching her, I lean over and kiss her forehead. This is the closest I'm gonna get, but I just need to feel her skin against my lips once more. I crave her, I need her. Without her, I'm nothing. With her, I'm everything. I'm me, beast and all.

Not wanting her to wake up in the morning and freak out with me in the bed next to her, I quietly gather up my clothes and get dressed. I give her one last kiss, on her cheek this time, and then I leave her there to sleep.

I would love to be in that bed with her, holding her in my arms as we sleep through the night, but I know that, even though she showed a little bit of progress tonight, she's not ready for that. I won't risk any setbacks with her.

I'm grateful for what she gave me tonight. It means more than she will ever know.

CHAPTER TWENTY-FIVE

Harlow

STRETCHING, I let out a groan of pleasure. Fuck, that feeling of a good stretch is almost orgasmic. Blinking my sleep filled eyes open, I look around the red hued room. *I'm still in the dungeon; what the fuck?* What am I doing here?

The events of the night before come flooding back. Neo. Daggers, blood, cum, orgasms, blood... the fucking blood. I'm fucked up, I know it. I really do enjoy the copper taste, but don't judge me; there are people out there eating drywall and toilet paper. I've seen a few episodes of *"My Strange Addiction"*, and I know that I'm not as bad as *THAT*.

Although it had crossed my mind that maybe I'm part vampire. *Wouldn't that be awesome? Ripping people's necks out with my teeth.* I shiver with delight at the very thought. I really am fucked up.

Sliding out of bed, I pad over to the en-suite bathroom and take a hot shower, washing off the dried sweat. I look down between my thighs, expecting Neo's dried cum to be there; only there's nothing, I'm perfectly clean.

Furrowing my brow, I look around and find a dirty face cloth sitting on the counter. Did I sleep through him cleaning me up? How could I be so careless? And why would he clean me up? Fuck, and I fell asleep with him in the same room as me. I must be losing my touch.

Or the crazy fucker is finding a way into your fucked up and damaged heart, an unhelpful voice states in the back of my mind.

Ugh, just what I need... feelings. Shaking my head, I finish cleaning up and wrap the towel around my body.

Shit. I don't have any clothes here, and I'm not putting on my leather pants stained in my own juices. Oh well, this is my club, and it's not like everyone who works here hasn't already seen my naked body. So, me walking around in nothing but a towel won't be shocking to anyone.

Leaving behind everything to be cleaned later, I head upstairs. What time is it? There are no windows down here, and I didn't bring my phone with me, so I can't check the time.

When I get to the main part of the club, the room is lit up by the ceiling lights. Again, I still don't have a fucking clue what time it is because there are no fucking windows. But there are a few people milling around, so something tells me it has to be at least noon. No one but Evie, Roxy, me, or the guys are ever in earlier than that.

I get a few hellos as I walk through the main part of the club past the stage. I really should head upstairs to get dressed, but I'm so damn thirsty after everything last night; my mouth feels like sandpaper.

Roxy isn't at the bar right now, so I slip behind there and grab myself a bottle of water. Downing the ice-cold liquid, it hits me in all the right spots.

Wiping my mouth with the back of my hand, I see a tweaked-out looking Evie. She comes running out of her office like a bat out of hell. When she locks eyes with me, her face is filled with an excited grin.

"Oh, thank god, you're up. Neo told us you were probably gonna end up spending the night down there. I was gonna come get you myself since it's noon and no one had heard from you yet. I'm glad you're here. Oh my god, Low! Like, oh my god!" she rushes out, and I chuckle at her excited blabbering.

"E, breathe," I giggle. She snaps her mouth shut, closes her eyes, and takes in a deep breath. "Good, now what's going on?"

She smiles wide again. "I found something!" she squeals.

My eyes widen. "Really?" I ask, hope lacing the word. "You better not be fucking with me, E. I don't think my heart could take it."

She quickly shakes her head. "I'm not. Come with me," she says, grabbing my hand and dragging me back to her office.

She shuts the door behind us and takes a seat at the desk. She opens her laptop and presses play.

It’s security footage of the back alleyway of the Rack Shack. “I have been checking the footage of the previous night every morning like I have been since we set these up, and karma must fucking LOVE us because I just hit the jackpot. Well, it feels like it, since it's been months, and we’ve gotten nothing and nowhere,” she says just as a woman comes into the camera frame.

It’s the fucking cunt face, Dina. She stands there, looking around nervously. Then out of the dark comes another person, an older man.

“Low, do you know who that man is?” Evie grins. I look from the screen to her.

“He looks familiar. But I can't see his face.” My brow furrows as I continue to watch.

“Just wait,” she bounces in her seat.

We keep watching as Dina and this mystery man start to have heated words. The man rubs his face in frustration and turns to face the camera at just the right angle for me to see who he is.

It’s Richard fucking Baxter. “Dick.”

“Fucking Dick,” Evie giggles.

“Evie, this may not be much and may not hold up as evidence to the police, but I know, deep down in my fucking soul, that he has something to do with the missing girls, and I bet that bitch is helping him. There's no way that they are entering that club and never leaving. There's more to this, and we need to get to the bottom of it."

“I agree. But now we have a place to start.”

“That rat bastard. I bet the other old farts are in on it too. I knew giving them all this damn power was gonna bite me in the fucking ass,” I sigh, rubbing my face, forgetting I’m still only in a towel. It slips from my body and onto the floor.

Evie sucks in a breath. “Sorry about that,” I laugh, bending over to retrieve it, allowing my breasts to hang forwards. Evie lets out a little groan.

“Like what you see, E?” I tease.

Her eyes snap from my tits to my eyes, her face flushing red, almost the same color as her hair. She's so stinkin’ cute.

“I like women and can't help but appreciate a nice pair of breasts when I see them. Sue me,” she plays off her embarrassment.

Laughing, I head to the closet and grab a robe I keep in there. Tying it closed, I head back out to Evie.

“All I was thinking about were all the innocent people in the companies. I didn’t want thousands of people to suddenly be out of work, just because we chose to go after the owners by bankrupting them. And like fuck, there’s no way I’d been able to run all of those companies myself, so I put a few people in charge. I should have known that the people who I chose to replace the sick fuckers would possibly end up on the same path as the originals. Money is power and power can fuck with a person’s head. Guess these greedy fuckers chose evil as well,” I fling myself dramatically on the couch.

“FUCK!” I turn my head to the side and see an anxious Evie chewing her lower lip. “Well, like you said, we have somewhere to start. So, let's get on that. We have girls to save and monsters to slay."

Evie and I spend the next hour coming up with a plan. There's a yearly gala that all the ritzy-ditzy rich folks put on to network with others and further their businesses, while supporting a good cause. Or at least that is what they tell the press. The gala is a night for society's elite to condone their illicit behavior: getting drunk, drugs, and cheating. The guys used to attend until they realized what went on. That will all change because I need the guys to rub elbows with these snobs, to do some recon.

When Evie and I are done, we take a seat at the bar and get the kitchen staff to make us some chicken wings. Fuck, I love wings. I don't even feel bad when I make Evie uncomfortable with all of my over-the-top moaning as I eat every yummy bite.

After getting dressed for the day, I make my way back downstairs. "Good you're here!" I cheer, bouncing my way over to Axel, Neo, and Dean. I've been in a good mood since seeing the video and finally being able to have a plan.

"Hey, My Queen," Neo grins wickedly, telling me he's thinking of all the dirty things we did last night. My skin flushes and my heart flutters. What the fuck is this bullshit? I do not swoon! Someone kill me, please?

“Hello, my Pet,” I grin, playing along as if his smoldering stare isn't doing things to my pussy right now.

Axel grumbles something about sick fucks and blood play.

“What was that?” I ask Axel, faking innocence.

His eyes snap to mine. “Nothing,” he says casually.

I look at Neo and narrow my eyes. He holds his hands up. “I said nothing. He walked in on me afterwards, when I was showering, to bitch about something the duck did and how Daisy is becoming a bad influence on Susie and Bob. So, he saw my chest.”

“Pretty fucked up if you ask me,” Axel mutters. Who does this fucker think he is, kink shaming me?

“Don’t,” I warn. “Don't fucking judge us for our personal sexual preference. We don’t tell you what to like and what should get you off, so don't you fucking dare put your two cents in when it comes to ours. Got it?” I growl.

He grits his teeth. “Sorry,” he forces out.

“Like fuck you are. You’re on thin ice and, if I wasn't in such a good mood, I would give you another scar on the other side to match the first one.”

“What’s got you in such a good mood?” Dean asks, taking the attention off his cousin.

I turn to him with an excited grin spreading across my face, “I'm glad you asked. And you’re just the person I wanted to see too.”

“I am?” he asks with genuine surprise.

"Of course, Silly," I flutter my eyelashes, trying to butter him up, and hope I don't have to fight him on the date we are having tomorrow night.

"Okay..." he says with caution, not really trusting my sudden niceness. He's smart not to. It's all fake, but it's worth a shot. "What can I do for you?" he questions.

"You can take me on a date," I smirk.

His eyes go wide. "What?" he sputters.

Neo growls from behind me, and his sudden possessiveness is both a turn on and annoying. I'm not his, and he doesn't have the right to act like this.

"That's enough out of you, Pet, don't make me punish you," I heed. His eyes light up at my threat in hopes that it's a promise as well as a threat.

"What do you mean you wanna go on a... date?" The fucker looks panicked. What the hell, rude much? He would be lucky to have me as an actual date. Asshole.

"Well, Evie found something pretty big with the missing girls case, and you're gonna help me see if we can get some information."

"But why would I need to go on a date with you to get that?" Dean asks. Seriously, dude, the idea of going out with me shouldn't be that much of a turn off.

"Because," I grit out, getting annoyed with asshole number two. "There's a gala tomorrow night, and we are attending."

"What gala?" he asks warily. Fuck this shit.

"Listen up, buddy. There are a bunch of old rich men that I was stupid enough to put in charge of the companies I took over after burning the old owners to the ground. I'm 99.9 percent positive that at least one, if not all of them, are behind the girls going missing. I have video proof. Or at least proof enough for me. So, you, being a young businessman yourself who is looking to build a good image for your company once it's back up and running, will take me with you. I will cling to your fucking arm, bat my lashes like most of the gold diggers there, and say lots of nice and uplifting things about you, all while trying to get whatever information we can in regards to the missing girls. You are the leader of your company, so all the attention will be centered on you as the face of said company. You don't have a choice. This is how it's going to be," I admonish him.

He just stands there, blinking at me. It seems I've stunned him. "Alright," he calmly states.

I'm taken aback. "Wait, what? Just like that?"

"I'm not gonna argue about something so important. Your plan is a pretty good one. Only, won't they know who you are?" he cocks a brow.

"Not if I go in disguise," I grin.

He nods in agreement. "That might work."

"Trust me, I'm a good actress," I wink.

"I have no doubt about that," Neo says, amusement lacing his voice. I narrow my eyes at him. What the fuck does he mean by that?

He just laughs harder at my glower and drops a kiss on the top of my head before taking off to start his work. I just stand there, eyes wide. Did he... did he just... kiss me? I'm in shock. I'm almost never in shock. If this fucker thinks that what happened last night changes anything, he's sorely mistaken.

"Umm…" I say, then turn back to the other two. They both have looks of surprise on their faces.

"Dude, better watch it before he gets his balls chopped off," Axel says, cringing and cups himself like he imagined it happening to him before he follows after Neo.

"Well, then. I'm heading over to Redemption to start the elimination process. Turns out the only woman in that club who doesn't agree to the new rules under my ownership is Dina. Surprise, surprise," I roll my eyes.

"So, you're really going to go with my suggestion?" Dean asks.

"Yeah, why not? It's actually a good name," I shrug.

"Glad I could help," he nods, then turns around to find something to clean, while trying to hide a smile.

"Hey," I shout. He stops and looks over his shoulder, his green eyes showing so many unsaid things, almost catching me off guard. "I'll be getting ready at your place tomorrow. Be ready by 6," I instruct.

He nods and walks away, and I find my eyes glued to his toned ass that looks especially biteable in his dress pants. I may not like the guy, but damn, I would sure love to watch him get on his knees and beg for his Queen.

Oh well, I plan on having my fun tomorrow night. He's not even gonna know what hit him.

DEAN

A DATE. Tonight, I am going on a date with Harlow McKaven...

I don't think I've ever really been on a date. I haven't felt the need to get to know a woman well enough to go on one. I find my release in professional escorts. Not exactly the most traditional way, but I never really had the time to go out and meet women like my cousins did while I was busy running the company. I could just be with a woman, no strings attached, who was prepared to take care of my sexual needs how I saw fit. I had a few regular women who would come to me, all for different desires and all tested, so I didn't have to worry about catching any diseases. A very controlled and convenient way to have sex. Now, I've had a few very long sexless months and ever-growing blue balls.

Honestly, I've never even had a girlfriend before. The only woman I ever wanted, I ever had feelings for, I sent away. I banished her from our lives in hopes of saving her from the dark and twisted world we were transitioning into, but instead I ended up pushing her deeper into the belly of the beast.

From the moment I found out what my actions caused, I've been beating myself up, making it easy to lose the control I thrive on in my everyday life.

She pushes me, taunts me, gets under my skin. At first, I hated this new Harlow. She wasn't the quiet, compliant woman we all fell in love with back then. That I fell in love with. Now, she's this wild, carefree, unhinged goddess.

As I get to know her better from afar, I am able to see that she has also become a strong, powerful, and loving woman. Sure, she's unpredictable and ruthless, but she's also... kind of fun.

I've been second guessing my way of life, my need for control as of late. Whenever I'm around her, I feel like it's okay to let go, to let loose, to just live in the moment, because you truly don't know if you will get a tomorrow. And that fucking terrifies me.

I'm slowly starting to fall for this new version of the love of my life, and I wasn't the least bit prepared for it.

She's a breath of fresh air that I didn't know I needed to take.

I want to let her in, I do, but I don't know how to. So, I just come off as this quiet asshole who doesn't seem to give a shit about anything.

Maybe this date is a blessing in disguise. Tonight, I will have to act like we really are a couple. Maybe a few hours of acting will loosen me the hell up.

I can't give up control, though. I'm not ready for that. It's going to take time, but I'm hoping she's the one who can help me do it, unlike the multitude of therapists who have tried before her.

Unfortunately, this new Harlow is a lot tougher, and it's gonna be a lot harder to get through her walls. I just hope someday I can make it up to her enough for her to give me a chance, or at least forgive me.

My cousins want her, though. Neo is madly in love with her, and Cass is quickly getting there too. Axel? I really don't know what he's thinking. He is obviously attracted to her, and I don't blame him. She is one of the most stunning women I've ever laid eyes on. It's her face I see whenever I close my eyes and wrap my hand around my cock. The amount of jacking off Axel and I have done since she banned us from sex is unhealthy.

Right now, I'm getting ready for what is technically my first date ever. But why do I feel like a nervous virgin? This isn't even a real date. This is business, nothing more to her.

But why do I feel like I wish it was?

I've picked out my nicest suit, a gray Brunello Cucinelli, with a pair of black Hugo Boss dress shoes.

I've slicked my dark brown hair back and trimmed my beard so that it's about half an inch from my face. For some reason, I'm set on looking my best tonight.

Harlow did have a point. This would be a good opportunity to build our reputation back up and make a few potential future business deals. At least that's the direction I'm trying to point my thoughts towards, instead of daydreaming about what Harlow is gonna look like tonight.

Giving myself a light spray of cologne, I head out of my room in search of my date. It's almost 6, so at least I'm not the one who's late.

When I get to the living room, the guys are all there, sitting around laughing. When Cass sees me, he lets out an appreciative whistle. “Looking good, cousin.”

Grinning, I shake my head. “It's not all that different from what I normally wear.”

“I don't know. You look like you’re trying to impress someone,” Axel chuckles. “I can smell you from here.”

My eyes widen slightly. “Is this too much?” I ask, feeling like I may have overdone it.

“Nah, man. You look good. You're fine.” Cass claps me on the back.

“I think you look stupid. You should just stay here, and I’ll even help you out by taking your place. I look better in a suit anyways,” Neo grumbles, bitter that Harlow didn't ask her little Pet to go with her.

“Oh, shut it, Neo,” Cass grins. “You’re just sour that she didn't ask you.”

“I should be the one going! I'M her bestie. I'M the one who rocks her fucking world with my amazing cock. But she chose YOU over ME, and she hates you?!” Neo continues to bitch.

I flinch slightly at his words. I know I'm not her favorite person, but does she really hate me? Of course, she does. I'm the reason she went through years of fucked up shit that no one should ever have to endure. She does spend a lot of time with Neo, though, and they have gotten closer. Did she say something to him about me?

Maybe I don't have a chance in hell at making amends. I just need to make her understand that I never meant for anything bad to happen to her. I just wanted her to be safe and happy. I thought she ended up with the money and took off to live a better life, without us. Oh, how fucking wrong I was.

“As much as I don't like the woman, she was right. You are the best person to go and represent Pentagon Industries. You’re the level-headed businessman,” Axel comments from his spot on the couch.

“Aww, I'm crushed. The big, bad grizzly bear doesn't like poor, little, old me? Whatever shall I do?” Harlow mocks in a fake southern accent, her voice filling the room.

Quickly, I turn around to look at her. Holy fuck. My knees just about buckle, forcing me to kneel before the Queen that she so clearly is.

She is stunning, standing there in a black, form fitting, V-neck dress that shows the tops of her perfect breasts. It hugs every curve in all the right places.

My cock swells at the sight of her and pulses excitedly when I see that the dress has a slit all the way up one side, stopping just at her hip bone. Fuck me… This is gonna be pure excruciating torture to try and keep my dick down all night. I know there's gonna be numerous times that I’ll be excusing myself before tonight is over.

Her makeup is done beautifully too, her luscious lips painted in blood-red lipstick. Her silky, long, black hair is styled in curls and pulled to the right side of her head, so the curls flow down onto the front of her chest.

“Fuuuuuck,” Neo groans, hopping up off the couch and rushing to Harlow's feet. He kneels down before her, holding his hands up in a pleading motion, and throws his head back to look at her.

"Please, Mistress. Please leave this dickhead behind and take me instead. Hell, let's just skip tonight, and you can let me worship every inch of your perfect body," he begs.

"You have got to be fucking kidding me. Neo, get the fuck off your knees! You look pathetic, begging for her. God, you really have lost it," Axel's voice interrupts.

Harlow's face held a humorous grin at Neo's antics, but the moment Axel becomes his normal dick of a self, her face changes to an eerie, deadly stare as she glares at Axel.

She pulls back the slit in her dress, showing a gun that I didn't see strapped to her thigh. Sue me, I had better things to gawk at.

"You are so lucky that Rosie is in the other room because I'm moments away from taking this gun and putting pretty, little holes in your foot. Don't. Test. Me," she warns, and I get a chill that tingles all the way down my spine. Part arousal, part fear.

Axel says nothing, looking like he regrets ever opening his mouth. He mumbles something to himself and storms out of the room.

"You look beautiful, Harlow," Cass says, his voice in awe. She gives him a genuine smile.

"Thank you, Cassy boy." Her deadly persona, now gone and replaced with her sugary sweet side. She looks down at Neo. "And, as for you. I'll deal with you later. I'm going with Dean, and you are staying behind. But expect a spanking for this little outburst later," Harlow says, but I can tell that she means it in a light-hearted way.

Neo clutches his hand to his heart and dramatically falls backwards to the ground. "You killed me, My Queen. I've died of blue balls. I'm so fucking turned on by the idea of your deadly hands on my ass that my dick and heart exploded in unison."

Harlow starts to giggle, real happiness shining in her eyes. Fuck. My heart flutters at how gorgeous she is right now. I can't believe this woman is my date.

"I thought you were going in a disguise?" Cass asks.

"I was, but then everyone already knows you guys are working for me so, why hide? Also, if they are guilty, I'm sure seeing me will make them sweat. Maybe even slip up." An evil grin takes over her face.

She steps over Neo and makes her way to me.

"Well, don't you clean up nice, Mr. Lean Mean Dean Machine," she taunts with a menacing grin as she brings up that god awful nickname, she used to call me when we were kids.

I groan and close my eyes. She's gonna make it her mission to torture me tonight. The question is, will I hate it? I'm guessing not as much as I would like to think.

She cackles as she takes off for the garage door, leaving me with a view of her ass in that dress.

I bite my hand, holding back a groan. Fuck me. This is gonna be a long night.

CHAPTER TWENTY-SIX

DEAN

THE CAR ride here was... interesting. Harlow really has a thing for car tunes. She turned the radio to an all 90s station and was singing '*Wannabe*' and '*Stop*' by The Spice Girls from the top of her lungs.

It took everything in me to hold back the grin that kept threatening to take over my face. It was like a flashback to the past. That was the Harlow I knew and loved, once upon a time. It's nice to see she's not fully gone.

When we get to the Embassy Hotel, where the event is being held, we pull up to the front entrance.

"Um, don't we need to park?" Harlow asks, looking out the window.

I chuckle. "Not at places like this; you do know what a valet is, right?"

She narrows her eyes at me in annoyance. "Of course, I do," she sasses. "Just never been to a place that had them," she mutters under her breath, then blows a bubble with the gum she's been chewing. “Come on, let's get this show on the road.”

We get out of the car as the valet greets us at the curb. “Good evening, Sir. Shall I park this for you?” the man asks.

“Dude, what are we in a 50s movie? No need to sound like some fancy British dude,” Harlow says, eyeing the man up like she already has reasons to be suspicious of the guy.

The guy looks at her warily, “Umm… I am British, Ma’am.”

“Oh, well, cool accent. Would be hotter if you were twenty years younger and naked,” she smiles sweetly. So, this is what we have to expect when we go out in public with her? God, this is gonna get embarrassing fast. I knew the woman spoke her mind, but this is a little much.

Harlow takes out her gum. “This has lost its flavor,” she says, looking around for a place to dispose of it.

The man holds his hand out for my keys, but before I get the chance to place them in his palm, Harlow smashes her chewed gum into his hand. The man's eyes go wide as he stares at her in horror.

“Here, get rid of this for me, will ya?” she asks, patting the guy on the back as she passes him and struts her way to the front door.

“I am so sorry about her,” I say, pulling out my handkerchief from my pocket. “Here, I’ll take that,” I say, grabbing the gum from his hand. She really has a “gives zero fucks” personality. “She’s not really the best at social situations. She spends most of her time at her club, Evolution, so she doesn't get out much." Except when it's to find people to kill.

The man's eyes go wide again, and this time it's in fear. He looks behind him at Harlow's retreating back, then to me. "Is that... Queenie?"

"So, you've heard of her," I sigh.

"You know what, Sir, I'll take that," he says, quickly taking the handkerchief. "And I'll be sure to get this cleaned and sent back to you as soon as possible. At the latest, you will have it before you leave for the evening."

"That's okay. Just toss it," I say. I mean, it was 50 bucks, but I'm not attached to it.

"Nonsense. And I'll take these too," he says, taking the keys from my hand. "I'll take the utmost care of your vehicle, Sir. Have a good night," he says, then rushes to get into the front seat of my car, starting it up, and takes off.

We just got here, and already I know this night is far from over.

We've been here for about an hour, and Harlow seems to be doing better, not too many rude comments. She's actually been really quiet, clearly concentrating on listening to everyone else's conversations. It doesn't seem like anyone has realized who she is yet, because no one looks ready to shit their pants.

"Oh, oh, look, there they are!" Harlow says with glee. In walk five men of various ages, all in tuxedos. As they make their way through the crowd, people around them wave and greet them.

"That's the Council of Dipshits," Harlow says, rolling her eyes as the men walk in like they own the place.

"So how exactly do you know them? You don't really talk to us about much, other than Rosie and things currently going on in the club. We don't know all that much about the past eight years of your life," I say, taking a bite of a pastry I just snagged from the table of desserts. We found a spot against the wall and have been standing here, eavesdropping on people who see us as invisible because they don't know who we are and don't feel the need to interact with us.

So far, I found out that one man is sleeping with his business partner, who is also of the male gender, and then later found out that the man's wife is also sleeping with that very same man.

I've also had the privilege of knowing that some stuffy, old lady thinks it's appalling that gay people can get married now. What a fucking bitch.

But nothing even close to what we need.

"Well, you don't really have the right to know anything I don't want to tell you," Harlow says and cocks a brow, bringing me back to our conversation.

"True, but can you at least tell me exactly who these men are and how you know them?" She mentioned something before, but it wasn't enough to give me an idea of the situation we are walking into.

"Fine," she sighs dramatically, looks around, and lowers her voice, leaning in so that her arm is touching mine. I can feel the heat of her bare arm and have a direct view down her dress, giving me a better look at the curve of her breasts. My cock starts to stir again, and I mentally tell it to chill the fuck out before I give this woman a reason to embarrass me more.

"So, the night that the girls and I made it out of the club and started over was also the night that some of society's elites lost their lives. Most of the men who, you know, went up in flames like a couple of burnt marshmallows, well, they were all the owners of multi-million, some even multi-billion, dollar companies. Which is when I found myself with an opportunity to pick who would be in charge and take over said companies. I wanted to make sure that they played by my rules and did not become what the people before them were. At the time, they all seemed like reliable businessmen who just wanted what was best for the company they worked for; to do good in life and do good by their families. None of them had any criminal history and seemed like a perfect fit at the time. Guess I was wrong. I might not have any proof. But seeing Dick," she points to an older gentleman with salt and pepper hair and beard, "With that cunt face in the security video makes all this fishy. Reeks of twenty-day old tuna left out in the sun if you ask me."

I grimace at her words. Nasty.

"Anyways, so yeah. There seems to be a lot I don't know about these guys, but I can't find anything on paper to nail them. It makes me feel all stabby," she grumbles, her eyes never leaving the men. They move to a table on the far side of the room where some really tall plants stand. They really don't go with the rest of the decor.

"I'm gonna go all Nancy Drew and see what I can find out on a solo mission. You schmooze with the rich farts here. Make friends, but play nice," she winks, then takes off, leaving me standing there by myself. God, she's an oddball. One of the things I loved about her when we were kids. She never tried to change herself to fit in with others. She was always a "take me as I am" kind of person.

"Dean Beckett, is that you?" a vaguely familiar man says, getting my attention.

"Yes?" I ask with caution.

"Leonard Pinkson," he says, holding out his hand. "I met you a few times back when I did business with your father and uncles."

"Oh."

"I haven't seen you at one of these parties in a while."

"Well, when the owners of the company you're set to inherit decided to bankrupt it and damage its reputation by stealing from everyone they're doing business with, it doesn't leave you with too many friends," I shrug, looking around but I can't find Harlow anywhere.

He gives me an understanding chuckle. "What brings you here tonight?"

"Hoping to start afresh. My cousins and I have been working hard to get our company back to its former glory, minus the corruption."

"I like the sound of that. Come talk to a few buddies of mine; let's see what we can do for you." Looking back at Leonard, I'm stunned. May as well take the opportunity if it presents itself to me.

I spend a good half hour talking about business opportunities, and although we are nowhere near ready to start the company back up, I may take these men up on their offers.

Saying my goodbyes, I step away from the group; my eyes search for Harlow, finding her by the buffet table stuffing her pretty face.

That woman has curves in all the right places, but I don't get how she's that size when she eats like a man who hasn't seen a meal in weeks.

I wanna look away, but I can't.

I start heading over to her when I see her struggling to get the cork out of a bottle of wine with a corkscrew. She looks so cute with her tongue sticking out in concentration as she pulls. With one more big tug, the cork pops off with force, flying through the air, just grazing the top of a man's head, taking his toupee with it.

I stop, just standing there watching with my mouth parted as everything unfolds. Harlow stands there, clamping her lips shut to keep herself from laughing, but when the man turns around to look at her, grasping at the bald spot on his head with absolute horror in his eyes, she lets the giggles bubble out.

She gives him a shameless shrug and takes a big swig of her wine, straight from the bottle. You really can't take this woman anywhere nice.

I'm almost to Harlow when a woman steps up to her. "I believe this belongs to you," she snarks.

Harlow wipes her mouth with the back of her hand and looks at the woman, then down to the champagne glass she's holding out.

"Oh, thanks," Harlow says, taking the glass from the woman, sticking her hand into the glass, fishing out the cork, and chucking it blindly behind her, hitting someone else in the head with it, then downs the entire glass of champagne. "Damn, this shit's good."

The woman scrunches up her face in disgust and huffs at Harlow, "You are a very uncivilized young lady. You really ought to get a little class."

Harlow gives her one of her signature Cheshire cat smiles. "Well, maybe you can help me find some, or maybe I can just put a bullet between your pretty hazel eyes," Harlow coos, lifting the slit in her dress to the side, exposing the gun strapped to her thigh.

The woman pales and swallows hard. "Who do you think you are? Coming in here, behaving like some common street criminal?" the woman asks, her voice shaky with fear.

Harlow's smile slips, and in its place is a look that would have grown men begging for their lives, as she steps close to the woman, getting in her personal space. "I think I'm the mother fucking Queen. So, how about you learn a little bit of respect while you're still breathing."

A man rushes over to the woman's side, panic and fear radiating off him. He leans in to whisper into her ear and I watch her face slip into one that matches his. She swallows hard.

"My apologies, Queenie. I... I didn't know it was you," she stammers out an apology.

"You're lucky I'm not done with this party yet. I don't put up with that kind of shit from anyone, and not from some dusty, old cunt like you. Now get the fuck out of my face."

The woman and man get away as fast as they can, and Harlow watches them go with a big grin. It grows even bigger when she sees me.

"That was fun," she says, giggling. "I should come to these things more often."

I can't help but grin. "They definitely wouldn't be boring with you around."

"Never," she beams.

"So, how did it go? Get anything good?" I ask. Her face drops.

"No," she grumbles. "All they fucking talked about was golf." She rolls her eyes.

"Did you want to go?" I ask.

"Well, how did you make out?" she asks, brushing off my question while putting the bottle of wine on the table and sweeping some of her black curls away from her face.

"Not bad, actually. May even have some potential business opportunities with a few of these companies."

"Nice!" she smiles again, nodding her head appreciatively. "Well, the night is still young, and so are we. Let's mingle and see if we can make a good name for you. I'll be good, I promise," she winks.

"Really, now?" I smirk, and she just shrugs. She slips her arm into mine and drags me off.

We spent the next little while talking to most of the people here; everyone but the men she wanted information about. At some point, they noticed Harlow was here and some even had nervous looks on their faces. Some may think it's due to a guilty conscience or in fear of being exposed.

There was a moment when I had to excuse myself to the bathroom and rub one out, because the amount of touching she was doing caused all of my blood to rush right to my dick. After that, when it happened yet again, I just tucked my dick into the waistband of my pants. There was no ridding me of this guy right now.

She laughed as she told everyone nothing but good things about my cousins and me. She would pet my chest and squeeze my arm; a few times she even placed her head on my arm.

How can such simple things have this much of an effect on me? I know it's all for show. Deep down she hates me, only putting on a show and playing nice for Rosie's sake. But her act is anything but nice tonight. It's pure fucking torture and is testing every ounce of my needed control.

She makes me feel things. Things I've never felt about anyone before. I don't know how to handle this. Knowing she won't ever feel the same things I do, makes me feel even more out of control.

My cell phone goes off, and Harlow looks at me in question, interrupting the conversation she was having. I shrug and step to the side to take the call.

"Hello," I answer.

"Put Harlow on," Evie says as her greeting.

Without another word, I hold the phone out, wordlessly telling Harlow it's for her. She wraps up her conversation and makes her way over.

"It's Evie," I explain when she cocks a brow in question. She snatches the phone from me.

"E?" Harlow answers. I look between Harlow and the councilmen as she talks to Evie. Harlow doesn't say much, just cursing at whatever Evie is telling her. The men watch her with wary eyes, but I can see them trying hard to hide it.

"Fuck," Harlow hisses. "Another girl."

"Shit," I sigh, running my hand through my hair.

"I need to get out of here and cool down before I take this motherfucking gun and shoot all of the fat fuckers point-blank right here in front of hundreds of witnesses," she growls.

"Might be a good idea. I can drop you off at the club if you want," I tell her. "I need to head over to our downtown office building. There's a few old files there that might help with some business dealings that these guys have been going on about."

"Your building isn't too far from the beach, drop me there. I'll take a walk, maybe dip my feet in the water, and meet you at your office in an hour."

I pace around my office like a caged animal as I try to get myself under control. I have a raging boner that won't go away. I've masturbated three times now, and it won't fucking go down. I'm slowly going out of my fucking mind! I can't get her out of my head.

I knew I was falling for her again. Back then, she was the person I pictured in my mind every night when I took care of my aching cock.

But spending this much time alone with her, laughing and talking as if we were a couple, with her touches and caresses all night... I can't take it anymore! My hand isn't doing the trick.

Picking up my phone, I dial a number I haven't called in a while. I just don't have it in me anymore to keep going on like this. I thought I was stronger, I thought I could abide by her rules, but I can't.

I'm not some sex-crazed addict, but I used to have a routine. Anytime something happened that I couldn't control or when I was too stressed because of work, I would call in a girl to come take my mind off everything. To get rid of the pent-up energy, and clear my mind so that I could find a solution to my problem.

The problem is that I haven't been able to do that for months, and tonight is my breaking point.

I can't go the rest of my fucking life without sex. I can't just live off having my hand do the job, especially since it's not doing anything for me anymore. It's not possible.

I'm a fucking fool to even think for a moment that I stand a chance with Harlow. I ruined her life, no matter how good my intentions may have been back then. They led her to be homeless, kidnapped, and raped for years.

My mind can't shut down, and I feel like I'm slowly losing it. I need something, anything.

"Hello. Finding Pleasure Escort Service. How may I help you?" a woman answers after a few rings.

"Hi. Dean Beckett here. I'll be needing Cindy over here as soon as possible. I'll pay extra if she can be here within 10 minutes," I say, my voice tight and my stomach uneasy at what I'm about to do, but I'm desperate.

"Oh, Mr. Beckett. So lovely to hear from you again. It's been a while."

"Yes. Life has been busy. Please send her to my office like always," I ask, growing impatient. My foot taps rapidly as I sit at my desk, trying to keep calm.

"She lives nearby. I can have her over in five."

"Perfect. Thank you." I hang up my phone and stand up to pace again. I lose my tie, needing to get it off. I feel like I'm being strangled.

Sweat starts to drip down my spine and bead on my hairline. Fuck, why is it so hot in here? I take my suit jacket off and toss it over the couch in my office.

A few minutes later, there's a buzz from the main door. I let Cindy in. After a few moments, I hear a knock on my office door.

"Come in," I command, and she obeys. Cindy is a tall, pretty lady with red, curly hair. I've never had an overwhelming attraction to her, but she's good at what she does.

"Hello, Dean. I was starting to think you forgot about me," she purrs.

No. This isn't like how it normally is. I don't have time for her flirting. I need this now. Hard and fast before my brain can tell me to smarten the hell up.

"No. Life has been keeping me busy. Look, I don't mean to sound like an asshole, but I really just need you to take care of this," I say, pointing to my never-ending boner. "I'll pay you extra for getting here as fast as you did."

"Okay. I can do that," she shrugs, stalking toward me. She wastes no time dropping to her knees and unzipping my pants. She takes out my thick cock and licks her lips.

"This is gonna be hard and fast." I know she likes it rough, so there are no complaints from her.

She wraps her lips around my cock, and I moan at the contact. It's been so long since I've felt the heat of another; the wetness of someone's mouth.

I grip a large chunk of her hair, holding her in place, then I try with everything I have to purge these urges. To use her mouth to try and fuck all of my thoughts of Harlow out of my head.

Tossing my head back, I try to concentrate on the feeling. Thrusting my hips ruthlessly as I continue to hit the back of her throat, making her take my whole cock.

I don't stop when she gags.

I don't stop when the saliva pours out of her mouth from not being able to swallow.

I don't stop until Harlow's face flashes behind my closed eyes and I cum hard down Cindy's throat, moaning Harlow's name.

I'm ruined. She's embedded herself into my subconscious, my heart, and my soul. She owns me, even as some other woman sucks my cock.

My life is no longer my own. She owns that too.

I'm ruined, and I don't know if I'll make it to the other end alive.

CHAPTER TWENTY-SEVEN

Harlow

FUCKING BULLSHIT if you ask me. When Evie called, I rushed right over, unable to enjoy any walk on the beach I was planning on having. This is me we are talking about; I can't just sit back and do nothing. I called Miller after Evie showed me the most recent news report. He told me that the girl went missing the night before I took ownership of the Rack Shack.

I was one day too fucking late! And it cost me another girl. Not one of mine, no, but that doesn't mean that the young lady's life isn't just as important.

I asked Miller if anyone else has been reported missing, and he said no. That this girl was the last one for now.

Ever since the moment I took over the club, no more girls have gone missing, which is too much of a coincidence if you ask me. It's been a few months, with ten girls missing in total, which means that one girl has gone missing almost every week.

I need to stop beating myself up because if that's the case, I've saved at least two girls and possibly hundreds more.

After finding nothing useful on the club security cameras, I take off. Dean is waiting for me at his office, and a part of me is anxious to get back to him.

Maybe he can take that walk with me, and we can finish the night with a nice ending. Surprisingly, I was having a really good time.

I mean, yes, I was being all touchy-feely with Dean, but that was just for my enjoyment. It's fun to mess with him. I don't know who he was trying to fool, but I know when he went to the washroom to spank the monkey. I felt powerful to have that effect on him.

For a while, I thought he was some alpha asshole. He never talks much and always has a resting bitch face on, but tonight he just did what I asked with little to no complaints. Unlike his meathead of a cousin, Axel.

After spending time with him tonight, as well as seeing how he's acted with the guys and Rosie whenever I am at their place, I'm coming to realize there is a whole lot more to Dean Beckett than what meets the eye; he just hides it well.

Turns out he's not all that bad of a guy. A little too much of a robot personality, but I can loosen him up. No one can resist my charm and award-winning smile for long.

Life's too short to hold on to hate. Well, hate on people who don't deserve it. I've allowed what Dean did to hold too much power over me, and I didn't even know until I started to slowly change my opinion of him.

In the end, yes, I ended up in a horrendous life, but there was no way he could have known that. He thought the fucker they hired to bring me money did his job, and that I was living a decent life somewhere. So, should I hold this against him for the rest of his life? Can I? No, I don't forgive him. But I'm done hating him when there are plenty of other people who deserve my hate. Plus, he's not being a butt munch, so brownie points for him.

When I get to his building, I head to the elevator, punch in the code, and press 10 to get to his floor. I can't help but hold my breath the whole ride up.

I hate elevators.

Every time I'm in one, the image of Triver right before the doors closed flashes through my mind, and I can hear the faint sounds of gunshots from when I shot and killed him, letting the fire rid his body from this world.

When I get to the floor, the elevator door dings, and I shake my head, bringing myself back to reality.

I've never been to their office before, so I don't know what room is his, but considering he's the only one on this floor, it should be whatever one has the lights on.

I walk down the hall, looking around to find the right one, when I hear noises coming from down the hall. As I get closer, my ears are met with moans and choking.

What the fuck is going on?!

Fury fills my veins at what I'm about to walk in on.

When I get to the door with the lights, I crack it open to see Dean standing in the middle of his office, his face contorted in pain and pleasure as some bitch on her knees gags on his cock.

My hand wraps around the handle of my gun. I'm ready to fucking murder them both. How dare he disobey me?! How dare he go behind my back. Has he been doing this the whole time right under my nose?

Just as I flick the safety off, ready to put a bullet in someone's brain, Dean lets out a groan as he cums down the chick's throat. Moaning my name.

I'm stunned momentarily.

Why the hell is he thinking of me while this chick's lips are wrapped around his cock? I thought he hated me. I mean, sure, I'm hot enough for spank bank material, but I didn't know he would go as far as think of me while doing shit like this with another woman.

“Bravo. What a show,” I say, kicking in the door, aiming the gun in their direction, unsure who I wanna shoot first.

Dean's eyes snap open. With wide eyes, he gawks at me, frozen in place with a look of pure fear and shame.

The chick on her knees releases his cock with a pop and wipes her lips with the back of her hand.

That does it.

“I hope you said your piece to whoever is important to you, because tonight you fucking die!” I laugh like a person fresh out of the loony bin. I'm vibrating with anger. This isn't like me. I'm normally level-headed and rational when I kill. Sure, I'm not really all there in those moments, but I never do something that would get me caught or cloud my judgment. Not when killing, it's too risky.

"Queenie. Please, don't kill her. This isn't her fault, she didn't know. This is all me," he says, holding his hands out like you do when dealing with a wild animal.

I mean, he's not really that far off. I'm sure the look in my eyes is pretty feral.

But he does have a point. From what I know, Dean only does things with a paid woman; they are just doing their job and don't deserve to die over it because this fucktard screwed up.

"Get out," I growl at the woman, and she quickly scrambles to her feet, crying now, clearly knowing I'm not bluffing. She goes to race out of the office, but I stop her before she gets out the door. "Let all the women in your company know that Dean Beckett and his cousins are no longer customers. They are MINE. Don't fuck with the Queen if you don't want to fucking die!" I don't know if the other guys have ever used this service before, but a warning doesn't hurt.

She nods her head, sobbing, and I push her out the door.

Slamming the door shut, I lock it and spin around back to Dean, finding him tucking his cock back in his pants, but he does not take his eyes off me, knowing that could be a big mistake on his part.

"I'm sorry, Harlow. I'm so fucking sorry," he croaks, his voice breaking with emotion. "Fuck. FUCK!" he screams. He grips handfuls of his hair and starts pacing.

Wow... Okay, how do I go all crazy bitch on his ass when he looks this destroyed. This is not the Dean I know. He's finally lost it, like full on Humpty Dumpty cracked. From the moment he came into my life again, I made it my mission to watch him slowly lose control, but I had no idea I'd feel this way when he finally did.

"Gah," he shouts, punching a hole in the wall. "I just couldn't take it anymore! I've never felt so out of control in my life. You drive me insane; you make me want to rip my fucking hair out. Yet for some reason, you're all I can think about," he lets out a laugh like he's the one who's crazy.

I just stand there, stunned at his outburst, and let him continue, but I don't lower my gun.

"I tried. I really tried. But come on! Do you know how cruel it is to just ban us from sex because you can? Because you want to control us. I get you want revenge, and we deserve everything you throw at us, but fuck! If you don't want us in that way, then why not let us have someone else?" He's breathing hard, his chest heaving.

Why was I doing this to them? At first, it was just to fuck with them. I was doing it to watch them suffer, but over time, it became more. They are mine, and the idea of someone else having their hands on them makes me want to shoot someone until they look like a piece of Swiss cheese.

Fuck. Fuckity fuck. I'm starting to... like them. Ah, hell. Maybe I should just take the gun and shoot myself in the head; it would keep me from having to deal with the shit show that is my heart and brain battling to the death right now.

Okay, maybe not Axel. I just enjoy watching him suffer. The fucker has been nothing but a grade A asshole, but Dean, Cass, and Neo? They haven't. Sure, the other two have behaved a hell of a lot better than Dean, but still.

"I just needed to clear my head. And I can't do that with you invading it every second of every day. I haven't felt this out of control since we were kids. Back when every time you walked into a room, my brain would go blank, and my heart would threaten to break out of my fucking chest. I just needed to get rid of this motherfucking boner!" he shouts.

I can't help it. I giggle. I know, not the right time, but how he yelled boner was just too funny.

He stops pacing and looks at me with shock, making me laugh harder.

"What's so funny?" he growls. Oooh, he's extra spicy right now, but he's having a meltdown, so I'll let it slide... for now.

I just shrug, not really having an answer.

"Is it the fact that you're the only one who can make me lose it like this? That this new version of you is making me feel things that I used to feel about you when we were kids? Or is it just because you like to see me suffer? Dammit, Harlow, I don't know what to do anymore. I need control. But I can't find it anymore." He looks lost, broken, and destroyed. All because of me. I know I shouldn't feel bad, not after everything he caused in my life, but my stupid, newly developed heart does.

I blame Rosie and all her awesomeness for this.

With my need to help him find control again, I do something I have never done before. I offer to give up some of mine.

“Take it back,” I tell him, putting the safety of the gun back on and placing it on the table by the door.

“What?” he asks, face contorted in confusion.

“I said take it back. Your control. Take it.” I stalk towards him, slipping the straps off my body and shimmying out of my dress.

The dress didn't need a bra, so now I stand there in nothing but a pair of lace panties.

His eyes switch from feral panic and fear to pure lust. His eyes devour my naked body as I slip out of my panties. He’s seen me naked before, but this is different. This is me offering myself to him, to only him. Something you can see in his eyes that he's been desperately wanting, needing for a very long time.

I know what I'm doing, and I’ve officially gone full cuckoo bird to allow this, but that's just it. I'm choosing this. I'm giving him the illusion that he's in control, when really, I am because I'm allowing him to do this to me. But fuck if my heart isn’t about to flat line from how overworked it is right now.

The idea of him fucking me, taking me, which is something he desperately wants and apparently is making him go insane without, is a major turn on. My thighs grow wetter with each passing second. I’ve never willingly allowed someone to take control with sex. Yes, Neo grips my hips, bends me over shit, and fucks the life out of me, but I know this won't be the same.

Deep down, I want this. I want to help him.

He keeps staring at me like if he blinks, all of this will disappear, and it would have only been a dream.

I hop up on his desk, lean back on my arms, and open my legs for him, putting my dripping pussy on display for him.

The way he looks at me makes me feel so fucking powerful, settling some of the unease I have about doing this.

He slowly walks towards me until he's standing in front of me. He forces his eyes off my center, to my breasts, then finally my eyes.

“I'm offering myself to you, Dean, and if you don't take what you need from me in the next minute, this offer is gonna expire, and you won't get another one,” I smirk.

He looks at me skeptically. “This isn't some ruse to get me to touch you so that you have a reason to kick my ass, is it?”

“No,” I giggle. “Look. Don't overthink it. I have no idea what's come over me, but do you really want to pass up this chance to fuck me? Because I'm pretty sure it was my name you were moaning before as you came.”

He takes a moment, debating his next move before stepping between my legs and taking his cock out again. I don't think the damn thing had gone fully down yet. “What can I do to you?” he asks, still not sure what I'll allow.

“Anything you want, but I only ask you to let me know beforehand.”

He nods his head in agreement. He understands that this is big for me to offer anyone something like this.

"I want to taste you," he whispers, looking back at my pussy.

"So have a lick," I taunt, widening my legs further.

He drops to his knees as I lay back and wait. Then I feel something press against my clit, causing me to gasp. "God, you smell amazing," he groans, inhaling my scent. I never got why guys smell a woman's vagina like they're doing a line of coke. I can't imagine they smell very nice.

He grips my hips and licks me from bottom to top before going to town on my clit. Fuck, his tongue is amazing. I haven't been eaten out in years; it's just not something I did with my relievers. Neo has been bugging me to do it, and maybe now I'll let him because fuck, this feels amazing.

He growls against my pussy as he licks, sucks, and nips at my clit.

I moan, rocking my hips as I grip his hair, forcing him in place. He doesn't stop me, letting out a moan of his own as I rock my pussy into his face.

He inserts two large fingers into my cunt, hooking me in just the right spot.

I'm worked up over everything that has happened tonight, and I'm desperate for my own release to get rid of this extra energy, so it doesn't take me long to cum.

After a few more pumps of his fingers and sucks of my clit, I clamp my legs around his head, crushing him to my pussy, probably smothering him. But I don't give a fuck; I ride his face as I scream out my release, enjoying every twitch, flush, and tingle.

When I'm done, I release him from my death grip.

He rises to his feet with a look of awe on his face. “You have no idea how many times I’ve jacked off to the thought of my face buried between your sinful legs.”

“Well, thank you for thinking of me while you're alone,” I wink. “I hope this was better than whatever you conjured up in that brain of yours.”

“So much better,” he grins. “I need to fuck you now, please,” he begs.

He grabs a hold of his cock, ready to put it to use, but then I remember something. “Wait!” I hold up my hand. “This is probably gonna ruin the moment, although something tells me we will both recover from that fast, but you just had some call-girl’s mouth on your cock. You're not sticking that in me. So go clean it.”

His eyes widen, looking from his cock, then back to me. “Fuck! I'm sorry. I wasn’t thinking,” he apologizes sheepishly, and it’s fucking adorable.

Using the sink in his office, he takes the bar of soap from the dish next to it and scrubs his cock good, hissing at the obvious pleasure he's getting from it.

I should be turned off by the fact that he was just with someone else, but the need to wipe her from his mind takes over all my senses. I want to be the last and only one to touch his cock. I want him to fuck me so good that I ruin him for anyone else.

I should hate him. I should want to slice his fucking dick off... but I don't. I don't forgive the fucker. Not by a long shot, but I mean, it is cruel to cut him off from sex with anyone for forever, so if he needs to find release, why not take advantage of the situation and get myself a few orgasms out of it.

With Neo, he craves to be dominated, but this is a nice change. I didn't think I would enjoy this so much after years of being forced... actually let's call it what it is, raped. After years of being raped. But the way he looks at me, this isn't the Dean I'm used to. He looks at me like I'm the most precious thing in the world, like I'm some rare find. I feel sexy right now, naked with my legs open and waiting for him. On the other hand, all the feels are making me ready to bolt.

I keep reminding myself that I'm the one who is really in control by giving him this, and there's the fact that I'm currently being fueled by jealous rage. I might look calm on the outside, but trust me, it's taking everything in me not to grab that gun and shoot him in the fucking leg for allowing some bitch to touch him when he is MINE. Oh, and I'm really fucking horny.

At first, my plan was to get him all hot and bothered and watch him suffer, but in reality, I've been drenched most of the night.

He looks fucking amazing in a suit, his muscles bulging out of his tight dress shirt right now. He's tall, dark, and handsome for sure. With his dark brown hair and perfect beard that is currently soaked in my juices. My pussy clenches at the thought that I've marked him with my scent.

All his rage is gone now. He looks really cute and awkward, walking back over here with his cock still out and bobbing with every step. I can't help but giggle.

"What's so funny this time?" he grins as he steps between my legs again. He rubs my thighs as his eyes roam over my body. "Fuck. You're perfect," he whispers.

I get this fluttery feeling in my belly. No! This is only meant to be about control and sex. He shouldn't be able to make me feel like a giddy schoolgirl. It's already bad enough that Neo is breaking down my walls, and Cass is not far behind him. I can't let this happen. Especially, with Dean!

This needs to be about only sex. The best they will get from me is friendship, even if my stupid traitorous heart seems to be wanting more.

I thought we had a deal? We locked that shit down years ago to avoid being destroyed again, but here you are, breaking that contract. Dumb bitch.

"Fuck me, Dean," I demand. I can't keep playing this game, he needs to know that I'm still in control, even if I'm allowing him a little of his own. "This is a one-time offer. After this, you're going to need to learn to let me take control if you want any sex. I'm offering you me as your release, but under my rules. This might be only sex between us, but I am in charge, always." His face drops, and I don't know if it's from the part where I said this is a one-time thing of him taking me like this, or the only sex between us part. Am I being a bitch right now? Probably. Do I care? A little. Am I gonna change my mind? No, because I'm stubborn, and I won't and can't admit to myself that these guys who once owned my heart may still have a piece of it.

I may have only dated Cass, but I was just as crazy about the others as I was him.

“Harlow,” he says, stopping just as he places the tip of his cock at my entrance. My eyes find his as I lay back and wait to be fucked within an inch of my life. “I'm sorry,” he whispers. “About everything. I loved you so much that I was willing to lose you if it meant you had a better chance at a good life. And all I did was make it worse. I hate myself every day for what I did.” His voice is filled with so much pain and regret that my breath catches. Before I can tell him to go fuck himself for making me feel anything for him, he grips my hip and thrusts his cock all the way in.

“God!” I scream, tossing my head back, and arching towards him.

Dean chuckles, the sound sending shock waves right to my clit. “Nah, sweetheart, I’m no god, but I can fuck like one.”

Dean pounds into me, letting out groans and curses. The force moves the desk with every thrust. My tits sway, and my pussy throbs. Fuck, his cock feels amazing. Thank god that all of them are big because I love a good sting with my fucks. Pain and pleasure go hand in hand for me.

My brain is hyper focused on everything this man is doing to my body. I thought about this moment for years when I was younger.

The feeling of his thick cock sliding in and out of my tight, soaked pussy. His strong hands gripping my hips, holding me in place as he fucks me like an animal. Wild.

It doesn't take me long before my belly fills with heat and my inner walls quiver around his cock.

"Fuck. Oh god, fuck!" I cry before gripping his dick like a fucking boa constrictor; I cum so fucking hard that I squirt all over his cock until it's soaking both our thighs.

"So fucking sexy," he groans, watching me with fascination as I shake out my release.

When I come down from my high, I find Dean still hungry as ever for my body. For more.

"Get up and turn around. I want to take you from behind," he demands. I cock a brow and give him an 'are you shitting me' look. "Please?" he adds.

I roll my eyes, but do as he asks. I mean, he did say please, so it lessened the demand.

I thrust my ass out to him, and I hear him groan. Looking back over my shoulder, I find him eyeing up my round cheeks. "You have no idea how much I want to bury my face between these cheeks, to bite them and leave my mark."

"Not today," I warn, his eyes snap up to mine. "Don't think you're an exception to my three-orgasm rule. Get to work," I say, wiggling my ass and taunting him to continue.

He growls then slaps my ass, as he goes to enter me. My head snaps back to him with murder in my eyes. His go wide with fear. "I'm so fucking sorry. I don't know what came over me." I can tell his natural dominant personality is still hovering on the surface, so I let it go.

"Fuck. Me. Now. Before I take what I want." I don't mean it. I'd never force myself on anyone. But something tells me he would not be opposed to me going all Yankee Doodle on his ass and riding him like a pony.

He doesn't argue with me, just grips my hips, entering me again. I moan as he slides back into my slick pussy.

He fucks me hard and fast like before, and I feel his hand graze the top of my head like he's debating on grabbing my hair, but retracts his hand. I love my hair being pulled. I love the pain, as long as it's not a man doing it to force my mouth on his cock.

I reach back and grab both of his hands, standing up a little, so he can have better access. I bring one hand to the back of my head, and the other to my breast.

"Do it, Dean. Give me a little pain with my pleasure," I purr.

His fingers thread through my hair, getting a good grip. The other hand kneading my breast and pulling at my nipple. I moan as he starts to work me into another orgasm.

He's spewing all these dirty words under his breath. I don't think he knows I can hear him over my own sounds, but fuck, his words make me even wetter.

He ruts into me like a wild animal. One of my hands is holding me up on the desk, and the other I slip between my drenched thighs. I find my swollen clit, throbbing with need, demanding attention. As soon as I start to rub my oversensitive bud, I feel another orgasm coming on fast. With a few more flicks, I'm done. My back bows and I thrust my ass into him. A scream rips from my throat as I cum, flooding his cock again. My knees almost give out, but his arm comes around my waist as he keeps fucking me.

"Fuck. I don't... I don't think-" he struggles to get words out through his gritted teeth, his hips smashing into my ass. "I don't think I can last. Oh fuck!" he groans, before biting my fucking shoulder, as he cums hard and deep into my pussy. The feeling of his hot cum mixed with the pain of his bite sends me into another climax.

I collapse over his desk, breathing like I'm dying. He leans over me, his forehead to my back.

"Thank you," is all he says, before kissing my back. Why! Why does he have to go and ruin it by being all... sweet? Ugh!

He pulls out of me and falls back into his chair. Cum starts to drip down my thighs and onto the carpet, but I don't give a fuck.

Standing up, I turn around and hop up on his desk. His eyes devour my sweat coated body down to the puddle of our combined juices on his desk. Again, no fucks are given at this moment.

"Well, that was... fun," I grin.

His eyes go wide. "F-fun!" he sputters in disbelief. "That was better than just fun," he scoffs, making me giggle. "Don't try and act like I didn't just rock your whole fucking world. Because you sure as fuck rocked mine."

I just grin harder, giving him a shrug, making him narrow his eyes at me, sending me into a fit of giggles.

"Fine, it was a lot of fun," I tease, walking over to grab my discarded dress from the floor and slipping it on, then I turn back to him.

"What just happened stays between us. I like what I have with Neo, and I'm starting to think Cass might be into being dominated soon. So, I don't need them thinking I'm going soft and that they can have any control."

He smiles and nods.

"Also, this," I say, pointing between me and him. "Not gonna happen again. Well, at least not like this... any time soon." He just grins harder like I'm full of shit.

"Don't look at me like that!" I snap. "And don't think you're getting off with that little stunt you pulled tonight. You're being punished. I think a nice, thick dildo up your ass will do the trick."

His eyes go wide. "You can't be serious," he protests.

"Nah, I'm just fucking with you," I giggle.

"Thank god," he breathes.

"But you still need to be punished. Hope you don't hate me too much after this."

"Huh?" His brows pinch in confusion.

In one fluid motion, I snatch my gun off the table and shoot him in the shoulder. He lets out a scream. "Oh, come on now, you big baby, I didn't hit anything important. But hopefully, this will teach you not to disobey my orders. Like you think I would just let you get away with you having your cock down some bitch's throat." I laugh and shake my head. "You might wanna go to the ER right away. You're bleeding a little."

"You think?!" he shouts, hissing in pain as he holds his hand to the bleeding wound.

"Well, good luck with that!" I chirp.

"You're not seriously leaving me here bleeding, are you?" he cries.

"Like a fucking heart attack," I smirk before turning around, leaving him there sitting in his chair with his limp dick out and bleeding as he shouts his disagreement. At least I got the fucker to go down. I call this whole night a win.

CHAPTER TWENTY-EIGHT

SO, LAST night with Dean? Yeah, that *didn't* happen. I refuse to let myself think about it. I didn't open up a small piece of myself to the man who sent me straight to hell. And I *didn't* like it. Nope, not at all.

Try telling that to your sore pussy. She seems to think it was very real.

Damn it!

This morning I checked in with Roxy, Lucas, and the guys to make sure everything for tonight was set up and ready to go. Evie and I spent the day at the Rack Shack... well, now it's called Redemption.

Cass and Dean did a pretty good job at getting newly hired muscle for the place. Even a few guys they trust who used to work security for them. Of course, I gave them a mini show to let them know what happens when you fuck with me. I think I drove the point home.

"You know, it's weird, me coming here with you," Evie says as we get out of the car, looking up at the guys' mansion.

"Why?" I laugh. "You see them almost every day anyways."

"Yeah, but this feels more... personal. It's different when it's just you and Rosie, but with the guys, seeing them in their natural habitat, it's... like I said, weird. And what's up with Neo always being shirtless?" she asks, scrunching up her nose.

I burst out laughing. "I think he does it to try and entice me to fuck him for fun. You know, outside of kill fucks and the dungeon. But trust me, I'm not complaining. He's so... edible."

"Eww... Just eww," she says, covering her ears, making me laugh harder.

"Come on, you. Rosie is waiting for us." I grab her hand and drag her towards the front door. She mutters under her breath, calling me a "Pushy Bitch" but I just smile. She's the only one who can talk to me like that and well... not die.

"Honey, I'm home!" I shout. "And I brought a friend!"

Little feet stomp through the hallway, and I let go of Evie's hand, opening my arms while crouching to get ready to be tackled.

"Mama, Mama!" Rosie squeals, her little, dirty blonde pigtails bouncing with each step. My face splits into a wide grin. She is my happy place, my safe place, my favorite place. When I'm with her, I forget about everything bad in the world. It's impossible to be unhappy around this little ball of sunshine.

"Hey, Kiddo!" I say as she plows into me. I scoop her up, spinning her around in circles, making her giggle in delight.

"Auntie E!" Rosie cheers, running over to Evie when I place her down. Evie smiles at Rosie clinging to her leg.

We make our way into the kitchen, finding the guys spread out around the room. Cass is making a cup of coffee, Neo is sitting on the counter chatting Cass up, Axel is at the table cursing at whatever video he's watching, while Dean sits next to him, his eyes closed and head leaning back.

"Well, good morning, everyone," I greet cheerfully and ignore the flutter in my belly at the sight of all my sexy as fuck men. Yes, they're mine. I mean, no one else can have them, so why the fuck not.

"My Queen," Neo greets, hopping off the counter and bowing to me. I giggle at his antics, and he looks at me with a sassy smirk and wink. I slap his ass while I walk by him to get to Cass. He lets out a yelp/groan combo, making me grin.

When Cass goes to take a sip of his coffee, I take it from him and bring it to my own lips, taking a drink.

"Eww. This is black." I spit the coffee out into the sink.

"Yeah, because it was my coffee," Cass smirks. "But be my guest. You can have it."

"I will, thank you," I snark back playfully before adding a shit ton of sugar and cream.

"How can you drink it like that? You're gonna get diabetes or something," Neo laughs.

"Oh shush, you! Tomorrow isn't guaranteed. Let me live a little," I say, tossing an apple from the bowl next to me, aiming for his head. He catches it before it hits him, then takes a bite. My eyes follow his movements; the juices dripping down his chin, his tongue darting out to lap it up, his jaw muscles working as he chews. Fuck, who knew eating a damn apple could be so hot.

When my eyes finally move from his mouth back to his eyes, they are filled with heat. My belly flutters and I clench my thighs together. Maybe sexy time with him for fun wouldn't be all that bad. I mean, I think he's earned it. And my pussy is in a never-ending loop of horniness. As much as I'd love to, I can't just go find people to kill just to fuck. I mean, it would be fun, but you know, Miller would have a bitch fit.

As if he could read my thoughts, Neo gives me a wink.

Needing to distract myself, I make my way over to Dean. Rosie has dragged Evie out into the backyard to show her some tricks she taught Daisy. It's just the duck quacking on command, and I'm sure she would have done it anyways, but are you gonna be the monster to tell the adorable, little girl that? No, I didn't think so.

"So, Dean. How are you doing, buddy?" I say, slapping him on the back. He lets out a pained grunt.

"You okay?" Cass asks.

Dean sits up straighter, gritting his teeth as he does. "I'm fine, just a gunshot wound. I'm all stitched up," he says, shrugging like it's no big deal.

"A gunshot! Who the fuck shot you?! I'll fucking kill them," Axel growls.

"No, you won't, silly," I say, leaning over his shoulder to see his face. "But I'd like to see you try," I taunt before licking the side of his cheek and snatching his muffin.

"What the fuck?!" Axel bitches, wiping the side of his face. I giggle, taking a bite, backing away. "You're fucking weird, you know that, right?"

"Ah, Axel, with you sweet-talking me like that, I might think you liiiiiiike me," I sing-song with a smile, and biting my lip to keep me from laughing at his resting bitch face.

"Dean. Who shot you?" Cass asks.

"Harlow," Dean says, looking quickly at me, then back to Cass.

"Why?!" Cass asks, looking from Dean to me and back to Dean.

"I was a fucking dumbass and broke," Dean sighs.

"Broke how?" Axel asks.

"Harlow found me with a girl on her knees and my cock down her throat," Dean won't meet my eyes, shame filling his face.

"Son of a bitch," Axel curses then huffs out a laugh. "I thought I'd be the one to break first. Now I definitely won't even risk it. Knowing her, she would aim for my cock."

"Wanna test out that theory?" I coo.

"Fuck no," Axel scoffs, getting up and leaving the room. What a fucking asshole. Whatever, I don't need him putting a damper on my day.

"Damn, dude. She got you good," Neo crows, looking at the stitches under the bandages. "I don't have to worry about ever wanting to stray. I already have the best pussy to ever exist. A rare, golden pussy that men would literally die to have. Too bad you can't speak from experience yourself," Neo says, sounding like he actually feels bad that Dean will never get to fuck me.

Little does he know.

My eyes are focused on Dean, waiting to see if he says anything about what happened last night and if he will go against my word, again.

"Yeah. Too bad I'll never know the feeling," he says, slapping Neo's hand away when he goes to poke at the wound.

"Come on, My Queen, I know Susie will be happy to see her mama," Neo grins, holding out his arm for me to take. Cass chuckles, heading out into the backyard ahead of us.

Hooking my arm through Neo's, I look back at Dean over my shoulder.

He's staring at me with a mix of emotions; pain, regret, shame, guilt, and... love.

Unable to deal with the mixed feelings, I break eye contact and head to the funny farm.

Because why the fuck not.

Evie, Rosie, and I are sitting on the ground in the backyard, taking turns tossing grapes for Daisy to catch when there's a big crash followed by a loud curse and "You fucking bastard!".

Neo comes storming over to us, his face a mask of fury. "You!" he growls, pointing to Daisy. "I'm gonna murder you!"

Rosie's eyes go wide before breaking down crying. She buries her face into Evie's chest. Evie consoles Rosie, and I jump up fast, getting into Neo's face.

"What the fuck is your problem?" I hiss. "You can't just come up to a little girl and threaten to murder her pet!"

"Fuck. I'm sorry," he sighs, running his hands through his hair, then down over his face. "It's just that since that little demon bird came into this house, Bob and Susie started copying the little fucker, and now they think it's okay to bite me! Look," he says, pulling down the back of his pants to show me a big, red mark with teeth imprints. I can't help but giggle.

"It's not funny!" he snaps.

I raise my brow at him in response to his outburst. His eyes go wide. "Sorry, Mistress. I didn't mean to snap at you." He looks sheepish, and it's pretty fucking cute when he rubs the back of his head.

"Naughty boys need to be punished," I say, trying to sound as serious as I can, when really, I'm holding back my amusement. What does he expect, they're damn farm animals.

Before he can say anything else, I bring my hand back and slap him really hard over the bite mark.

"Ahhh!" He jumps away from me, shock written on his face. He gapes at me like he can't believe I just did that.

Dude, are you new or something?

I burst out laughing so hard I almost piss myself.

"That's not nice," he pouts. "My ass really hurts."

“And it's not nice to say shit like that in front of Rosie. That duck is a hell of a lot more than just some pet to her. It’s helping her heal.”

“Okay, fine, I deserved that,” he says, rubbing his ass.

“Pull up your damn pants, dude, there's a child back here!” Cass yells from the barbecue.

But Rosie is too busy crying to see anything.

Neo looks over at Rosie. She’s still crying, but her sobs have slowed down. Neo better make this right before papa bear sees his little cub crying and beats the shit out of Neo. I’m pretty fucking close to doing it myself, but I know Neo didn’t mean anything by it; he was only reacting in the moment.

“Rosie Posy. Uncle Neo is sorry,” Neo soothes, rubbing Rosie’s back as he crouches down.

She peeks up at him with red, teary eyes, giving him a little sniff. Ugh, my fucking heart! Dude better make this better, like right now.

“You're mean,” she whispers, and Neo flinches like he's been hit. “You wanna hurt Daisy.”

“No, Baby Girl. It’s just that Susie bit me like Daisy does, and it caught me by surprise. It hurt my feelings. Like if Daisy were to bite you, you would feel a little mad and sad, right?”

She nods her head. “I'm sorry Daisy’s not nice to you.”

“It's not your fault,” Neo smiles.

Rosie gets up, wipes her eyes, and starts stomping over to Susie’s pen with a look of sheer determination on her face. Neo and I follow, wanting to see what this little spitfire is up to.

She stops next to Susie by the fence. "You've been a bad girl!" Rosie scolds, and I bite my bottom lip, holding back my giggle at how adorable she looks right now.

"You bit your Daddy. We don't bite daddies! So, say sorry. RIGHT. NOW," she shouts, wagging her finger at the alpaca. I can't believe she's disciplining a five-foot tall animal with no fear. I'm so proud.

And, what do you know, the damn thing turns to Neo and makes a noise that sounds like a squeak toy, then licks his face. Neo's face melts from anger to love like he's mush over this animal. He gives Susie a hug around the neck and starts petting her, telling her he's sorry for getting mad.

I just stand there shaking my head that this big, crazy killer of a man, who helps me mutilate people, then fucks me like a beast, is a puddle of fucking goo for his pet.

He really does surprise you.

"Hey, Low. Are you ready? We should head over there now if we want to get anything done today," Evie says.

"Yeah, let's go." I turn to Rosie, and we say goodbye. I shout my goodbyes to the rest of them. Neo looks at me like a sad puppy.

"What?" I laugh.

"No goodbye for me?" he pouts again.

Feeling the need to fuck with him and take him by surprise, I do something that I haven't done with him or anyone but Evie and Rosie. I hug him. I step up to him, wrap my arms around his waist, and give him a quick squeeze, then quickly back away.

He's in shock, his mouth slightly parted as he stares at me like I'm some alien, just blinking.

Giggling, I back away. “Bye bye, Pet. See you tomorrow,” I wink.

He snaps out of it. “Wait! Do that again. It was too fast; I missed it.”

“Sorry. Gotta go.” I wave, disappearing into the house. Evie shakes her head with a light smile as we walk out the front door to the car.

She pokes me in the belly. “You're getting a little soft there, Low,” she grins.

“Am not!” I gape at her.

“I think those men are slowly getting to you. And I think that's a good thing,” Evie says.

“You do?” I ask, my brows pinched.

“At first, I’ll admit, I was jealous. I wanted you all to myself like it has been for eight years, but since they came into your life, mostly Rosie, I’ve seen you laugh more, smile more. There's a lighter presence to you. I like this Harlow. It gives me a good idea of who you were before you were beaten and broken.”

Her words hit me hard. I don't want her to think she isn't enough, but I can't argue with her. I’ve been seeing it too. It fucking terrifies me, but also thrills me.

“You deserve to be happy, Low. You deserve to love and be loved. And those men in there,” she points back at the house. “They love you. You just need to learn how to let them in.”

“I don't need them, Evie. I have you,” I say. “You’re enough for me.”

She gives me a sad smile. “I know. And I’m so fucking glad for that. But it doesn't just have to be me, I'm willing to share. But I'm still number one. Next to Rosie, of course,” she laughs.

I say nothing more as we get into the car and drive over to Redemption, my brain processing her words.

Fuck. Why does life have to change? I was just enjoying life, killing, dancing, singing, and spending my free time with my bestie. Now I have all these... feelings... eww.

Karma, I thought the deal was to be a bitch to them, not me. I want a refund.

“God, this place looks even worse with the lights on,” I cringe. “It's like going to a bar and taking someone home when you’re wasted. You’re thinking that they’re pretty cute, but then when you wake up in the morning, you don't know if you took home a human or a zoo animal.” I shudder, looking around at the now empty building.

When we came here that night, I thought it had potential. Looking at it now, I wasn't exactly wrong, but it's gonna need a lot more work than I was expecting.

"I want to change everything to silver and black. The bar top needs to be replaced. Everything that's fabric needs to go. God knows the amount of blood, cum, piss, and sweat that has soaked into all of that," I say, waving my hand at the chairs and couches.

"The stage needs new flooring. The bathrooms need to be gutted and everything replaced. Oh, and the carpeting has gotta go but other than that, I think we're good. And I want EVERYTHING bleached, at least like ten times."

"Is that all?" Evie giggles.

"Oh, shhh, you. You know this place will do well, once it's done," I laugh, slapping her on the arm.

"I'm wondering how this place would light up under a black light," Evie says, then looks around to make sure she's not touching anything.

"No, girl. Just don't." I shake my head and shiver.

"You're kidding me, right? That grosses you out, but you can bleed multiple men dry and disembowel them. How does that even make any sense?"

"Well, with like 99% of them, I've had them tested. You know how much I love my blood play, but I would never risk my health."

"Excuse me, Queenie. Sorry to interrupt you, but I think you should see this," one of my outside workers, who I hired to do a building inspection, says from behind me.

"What is it?" I ask.

"Well, we were down there, checking every room, when we found a door that was hidden. It's not on the blueprints you gave us. I think you should see it."

"Lead the way."

He leads us down to the door. At first glance, you don't notice anything because the light is so dim in this room, and the door is in the back, covered by a bookshelf.

"How did you even know to look for this?" Evie asks.

"There was a breeze coming from this side of the room; we checked it out and found it," he shrugs.

"What's behind it?" I ask.

"I don't know, we didn't want to open it until we talked to you."

"Well, what are you waiting for; open the damn thing," I say, impatient because I really don't like secrets, and this door smells like trouble.

He slides the bookshelf out of the way, revealing the door. Well, here goes nothing.

When I open the door, I'm hit with the smell of sewage. I gag as I cover my nose, trying not to inhale the foul scent.

"What the fuck is that smell?" Evie gags.

"My guess, shit, piss, and other bodily excretions. I wouldn't be shocked if there were some mystery things mixed in," I cough. "You, give me your shirt and flashlight. Evie, stay here." She looks like she's about to argue, but the look in my eyes tells her this isn't up for discussion.

The guy slips off his shirt, and I wrap it around my mouth and nose, thankful at least that it smells like clean laundry. Then take the flashlight he holds out for me.

"Be careful, Q," Evie says.

"Always, Babe, always."

The door leads down a long flight of steps into an empty room with another door. When I go through that door, I find myself in the motherfucking sewer. Like no joke, there is waste everywhere. Following the little path against the wall, I keep going until I see another door. Not wanting to be in this smell anymore, I take the chance and open it.

Well, fuck me! This just leads to a bunch of tunnels. If I had to guess, they probably lead all over the city. Not wanting to get lost, I decide to go back to Evie.

Heading back to the door that leads to the flowing river of shit, I almost face-plant when I trip over something. I shine the flashlight on whatever it is, getting a sparkly reflection in return.

It's... a shoe. A silver-studded high heel to be exact. What the fuck would a single heel be doing down here in the tunnels?

Then it hits me. This! This is what whoever-the-fuck-is-taking-the-girls uses to get them out without being seen!

Holy monkey balls!

I can't help the massive grin that slips onto my face right now. This, this is the big break we needed!

Doing a little happy dance, I pick up the heel and head back to Evie.

I find her pacing back and forth in the basement room.

"Q, you're okay," Evie breathes, relaxing when she sees I'm safe.

"Oh, Evie, my cold, little heart hurts that you ever doubted my survival skills for even a second," I say dramatically, bringing my hand with the heel up to my heart.

Evie's eyes lock on to it. "What's that?"

"Come on, E. Are you telling me you don't know what high heels look like?" I grin, fucking with her.

She crosses her arms and gives me a stern look. "I know it's a heel, butthead. But why do you have it, and where did you find it?"

I gasp. "Did you just call me a butthead? What are we, six?" I laugh.

"Don't dodge the question," Evie huffs.

"Well, my dear, bestest friend in the whole wide world, I found this through a door. A door that leads to an opening to a shit ton of tunnels that probably lead all over the city."

"How did it get there?" she asks.

I just grin at her, waiting for everything to click. When it does, her eyes go wide, and she gasps.

"Oh my god! That's gotta be from one of the missing girls! Q, this must be how they got the girls out undetected."

"And now we have a solid lead," I slip past Evie, and we start to head back up to the main floor of the club.

"But Q, there's gotta be hundreds of tunnels. It would take months to look through them all."

"See I thought of that on the way back up to the basement. If it is a trafficking ring, then they are going to want to use only the tunnels leading outside of the city. And this club is already pretty close to the outskirts of LA. That lessens the options by a shit ton."

When we get to the main part of the club, I pull out my phone and call Miller.

"What can I do for you?" he greets me.

"I need every blueprint the city has for the underground sewage tunnels," I demand.

"And why do you need these?"

"Because I do. So, get them for me. Or I'll fucking stab you," I say sweetly. Not the best idea to threaten a cop, but I'm strung tightly, and we just got a big lead in this case.

"Does this have to do with the missing girls?"

"Maybe," I say, not wanting him to know my plan. I don't need him having the police taking over and getting in my way.

"Alright, I'll have them sent over as soon as possible."

Last night, Rosie and I had a sleepover. I was in a really good mood, excited because of what we found. I needed some fun with my girl to keep me from going crazy until Miller could get me those blueprints.

I'm making Rosie and the guys some breakfast, feeling oddly like a domestic housewife, which is so not me, when my phone rings.

Seeing that it's Evie, I answer right away. “What up, Babe?” I greet, flipping a pancake.

“Low. Oh. My. God. Low. You have to get down here, like right NOW,” Evie says, sounding like a cracked-out chipmunk talking a mile a minute.

“E. Chill. Slow down. What's going on?” I say, putting the pancake on the plate and giving it to Neo. He gives me a panty melting grin and a wink before diving in. On the outside I’m playfully glaring, but on the inside my body fucking flushes. Ugh, this man.

“You know how you thought you found the pot of gold at the end of the rainbow with what you found last night?” she asks, her voice giddy with excitement.

“Yeah...?”

“Well, I’m Charlie from Willy Wonka, and I just got the motherfucking golden ticket,” she squeals. It’s so un-Evie-like to hear her swear like this. It’s kind of hot.

“What did you find?” I ask, her excitement has me really invested now.

“I'm sending Penny over to watch Rosie. I have a feeling when you see this, the guys are gonna want to be here too.”

Hanging up, I tell the guys, and we wait until Penny arrives, with a few of my men.

When we get to my club, we head right to Evie’s office.

“Oh good, you’re here, come, come!” she says. “Okay, so you know how we had Dina tailed. Well, I’ve been going over the footage since last night, hence the red, tired eyes, but just as I was about to go to bed, like a half hour ago, I got sent this," she says, turning the laptop to the guys and I, pressing play.

The video angle is from the top of a building, looking down over Dina and the whole motherfucking council of dipshits!

"I'm sorry, there's nothing I can do! She took over the club and fired me," she sobs.

"I know, and that's such a shame. It was all going so smoothly. But now you're no use to us. You know too much, and we just can't allow you to live. You're too much of a liability," Dick says in a cold voice.

Before Dina can beg for her life, Dick raises a gun and shoots her in the head. Her body falls to the ground, and the men pay her no more attention as they continue to talk.

"Get a cleanup crew out here," Dick says. "Damn it. That whore was only good for one thing, and she somehow managed to fail at that."

"What do we do now?" Rick asks.

"Find another building with access to the tunnels. The auction is next weekend, and if we want a good profit, we need a few more girls," Dick says, taking out a smoke and lighting it up.

"We have ten already, that's plenty," Bill says.

"NO!" Dick snaps. "We have enough time to get at least a few more."

With that, they leave the alley, and a few seconds later, a cleanup crew comes into view and start dragging Dina's lifeless body away.

"Holy fucking shit!" Neo laughs. "We hit the fucking jackpot."

An eerie calm takes over my body. I'm not Harlow anymore. Nope, now that I know everything, or at least enough, Queenie is coming out to play. And, boy, is it gonna be a glorious bloodbath.

This is personal. They went behind my back, making me look like a fucking fool. They will not make it through the day alive.

"Where are they right now?" I ask.

Evie sees I'm not really Harlow right now, and all her playfulness is gone. She types a few things on her laptop. "Business meeting downtown."

I turn around without another word, and the guys seem to know what to do, following behind me.

Welcome to the mother of all D-Days. Get yourself an umbrella because it's about to rain with the blood of my enemies.

CHAPTER TWENTY-NINE

Harlow

THE ELEVATOR dings and the doors start to slide open at a painfully slow pace. It's taking everything in me not to kick open the fucking thing. I'm fuming. I am so enraged that I may need the guys to keep me from murdering the whole damn building.

These old-timey sacks of shit thought they could pull one over on me? Well, I guess in a way they did, because they did manage to start a whole new, fucking trafficking ring right under my nose. God, don't ever tell this to the guys or any breathing soul, but I feel really fucking embarrassed and stupid for not knowing what was going on and allowing them to make it this far.

But don't worry. That all ends today. I have very exciting plans for these geezers. Hope they enjoyed whatever pathetic excuse of a life they were living because that all ends today... Or tonight.

The guys are quiet behind me as I storm into the building. Quiet, but alert and aware. Not that I'd need them to watch my back or anything. It's just who they are.

The guys trail behind me as I plaster a big smile on my face, masking my true feelings.

"I'm sorry, ma'am, but they are in a meeting," a young lady tells me from behind a desk. One of their secretaries. I wonder which wrinkly dick she's sucking? Because I know for a fact that each of these men are cheating on their wives. Fucking scum.

"Bite me," I say, voice dripping with sugary sweetness. Her eyes go wide, and I keep heading towards the boardroom, where laughing and chatting makes its way through the cracked door.

Neo snaps his teeth at her in a biting motion, making her squeak in fear and rear back on her chair, almost losing her balance and tumbling over. He lets out a deep belly chuckle, and I smile for real. I love my crazy Pet.

"Hello, boys," I purr, busting the door to the boardroom open. All chatter stops, and each head whips in my direction. Their eyes go wide, and a few swallows hard, the sounds easily noticeable in the deadly silence.

"Queenie. To what do we owe this pleasure?" Riggs finally greets. He puts on a fake smile. I can see it in his eyes. He's pissed at my unexpected arrival but desperately trying to bite down his outrage.

"A little birdie told me that you lot have been very naughty boys," I tsk. My guys file into the room and take a place against the walls next to the doors. I'm pretty sure it's so no one escapes. They don't know what I'll do, but they are ready for anything.

“And what might this birdie have said?” Richard asks from the other end of the table.

My smile turns wicked. I jump onto the table and strut to the other end towards him, kicking their coffees and waters over as I go, just for the fun of it. They let out gasps and curses as the liquid makes contact with them. I can tell which ones are scalding hot, and I get a sick sense of pleasure at their little cries of pain. Silly men, this is just the tip of the iceberg compared to what's to come.

My heels click against the wood tabletop. When I reach Richard, I squat down in front of him. Thank god, I chose the stretchy leggings for a change because if it was my leather pants, I would probably have a rip down to my crotch right about now from bending so fast. Then I'd have to kill the fucker right here and now for getting a look at my pussy, and I can't have that. I have big, fun, exciting plans for these dudes tonight.

“Well, Dick, it just so happened to tell me all the dark and dirty things you boys have been doing behind my back,” I say, then grab his tie and yank him to me so that we're face to face. “You see, I didn't like that. I thought we had a nice thing going. You guys keep your businesses and everything else all squeaky clean, and in return, I let your pathetic asses live. I thought I was doing you all a solid by not killing you because of who you were connected to by blood or business.” I start to undo his tie as I talk and slip it off of him. He says nothing, refusing to lose eye contact with me, afraid to be caught off guard. "But nooooo, you guys just had to go and take the wrong road, thinking you could pull a fast one on me by keeping everything clean on paper, so that my little birdie couldn't find your secrets. Well, sooner or later, karma comes to bite you in the ass. And guess what?" I ask, voice low. I take his tie and quickly loop it around his neck a few times and fist both ends. I yank my hands in opposite directions, making the tie constrict tight around his neck. He starts to gag, coughing as he scrambles to get the tie loose. I keep my hold on it until he starts to turn blue, and his eyes bug out, but then I loosen my grip. I don't want him dead yet.

I let go, pushing him away from me, causing his chair to topple over. He scrambles to get the tie off, and when he does, he sucks in big gulps of air. "Karma has arrived," I smile.

I look at the other wastes of space. They all have fear in their eyes, but Riggs, the cocky fucker, has a blank face as if I don't intimidate him. That pisses me off. But I won't take the bait. He wants me to lose it in front of witnesses. To have his secretary call the cops and end me. But little does this fool know that I already have everything planned out in my head, and after this little meeting, I'll be calling Evie to get everything put in place.

"So, be sure to remember that. Just when you think you're safe, when you close your eyes to sleep at night, ask yourselves, are you really safe? Or am I lurking in the shadows?" My smile turns dangerous as I click my way back to the other end of the table. I hop off and head for the door. Just before exiting, I turn around to look at the whole room.

“Toodles,” I wave my fingers, my voice perky. Blowing the room a kiss goodbye, I head back to the elevator. My guys follow close behind, none of them has yet to speak a single word.

When the elevator doors close, locking us all into this tight space, Axel goes to speak. I put my fingers to my lips and then point to the camera in the corner of the elevator. He looks, then sighs in frustration, crossing his arms and leans against the wall. Grumpy fucker.

When everyone gets in the car and the doors have been shut, Axel can't keep his trap closed any longer. “What the fuck was that!?” he snaps. “These fucks are doing EVERYTHING that you normally kill someone for. How do you just walk out of there, leaving them alive?!”

I look at him in the rearview mirror, where he sits between Cass and Dean. “Okay, first off. I'm gonna advise you to watch your tone with me because that lovely sized cock in your jeans would make a nice decoration on my mantel,” I warn, voice dripping with venom. He shuts up fast, pupils wide as he puts a hand over his junk. “And second,” my voice goes sugary sweet again. “There were too many people and cameras in there. There's no way I could have killed any one of them, let alone all of them, without being put behind bars by the end of it, and all of you by association. Even Miller can’t get us out of something like that. At least not in time for what I've got planned for tonight.”

“And what do you have planned for tonight, My Queen?” Neo purrs, his eyes glazed over with lust, and his cock is hard in his pants as he daydreams about what I'll do.

"I'm so glad you asked," I say, voice giddy. "I have big plans. It's gonna be one of the biggest, messiest D-Days to date." I'm bouncing in my seat as I think about all the blood I'll be spilling tonight. "Nothing but the best for the traitors who outright fucked me over. No one makes a fool of Queenie and lives to tell the tale."

Neo groans. "Fuck me, Mistress. You're gonna make me nut just thinking about it."

I give him a girly, little smile. "After, I promise," I giggle, and his smile spreads even wider. He bites his knuckle as he shamelessly checks me out while adjusting his tight crotch.

Dammit, just thinking about the mass murder tonight makes me want to crawl right over to Neo, mount him like a horse, and ride his cock like a mechanical bull, all while his cousins watch and listen as he screams my name.

But no, not now. Gotta wait a little while longer. Too much to do. Too much to plan.

"I want all of you present tonight. Doesn't hurt to witness what could happen if any of you ever decide to fuck me over again," I say, looking directly at Axel but he's trying to avoid my gaze. "And not in a fun way," I wink at Neo. He just gives me a small smile.

"I wouldn't miss it for the world," he says.

My face falls. Damn it! Why does he have to be so chill and easygoing all the time. He, like... supports me in everything I do, doesn't complain at all, not like his cousin does.

I don't like it. I mean, I do but... It makes me feel shit... Deep breath, hussy.

We drive back to the club, and the guys head straight home to spend some time with Rosie before putting her to bed for the night.

"Alright, everything is good to go," Evie says, closing her laptop. "Our guys will be picking them up from the airport a little bit before the plane departs. It will be set up to look like everyone got on board. I've hacked into the system and set a timer to have the plane shut down in the middle of the ocean on its way to Hong Kong."

"What about the pilot? You can't send him home because then the feds will investigate," I point out.

"Did some digging on him, fortunately he's dirty too. Has been helping fly in girls for other rings, but he was easily bought off to supposedly fly the empty plane to Hong Kong. No one will miss him when he goes down with the plane midway," she smiles with this beautiful, menacing glint in her eye. Oh, I love wicked Evie.

"Perfect." I strum my fingers together like an evil mastermind, and Evie giggles. My face probably looks like a crazy fucker, but that's nothing new.

"Have Lucas, Tommy, and Max set everything up. I want my katana for tonight."

Her brows pinch. "That's it? No daggers, no guns? None of your other toys?"

"Nope," I say, popping the 'p'. "We're having sushi tonight," I cackle.

She wrinkles her nose, and I know she's picturing what that would mean in her mind. "It's gonna be messy, isn't it?" she groans.

"The worst, by far," I smile. "If you're gonna watch, maybe don't eat beforehand," I giggle.

She just smiles and shakes her head. "Right. I'll get the cleanup crew on standby. Maybe call in for back up," she says, dialing a number on her phone.

"That would probably be for the best," I sing, then kiss her cheek before skipping out of the office to get ready for the big night. I'm so fucking excited right now, it's not even funny.

Neo

"I FEEL like a giddy schoolgirl," I exclaim and bounce in my seat a little. I've been allowing my mind to wander with all the possible ideas of what Harlow is gonna do to these slimy fuckers.

I wish I could slice every one of their necks and watch the blood flow like a water fountain, watching the light drain from their eyes.

But I don't get to have fun. Well, I do, but only when My Queen allows it. I guess I can live with that. It's not like she never lets me play. But like the guys, sometimes when I'm in the zone, I'm like a dog with a bone that locks its jaw and won't let go until the prey is dead. Or, you know, someone might have to beat me in the head until I let go. I'm speaking from experience.

We're on our way back to the club after spending a few hours with Rosie. How strange is it that just moments before we were tucking a sweet, little girl into bed for the night, and now we're heading off to watch a mass murder.

We may live a fucked up and dark life, but Rosie won't see that side. We've talked it over, and as long as we can help it, Rosie will never know what Harlow does, or what we help her do.

Harlow was really set on doing her kills solo, but after letting me join in on putting down Rosie's mother and that pig of a husband she had, Harlow has let me play a little more. It all depends on who the kill is and where.

Tonight though, I know I won't get to play, but I'm more than happy to sit back this time and just enjoy watching My Mistress at work. I know we're in for one hell of a show. I'm getting hard just thinking about it.

When we get to the club, it's packed. I look around at all these people enjoying their night, oblivious to what's about to happen under their feet. Good thing Harlow had that room soundproofed, because something tells me that even with this blasting music and the bass, it wouldn't be enough to drown out the screams we will be getting tonight.

"Just in time," Lucas says, coming up next to us.

"Would she have started without us?" Axel drawls.

Lucas narrows his eyes at him. “No, she wants you all there. But she also doesn't like to be kept waiting. She’s down there like a caged animal, pacing around all hyped up on energy drinks.”

“Oh, such a shame. Well, let's not leave the Queen waiting anymore, shall we?” Axel snarks.

“You know, your mouth is gonna get you killed one of these days. I think Queenie only allows it because you’re Rosie's uncle. But there's only so much she's gonna allow,” Lucas warns, before leading us toward Harlow's playroom.

He stops at the door leading downstairs and looks back. "You wanna know why she treats us better? It's because the difference between us and you,” he says looking at Axel, “Is that we have respect for Queenie. We owe her our lives, and therefore we are loyal and treat each other like family. You have yet to see who she really is. All you see is a crazy bitch who wants to rule the world. And that's stopping you from seeing who she really is. I'm sure after tonight your opinion won't change, because I know this is gonna be the bloodiest D-Day to date, but when you see her with Rosie, remember that that's who she really is deep down.”

Lucas stares at us for a second longer, then pushes the door open, and we all head downstairs. When we get to the room, there are seven men bound and gagged to chairs. They are spread out around the room, making a wide circle.

They all look petrified, struggling against their restraints, screaming against the cloths in their mouths. Looking around the room, I see most of her... family? I guess that's what she would call them. Anyways, most of them are here, standing against the far-left wall, away from the soon-to-be war zone.

Plastic covers the whole floor and all of the walls. Looking up, I see that it's even taped all over the roof. My face slips into a grin. “Hell fucking yeah,” I chuckle, rubbing my hands together. “Tonight is gonna be a bloodbath, isn't it?” I ask, looking at Evie. Her face looks a little green. Fuck, it must be bad if she looks sick. She's been there for every one of Harlow's D-Days, so if she’s already like this, before anything has even happened, then it's gonna be fucked up. I'm even more excited. She nods and looks away.

The sound of clicking heels draws everyone's attention to the other side of the room. Harlow is dressed in her signature black and red corset. Her hair is long and straightened, ending just above her luscious, plump ass. Which, by the way, looks amazing in her matching booty shorts. I shamelessly eye fuck her body. Damn, My Queen looks extra yummy tonight. I can't wait to get my cock inside that tight pussy after this is done and over with. It’s gonna be hard and dirty. My cock is practically like a stone and ready to go. I'm gonna have to try not to blow my load in my pants once they start screaming.

My eyes find her feet, and I tilt my head to the side as she slides her heels off so that she's barefoot.

“Alright, my lovelies,” she says, her raised voice showing authority. “If you don’t think you can stomach what's about to happen, I am giving you an out.” A smile takes over her face, and she looks more playful. “Leave now or forever hold your peace,” she giggles.

I look around to see who is too pussy to see their Queen at work. No one leaves.

Looking back to Harlow, I finally see what she has in her hand, too distracted by her banging body to have noticed it before. A long blade gleams in the light. She twirls it around a few times. Is that a katana?

The lights go out, engulfing the room in complete darkness. The room is silent except for the men's muffled screams and the sounds of them desperately struggling against theirs binds.

"Remember this as you take your last breath, boys. Fuck with me and die," Harlow voices break the silence. Then music starts to play.

The eerie melody is one I recognize. One of my favorites, *Cradles* by Sub Urban.

The room is pitch dark until the base of the song starts up. As each beat pulses, a strobe light flashes, allowing us to see the room for the briefest of seconds. Harlow is still standing in the spot she was moments before, but she's staring right at me. The bass keeps going, and the lights keep flashing on the beat. A smile creeps onto Harlow's face, and she places a finger over her lips and in unison with the song she mouths the word Hush. And just like that, the show has begun.

As the strobe lights flash, it makes the scene in front of us look like it's moving in slow motion. On the other hand, when it goes dark again, everything speeds up. One second, she's in one place, and the next she's across the room. Almost like a flip book. The combined effect is captivating. Her body moves in fluid motions. Dipping and flipping her way around the room. Her katana occasionally catching the strobe light as she wields it like some kind of fucking samurai master or some shit.

I pay no mind to the sacks of shit she's dismembering right now, too lost in the beauty of her performance. But I hear them. They are screaming at the top of their lungs in extreme terror and agony as Harlow slices and dices them. It's like she's playing that Fruit Ninja game. Not even the gags or music is masking their screams. I can hear the sounds of body parts hitting the ground.

When the song is over, the room is completely dark again, and all you can hear is the sound of Harlow's heavy breathing. It's almost like everyone else is holding their breath, waiting for what just happened to be revealed.

The lights flick on, and the sight I'm met with has me wanting to piss my pants but also cum at the same time. God, it's the most fucked up, disturbing thing I've ever seen or could imagine.

Body parts litter the floor. Legs, hands, feet, toes, fingers, arms, and even severed heads. All that is left is their torsos and bottom halves, but their stomachs are gutted like a fish. Their intestines hanging out, half draped down onto the floor. But because Harlow cut them all into pieces, the ropes are no longer holding them onto the chairs. One by one, the remains of each body topple to the ground.

“Ooops,” a giggle brings my eyes to the woman of the hour. The mastermind behind this masterpiece.

Holy fuck! My eyes widen and my cock pulses at the sight of her. She is drenched from head to toe in blood. Not one speck of her is left untouched. She looks like Carrie when they dumped the pigs' blood on her at prom, or like if they tossed her into a pool of it instead.

Blood drips from her hands onto the floor. My eyes travel back to hers. She's standing there like a statue. A smile, that would leave any sane person petrified, creeps onto her face. Thank god, I'm the furthest thing from sane.

A smile almost identical to hers makes its way onto my own face. She gives me a wink. That's it. That's the signal I've been waiting for. Her permission to touch her, to fuck her until she passes out.

She runs across the room, jumping into my arms. I catch her with ease. Her arms come around my neck, her legs lock around my waist as she smashes her mouth to mine.

I spin her around and crush her against the wall. She lets out a little grunt that sounds more like a moan. I don't show my shock, allowing myself to go with the flow, but what the fuck is happening? Harlow doesn't kiss...? We fuck like wild animals, lips everywhere on each other's bodies except on the mouth. Well, mine are mostly on hers, but still.

Kissing is intimate to someone like Harlow. Like me.

I quickly block out the shock and focus on this vampire queen in front of me, and I love the taste of blood on her lips. She rams her tongue into my mouth, moaning as her nails dig into the back of my scalp. The sting of pain as they scrape hard into my skin, enough to make me bleed I'm sure, makes my cock painfully hard. I'm already stiff as a board from watching that sexy foreplay she just did. Part of me likes to think she does it just for me. A man can dream.

She withers against me, and the sounds coming from her tell me that she needs me, and she needs me now!

Not wasting any more time, I rip away any fabric separating me from the promised land that needs to be thoroughly explored by my cock.

She rips her lips away from mine and tucks her head into the crook of my neck. At the same time as I thrust my cock into her dripping and ready pussy, she bites down hard, latching on to my neck. I let out a strangled moan at the pain, and thank the devil I didn't cum like a virgin. But fuck, the pain and pleasure mingling together is the best fucking feeling. I can't have one without the other.

I start to rut into her, losing myself because all of my senses are focused on her. The only thing I can think about is how her tight cunt feels, gripping my cock like it owns it. And fuck if I don't enjoy being pussy whipped by this goddess of mine.

I'm pounding her harder into the wall with each thrust, but she doesn't complain. If anything, she's enjoying it. "Fuck me dirty, Pet. Make your Mistress scream," And I do. She tosses her head back letting out a cry so loud that if there weren't about ten people watching this right now, someone might think she was the one getting murdered.

My breathing is rapid as grunts are spilling from my mouth. This is where I belong. My cock inside her pussy as I destroy her, and her drenched in blood. A teenaged Neo's wet dream.

She cums hard around my cock, and I grit my teeth, prolonging my release. I'm not done with her, and she likes at least three orgasms, or she still feels a bit stabby after.

Needing to obey my mistress, I haul her off my cock, spin her around, and slip back inside as I push her against the wall again. Her stomach pressed against it. Thrusting into her again, this new angle has her moaning and screaming immediately. I don't know how much longer I'm gonna last. The sight of her drenched in blood, the smell of it as well, is all too much.

"Fuck yes!" she chants. "Split my pussy in two, Neo," she cries. Neo. She never uses my name when we're fucking. Another intimate thing for her.

Do I dare to think that the big, bad monster might be warming up to little, old, crazy me? The thought has my blackened heart, that only beats for two people, swelling. I would cut off my left nut for this woman to feel even a sliver for me that I feel for her. Fuck, I'd cut off my dick and let her use it as a dildo if I had to.

"Right there!" she moans. "Don't you fucking move from this spot. If you make me lose this orgasm, I'm cutting fucking your dick off and using it like a dildo," she growls as if reading my mind. My cock twitches in delight. I'm fucked, okay?

The violent warning has my balls drawing up. Needing her to cum first to avoid looking like a two-pump chump, I slip my hand down and over her clit. Her "God, yes" tells me I get to live another day even after disobeying another order.

I'm not going to be able to last for three orgasms, so I better make this one mind-blowing.

I pay extra attention to her swollen bud as I thrust my hips, fucking her deep and fast. “Yes!” she screams over and over until she lets out one long yell, cumming around my cock again. This one is powerful. Her body starts to twitch as her knees give out, and if it wasn’t for me and the wall, she would have crashed to the ground.

I follow her climax with my own. I toss my head back and roar my release. I feel my cum fill her sweet center as my cock twitches hard.

We’re both breathing hard, choppy breaths. After a few moments, I open my eyes and find a half asleep, bloody Harlow leaning into me, my cock still buried deep inside her.

A growl not too far from me grabs my attention. Axel is staring at me with furious eyes. Dean's jaw is clenched, hands fisted at his side. Dude looks constipated. And Cass is looking at Harlow longingly, as if he wishes it was him who fucked her into a coma and not me.

“Totally forgot you guys were here,” I chuckle. “Well, did you enjoy the free show?”

“Fuck you!” Axel spits, making me grin wider. “And what the fuck was that?!”

“Umm, dude, I know it's been a while, since I'm the only one getting any, but it’s called sex. Mind-blowing, ball busting sex, but sex, nonetheless,” I laugh again.

“Not that, you moron! That!” he shouts, thrusting his hand out, gesturing to the body parts littering the ground.

Blood drips from the roof onto the floor, making the blood already pooled there splash.

“That would be Queenie unleashed,” Evie says, stepping over the body parts as if she's trying to avoid mud, not blood, to make her way over to us. “When it's personal, Harlow tends to be a little more blood thirsty. It’s been a while since I’ve seen a show this... wild. No one has had the balls to betray Queenie in a very long time.”

Looking around more, I see the guys and Evie are the only ones left. Evie sees the question in my eyes. “They left the moment Harlow jumped into your arms." Evie walks up to us and strokes Harlow's hair out of her face, looking at her with so much love shining through her eyes. Poor girl has it bad for the Queen. Mine, my beast snarls. Only she isn't... yet.

She looks up at me, and I see the hurt in her eyes as she tries to ignore the fact that she just witnessed me annihilate Harlow's pussy. “She's out cold. She's gonna be pissed when she realizes she left herself vulnerable,” Evie sighs. “Just get your dick out of her and take her up to her apartment, clean her up, and put her to bed. If she asks how she got there, I'll tell her Lucas did the lifting, and I did the cleaning.” She hands me keys. “Bring them back to me when you lock up.

I nod and silently thank her for giving me this moment to care for my Queen, like I’ve been dying to do since the dungeon.

She gives Harlow one last look and takes off across the room, pulling out her cell and calling for a cleanup.

I look back at the guys and give them a cocky smirk, then ignore them, not wasting any more time. I pull my still hard cock out of Harlow and lift her into my arms. She grumbles but snuggles into my chest.

Fuck, I want to tease her about this so bad tomorrow, but I also enjoy living. Living means worshiping her body, and I quite enjoy that. I'd fucking burn cities to the ground just to keep what we have. But I'd also decimate countries to have the possibility of more.

Leaving the room, I take one last look at the guys before taking Harlow up to her apartment, leaving them standing there amongst the battle-ground of dismembered bodies.

Best fucking night of my life.

CHAPTER THIRTY

MY EYES snap open from a dreamless sleep. Looking around, I find myself in my room. *How the hell did I get here?*

Groaning, I sit up and stretch. Looking down at my body, I see that I'm naked… but clean?

Last I remember, I was covered head to toe in blood and very much dressed in one of my dance outfits. I remember I was running across a sea of bodies, launching myself into Neo's arms, and that's it… my mind is blank.

FUCK! Don't tell me I was so fucking worked up that I blacked out! At least I can remember the show. All the screaming, all the blood. The sounds of the body parts hitting the ground. Fucking heaven.

With a shiver of delight and a smile, I head to the bathroom to get ready for the day.

As I'm brushing my teeth, my eyes go wide. How the fuck did I forget about the girls? Shit!

Spitting out the toothpaste, I quickly rinse my mouth, tossing my toothbrush in the cup beside the sink, and rush to my room. I race around, frantically trying to find something to wear.

I put on the first things I can find; a pair of sweats and a tightly fitted sweater. I grab an elastic off my dresser and toss my hair into a messy bun.

Snatching some socks and my sneakers, I head down to the club, ready to bitch everyone out for letting me sleep when we have shit to do and girls to find.

“Someone better have a good fucking excuse as to why they let-” I start, rounding the corner to the main part of the club.

I stop mid-sentence when I see that the place is packed. Everyone is here. And I do mean everyone; everyone who works for me inside and outside of the club.

“What's all this?” I ask, looking around the room.

“Well,” Evie says, moving out from in between the crowd of men. “We knew you would want to find the girls right away, but you're no good to anyone if you're not fully rested, so I made sure you got a full night's rest. Then I called everyone over to be ready when you woke up. I figured the more people looking, the better. There are a lot of tunnels to search, and we don't know how long it will be until we find the right one. Miller brought over the blueprints, and we have been studying them for a while now.”

“And we know you don't want to risk our safety, so the girls and I are getting some of the houses ready for whoever you find down there. Somewhere safe and warm for them to stay at, until we figure out what to do with them, or if they even have homes to go to," Lola says, jumping off the stage, heading towards me.

I give her a smile and nod. "Thanks. That's gonna be a big help." I look at Evie, then to Neo and back to Evie. "So, how did I go from being impaled on Neo's cock, because I'm assuming that's what came after I launched myself into his arms, and we fucked like demon bunnies, to being clean and naked in my bed? Alone."

"Oh umm, Lucas brought you up, and I cleaned you and put you to bed," Evie says, flicking her eyes from Neo to me.

"Riiiiiiight. E, you need to work on your poker face," I grin and look at Neo. "Thank you."

His eyes go wide in shock, then a little grin appears on his lips. "Anything for my Queen."

"And sorry about that."

"About what?" he asks, cocking his head to the side.

"For falling asleep on your dick," I giggle. "It's not because I was bored, I swear."

"Oh, trust me. I know," he gives me a wolfish grin. "It's because my magic cock pricked you so damn good, you fell into a fucking cum coma."

"Hey, when it's good, it's good," I shrug playfully.

"Good?" He cocks a brow.

"Okay, fucking epic," I smile.

"Damn right, it was. My little vampire." He steps close to me, taking his thumb and brushing it along my cheek. My breath gets caught in my throat. I want to back away, to slap his hand, to tell him to fuck off and not to touch me like that.

But I don't, because of how he's looking at me right now. It's pure lust, love, and affection that has my mind melting.

I want him to lean down and kiss me. And that fucking scares me, more than anything. A memory of last night flashes before my eyes. His lips on mine as we devoured each other's mouths. Fuck, a kiss never felt so good, so powerful.

When he doesn't and just backs away, giving me a sad smile, my heart hurts a little. I know this isn't rejection, it's fear. On both our parts. Fear that I'll be the one rejecting him, and fear for me with what all this might mean.

But I can't think about feelings and all that mushy gushy bullshit right now. We have girls to save!

"Everyone ready?" I shout. We spent the last hour planning, looking over blueprints, and arguing about who does what and goes where.

Rather than search every tunnel down there, we're going with every tunnel north of the club. We are already close to the outskirts of the city, so there are only twenty to choose from. With everyone we have to help us look, we should be able to find them. I hope we find them. We fucking better.

I went and changed into some leggings, a tank top, and my best running shoes. They are the best, ones that help me move with next to no sound.

I know those men would have people guarding them. They're not dumb enough to stash them, then leave them there. They are cash cows to them. They wouldn't have risked it.

All the better for me. I'm feeling extra stabby.

With my daggers strapped to my legs, and my guns on my hips, I'm good to go. Neo insisted on coming with me, but I shot that down. I don't need any help; I don't want it.

He looked like a kicked puppy, but he accepted my decision. Now he's all growly and snapping at everyone. I had to stop him from almost killing someone because they bumped into him.

I mean, it was totally hot. If it wasn't one of my own men he was threatening to kill, I probably would have touched myself as he beat him to death and had Neo finish me off next to the dead body.

Fucked up? Yup. But what else is new?

"Good to go," Evie says, looking up from her laptop. She's staying behind with the other girls. Evie is the best person to help get a bunch of scared and damaged women to feel as safe as they can after what they have been through.

Months of living underground, and who knows what their living conditions are. They wanted to collect as many as they could rather than just sell them one by one. But at least it worked out in our favor.

If they sold them right away, it would have been harder or next to impossible for me to find them. I mean, I've done it before with some of the girls that Triver sold, but it's a lot of work. So, getting them all back at once is the best-case scenario.

"Alright," I shout, addressing the room. "You know what to do. Let's go boys; we have girls to find, and fuckers to kill," I cheer.

Taking the lead, we all file down to the basement to the door that leads underground. "Masks up!" I shout. Everyone slips their bandana masks up over their mouths and noses. We don't know how long we will have to travel through the tunnels, so it's good to be prepared. According to the blueprints, there are about fifty maintenance rooms along the tunnels, meaning we have a lot of ground to cover.

"If you come into any trouble, remember that every five hundred meters, there are ladders that lead up to manholes. If you need to get out, do it. Don't play the hero, because you're no use to me or those girls if you get hurt or sick."

When we get to the door that leads to the tunnels, everyone piles in and starts down their assigned underground passage.

"Hey," Dean says, looking yummy outside of a suit for once. He has on a pair of black cargo pants that shows off his biteable ass, a gray shirt that is snug against his body, showing off his delectable arm muscles that I don't have the privilege to see much, and a pair of brown boots.

My mind goes back to his office, and I have to give myself an inner bitch slap because this is a serious situation.

But, I mean, there's always time for sex...

Damn it, Harlow! Tell your horny, little cunt to shut this shit down! Thirsty bitch.

“Harlow?” Dean asks, making me snap out of my nasty thoughts.

“What's up?” I ask, smiling wide as if I wasn't just imagining his thick cock pounding into me from behind.

“I just wanted to tell you to be safe,” he says, his voice stern.

Everyone has already left but Dean, Neo, Axel, and Cass. They look at Dean like he grew a second head.

“Since when do you give a fuck about her safety?” Axel snarks, leaning against the wall. I shoot him a glare. Maybe if I focus all my energy, I can make his gun move with my mind and make him shoot himself.

But sadly, I'm not a Jedi Master. Life sucks.

“How about you go take your gun and fuck yourself? Make sure to keep the safety off,” I smile sweetly at him, my voice girly and sweet.

He just narrows his eyes, doing something smart for once and shutting his giant pie hole. God, that man! I just want to punch him over and over in his stupidly sexy face. I mean, I have Cass, so it's not like the good looks are gonna go to waste.

“Look, you don’t have to always be a fucking dick to her!” Dean snaps, making everyone's eyes go wide.

He turns back to me. “Look, I know I haven't been the most easy-going person, but this shit could go south. So just be careful, okay?”

Okay? What the fuck is going on? Ugh, why does he have to be so... alpha male, and why is it so damn hot hearing him growl at me like that.

Normally, I would have stabbed him in the neck by now. Fuck, Evie is right; I am going soft. I'm three more swoons away from being a fucking squish-mellow.

"Yes, sir," I salute him like a soldier, making him crack a grin. "And you know, stay alive and all that bull shit. Rosie would be crushed if she lost any of you."

Not wanting this to turn into some love fest, I push past the guys. "Peace out, fuckers. May the odds be ever in your favor."

I've been walking for at least two hours. I've checked three rooms and found jack shit. Needing a moment's break, I take a drink from the water bottle that I brought with me.

Screwing the top back on, I retie my laces and get ready to continue down the tunnel when I hear people arguing.

Yes! Fuck yes! That's got to be the men they hired to watch over the girls. I'll be fucking pissed if it's just some random city workers.

Quickly but quietly, I creep my way down the tunnel, dimming the light on my flashlight. The tunnel turns off to the left, so I'm able to peek around the corner, keeping my body hidden.

"Look, we haven't heard from them in almost two days. Something must have happened. Reception is shit down here. I'm just gonna go up and call them to see what's going on. You're gonna be fine," a man with a buzz cut says, rolling his eyes at some blonde dude.

"Let me go. I need a break from all the bitching and crying these girls do. They're giving me a fucking headache."

"Fine," the first guy snaps, shoving the cell phone into the blonde guy's hand. "But hurry. When you get back, we can take that pretty, little redhead for a spin." His grin is sick and twisted, and I can't fucking wait to watch him bleed.

"You're fucked," blonde guy laughs. "They would kill us if they knew we were sampling the goods."

Buzz head scoffs. "We're down here for hours every day. It's just mean to tempt us and not to let us pass the time. It's what they're here for anyways," he shrugs.

Oh, yes. I'm gonna have so much satisfaction killing these guys. My only problem is that I don't have the time to knock them out and tie them up to bring them home as my next playdates. Insert pouty face.

Blondie starts heading down the tunnel towards me as the buzz head dude goes back into the room. Plastering myself against the wall to avoid the light of his flashlight, I wait until he rounds the corner.

Thankfully, the light misses me, and he continues down the tunnel. The light is bright enough for me to see what I'm doing, so I slip out my dagger, not wanting to use my gun and end up drawing attention to us. I don't know how many more men are in that room.

Creeping behind him, I wait for the right moment, before leaping on him like a little spider monkey. I know there's probably more graceful ways of doing this, but where's the fun in that?

“What the fuck!” he grunts, but that's all he has the chance to say before I wrap my legs tightly around his waist, grip his hair with one hand, and bring my dagger up. With one swift motion, I slice his neck. Blood starts squirting out of his neck almost as hard as Neo makes me squirt during our fuck fests. Almost. I still hold the gold medal for that.

The flashlight falls from his hand, and he drops to his knees. Hopping off his back, I kick him the rest of the way to the ground for the fun of it.

“Well, that was fun and all, but I got more of your friends to kill and mine to save. Bye-bye.” I wave to his corpse. His eyes are wide and glazed over, his mouth parted, and a pretty, red pool of blood starts forming under his face.

“Ha, you look funny,” I giggle, wiping the blood on my dagger off onto his shirt, then turn around and skip down the tunnel back to the door he came out of. Killing always puts a pep in my step.

Getting to the door, I slowly pull it open. Thankfully, it doesn't make too much noise. Not that anyone would hear it over all the crying.

“Just you wait! When she finds us, and she fucking will, she’s gonna kill you all!” a woman roars. It’s Tracy! My heart skips a beat while a smile splits my face. Thank god, she's here. She just better be okay.

"Oh, shut the fuck up. No one is coming for you. You're just pissed that you were stupid enough to actually believe that I wanted you. I do have to admit that kidnapping one of Queenie's girls was a good 'fuck you' to the stupid bitch." That voice sounds like the dude with the buzz cut.

Looking around the dimly lit space, I see shelves and boxes. It looks like we're in some kind of storage room.

Keeping hidden, I do a quick sweep of the area. There are three men in total: one talking to Tracy and two fuckers sleeping in chairs.

I guess watching a bunch of kidnapped girls can be a pretty tiring job. That's sarcasm, by the way.

Moving around a few more shelves, I get a better look at the girls. I can't see them all, but it looks like the room goes further back into another chamber with wall to ceiling cages taking up the entire space. Fucking pieces of shit are chaining them in like cattle.

Flashes of my past flicker across my mind. Being locked in my cell every night for years. Seeing those helpless girls getting ready to be sold on the night we burnt the place to the ground.

I swore I would never let something like that happen again, but I failed. I won't allow that to happen again. I will take down every motherfucker who ever entertains the thought of crossing Queenie. I will show no more fucking mercy.

Needing to take out the sleeping beauties first, I creep back over to where they are propped up. Luckily, Buzz cut's attention is firmly on Tracy, still arguing away from her cage on the other side of the room, leaving me with the chance to play with his friends.

All I have on me are my guns and daggers. A gun is out of the question, so daggers it is. They're my favorites, anyways.

Tiptoeing over to the first guy, I lean in real close, my dagger gripped in my hand, ready to go.

"Hey, you. Are you awake?" I whisper so the guy a few feet away doesn't hear. The guy's eyes snap open. Oops, guess he was just resting his eyes. "Shit," I giggle, eyes going wide in surprised amusement.

He opens his mouth to talk, yell, I don't fucking know, but I don't need him blowing my cover, so I shove the bandana I have tucked into the top of my shirt into his mouth. I ram the tip of my blade into his neck as he gags around the piece of cloth, but thankfully it muffles the sound. Just for good measure, I yank the dagger out of his neck and plunge it into his chest, hopefully hitting his heart. Fingers crossed.

When I know he's dead, I do what I did with dumb fuck number one and wipe the blood off my blade using his shirt.

Loud snores get my attention from buddy number three. Yay!! This one is actually asleep. It gives me a better chance to have more fun with him.

Looking around for something to use, my eyes land on some rope in a pile on the floor. Cutting it into five pieces, I check how deep of a sleeper this guy is by poking him in the chest a few times. When nothing happens, I take both his hands and tie them to the chair. Then I do the same with his feet. Taking the last piece of rope, I loop it loosely around his neck, then straddle his thighs. Fucker is lucky that he gets to die with me on his lap. He should see it as a fucking honor.

Bringing my ass down hard over his crotch, his eyes fly open as he lets out a pained grunt. Thankfully, no one hears him over Tracy's loud voice as she continues to bitch out buzz head. God, I love that feisty bitch.

Before he can say anything, I pull both ends of the rope, like I did with the tie back when I crashed the business meeting, only this time I go really fucking hard. When his body thrashes in his chair and his face starts to turn blue, I don't let go. Nope, I just sit there with this creepy and crazy as fuck grin plastered on my face, until his body goes slack. What a sight to have as the last thing you see, huh? Priceless.

Crawling off him, I stand there admiring my work. "Nice," I smirk. Now, it's time to get the real show on the road.

"You know what. Your mouth is gonna get you killed. You're not even that fucking pretty. I bet they wouldn't even be mad if I killed you right now," Buzz says, making Tracy start up with another line of curse words. "I have another way to shut you up, though. At least then you might be good for one thing."

Oh fuck. Nope, not gonna happen.

Stepping around the shelf, not quite in their line of sight, but enough for me to be able to see what's going on, I watch this fucker open the cage she's in and start unbuckling his belt.

Tracy realizes what he's about to do and snaps her mouth shut. Horror and fear take over her face as she goes white as a ghost. She scrambles to the corner of the cage, trying to get away from him.

"Got nothing to say now, do you?" he chuckles darkly.

"Fuck you!" she spits, her voice wavering.

"Nah, baby, but I plan to fuck you," he sneers.

From the angle I'm at, they are both sideways. He takes out his pathetic excuse for a dick and starts jacking off as he looks at her with a sick satisfaction.

"At least this job comes with some perks," he leers at her.

Tracy does nothing. She's too proud to beg. We all learned a long time ago that there was no point in wasting our breath on pleas when we were in that basement. But fuck if I'm gonna ever let her be a victim like that again.

I slip my dagger out of its holster and wait for my opening. I need him to be lined up with the gap in the bars for this to work. Come on, target practice, don't fail me now.

Taking a few deep breaths, I focus on my target, and just as he steps into place, I let my baby soar.

I watch as it twirls through the air, right through the bars, slicing his dick clean off.

There's a moment of silence as everything registers in his brain. His eyes go wide as a scream of agony rips from his throat. Blood starts shooting out everywhere. His hands go to his crotch as his knees give out.

Blood splashes onto Tracy as she looks at him in shock, then over to me. Her face splits into a relieved grin.

Taking my gun out, I'm about to shoot the fucker, and get this over with, when Tracy's smile falls. "QUEENIE!" she shouts.

But it's too late. Someone body checks me, barreling into me from the side, sending me crashing into the wall, and knocking the gun from my hand.

Pain radiates through my body as I struggle to breathe from the blow I was just given. My head feels heavy, and ringing takes over my sense of hearing. I almost feel like I'm high.

"Stupid bitch," the guy growls, pulling me up by the shirt, getting in my face. "Can't believe I get to be the one to put down the one and only, all powerful Queenie," he grins.

I struggle in his hold, unable to properly make sense of anything right now. He laughs and laughs as he tells me all the fucked-up things, he wants to do with me, but I can't do anything. My brain is betraying me. I'm useless right now.

Then, there's a bang. Warmth sprays across my face. My body sways back, no longer being held up. Using the wall to keep me from crashing to the ground, I look over to see Tracy standing there with a smoking gun, breathing hard.

She looks at me, then rushes over. "Harlow, thank fuck you're okay. I really thought he was about to kill you," she cries. She helps me stand and brings me over to a chair to sit down.

"Never, Trace. Like fuck I'll go down that easy," I laugh, trying to get the rattling feeling to leave my brain. "But between you and me, it was kind of a hit to my pride, having him get one up on me. But hey, I guess there's always a first time for everything."

"Fuck, I've missed you," she laughs, pulling me into a hug. I hold her tight as an overwhelming feeling of relief and happiness takes over, replacing the pain... for now.

"I knew you would come. I never let myself doubt it for a second."

"From the moment you went missing, and the news reports started up, we did everything we could. But girl, they were good. I'm just sorry it took us this long."

"Don't be. What matters is you found us in time. We're all okay and alive," she says.

"Alright, girl. You okay enough to help us get these girls back to our little village?" I grin.

"More than okay," she smiles. She walks over to the guy who I dick filleted. Fucker is already dead from bleeding out. I'm just sad I didn't get to shove it down this throat.

She takes out a ring of keys and tosses them to me, then walks over to the guy she shot in the head and takes out another set. "I'll take the left side; you take the right?"

"Let's get this done and get these girls home."

It doesn't take too long to get everyone out. I made sure to check them over; some are scared, others are wearing brave faces. They've survived a lot, but I know some of them were not lucky enough to be left untouched. Some of them flinched away at first, and it broke my heart to see, reminding me of too many bad memories.

We gave them some bottles of water and granola bars that the guards had stashed down here. From the looks of these girls, and how they devoured their food, they were not being fed much.

Doing a headcount, I see that we have all ten women. “Alright, Tracy, are you ready to go? We can find the nearest manhole, get to the top, and call for help.”

“Wait, we're missing Sam,” Tracy says, slipping past me and heading down the line of cages, all the way to the back. Sam?

Following her, I see her disappear into the dark. “Tracy!” I hiss, wondering where the fuck she went.

“Over here,” she calls from the dark. Getting the flashlight from my pocket, I follow after her.

There in the dark, away from everyone, is another cage. Only this one doesn't have a girl in it. I shine my light on Tracy and find her squatting next to a man. A very gorgeous man with long, blonde hair and striking blue eyes.

He's huddled in the corner like a scared little mouse, and my heart breaks. His eyes dart between Tracy and me.

“Hey. It's okay. She’s here to help,” Tracy says in a calming voice. “You're okay now.”

Something tells me this man is far from okay.

The beast roars within me. She tells me that this man must be protected at all costs. The overwhelming need to kill every fucker who ever hurt him takes over, and I don't even know this man. I don't know his story or even his full name.

But I do know, from just that one look, that this man has had it much worse than me, and that says a lot.

He's in nothing but a pair of gray sweatpants. Tattoos on display over his naked chest. He looks a little on the scrawny side, but he's still one of the most beautiful men I've ever laid eyes on.

“Tracy. Go back to the girls. I got this,” I tell her.

She looks a little unsure, but does what I ask.

When she's gone, I slowly make my way into the cage. “Hi,” I say, lowering my voice to a softer tone, giving him a sweet smile that probably comes off as sad. “My name is Harlow.”

He just blinks at me. I need him to trust me enough to come with me. I can't and won't leave him behind. My beast has to do this. Needs to.

I sit down on the other side of the cage, facing him.

“You don't have to talk to me. You don't have to tell me anything you don't want to. But I want to help you.”

“Y-you don’t want me?” he asks, his voice cracking.

My brows pinch. “Want you? How so?”

“Like all the others,” he whispers. Others. As in people who fucking held him captive. I don't need him to tell me that he's been beaten and raped for years.

“No,” I say softly. “Can I tell you my story?” I ask. Maybe hearing that I understand what he's going through and that I'm no threat to him will help.

He slowly nods his head.

“When I was 18, I was taken by some really bad men. They held me in the basement of a club for years. But this wasn't just any club. They took girls and sold them to the highest bidder."

"You were sold?" he asks, sounding unsure.

"No," I shake my head. "They saw me as something more valuable than most. They saw a pretty woman who could dance, so they kept me in a cell and only let me out to dance, and well... whenever they wanted my body."

His eyes flush with understanding. "You were raped," he states, knowing there's no question.

I nod. "Every day. More than once, for years."

"So, you don't want me like they do?" he asks, meaning to keep him as a prisoner and take advantage of him.

I try my hardest not to let my anger show, not wanting to scare him. "No. I would NEVER do something like what they did. I want to make sure nothing like that ever happens to you, ever again," I swear.

"My name is Sam," he says.

A bright smile takes over my face. "It's nice to meet you, Sam."

"Are you my guardian angel?" he asks in a whisper.

My heart flutters at his words. How do I answer that? I'm far from anyone's guardian angel. If anything, I'm more like the angel of death, the grim reaper to all things evil.

"I'm whatever you want me to be," I say.

"Good," he says and gives me a beautiful smile, and fuck me, I'm almost knocked on my ass from how stunning he truly is.

"I have nowhere to go," he confesses, his smile slipping. "I lost my home years ago."

Fuck.

"If you're okay with it, I'd like to take you back to my place. I have a little community of town homes that I own. All the women who were in that club with me live there. You will be safe. I promise." Sincerity ringing true in my words.

"I trust you," he says hesitantly, but getting off the ground and giving me his hand. "I don't know why, but something tells me everything is gonna be okay as long as I'm with you. Thank you, Harlow," he whispers, and his gaze is intensely searching mine with a mixture of hope, relief and gratitude written all over his gorgeous face.

I'm speechless. To be granted such trust from someone who's so truly damned from his past is a major fucking honor.

Well, that just set his fate. I'll be his protector for as long as he will allow me, and if for some reason I can't be, Evie will take my place. Something tells me these two are gonna be like two peas in a pod.

Lacing my hand into his, we make our way to the waiting girls.

"Come on, ladies. Time to go home. Your nightmare is over."

CHAPTER THIRTY-ONE

AS WE walk down the tunnel, Sam clings to my arm like I'm his life raft. The poor guy is shaking. There is only pitch-black darkness down here, except for the flashlights the guards had and the one I brought with me.

"How are you doing?" I whisper, not wanting to draw attention to us. Sam tightens his grip on my arm but relaxes when I give his hand a reassuring squeeze.

"I don't like the dark," he whispers back, sounding ashamed. "They always had some kind of light when I was in my cell. And when I wasn't, bad things happened in the dark."

The thought of what they did to him makes me so fucking mad and makes my heart hurt for him. "We're almost to the nearest ladder; then we will be above ground and in the light," I say, smiling up at him. His face is just barely visible in the flashlight's glow.

"Will there be sunlight when we get there?" his eyes light up.

I think for a moment, calculating the time. “I left around 8 this morning. It took me two hours to find you and about an hour and a half to get rid of the guards, gather everyone, and leave, meaning it should be around noonish, so yeah, the forecast is calling for a bright and sunny day,” I chirp.

“Sun,” he sighs happily. I don't say anything more. From the way he just reacted, I don't think he's seen the sunlight in a very long time.

When we get to the ladder, we all gather around.

“Alright, I'm gonna go up first and see how hard it is to get the manhole cover off. If I can't get it open, I'll be close enough to the top to get some service, and I’ll call for help,” I say, letting go of Sam's hand and starting towards the ladder.

He grabs a hold of my hand. Looking back, his eyes are filled with fear. “Don't go,” he whimpers.

“I won't be long, okay. I'll be right back. You're okay now. I won't let anything happen to you. I promise,” I soothe him, rubbing my hands up and down his arms. Then, I realize what I’m doing. I look up at him, seeing if he's uncomfortable or has any fear of me touching him like this.

But his face relaxes, and he leans into my touch. He closes his eyes and takes a deep breath. “Okay. I can do this.”

“Fuck, yeah you can.” I beam up at him, and he gives me a matching one. I can see his face wrinkle on the side, like his face isn't used to that movement. It’s gonna be my mission to make this man smile so much his face hurts.

Hesitantly, he lets my hand go.

The climb up the ladder is a bitch. I didn't know how fucking far underground we were. It's just our luck that when I get to the top, I find myself in one of the main, above ground, maintenance rooms. Looking around, I find the door, then another, and by the 3rd door I am able to step out onto a sidewalk. Looking around, I see a sign that says 34th street, and I know we're not too far from my place.

"Karma, my main bitch, I wish you were a person right now, so I could ram my tongue down your pretty, little throat and kiss you for this stroke of luck," I shout, scaring off a few crows from a nearby power line. For a second, I wonder where the guys ended up.

"Alright, everyone," I say, hopping down off the ladder. "I have good news and just some small, inconvenience news."

I walk back over to Sam, who is a few steps away from the group, sitting on the ground huddled into himself.

"I tried to keep him calm, but the longer you took, the more anxious he became. I didn't want to make it worse," Tracy says, looking at Sam with a sad smile then back to me. "He's gonna need you to get through this."

"I know." I pat Tracy on the back and make my way over to Sam.

"Hey," I greet him calmly. He peeks up over his arms. "I'm back. Just like I told you I'd be." I hold my hand out for him, and he takes it eagerly. When he's standing, he pulls me into a hug, holding me in a death grip.

"I don't think I can do this, Harlow," he whispers shakily.

"You can. And I'll be right there next to you, holding your hand," I grin up at him. He gives me a brave nod.

"So, good news. Getting out of here is gonna be easy, but the ladder is pretty high up, so it's gonna take some time to get everyone up. And my place isn't too far from here. Bad news, I called my guys, and they are all still underground looking. They were ordered to go back to the club if they didn't find anything, so I'm not worried about them. But there's no one at the club to come pick us up. My friend Evie could, but it would just be quicker for us to all walk there together. It's only five blocks north. If you're up for it?"

"We've been down here for months. I think a little extra time, breathing in the fresh air, and having the sun on our faces will be nice," a blonde girl pipes up, smiling gratefully at me. The rest of them agree and with that, we start making our way to the top.

It takes us about a half hour to get everyone out, leaving Sam and me till last.

"Are you ready?" I ask.

"I think so," he says, sounding unsure as he looks up the ladder. "Do I really get to stay with you?"

"We have a house we can set you up in," I nod with a smile.

"I don't want to be alone anymore," he says, his voice filled with despair. My heart is about to flat line right now with all these feelings that are rushing through me for this guy, whom I've never even met before.

"We'll think of something, so you won't have to be alone." The idea of him staying at my place feels funny. I never had a roommate after we escaped and moved here. Even Evie got her own place. Not that I didn't enjoy living with her for all of those years in our cell. She was the best person I could have asked to be trapped with. But once we were out and free, I had a strong need for independence and finding a new normal.

He accepts the answer, knowing there's nothing left to lose at this point, and it's sad.

"I'll go last," I say when he looks around like someone's gonna jump out at him.

He gives me a grateful smile and a sigh of relief, as he starts up the ladder while I shine the flashlight up so that he can see. When he gets up to the top, he calls down for me.

Time to end this fucking nightmare.

Sam stands there, eyes closed with his face directed towards the sky. He has a content smile on his face as he soaks in the sun. "I forgot what it felt like to have the sun warming my skin, the smell of fresh air," he says softly, lowering his face to look at me.

"Sam, I don't know your story, but someday, I hope you trust me enough to tell me," I say, giving his hand a squeeze. I want to be able to help him, but until I know his story, I can't fully understand. All I know is that it's similar to mine, but at the same time it's completely different.

"Someday," he says, giving me a soft smile.

We start following the girls in the direction of our home, but we keep lagging behind, and I can tell it's because Sam feels more relaxed around fewer people. Maybe it's because he is used to being alone, or because he doesn't know who he can and can't trust. My guess is that he trusts no one, and rightfully so.

He sure seems to trust you.

Looking up at Sam, I see him taking in his surroundings with wide eyes, looking like he's ready for someone to grab him at any moment. I really hope that someday he can feel safe in his new home. He will always be welcome in our little family, no matter what.

When we get to the club, the guys are all standing around. Some look stressed, others look tired.

Neo is pacing back and forth like a caged animal as Cass tries to calm him down. Evie is standing by the door, talking to a few of the guys when she sees me, spotting the whole group.

"They're here!" she shouts excitedly, staring at us like she can't believe her eyes. Everyone starts to look our way, and the cheering begins. Sam flinches at the noise.

Evie runs over to Tracy and wraps her arms around her in a big hug. Evie sees me, and her face lights up. She's about to come over when she notices Sam. She looks him over, then back to me. Shock takes over her face when she realizes that the girls were not the only ones down there. Looking at me for a moment longer, she turns toward the girls and ushers them into the club, following after to start making all the necessary calls. We have a doctor there waiting to check them over. He's one of Miller's best friends. He never asks questions, which is nice.

"Thank fuck, you're okay," Neo growls before crushing me to his chest. I let out a hiss of pain. He quickly lets go of me, holding me out at arm's length. "You're hurt?" He doesn't look very happy about that.

"Nothing I can't handle, Pet," I wink. "I mostly just hurt my pride. I think I'll live, though. But the fewer people that know, the better," I say playfully. Neo's not having it. At all.

"Let me see," he demands.

"Whoa there," I laugh in surprise. "Who the fuck do you think you are?"

"Sorry," he deflates. "It's just that we all got back here, and you weren't here, and none of us found the girls. I was starting to think you did, but the job was too much for just you, and now you were stuck down there with them."

"Took a lot to keep him here. He was ready to go down there and find you himself," Cass says, giving me a smile. "I'm glad you're okay though."

"Harlow," Sam whispers from behind me. Crap, I forgot about him for a moment. He's looking at Neo with pure fear, like he's about to drop into the fetal position.

"Hey, it's okay. He's not gonna hurt you," I say, stepping closer to him, caressing his face. I don't know why the fuck I'm doing this, I've never done this, but it feels... right?

He closes his eyes, relaxing into my hand.

"Deep breaths," I say soothingly.

"Who the fuck is this?" Neo's voice is low with pure venom. My eyes snap over to his. Raging jealousy is swimming in his pretty, blue eyes. He looks seconds away from shooting Sam. Fuck me. Sam backs away, whimpering.

"That's enough," I command Neo.

When Neo does nothing and continues to shoot daggers at Sam, I slap him across the face.

That snaps him out of it.

"When I give you a command, Pet, you obey. Do. You. Understand?" I ask in a deadly tone.

His nostrils flare, his eyes wild. His beast is hovering on the surface, and as much as I've been dying to see him, not just the glimpse I've gotten, now is not the time for that.

"Yes, Mistress," he forces out through gritted teeth.

"Good. Now go inside. Evie has the girls under control. I need to help Sam."

Neo tries to look back at Sam, but I tightly grip his face between my fingers. "Go!" I growl. He lets out a pissed off huff and storms towards the club, passing Axel and Dean who are watching the whole interaction.

"I'm getting drunk, and all of you can kiss my tight, fucking ass!" Neo shouts before disappearing into the club.

"I don't know what's going on, but I'll let you do what you gotta do. I'm gonna go see if Evie needs any help," Cass says, looking a little uneasy about Sam, but gives me a tight smile.

"Thanks," I smile back.

When he's gone, the others give me one last look before turning to follow Cass.

"I'm so sorry about that," I say, turning back to Sam.

"I don't understand," he whispers. "Why did you call him Pet? Do you...? Do you own him?" he asks, his eyes wide as he gives me a look of fear for the first time, and fuck, does it ever hurt.

"No. No, I don't own him, I promise. Neo and I... we have a different kind of relationship. It's a little complicated to get into right now, but I can assure you, he is his own person, free to do whatever he wants." Okay, that's not exactly true, but he doesn't need to know that right now.

"Sam, there's a lot you don't know and probably won't understand about me and this life that I've built," I sigh, not sure how to explain to him that I'm a serial killer, or that how I've been with him is not like my normal persona.

"I heard Tracy call you Queenie?" Sam says, looking a little less fearful of me.

"Yes. That's what the world knows me as. Only the people I trust know my real name."

"But you told me?" he asks, sounding confused.

I take one of his hands in mine, and he laces his fingers through mine. "You know how you didn't fear me, talked to me, and trusted me enough to get you out of there?" He nods. "Why did you do that?"

"I don't know," he says, brows pinching. "Something in me felt like it was okay. That, with you, everything was going to be okay," he whispers.

I smile up at him. "Well, the first moment I laid eyes on you, I just knew I could trust you too. I want you to know me how everyone else that I trust knows me. How my family knows me."

"I've heard of you before. Queenie, I mean," he says, a bit of amusement laced in his voice.

"Oh god," I groan.

"Is it true that you kill people for a living?"

I bite my lip. "Well, not for a living. More as a... hobby? I mean, I don't get paid for it." I give him an awkward smile.

"I've heard the name Queenie mentioned in almost every place I was held. They acted like you were a joke, not to be feared, but I could tell it was all false bravado. Why would they fear you like that?"

"Because I put people like them down. Mostly rapists and abusers, but any kind of scum will do," I shrug, not wanting to lie.

"So, would you ever hurt someone who didn't deserve it?" he asks.

"Never," I say, strongly. "I don't hurt innocent people."

"What about the people who are bad, but not that bad?" he asks, tilting his head to the side as if trying to understand me.

"Oh well, I'd kick their ass of course," I snort shamelessly. Sam grins.

"Okay," he finally says.

"Okay?" I ask. "That's it?" He nods. "Alright then, let's get you up to my place. I can get you settled in the spare room before I go downstairs to deal with everything else."

We head up to my apartment through the side door of the club to avoid the crowd of people.

"As you can see, the kitchen's here," I say, pointing to the left as I flick on the light. "Living room. Down the hall is the bathroom and bedroom." I toss my keys on the counter and turn to Sam. He takes in the room slowly.

"The fridge is fully stocked. Feel free to help yourself. There are clean towels and stuff in the hall closest. I don't really have any guy clothes, but I do have a few oversize shirts that should fit you. And I find men boxers comfy, so I like to use them as sleep shorts; they should also fit you."

I stand there awkwardly. No one but Evie has ever been in here. I don't allow just anyone in my personal space; this is all so... new to me.

"You can stay in here," I say, turning on the light to the guest room. It's nothing fancy, just a queen size bed with a black and white bed set. A side table with a lamp and a dresser. "There's extra blankets and pillows in the hall closest as well. You can take a shower if you want," I say, heading back to the living room. A shower... Fuck that sounds amazing right about now. My hair is a wild mess, there's blood dried to my skin, and I smell like BO. Eww.

"I know you said you don't want to be alone. And I'd stay if I could, but I really do have to deal with everything," I say, biting my lip, hoping he doesn't freak out.

"I understand," he says, looking a little disappointed.

"I'll lock the door when I leave. No one can get in but me or Evie, and I trust her with my life. If you turn on the TV, it should help with the silence." I know this from experience. When I first started staying here alone, I hated the silence. It made me jumpy as fuck. Sleeping with a fan at night helped me close my eyes, and the TV helped my mind not to wander.

"Harlow," Sam says softly. "Thank you. I owe you."

"You owe me nothing," I say, shaking my head.

"I owe you everything," he says, before turning around and shutting the bathroom door behind him. I head to my own bathroom to take a quick shower before I head out to see how everything's going.

When I get down to the club, the place is packed, but only with the girls. "Where did everyone else go?" I ask, wondering where all my men went.

"They wanted to give the girls some space. Plus, our girls wanted to check on them," Roxy says, fixing me a drink. The woman knows me well.

"Queenie," a voice comes from behind me. Turning around, I see Miller heading towards me. He's out of uniform. Probably a good idea.

"What's up, Milly?" I smirk. He rolls his eyes, but I see a slight smile forming on his lips.

"I wanted to go over a few things. Your girls are going to take these young ladies for the night. Let them clean up, eat, and rest properly before those who have homes to go back to face their families."

"What are they going to tell them? What are you going to tell your boss?" I ask Miller.

"Don't worry, I'll come up with something. You won't be involved in this as far as anyone outside these girls and whoever works for you is concerned."

I nod. "Good, let me know whatever cover story you're going with. So, how many have homes to go to?"

"All of them."

"That's amazing," I grin. I would have given any one of them a place here, but knowing they have people to go home to is even better.

Miller and I chat for a little longer. When he leaves, I realize that everyone else has left as well, with only a few of my girls sitting scattered around the club.

"What the...?" My brows furrow.

Roxy laughs. "Evie came and told me, while you were busy with Miller, she and the others were gonna get the girls settled in for the night. As for your guys, the asshole one and the silent one took the now drunk crazy one home."

"What about Cass?" I ask.

"The sweetheart?" she grins. "I saw him going up to the roof not too long ago. Poor guy looks like a mess."

Downing my drink, I head up to find Cass.

CHAPTER THIRTY-TWO

Harlow

I FIND him just sitting there on one of the lawn chairs. We had the whole roof renovated. A nice seating area, a barbecue, and couches.

He's leaning over with his elbows on his legs, head in his hands.

At first, I think he's just relaxing, but when I get closer, I see a slight shake of his shoulders. He's... crying.

"Hey," I say softly. "You okay?"

His head snaps up to me, and I can see his eyes are red, tears staining his cheeks.

"Oh, hey," he forces out a laugh, wiping his face. "I'm fine," he says, his voice cracking a little.

"You don't look fine," I say with caution as I take a seat beside him.

"Alright, I'm not fine," he sighs.

"Want to talk about it?" I ask.

He looks at me with wide eyes, shocked. It's almost comical. “YOU want to talk to ME about my feelings?” he asks.

“What?!” I huff. “*I* can be a good listener when I want to. Who do you think all the girls come to with their problems?” I give him a cocky smirk.

“I guess that’s true,” he nods his head. Closing his eyes, he sighs. “It's a lot, Har. A whole fucking lot. And if I start talking, I don’t think I'm gonna be able to stop. I’ve been holding a shit ton in for a very long time. And it's not just about Rosie.” He looks at me, and his green eyes are swimming with the emotions of everything he’s ever wanted to say to me, and a part of me is dying to hear it all; the other part is terrified.

Pulling on my big girl panties, I go for it. “I want to hear it. All of it.”

He looks at me like he's trying to memorize every inch of my face. Like I'm going to disappear again after he tells me.

He looks away from me, staring out at the city far off in the distance. “I went to the therapist again the other day. I thought I would give it another try.”

“How did it go?”

“Better than last time. But no matter what she tells me, I will always blame myself.”

“You couldn't have known, Cass. The whole situation is fucked up. It’s not something you can easily tell when it comes to a child so young.” I, myself, didn't know how fucked up and wrong everything I went through was, until I heard an older girl crying about it one day. Talking about how fucked up and wrong what happened to us in that place was. Her parents just died, and she was forced into the system. She had a normal life, until she got to the group home.

"I'm her father, Harlow. I should have been able to protect her. I'm supposed to be the one who keeps the monsters away, but I did nothing!" he growls, growing angrier by the minute. I'm not gonna tell him it's not his fault anymore. Clearly, that's not what he needs. He needs to vent, so that's what I'll do. Let him vent, while I just listen.

"She was with that man for two years. Two fucking YEARS of my child's life. How long was it going on? Was he doing all of that to a fucking two-year-old?! Fuck!" He punches the side of the building, breathing heavily as he closes his eyes, trying to get himself under control. His eyes open, searching for me. They soften as they fill with love and gratitude. "You," he breathes.

"Me?" I ask, pointing to myself like an idiot. "What did I do?"

He starts to laugh. I think he's lost it. "What did you do? Harlow, you did everything. Everything I couldn't. Because of your past, you were able to see the signs we couldn't. You saw a little girl in pain, afraid, and helpless, while we thought she just hated her mom. You saw the deeper meaning behind her cries. If you didn't come back into our lives, Harlow..." He sits back down next to me. "Something so much more horrendous would have happened. If he'd ended up raping her, god, I don't know *what* I would have done." He looks so broken as tears start to fall down his cheeks again. My heart breaks right along-side his. I love that little girl just as much as he does, and the idea of her having to go through that makes me sick to my fucking stomach.

"Thank you," he chokes out. "Thank you so fucking much." He cups my face, rubbing his thumbs against my cheeks as he looks at me like I'm his whole fucking world.

I let him, conflicted with what my heart and mind are telling me. My mind is telling me to back away, to shut down, but my heart is telling me to kiss him, to consume him in every way possible, and more.

"You're exactly what we didn't know we needed in our lives. You saved that little girl and, in return, became the best damn mother any kid could ever have. I don't care what you do in the basement of this building; I don't care that you have something with Neo. I don't fucking care about any of that." He closes his eyes and exhales before looking back at me with a look of determination in his eyes. "I need to tell you, Harlow. It's been eating at me for a while now."

Fuck. Here it is. Something I never wanted him to say to me again. Something that I know, at this point in my life, will break the dam built around my heart and send it flooding, destroying so much in its path. But I won't stop him. I don't look away. I don't say a word. I don't even fucking breathe.

"I love you, Harlow. So much that it hurts. I fell madly in love with you the moment I saw you when we were teenagers, and I never looked back. When you left, it destroyed me. I lost pieces of myself I never thought I'd get back. Parts of me were put back together when Rosie came into my life, but there was always something missing.

"When you took my little girl and made her your own, not once caring that she wasn't your blood. When you killed to protect her, like I would've, that's when the last few pieces clicked back into place. No, you're not the same Harlow you were back then, the one I fell in love with. But you are something better now. You're strong, beautiful, fierce. You were dealt a fucked-up hand your whole life, but you never let it break you. You are the perfect woman to raise my little girl. OUR little girl. And you're the perfect woman to spend the rest of my life with. I love you, Harlow McKaven. And I'm never letting you go," he growls, right before he smashes his lips against mine.

My heart is pounding, my breathing erratic, and I feel like my soul just left my body. *That part of me that's telling me to run? Yeah, I just shot her in the fucking head and buried her tiny, little body.*

I should castrate him for touching me without my permission, but instead I open for him when his tongue licks the seam of my lips.

He devours my mouth with his tongue as mine battles with his. I moan and move to straddle his lap. He's hard as fucking steel.

My hands thread through his long locks as I grip them hard, making him grunt. He moves his hands from my face to my ass, grasping my cheeks and grinding me against him.

But that's as rough as it gets. We move with each other, kissing, consuming, as I rock against him.

I'm so fucking wet that I bet there's a damp spot over his crotch right now, but I don't care. My beast is roaring inside. She wants him. She wants to let him in, in every way possible.

So, when he lays me back on the lounge chair, I let him cover my body with his.

He settles between my legs as he moves his lips from mine to my neck, sucking and nipping at the sensitive skin. I mewl at his touch. I fucking mewl like a bitch in heat, and I fucking love it.

“Let me make love to you, Har. Let me make you feel good?” he asks as he trails kisses down my chest. When I say nothing, he looks at me, knowing he won't get further without my permission. “Tell me to stop, and I will.” His pupils are wide and black. His own beast hovering right behind them. He needs this. He needs me more than I understand. A part of me didn't know that I needed him too. *Fuck*. I say nothing. But I also don't deny him.

He takes that as a yes. Because he knows that if I didn't want this, he would be dead by now.

Lowering his head back down, he moves my top down so that he can take my hard nipple into his mouth. I moan, closing my eyes as he swirls his tongue around the hardened peak.

My body is on fire, every nerve ending going off like the Fourth of July. My pussy is pulsing, demanding he fill us up, my clit aching with need.

One of his big, strong hands slides down the front of my pants, right over my soaked core. Fuck, I shout in my head, scared that if I speak out loud, I'll come to my senses, and this will be all over. I hiss as he rubs my clit with his finger.

"I've been dreaming about this every fucking night," he groans against my skin as he makes his way down to my needy core, pulling my pants down as he does.

"My lips against your soft, creamy skin." He kisses my belly. "My hands on your body." He kisses my mound. "And my mouth, feasting on your perfect pussy," he growls as he stares at my dripping cunt like a man who hasn't eaten in weeks.

Wasting no time, he dives between my legs. He starts lapping up my leaking core, not wanting to waste one drop. My body arches off the chair, and I cry out at the contact of his tongue against my over sensitized bud.

He sucks it into his mouth as he devours his meal.

My hands fly into his hair to hold him tight against me as I start riding his face. He groans against my center, vibrating against it, making my body shiver in delight. My fingers dig into his scalp, and I'm sure I'm drawing blood, but he loves it. He grips my ass, bringing me closer to his face, as if I wasn't already smothering him.

Then my orgasm hits me like a fucking freight train. My head flying back hard and fast. I'm surprised I didn't break my neck. My back arches off the chair so high, I probably look like I'm possessed by a demon and his mouth is the one performing the exorcism.

The scream that rips from my throat is so loud that I think I broke the sound barrier. Fuck. I'm dead. Like no, really. I felt my soul exit my body with that scream.

I will my lungs to take in air as I come down from that earth-shattering climax.

Licking his lips, with one of the most fucking adorable smiles on his face, he crawls between my legs, and hovers over me. “I don’t want to fuck you, Harlow,” he says, kissing me hard. I can taste myself on his lips. My tongue darts out, licking his, wanting a better taste. He growls with approval. “I want to make love to you. Please.”

My heart flutters. Make love. I haven't made love to a man since... well, since him. The part of me who fell in love with him all those years ago craves this, needs this.

“Okay,” I say, hearing my voice for the first time since we started kissing.

We strip our clothes off and lay back down on the chair. Cass holds himself up so that he can take in my naked body. “So fucking perfect,” he breathes. “Everything about you is. Even the parts that aren't.”

Looking down between his legs, I find his cock hard and waiting. Pre-cum covers his tip. It looks magnificent.

My eyes find his. We don't break eye contact as he settles between my legs. He claims my mouth again, before thrusting his cock into my needy, little pussy.

We both moan into the kiss. My nails are digging into his back.

Slowly and softly, he makes love to me. My brain is hyper focused on the feeling of his cock deep inside me. How my body tingles all over. It's one of the most intense experiences I’ve ever felt.

All my love for Cass, past, present, and future rushes to the surface. Tears fall down my face as I start to feel something I swore I never wanted to feel again. Something that made me feel weak and vulnerable. Something that could be used against me, to break me.

Cass makes love to me until I'm a shaking, blubbering mess under him. Who the fuck am I right now? This isn't a Harlow I'm used to.

All too soon, I feel another orgasm teetering on the edge. "Cass!" I cry, my voice cracking with emotion.

"That's it, Sweetheart," he says, sounding like he's holding back his own release. My legs tighten around him as my climax takes over. My nails scraping down his back as I hold on to him for dear life, and then I cum, so hard that I see stars, crying out his name.

With a few more thrusts, he follows after me with my name on his lips like he's uttering a prayer. His cock jerks in me, filling me with hot cum.

When he's done, he relaxes on top of me, holding himself up so that his weight doesn't crush me. Tucking his face into my neck, he kisses me, and sighs contently. "That was better than I could ever imagine." He smiles against my neck. "Thank you."

I don't say anything. I just blink up at the sky. I can't breathe. I feel smothered. What the fuck just happened?!

Cass told me he loved me. He told me he wanted to be more than friends. He kissed me. We made... love.

I can't breathe.

"Get off me," I croak.

"What?" he asks, pushing himself up so that he can look at me.

With panicked eyes, I repeat my words. "Get off me!"

He quickly detaches himself from me, standing up next to the chair, his cock still semi hard. Scrambling to get up, I move away from him.

"Harlow," he sighs, like he expected this.

"Don't you Harlow me!" I snap, narrowing my eyes at him. "What the fuck was that?" I say, waving my hand around in the direction of the chair.

His face softens. "Har, I know you're freaking out because this is all new to you. This isn't the person you molded yourself into to protect yourself. But I'm not letting you regret this," he says, crossing his arms.

"Don't tell me what to do." My voice is rising. "Fuck. My brain. God, my brain is so messed up right now."

"I know," he says softly.

"I don't know how to feel this way, Cass," I say, looking up at him with helpless eyes.

"I know," he repeats.

"This isn't me," I say, as I start to pace back and forth.

"I k-"

"Don't you fucking say I know again, or I'll bitch slap you!" I warn.

He smiles at my outburst and says, "This is all new and scary. But tell me, did you not feel the same? Did you not feel the love I have for you just now?"

"Ugh!" I shout, rubbing my hands down my face. "Yes! Okay, I did."

"And what did you feel?" he asks.

Looking up at him with frustrated tears, I wipe them away angrily. "I worked so fucking hard to never feel that way again, Cass. I can't survive that again." Tears start to flow for real now.

"What did you feel, Sweetheart?" Fuck, when he calls me that I feel all gooey.

"Mind numbing, soul crushing love," I whisper, feeling overwhelmed by a slowly spreading sense of dread.

He smiles so fucking bright that I think I'm gonna go blind if I look too long. "I love you, Harlow. Neo loves you, and I'm pretty sure Dean does too. We don't care who you became; we love whatever version of you, you're willing to give us now," he says, cupping my cheek, and I'm too shell shocked to move.

Like... is no one gonna point out that we're having this grand confession of love butt ass naked on the roof of my club while Cass's cum drips down my leg...? No? No one? Kay, cool.

"I need time," I whisper. "This is all too much. I can't think straight. I need to go. I need to get out of here. Just for a little bit."

He gives me a sad smile, "I know."

I narrow my eyes at him. He's so calm... Why is he so calm?! But he just chuckles. "Go. Take as much time as you need to come to terms with everything that's changing," he tells me.

"But what about the club? Rosie? What about the girls?" I say, exasperated.

"Rosie will be fine. She has me and her uncles. The girls will be fine with Evie. And the club will run smoothly with all of us working together," Cass says, leaning over and kissing the top of my head.

"Well, don't you just have everything figured out?!" I huff, crossing my arms with a pout.

He chuckles again. "I've just been playing how this moment might go in my mind a little too much."

"And how did it end?" I snark, and the fucker laughs. Again!

"It went one of two ways. The first being, I told you my feelings, and then you stabbed me in the neck," he smirks. My smile goes wide because that was a big possibility.

"Or the second, where you were so freaked out over everything that you ran," he says knowingly. My smile instantly drops.

"I'm not running!" I say, voice dangerous. Maybe it's not too late to stab the fucker. "I don't run from my problems. I face them and fix them," I insist.

"And that's exactly what this time away is gonna be for you. Harlow, you don't have to explain yourself to me. I get it. With Neo being attached to you like a leech, and everything that's going on with the club, the girls, and becoming a mom overnight, it's a lot to take in. You can't think straight, and you need some room to clear your mind." I HATE that he knows me so well. When the fuck did that happen, again?

"Neo," I groan. "He's not gonna like this."

Cass's face darkens. "No. But we will deal with him."

“Cass. I see how that man looks at me. He's gonna be fucking crushed.”

“Like I said. We will deal with him,” Cass insists, stubborn bastard. “You have been putting everyone else before yourself for years. It’s time you take care of yourself for once.”

“But-”

“No buts,” Cass says, holding his hand up to stop me.

“Okay, you need to fuck off with that. You may have caught me in a mood with all the feels, but that doesn't change the fact that I can still shoot you if I wanted to,” I snap.

“But you won't. Because you looooove me,” he teases with a cheeky smile.

“Do not,” I grumble.

“Do tooooo,” he sing-songs, and I can't help but smile at this big muscle man acting like a little, love-struck fool.

“Go. While everyone is sleeping tonight. Write Evie a letter. I'll tell the rest tomorrow.”

“I wanna say goodbye to Rosie. I don't want her to ever think I’m abandoning her.” The thought of leaving that little girl for any amount of time makes me wanna cry again.

God, what is wrong with me? I haven't cried in god knows how many years. I'm not a fan. I give it a -100 out of 10. Would not recommend.

“You’re not abandoning her. It takes a strong woman to admit when she needs help, even if it's to help yourself. Go. Take your time and come back being the best version of Harlow you can be.”

"You do know Queenie isn't going anywhere. Harlow may be rising from the dead, but the Queen is here to stay. Till death do us part, and all that jazz," I warn.

"I wouldn't have it any other way," he grins.

After saying goodbye to Cass, I head back to my apartment. I pack a small bag with clothes and my daggers. I'll get whatever else I need as I go. Sitting down, I write the best letter I can to Evie, hoping she understands why I need to do this. I sit there for what feels like hours, trying to find the right words. When it's finally written, I leave it on the counter.

I head back to my room and grab my passport from the safe in the hidden compartment of my closet floor, and all the cash.

I'm pissed I gotta leave my gun behind, but I'll be able to find one easily where I'm going.

Exiting my room, I look over to the guest room. Fuck. Sam. How could I forget about him? Damn it.

"Sam," I whisper into his room, expecting him to be asleep. But he's not. He's sitting on the bed with all the lights on, watching something on the tablet I let him use.

"Hi," he says, smiling brightly. God, this makes it so much worse.

"Can we talk?" I ask, stepping farther into the room. He looks at my bag and frowns.

"Are you going somewhere?"

"About that," I say, biting my lip. "That's what I need to talk to you about." I place the bag on the ground and take a seat on the edge of the bed. "There's a lot you won't understand about me or my life. And I know we just met, but I feel this connection to you. I want you here. I want you safe. I have to go away for a little while. But I'll be back. You can stay here; this apartment is yours. No one but Evie is allowed in here. She will be here for you when I can't." God, I hope he understands because I'm already about to piss off enough people.

"Oh," he says, looking down at his hands.

"Sam..."

"No. I get it. I don't know why you have to go, but I just hope you come back the same... you," he grins sadly.

"And what "me" would that be?" I laugh.

"My guardian angel," he whispers.

Like a fucking ninja, I sneak through the guys' house. I waited until night to say goodbye to Rosie. Cass isn't home right now, and I don't want to risk waking up the others. If Neo found out that I was leaving, there's no way he would let me go. I would have to shoot him, just to slow him down.

Cass asked me where I was planning on going, but I didn't tell him. I didn't want to risk Neo beating the answer out of him to come after me.

As hard as it is to admit to myself, I am falling in love with the crazy bastard. And I feel like shit with what I'm about to do. But Cass is right. I need this. I can't think right with everything that's going on. Big changes are about to come, and I need to be ready. Mind, body, and soul.

Just when I think I'm about to make it undetected to Rosie's room, I almost trip over something. "Quack!" Daisy practically yells at me.

"Shh! Don't blow my cover, you little shit," I whisper harshly at the duck. "Shouldn't you be in there with your mother? It's way past your bedtime." She just quacks at me again.

Quickly I scoop her up and dash into Rosie's room. Placing Daisy down on the bed, she ruffles her feathers before getting comfy and falling asleep. Shaking my head, I slightly chuckle. Silly bird.

"Mama?" Rosie's eyes blink open. Her beautiful, blue ones find mine. I'm hit with a wave of guilt and sorrow. How the hell do I leave this amazing, little human behind for any amount of time? God, I hope she doesn't hate me.

"Hey, Kiddo," I smile.

"What's wrong?" she asks, sitting up.

"Nothing's wrong, Sweetie, Mama just wanted to see you."

"Oh," she tilts her head. "No. That's not it," she shakes her head.

Smart kid.

"You're too smart for your own good sometimes," I grin, and she giggles. "Mama wanted to talk to you before she leaves."

"Leaves? Where are you going?"

"I have to go away for a little bit. But I'll be back. Mama's been working really hard, and I need to get away for a little while."

"Can I come?" she pouts. Fuck.

"No, Baby Girl. Where Mama's going, little girls aren't allowed," I say, wanting to shoot myself in the foot for crushing my baby girl's heart.

"But you're gonna come back?"

"Always, Sweet Girl. Mama will always come back. And we can FaceTime every night that I'm away."

Her face lights up. "Okay!" But then it falls. "But I'm gonna miss you."

I bite my lip, holding those fucking tears at bay again, and climb over to her side of the bed, snuggling in next to her. "I'm gonna miss you too. Soooooo much. But your Daddy and uncles and even Auntie Evie will keep you so busy, time will fly by."

I hold Rosie in my arms, playing with her hair until she falls back asleep. Giving her one last kiss on the cheek, I quietly slip out of the house.

Once I'm on the highway, I blast Check it out by Nicki Minaj and will.i.am, trying to get my mind off all the emotions swimming around in my brain.

This is what I know. I'm changing. As much as I wanted to deny it, since the guys came back into my life, the walls around my heart have been slowly chipped away, but I've been too busy, too... happy to notice.

Rosie is a big part of that. This little girl reminded me so much of myself; she won me over with just one look.

I spent years hating the guys for what they did. Thinking they never loved me, never wanted me. When really, it was all one big clusterfuck.

Dean cared about me so much that he was trying to save me from the life their fathers were forcing them into, when really, I ended up in one much worse.

When Dean lost it in his office, I knew he was in anguish about what his actions caused.

These boys, now men, always have ended up being an exception to my rules. I guess nothing's changed. Well, except Axel, that fucker can go eat a dick.

I don't know what I want to happen, or what will happen with each guy, but I guess that's what this little trip is about. Time for me to think about what I truly want, so that I'm not going into this blind or making myself suffer more, just because I'm too chicken shit to try.

I'm a big, bad, motherfucking bitch, but I'm also human, and it's human nature to have these feelings, no matter how much they suck.

"Have a nice trip, Miss Snow," the airline worker smiles, handing me back my passport.

You didn't really think I'd have one in my actual name, did you? Nah, until I get back, I'm Ruby Snow.

Walking past the window, I look at the tiny airplane I'm about to board. Excitement takes over me. This is the first time I've gone anywhere in the world that wasn't for work.

Catching a glimpse of myself in the windows of the plane, I grin at my reflection. The short, white-blonde wig is a big change from my long, raven-black locks, but it's kind of sexy. Maybe I'll wear it in the dungeon with Neo sometime.

Just thinking about all the yummy things we're gonna do when I get back has me clenching my thighs. Fuck, this is gonna be a long flight.

Neo's gonna be pissed that I'm gone. Okay, that's nowhere near the proper word for what he's going to be. Something tells me the beast he's been hiding is going to be coming out to play. And as fucked up as this sounds, I'm excited to see him in all his glory. My beast is dying to meet his. Oh, and just think about all the bloody, messed up things we could do together.

I don't know exactly where I'm going to end up on this trip, but I do know how I plan on spending it.

What better way to clear a killer's mind than a good, old mass murder.

Get ready world, because Queenie wants to play.

The end... For now.

Want to find out what's next for Queenie and her gang?

Find out in

Blood Empire - Book Two: Crowned Queen

BOOKS BY ALISHA WILLIAMS

EMERALD LAKE PREP – SERIES:

Book One: Second Chances (February 2021)

Book Two: Into The Unknown (May 2021)

Book Three: Shattered Pieces (September 2021)

BLOOD EMPIRE – SERIES:

Book One: Rising Queen (July 2021)

Book Two: Crowned Queen (Coming soon)

ACKNOWLEDGEMENT

I would love to give a big thank you to anyone who has supported me on this journey. A big thank you to every single person who helped bring Queenie's story to life. Without each one of you, this book would not be possible.

I'm also beyond grateful for Jessica Pollio-Napoles, Lærke Gade Villemoes, and Catherine Kilkenny Kroeger. You ladies are more than just my Alphas, you're family now! Thank you for all the time and energy you put into Rising Queen, and helping it become the awesome book that it is! I don't think I would have had as much fun writing it without you three! Can't wait to make way more books with you!

And a big shout out to my best friend of 24 years, Brittany Loubert. Thank you for being my cheerleader to my fucked-up, dark mind with this book. Thank you for always rooting for me no matter what I write.

Many thanks to my Beta and ARC teams. You all helped me make my book even better, and I look forward to sending you way more work in the future.

And finally, thank you to all my readers. It was an honor to write this book for you. Thank you for giving our crazy Queen a chance.

ABOUT ALISHA

Writer, Alisha Williams, lives in Alberta, Canada with her husband and her two headstrong kids, and two kitties. When she isn't writing or creating her own gorgeous graphic content, she loves to read books by her favorite authors.

Writing has been a lifelong dream of hers, and this book was made despite the people who prayed for it to fail, but because Alisha is not afraid to go for what she wants, she has proven that dreams do come true.

Wanna see what all her characters look like, hear all the latest gossip about her new books or even get a chance to become a part of one of her teams, join her readers group on Facebook called **Alisha's Ally Cats**. Or find her author's page - **Alisha Williams Author**, where you can also sign up for her **Newsletter**.

Of course, she also has an Instagram account to show all her cool graphics, videos, and more book related goodies, just look for **Alisha Williams Author**.

Got TikTok? Just follow **alishawilliamsauthor** for more of Alisha's book ideas and character gossip.

We look forward to you joining us.

Printed in Great Britain
by Amazon